ROBBER BARONS

— A —
GRITT FAMILY
NOVEL

RODGER CARLYLE

ROBBER BARONS. Copyright 2025 by Rodger Carlyle. All rights reserved.

Cataloging-in-Publication Data is on file with the Library of Congress.

Published in the United States by Verity Books, an imprint of Comsult, LLC, Anchorage, Alaska. Inquiries may be directed to *comsultalaska@gmail.com*

First published in 2026.

ISBN 978-960268-13-6 (paperback)
ISBN 978-10960268-12-9 (ebook)

Cover design and interior formatting: Damonza

BOOKS BY RODGER CARLYLE

THE TEAM WALKER SERIES

The Eel And The Angel
The Shadow Game
The Dragon, The Eagle And The Jaguar

THE GRITT FAMILY SERIES

Tempest North
Two Civil Wars
Robber Barons

PREFACE
1895

Kukwa Inlet, Southeast Alaska

THE TWO GUARDS at the site of the new fish-trap had spent the day throwing rocks at passing seagulls. The birds turned their efforts into a game, swirling above the men's heads, squawking and covering the rough wooden dock with white sticky bombs. Around the site, spruce trees soared into a soggy sky; tiny drops of rain creating texture on the saltwater inlet in front of them. The whistle of the workboat signaled the end of their twelve-hour shift protecting the craftsmen building the fish trap.

"Reed, it's that old Native again." The burly guard punched his partner's shoulder. To their left an ancient canoe approached the dock, a graying man with long hair driving the paddle with amazing strength for someone whose face wore the scars of more than eight decades of harsh living.

"What do you want old man?" called Nestor.

"I want you men to go home and leave my village and my people's fish," said Joe. "You got your cows where you come from, you don't need our fish."

Reed picked up his and Nestor's knapsack and started down the ramp to the boat. "Let it be, Nestor," he called, "that old man comes here every day. He is all talk. There's nothing he can do to stop us."

Joe maneuvered his canoe past the trap, the barking of the gray-nosed mongrel with him making so much noise that it drowned out Joe's words. The wrinkled face of the man twisted into angry contortions, his demands ignored by tired men on their way back to a warm bunkhouse.

Nestor pointed at the man in the canoe. "You get da' hell out of here old man before you piss me off."

"Leave him be," snapped Reed. "It's time to go get some hot food and sleep."

"I am full up on that old man whining at us every day," replied Nestor, finishing the last of his rye whiskey and shattering the bottle on the rocks below the dock. "What if he waits for us to leave and starts tearing things up?"

"Nestor, what damage is one old man going to do to a bunch of logs and decking cut from green wood? Come on, you're holding up the whole crew."

"Like I said, I am full up of that old man," snapped Nestor.

The guard raised his rifle and fired a shot in front of old Joe's canoe. "Get the hell outta here old man and don't come back."

Joe began paddling back toward the village of Kukwa, then stopped. "You men who steal our fish will face God. He will make you pay for you stealing. Joe raised his arm into the air and began shaking his fist. "There be no trap here!"

"I said get, old man," screamed Nestor as he emptied his rifle in the direction of the village shaman, kicking up sprays where the bullets skipped across the water's surface. "You come back and you're a dead man."

Nestor stumbled down the ramp, falling into the crew boat. Reed helped him to his feet and then to a seat. "I think you hit that old man," he whispered. "Did you see him double over after your last shot?"

"I didn't hit nobody. I shot into the water around that old fart," mumbled Nestor. "Besides he is just some dumb old Indian. Who would miss him?"

Reed turned to the crew in the boat. "You men there, you didn't see nothing. Anyone here who talks will have to deal with me."

Reed watched the old man beach his canoe and stagger toward the forest across the inlet carrying a small bag. His dog pressed his nose against the old man's leg, then erupted, barking at the retreating crew boat.

Yukon River, Alaska Interior

The five men were behind them before Ned and Jake heard them. The sound of the water running through their sluice box and the scrape of their shovels over lath and wire in the bottom of its wooden flume masked their approach along the moss-covered trail.

"You men doing any good?" asked a huge man with a pistol resting on his hip. Below the sluice he could see two gold pans resting at the water's edge and next to them a mason jar, half full of gold.

"We aren't getting rich, but we found some color," answered Ned leaning his flat scoop shovel against the sluice. "You boys will have to go find another stream to prospect. This one is staked by Jake and me, but there bare probably thirty more creeks on up the Fifty-Mile River."

While his companions stood back, the big man walked over to the sluice and ran his finger along the upstream edge of one of the crosscurrent wooden riffles. A line of black sand mixed with specs of gold slipped over the boards, sparkling as they rode the water down the sluice. "That looks like a lot of color for the small area you are working," he laughed. "How long ago did you two file your claim with the marshal down in Falcon?"

"We been camped right here since we found color back in May," replied Jake. "We staked it from where this stream hits the river upstream for about a half mile. We haven't taken the time to go down to Falcon. We have nobody to watch over our diggings while were gone. Filing can wait until fall when it freezes up."

"That won't be necessary boys," snarled the big man. "Why would you want to file on my claim?"

Ned looked up, fire in his eyes. He picked up his shovel and swung it. He had aimed at the man's head, but before it connected the man reached out and caught the handle, jerking it out of his hands. That same handle, aimed right between his eyes was the last thing Ned saw before he hit the ground. Jake dropped his shovel and crawled under the sluice. He tugged his stocking cap from his head and pressed it against the gash on his partner's forehead. Blood saturated the hat and dripped from his fingers.

"I think you killed him," screamed Jake. "Why did you have to whack him so hard." Jake turned to glare at the huge man.

With his hands busy trying to stem the flow of his partners blood he was helpless to defend against the shovel handle which broke over his own skull.

"Toss these two into the river," ordered the big man.

"Pug, these two are out cold. They will drown if we toss them in right now," responded one of the men pulling the injured men away from the sluice.

"You're right, and they done the boss and us a favor," replied Pug Wolcott. "Go check in their tent and gather up their belongings and anything that might indicate their names and pile it in that flat bottom boat up on the shore. Link and I will ride downstream with them back to the main river. We'll wait until they wake up and then send them on down the Yukon. You three keep working this claim. I'll set your kit out on the beach when we leave. Make sure you get rid of any sign of these two," he added tapping Ned and Jake with the toe of his worn leather boot. "After we file, we'll come back for you."

The two claim jumpers slid the rough wooden boat up to the side of their twenty-five foot steam launch. While Pug rekindled the fire in the firebox, his partner slid the miners tiny flat-bottom boat out into the current of the Yukon.

Two hours later, the two injured miners were floating down the middle of the Yukon trying to clear their heads, when the steam launch ploughed over their small boat, spilling the dazed men into the bitter cold water.

Washington D.C.

Senator Fess Bolt sat at a quiet table in the hotel bar with two friends. A senator from New York and one from California had invited him for an afternoon drink. "You two are buying, so this time it's me doing the listening," smiled Bolt.

"Fess, your sister's company has more than a hundred years' experience in Alaska so your support for our two bills would carry a lot of weight," offered Ulysses Smark. "My friends in California would be real happy to have your support for a bill to transfer the management of fish within five miles of any Alaska cannery or fish trap to the company who puts up the capital to build it."

"The folks exploring the interior of Alaska would feel the same if you could help them overcome the limitations of one claim per prospector. We all know that a lot of prospectors are already staking claims in the names of friends and relatives, to insure they assert title to the location where the gold they find originates." Bixton Bradford represented New York and probably would for life since he raised more campaign money than the next two members of the senate combined. "Proxy staking is taking place, all my bill does is make it legal."

"Just to humor you two, how pleased would your constituents be to corner the fishing industry in Alaska and to dominate the development of mining in the territories interior?" asked Bolt.

"Together, maybe enough to double the tonnage your wife's shipping company hauls," answered Smark. "Maybe even enough to make the family an offer to buy the whole business for twice what it is worth."

"Let me get this straight," smiled Bolt, "the same folks you work with in New York and the folks Ulysses works with in California somehow got together and asked you two to team up to hand them Alaska on a silver platter?"

"Fess, there are some overlaps," responded Bixton. "Quite frankly these folks scare us a bit, but they can do a lot of good for that territory. It's just that they would like to reduce the risk on the millions they are willing to invest. If Gritt Russ Am became more successful at the same time they would welcome that."

"Bixton, just how do these people scare you?" asked Bolt.

"Senator, they somehow always get what they want. Ulysses and I would rather help them succeed and work with you to help your wife's firm succeed than have them roll right over all of us," finished Bixton.

"Well gentlemen, I know the Gritt family. They have become successful, not rolling in money, but successful by working with small guys and helping them grow. I don't think they would be happy marching to someone else's music. No, I think that my supporting either of these two bills would create all hell in the family, especially with my wife and her brothers. I can probably live without the brothers, but my career depends on listening to the smart one in my family."

"Fess, without your support, neither of these bills are going anywhere, but we will push real hard with the departments and the administration to see that they read existing law our way," answered Ulysses. "Don't come to us later and tell us we didn't warn you. The man at the top of this group can be very persuasive."

Bolt stood, shaking his head. "Seems the man who would be king, is already taking most of what he wants. Just tell him not to push this so far people get hurt."

CHAPTER 1

1896, Sitka, Alaska

A YOUNG WOMAN IN a high collar white cotton dress rushed the gangway determined to be the first passenger off from the ship from Seattle. Hundreds of prior shoes and boots had worn the steep wooden walk from the ship to the dock smooth, rain making it slick. The young woman's arms flailed as she slid to the bottom tumbling face down on the dock. A bystander in a plain blue suit and felt hat reached down and grasped her arm, lifting. The woman looked up to thank him. Seeing her brown face, the man dropped her and absent mindedly wiped his hand on his trousers. Belinda Medev had been away from Alaska for almost five years. The time forever changed her, introducing her to a different culture and lifestyle. But, close to home, some things had not changed very much.

Belle, the nickname given to her at The Society Of Mission Friends, felt blessed that she had been given the opportunity to attend the University of Oregon. Still, there was no place like home, and from Sitka it was only one day's journey to the village of Kukwa where her family eagerly awaited.

"Gracious child! It is so good to see you again!" Irma Gillam, wife of the Reverend Max Gillam, placed her hand on Belle's shoulder and then helped her to her feet. "Max is over in Juneau or he would be here to welcome you home himself. Let's get you into some dry clothes and see what can be done for your traveling dress. We have a week of work getting you ready to open the new school."

"Oh Mrs. Gillam, I am ready to open Kukwa's first school. I have been working on my lesson plans. I am ready for your and Mr. Gillam's help preparing to share the gospel."

"And you shall child, but not for a few days, I have arranged passage for you on one of the Russ-Am trading boats for tomorrow morning."

"I don't understand Mrs. Gillam, wouldn't it make more sense to complete my preparation so that I am ready the minute I feel the beach at Kukwa beneath my feet?"

"Please do not fret child, but your family sent word that they would like to have you at home as soon as possible. Your grandfather has been missing for more than a week now. The entire village has been out looking for him."

Belle's face lost most of its color.

"The fish processors and mining companies are running Alaska now. Your grandfather has been in a fight with North Pacific Fisheries over their fish trap near the Kukwa River. He went out to demand the removal of the fish trap. He went alone, believing that the power of the Lord and those silly powers as the village shaman would give him protection. The searchers found his canoe adrift, but they have found no trace of your grandfather or that old dog that never leaves his side."

Belle picked at the crab casserole dinner. Just before the bells summoned the faithful to the evening bible study, there was a knock at the door. Irma ushered two men into the parlor and slipped into the kitchen to prepare tea.

"Mr. Johanson," pronounced a smiling Belle, "Mr. Gritt, how are you? It is so nice to see both of you."

"And you, young lady, have grown up," responded Strom Johanson. Irma guided the two men into the small parlor, seating them next to the potbellied stove.

Johanson plopped into the deeply padded chair that he knew would have already been occupied if the Reverand Max Gillian had been in town. "We stopped by to tell you what we know about your grandfather."

"There is not much to tell about his disappearance," added Chad Gritt, taking a seat on the bench next to Irma's prized piano. "One of our boats stopped in Kukwa the day after he disappeared and spent a day helping search. What old Joe was doing before he went missing is important."

"He's right as always," said Irma, as she set a tray with four cups and a pot of steaming black tea on the table. "Tell Belle about North Pacific's new cannery."

Strom began packing his pipe. He struck a match on his canvas pants and sucked flame into the packed tobacco. He held the pipe in his smoke stained left hand. "After you left for school, a slick San Francisco fisheries executive showed up and announced that his company was going to take over the cannery business in the Alaska Panhandle. No one took him seriously until the next summer, when the first ship of the North Pacific Transportation Company arrived with twenty-five workers and the equipment to build a cannery twice the size of mine. They claimed a piece of land on Chatham Straight and had a cannery up in less than three months. A second ship arrived in late June, with even more machinery and supplies, and they were in business. That first season North Pacific hired about forty villagers to tend nets and work on the slime line. These were supplemented by five net boats that ran up from Seattle. Their pack that year was almost as big as mine."

Chad stretched his six foot-three frame, the heels of his boots making the sound of a rusty hinge on Irma's painted wood floor. He brushed hair from in front of his blue eyes. "The next year they began buying up every bit of lumber they could. They started building fish traps at more than a half-dozen streams and rivers in the area. Even streams next to villages were not off limits. That year, they brought Chinese and Filipino workers from California to work the lines and only hired handful of villagers to help move fish from the traps to the cannery."

"I've never seen a fish trap," commented Belle, still not quite sure what they were telling her.

"You will tomorrow," said Chad. "I'll run you right past the one at Kukwa."

"The local jobs went away," added Strom. "The pack was so big that they were still running ships south in November. Worse, they took almost all the fish from those streams. By the time that the villagers knew what was happening there weren't enough fish left for winter. Gritt Rus-Am boats hauled tons of dried fish from other villages to feed those people, but that was a hungry winter."

"That's terrible. What did the government do about it?" asked Belle.

"Nothing," replied Chad. "The new magistrate said it was all legal. The Revenue Cutter was sent to the area to protect the cannery and their people from the angry villagers." The only concession was an order directing that the fish traps be left open for the first ten days after the arrival of the first salmon."

"That had to get enough fish to the rivers to feed the people."

Chad laughed. "You remember how a few fish come into the rivers, often weeks before the main runs? Well, that's what happened. Not enough fish got into the rivers to provide brood stock, let alone feed the people."

Strom stroked his huge handlebar mustache. "Other villages without fish traps agreed to allow hungry villagers to fish in their streams."

"That is the old way," smiled Belle.

"That is the Christian way," added Irma, circling the room filling teacups.

"The problem was, North Pacific Fisheries began work on a second cannery the next spring," continued Johanson. "By July, they were building the first fish traps in southern Chatham Straight. One by one, they began taking the fish from the remaining villages. A few men from each village were offered jobs building fish traps that would starve their own families, but they had no choice. A few were offered tender jobs, but just as before, most of the jobs went to immigrant workers imported from California."

"This year, they started a third cannery down on Frederick Sound," said Chad, placing his hand on the young woman's arm. Belle blushed. "The first fish trap that they started building was at Kukwa Inlet only miles from your village."

"That is what your grandfather was trying to stop," finished Irma.

"If they take all the salmon, there will be no fish in a few years. What will the people eat?"

"The fish traps compete for the same fish my small cannery needs," replied Jophanson, "so not only will it take food off from the plates in the villages, but it will take away the summer jobs that provide the cash income that they need."

CHAPTER 2

Southeast Alaska

THE SMALL STEAM ship *Miles Pierce* rounded Cape Ommaney and turned into Chatham Straight at noon the next day. With 18 hours of spring sun, the daylight allowed a man to work until he dropped if he didn't show some restraint. The men on the Gritt Russ-Am wharf arrived at 3:30 in the morning and finished loading freight by the time Captain Gritt arrived at 5:00am. The six man crew had steam up when their five passengers arrived, and the departure was delayed while the workers located Belinda Medev's trunks and boxes from the warehouse and slung them onto the deck next to the forward hatch. A heavy oiled canvas tarp covered them.

A fine mist shrouded the ship where the southern entrance of Chatham Straight met the Pacific Ocean. There was not a ripple on the water. The eighty feet of hull, sliced through the slate sea leaving a wake that spread from her bow like a line of geese in the fall sky. The gentle rumble of the steam engine below and the hiss of steam escaping from a rusted pipe below the ships whistle were the only sounds. Black smoke from the burning coal, escaped the ships stack and was lost within a quarter mile as it mixed with the mist. On the starboard beam, the trees along the shoreline appeared only as gray silhouettes and the mist went on forever to port.

Six of the souls aboard huddled in the small ship's cabin where a samovar of black tea and a huge pot of coffee on a flat topped coal stove offered respite from the damp chill. On the small, enclosed bridge, Chad Gritt stood at the huge, spoked wheel that directed the ship's rudder. Leaning against the chart table, Anthony "Tex" Walker stretched his lanky frame and watched. Belle Medev stood on the wing just outside the door of the bridge, her heavy raincoat and hat shiny from the moisture.

"Miss Medev is real unhappy with the situation."

"We all are," replied Chad. "It's not right that one company can come into a country and interrupt so many lives."

"I agree Chad, but Congress and the administration both want a return to the treasury from what most of them still call Seward's Folly. The only title to lands that the federal government recognizes are industrial sites. Men who are willing to invest in Alaska are given almost total latitude in how they run their business as long as they pay their taxes on each case of fish, or each hundred measure of lumber. The damned fool who decided that Alaska should operate on a body of law transferred directly from Oregon with only a note in the front of the law book tellin' ya' to substitute Alaska everywhere it says Oregon didn't know nothin'."

"Is the law silent on destroying the resources or taking so much that the people who were here first go hungry?" asked Chad.

"That wasn't a problem in Oregon by the time the law was

writ' I suppose, so the law don't address it. My orders from the magistrate are to protect the commercial interests."

"Is the law silent on murder too?"

"Don't get your horse before your wagon, Chad. Miss Medev is really upset, but even she don't know if there is any foul play in her grandfather's disappearance. That's one reason why I am out here with you, burning up my travel budget. I hope to find out and avoid more of a situation than already exists."

"I don't envy your position," responded Chad. "It must be hard to enforce a law that you know is wrong. You know that fish traps are the only talk I hear about outside of Juneau, and Alaskans won't rest until they are all gone. If Congress wasn't owned by the mining companies from the east and the California fishing companies, we would have a territorial legislature and the first bill they would pass would be to outlaw fish traps."

Tex began working out a kink in his back. "Maybe, or maybe it would be a law to give property titles to people who have built homes with their own hands. Or maybe they would outlaw proxy staking of mineral claims. Or maybe they would put more than a pittance into public school budgets. Or maybe they would even legalize alcohol and tax it since the territory is awash in booze anyways."

"Like I said, Tex, I do not envy your job, especially on what they pay you."

"It ain't so bad, the three marshals and the three judges all make twenty-five hundred dollars a year. That's a whole sight better than what I made as a deputy sheriff in Texas. With recon-struction and the carpet-bagger government, Texas is a shadow of itself before the war."

Belle Medev swung the door open and stepped onto the crowded bridge. She hung her soaking coat and hat on a peg at the rear of the cabin and pressed the back of her legs against the tiny steam radiator. "We will be in the sunshine in an hour."

"Now how do you know that?" asked Tex.

Belle just smiled at the tall Texan.

"You haven't had time to really get to know the Tlingit," offered Chad. "For generations they have relied on these waters for their entire livelihood. When Macky is on the bridge and he gives me advice, I listen. When he has the wheel, I shut-up. He and Belle are both half Tlingit and half Russian, but they were both raised in the villages where men still fish and hunt whales in canoes that you and I would expect to find for rent in a nice city park."

Belle's propensity to blush revealed itself, but the men watching the endless gray passage before them didn't notice. "Captain Gritt, there is a small inlet with a tiny stream only a short distance from the village. It must be close to where you say the fish trap is. Up that stream, about a quarter mile is a waterfall, with a jumble of logs from the top to the bottom. It is all covered in moss and the air always looks just like it does around your ship today. My grandfather used to take me there, especially if I was troubled. We would sit on a log and throw bits of dried salmon to the trout in the pool below the falls. We never talked, we just sat and let our minds run with whatever troubled us and by the time we got home it was always better."

"You want to stop and see if your grandfather is sitting on a log?" asked Chad.

"If you would not mind a short stop, it is my best guess on where to find Grandfather."

"But it's been more than a week," offered Tex.

"If old Joe is all right, he can live in the open like that for months," commented Chad. "Old Joe could live for a year with nothing but a pocketknife."

"And Captain Gritt," added Belle, "If he was injured, the waterfall would allow him a good death."

"What do you mean by a good death?" asked Tex.

"Marshal Walker, a traditional man like my grandfather would want to die where the only things around him were made by the creator, and where the spirits that he believed in, would feel free to take his spirit where he could look after his people. He would want a priest to read over his grave, and he would want his soul in heaven, but his spirit belongs with his shaman ancestors."

"I will have Macky hold the ship offshore, while the three of us go look for your grandfather," agreed Chad. "We will take a couple of rifles, Tex, just in case we find a brown bear along that stream. It is time for them to be moving close to the salmon streams."

Over the next hour, the sky grew lighter and the mist thinner until the *Miles Pierce* emerged from a fog bank into bright sunlight. After days of foul weather, it took only moments for everyone aboard, except the coal stoker, to find their way to the deck. In the distance, a pod of whales broke the surface with geysers of breath. Dozens of gulls circled the whales, hoping that they would push a school of herring to the surface.

The ship pushed north through the glassy calm until the captain could turn east around Kupreanof Island and then southeast toward Kukwa Inlet. All around the ship towering mountains, still capped with snow, fell away to dark green stands of evergreens that stretched almost to the rocky shorelines. A thin line of light colored deciduous trees and beach grass separated the dark green seawater from the stands of spruce and cedar.

"How far inside the inlet is the fish trap?" asked Belle.

"About seven miles on the north side of the inlet, west of the river."

The Kukwa River meandered through the relatively flat area between the mountains and the sea. A large bend in the river brought the river back toward the inlet about three miles upstream from its mouth. The village of Kukwa sat on a hill, not far from the shoreline at the head of the inlet. At the back of the hill, only two hundred yards from the salt water, the river ran clear over gravel and boulders.

"So that is a fish trap," commented Belle, lowering the field glasses that Chad had offered her. "The salmon travel along the beach toward their spawning river. With that monstrosity blocking their trip, how do any fish reach the river?" she asked.

"That's the beauty and the horror of a fish trap," said Strom. "The fish enter the spiral of the trap and herd themselves into the center holding pen. The tender boats simply tie up to the trap and ladle the salmon out of the pen with nets. Some canneries open gates after each tender visit to allow the remaining salmon to migrate on to their rivers, but the North Pacific Canneries run their boats all night and let the fish that they can't handle die and sink to the bottom of the pen. With fish traps there is no need to tend set nets, to spend money for boats, or hire fishermen."

"How many years until there are no more fish?" asked Tex.

"There is little real science. Some think that the fish return on the third or the fourth year after they hatch. Others think that they come back every two years. The facts will make themselves known within the next five years as the impact of the traps becomes evident," continued Strom. "I personally believe that each species of salmon has a different cycle and that each species can vary a year or two from that cycle. That would be God's way of protecting them against natural disasters."

"I think you're right," added Chad, who had just turned the bridge over to his number two, a five-foot six-inch fireplug of a man known only as Macky. "It would explain the differences in sizes of the fish in each run."

They watched a work crew from the fish trap board a steam scow. The boat turned east toward the huge cannery that they had seen on a bay north of Kukwa Inlet. As the scow passed the ship, two men with rifles stood at the bow. No one on the scow returned the waves of the *Miles Pierce* crew or its passengers. Belle pointed to a small stream across the bay, halfway between the fish trap and the main river.

"That is the stream that Grandfather used to take me to."

The fence at the entrance to the trap stretched out into the inlet more than two-hundred yards. "We will ease around the trap, and I will have Macky hold the ship out here with power rather than anchor," said Chad. He called down to a deckhand. "Thomas, please drop the small boat and grab a jacket. I want you to row us ashore and then hold just off from the beach and wait for us."

"I would be happy to row, Chad," offered Tex. "I could use the exercise."

"Thanks for the offer, marshal, but with the tide coming in fast, the boat would be gone if we left it beached at the mouth of the stream."

As the small boat pulled away from the stationary ship, a rifle shot rang out from the steam scow. "Don't nobody mess with that trap," came an order from the scow.

The marshal introduced himself and their mission to those on the scow. "A might testy don't you think?" he said to no one in particular. "Move on now or I'll arrest you for assaulting a federal officer," he called.

The boat grounded on a small gravel beach between two rugged rock bluffs. A stream, no more than six feet wide and a foot deep poured out of a cut in the alders and spread out over the gravel, running into the inlet only yards from the dark spruce forest. Belle, Chad and Tex crossed the small beach, headed for the trail that paralleled the stream on the left hand side. Belle stopped where the trail turned from gravel to dirt and pointed at the ground.

"Bear track," said Chad, reaching into the pocket of his red plaid coat for five cartridges for his Winchester 30-30. "Better load that rifle," he said to Tex.

Tex Walker fumbled in his coat pocket for a box of shells and began pressing four of them, one at a time, into the box magazine of the bolt action rifle he was carrying. The muddy trail cut through the moss of the rainforest, at times directly next to the stream and at other times it detoured around a huge fallen log or a boulder. Chad led the way, followed by Belle and then Tex. The only tracks on the trail were of a huge bear, so large that the deep tracks had become puddles.

The stream ran wildly along their path, echoing through the dark overhanging spruce forest. The sound covered their travel, growing louder as they approached the waterfall.

"By God, a dog barking," said Tex

"Its old Negra," said Belle pushing past Chad.

"Hold on Belle," said Chad grabbing the back of her coat. "You'd better let the marshal and me take the lead, we don't know what he's barking at."

Chad rounded the end of a massive moss covered log and found himself only twenty yards from the rear end of a huge brown bear. Sensing their presence, the bear spun to face them. The exhausted black dog between him and the waterfall simply laid down, too tired to attack. The bear was not that tired.

It rose onto its hind legs to get a better look, sniffed the air, extended its tongue to taste their scent, then dropped and charged. Chad had the Winchester to his shoulder in seconds and fired a shot. The bear ignored it and kept coming. Chad heard his second shot whack the bear, but it didn't even slow down. Chad fired a third shot just as Tex, now standing next to him squeezed the trigger of his rifle. The bear's right front shoulder collapsed, and it skidded onto its face, sliding to within feet of the men. Both men fired again aiming at the huge mouthful of snapping teeth, the animal shivered and lay still.

"What are you shooting?" asked Chad, trying to stop shaking.

"I picked this up in Cuba a couple of years ago," replied Tex. "it's a seven- millimeter Mauser, a Spanish army rifle. That solid copper clad bullet really socked that old boy. One of the Natives who works for the police in Sitka told me that old Mr. Bear is left handed and if you broke their right shoulder, they couldn't swipe you with their left paw. I don't know why I remembered that, but I did. Hell, I've never even seen a big bear in the six months that I have been in Alaska, until just now."

"You shoot well for a Chechako, and I'm dammed happy you do. I wasn't far from meeting my maker. I hit that bear in the chest three times and he just kept coming."

"He would have died."

"Maybe, but I wouldn't be around to see it."

"Then I would have had to pack two bodies out of this forest," replied the marshal, pointing at a man slumped next to a moss covered log."

The two men and Belle started toward the body but were stopped by the snarl of the gaunt old dog that lay next to old Joe. "Let me go first," directed Belle, "once old Negra recognizes me, he will be fine."

Belle walked slowly toward the dog and extended her hand. The snarls turned to a whimper and then the dog drug its tired body from the ground and managed one wag of its tail. Belle knelt next to the dog and rubbed its ears and then moved on to her grandfather. "He's dead isn't he."

The two men advanced only to stop at the growl of the dog. "You stop that, these are friends," she commanded. The dog dropped onto its stomach, its jaw resting on the ground.

Old Joe looked like he was sleeping, but the blood on his shirt and coat just above his belt told a different story. "The smell probably attracted the bear," offered Chad.

"He's been dead for a while, the bloating is already going away. I am going to take a look-see at that wound," said the marshal.

Tex pulled the shirt up and examined a small wound on the left of Joe's stomach and a larger wound on the right. "This man's been shot, gut shot. The bullet drilled right on through him and never touched a bone. It had to hurt like hell, and it probably took days for him to die. This might be a good place to die, but this is not a good way."

"Grandfather died a good death," sobbed Belle. "Look at that." She pointed at a small cross that had been carved from a broken branch and pressed into a crack in the rotting log. Next to the cross was an old leather bag with a sheep horn rattle and a spray of eagle feathers tied with a red string. "He honored both the new religion and his old faith."

While the two men fashioned a litter from their coats and old Joes, Belle sat on a rock, her face in one hand, tears running between her fingers, while her other hand slowly stroked Negra's head.

"I wonder how long that dog held off that Bear?" wondered Walker.

"He took care of the old man for a long while," replied Chad. "Look at the trout bones next to old Joe, the dog was fishing to feed him. Then after Joe didn't eat anymore, he fished for himself," continued Chad pointing to a small pile of fish heads next to the stream. "What he wasn't going to do was leave the old man."

It took two hours to move the body back to tide water. The incoming tide allowed Thomas to row the boat right up to the tree line and in ten minutes the party, old Joe and the dog were aboard the ship, and Macky had them underway toward the village.

"I will want to stop at the cannery on our way out of the inlet," directed Tex. "I have to try to find out who shot that man, but I doubt that we will find any witnesses. Unless a witness will leave with us, there is no one to stop a revenge killing for someone who speaks against his campaneros."

"We have to solve this," replied Chad," this could lead to a war. From what I can see the cannery has well-armed guards. This cannot end well for the villagers."

"I will speak to the people," offered Belle, walking up behind the men. "The good book talks about an eye for an eye, but it also says that vengeance is the duty of the Lord. Still, if that fish trap cuts off the fish that we rely on, one or all of us will deal with the North Pacific Fishing Company." Belle walked to her grandfather's body, now wrapped in a piece of canvas, and sat down. Negra finished a bowl of dried salmon without even sitting up and looked up at Belle, his eyes asking for more.

CHAPTER 3

Southeast Alaska

BELINDA WIPED AWAY a tear, then gave Tex a quick hug and turned to Chad. "Thank you for helping to find Grandfather. We will hold a celebration tonight in the old meeting house. Are you sure you can't stay?"

Chad paused for a moment. "I'm sure. The marshal wants to stop at the new cannery, and I promised Strom Johanson that I would get him and his freight to his cannery by tomorrow morning. Make sure you pass the word that Strom will be looking for fishermen and cannery workers in the next couple of weeks. One advantage of working without fish traps is that you can start fishing earlier and slowly work into the season."

Chad squeezed her hand. "I am really sorry about your loss." Belle turned away, a smile on her sad face. Her grandfather's old dog drug himself from the dock and followed.

It was after nine in the evening when the *Miles Pierce* tied up at the North Pacific Fisheries cannery. "Do you want me to tag along?" asked Chad.

"Nope," said Tex, "this has to be by the book—just these folks and the law."

The marshal walked across the deserted dock to the manager's office and pushed open the door. "I want to talk to everyone who has been working at the Kukwa fish trap."

"The men have just finished dinner and headed for the bunkhouse. It's been a long day with a summer of longer days just around the corner," replied the short, rotund foreman. "I don't want to disturb them."

"Perhaps you thought that was a request." The marshal laid the rifle on the counter in front of the man. "There has been a shooting and we're going to find out what happened. If I have to go to Juneau and get an order from Magistrate Tome, I will fine you for all the costs of coming back here."

A half hour later eight men sat in front of the marshal. "I asked to talk to all of the men."

"These are the only men who have worked on the trap in the last two weeks," replied the foreman.

"I saw two men today on the scow, both of them carrying rifles with those new telescope sights."

"You only asked for the men who worked on the trap," snarled the foreman. "Those guards are here only to keep trouble from our operation." He didn't like the look on the marshal's face. "I'll go find them."

An hour later Walker had determined that two of the workers were not at the trap the day that the village shaman had disappeared. The others had their story down to the same words, even the same gestures. "What about you, Rattler?" asked Walker. "Were you there?"

"Not that day, marshal, said one of the guards. He was a sandy haired man with a Spanish accent layered over his southern drawl. "I sent Reed and Nestor. Them boys are tellin' you straight, The old Indian came up in his canoe and asked politely to make sure we opened the gates to let enough salmon through to feed the village. These men agreed to do that and as a gesture offered the old man a pint of rye. Last they saw, he was headed back toward the village."

"And just what the hell was an illegal saloon operator doing out here anyway?" asked the marshal.

"Mr. Sontag hired me to help recruit security guards for his canneries. If and when the magistrate ever decides to enforce the liquor prohibition, I'm going to have to make my living outside the saloon business. I couldn't pass up this opportunity."

"I suppose that the Golden Goose Saloon is locked up while you're here," replied the marshal, rolling his eyes.

"You know better than that, Marshal, Flo and the boys will do a fine job while I break in Reed and his friends." Cobra Wilson patted a hulk of a man sitting next to him on the shoulder. "Reed used to be a prize fighter, then a bouncer, and lately worked on the milling line at the Douglas mine. He will be here all summer keeping the peace."

"Perhaps I was mistaken, but I thought that was my job."

"Marshal, everyone knows that you cover an area the size of Vermont by yourself, with no roads and no boat of your own. Sontag is damn smart to be looking out for the security of North Pacific Fisheries operations. Besides all three of us, you, me, and Reed are of the southern breed. We southern boys look out for each other. You can count on us to keep a lid on things."

Tony Walker found Macky and the captain waiting on the bridge. He looked down, just in time to see Rattler Wilson throw his travel case and two leather rifle bags onto the deck and then leap over the rail.

"Just as I expected, there is no one at this cannery who is

going to talk. I'm sure that hombre who just boarded had something to do with this, but I can't prove a thing."

"I recognize the face," said Chad.

"That's Rattler Wilson. He owns the Golden Goose in
Juneau. Now he's also running security for Sontag. He's meaner
than a wildcat with its tail in the door. His father was a colonel in
the Confederate army and smuggled his family and much of his
wealth, including his slaves out of Texas after the war. He named
his two boys Rattler and Cobra. That says a lot. The family lost
everything when Cuba outlawed slavery in 1886. He and his
boys went to work for the Spanish, suppressing the Cuban
revolutionaries, that is until the old man was hanged for black-
mailing honest citizens. I wasn't in this job more than a week
when it became clear that Rattler would need a lot of watching.
I could have arrested him a dozen times, but Magistrate Tome
just smiles and looks the other way."

By comparison to the cannery across Frederick Sound, The
Johanson Fishery Cannery was small and neat. The four buildings were freshly painted with rows of windows, even in the
ceiling, flooding every building with natural light. A dozen men
met their boss as Johanson leaped to the dock. As the crew from
the ship swung net after net of supplies from the hold of the small
steamer, half a dozen men with hand-trucks swept the supplies
from the dock to the warehouse. "Your main shipment should
be up here on the *MAXIMILIAN* in about three weeks," shouted
Chad from the bridge. What we put on the dock, should get you
through until then."

"You're going to want to get a little sleep after today," replied
Johanson. Why don't you tie up for the night and get an early
start for Juneau tomorrow?"

"I'll go see what my three passengers say, would that be
alright with you Marshal?"

"I can give everyone who doesn't want to bunk aboard a cot in the empty bunkhouse for the night," offered Strom.

"What about food?" smiled Chad knowing that the cook at Johanson's had a reputation as the best camp cook in southern Alaska.

"Fresh baked Halibut tonight."

"That ought to sell it."

Five minutes later, Chad tapped on the manager's door and accepted his offer of hospitality. "Only one shore bunker, that guard Wilson from the competition. That alright with you?"

"Sure, like everyone out here, you never know when you might need a favor."

"The marshal doesn't like him much."

"I prefer to judge men myself."

The fire-bell awoke everyone on ship at three in the morning, one of only four hours of darkness that time of year. The men rushed to the dock in time to see a bucket brigade forming from the beach to an open yard just north of the cannery. Taking a place midway in the line, Chad could see several gillnet boats burning in one corner of the yard. The flames pushed the men at the front of the line away from the burning boats, the heat scorching their shirts and hair. The man in front pouring a bucket of seawater over his own head to cool his scorched eyebrows. He used the next bucket to begin soaking an undamaged boat.

Before the fire was extinguished, three of the twenty-five foot sailing boats were a total loss and two more were damaged. Every man from the cannery and from the ship had been there to fight the fire or all ten of the tightly packed boats would have been lost.

"That will really hurt the early season," commented Johanson. "We'll need lumber to build three boats. When can you get it to us? The early sockeye run gives us our early cash flow. I just can't figure out how that fire started."

"I'll have to get lumber from Sitka or Ketchikan. All the lumber cut in the Juneau area goes to the mines. I'll see if I can rustle up a couple of boats that you can make do with," offered Chad.

The ship cast off its lines at six in the morning, the outgoing tide helping sweep it around the point in minutes. With Macky at the wheel, Chad went below to join the passengers for coffee, stopping a minute to enjoy the show of a whale breaching over and over.

"Damned shame about those boats, commented Rattler Wilson, I'll be sore for a week from slinging buckets up that hill."

Walker and Chad exchanged glances, but neither responded.

The paddle wheel at the stern of the *Miles Pierce* made almost no noise except the slap, slap, slap of water dripping from the blades as the ship pushed into Gastineau Channel. The long narrow water way divided the Juneau mainland from Douglas Island. On the right, an ocean steamer was tied to the Dupont dock unloading dynamite.

The hillsides along the channel were covered with a growing layer of brush, all the trees having been harvested for lumber and shoring for the large mines at the head of the channel. Gold had made the town of Juneau the largest community in Alaska in only a handful of years and the second largest town was on Douglas Island only a mile across the channel. Sitka remained the capital of Alaska, but Juneau was the center of commerce both legal and otherwise.

The small harbor was bustling with small craft of every type. At the wharf in front of the Rus-Am warehouse two boats from canneries and one from a mine, loaded freight. The *Miles Pierce* dropped its anchor waiting for a shuttle boat from the wharf to unload its passengers. The freight would have to wait.

CHAPTER 4

Juneau, Alaska

LIKE EVERY BUILDING in the boomtown of Juneau, the magistrate's office was a simple frame structure with multipaned windows on a wooden sidewalk. The town itself was carved into a narrow band of hills bordered by salt water on one side and steep, spruce covered forests on the other. The magistrate and the marshal were the only representatives of territorial government in a community of more than four thousand people.

Jorge Tome had been recruited from Chicago by Governor Karp after Congress appropriated funds for a handful of civil servants. Tome had been an attorney in Portland and an Oregon state senator prior to his appointment as an Illinois district judge. He'd made the mistake of believing that Chicago was a city of laws, and within months he had resigned. A letter, slipped under the door of his office gave him a choice of offers, only one of which extended his life. When he left Chicago, he'd sold his modest home on a downtown corner to an attorney representing an unknown buyer for ten times what he had paid for it. The sale gave him and his English-born wife a nest egg, making the twenty five hundred dollar annual salary of an Alaska territorial magistrate palatable.

Governor Karp had welcomed the Tome referral from his old friend Malcom Crier. Crier was the head of "Business Development Partners," a Washington D.C. investment company. The firm included a public relations and lobbying division that helped raise funds for political campaigns. Crier had been a major amalgamator of funds for Karp's own unsuccessful campaign for a congressional seat in Ohio. The only other law enforcement official in the area was standing in front of Tome's desk.

"It's good to see you Tony, I have a half-dozen warrants that need to be served, but after what you just told me, I guess they will have to wait."

Walker pulled up a chair and began rolling a cigarette. "I really don't know how to investigate the shooting in Kukwa, Jorge. There's evidence that it involves someone from North Pacific Fisheries, but no one at the cannery is talking. There don't seem to be any other witnesses, and it was clear that the actual shooting took place somewhere other than where Chad Gritt and I found the body."

"This may be one of those situations where we make a big push to show that we care and that we are working on this Tony, even if we know in our hearts that we probably won't find the killer," replied the magistrate.

"If we don't Jorge, the village and the cannery folks could tangle," replied Tex.

"I hope not. Our marching orders are to protect commerce. The villagers have no champion in the capital. Pat Sontag has a dozen congressmen and at least that many senators watching out for his interest."

"That's plain wrong Jorge, North Pacific is really hurting the villages. The Kukwa folks all tell the same story, old Joe went out to the new fish trap to demand that they move it away from the village. If that trap works like the ones from the northern cannery, there won't be enough fish in that river this summer to feed the village. I saw at least a dozen Winchesters in the few hours that I was in the village; they won't take this lying down."

"It will be your job to make sure that they do," replied Tome. "The territorial law makes it clear that the cannery will get title to that property as part of their commercial venture. Hell, Tony it's the only type of property that can get title under the law. Margaret and I can't even get title to the house that we built last summer."

"That don't make it right," replied the marshal. "Starving out villages just ain't right. The law also says that the villages are not to be disturbed, don't it?"

"It does, but that means that no one can go into a village and take the land. It does not guarantee them a living. Besides, maybe people like Sontag are right, the faster that the villages move to a cash economy the faster they will embrace civilization. There is nothing I can do, and you are sworn to keep the peace. That's the way it is."

Tome slid an ashtray toward the marshal.

"Governor Karp has petitioned congress for reform," continued Tome. "Hell Tony, you have a room in Sitka and know better than me that he is trying to get some home rule, and in the interim, make changes to the laws to better take care of the people. The folks here have been petitioning for changes since '81. But today we live with what we have. Now, the first warrant is for Wilson at the Golden Goose for illegal alcohol sales. You don't need to bring him here, just collect the two hundred dollar fine for the booze and drop it off with Elenor out front. Lotta good it will do. We fine him for selling stuff we all buy and can't do anything more. But we need the money to pay the light bill."

"Rattler was at the fish trap, working for Sontag. He was at Johanson's cannery when his boats were burned. I think he's involved somehow," offered the marshal.

"Maybe, maybe not. If we have proof, I will swear out an arrest warrant. Until then, we will use some of the ornery bastard's money to keep the doors open."

"Damn," was the only response from Marshal Walker. He tipped his hat to the magistrate's secretary on his way out the door.

The supply boats were all gone by afternoon and the *Miles Pierce* finally was moored against the dock. The crew was busy hoisting cargo from the hold. Rus-Am operated four large ocean going steamers between San Francisco, Seattle and Alaska. All of them called on Ketchikan, Sitka, Kodiak, and Juneau year round. From spring until freeze up Russ-Am ships operated all the way to the mouth of the Yukon River. They hauled supplies north and lumber, canned fish, and the occasional gold shipment south. They also hauled barrels and cans of fuel from Standard Oil to Alaska, shipments that supplemented the bulk shipments from the oil company's own fleet. Oil lubricated the equipment that made industry work. Kerosene lit the lights and ran the generators. Coal fired everything else. While Rus-Am didn't move coal, it operated a sales yard just about a mile south of the town. It brokered coal from a Canadian company that had a virtual monopoly in Alaska.

Smaller steamers, like THE PIERCE took supplies from Juneau, Ketchikan and Sitka and distributed them to the villages and commercial operators away from the major towns. Her sister ship and THE PIERCE were on a rotating schedule that allowed weekly service throughout Southeast Alaska.

Chad Gritt, an officer in the seventy year old firm didn't much like life in the East where the corporation continued a lucrative freight business to Europe and Latin America. The company had been divided into Pacific and Atlantic divisions, and his older sister oversaw the Atlantic division.

Katarina Gritt Bolt was an educated woman who couldn't set foot on a ship without getting seasick. Her husband, Fess, an older man, helped run the business until he had been elected Senator from Massachusetts. Fess and Katarina made a perfect team to run the business. His sister's marriage allowed Chad to return to his first love, Alaska.

While in college, Katarina became friends with a young woman who had started her education at the new University of Oregon and then gone on to Boston to study law. Danielle Post was the daughter of Sven Post, the former treasury agent and customs inspector for the territory of Alaska. The year after Chad moved north, Danielle followed. She had been unable to work Chad into her schedule that day but had accepted an invitation to dinner at the Romanoff Hotel that evening.

"No, I do not represent Patrick Sontag or any of his companies," answered Danielle. "I know them well; you are the fourth person to approach me with legal problems with North Pacific Companies."

Danielle paused as Chad refilled her wine glass before continuing. "Sontag has stepped on almost every toe in the fishing industry and in transportation bin the last three years. When Magistrate Tome sets up an inquiry on a complaint it is immediately halted by Judge Dischner. There is a possibility of redress through a civil case, but Sontag has deep pockets. Any judgement from an Alaskan court will be appealed immediately to the federal court in San Francisco, where his friends wine and dine the judges weekly."

"What about a criminal investigation over the death of old Joe? If we can get one of the people at Sontag's cannery to implicate Rattler Wilson or one of his hired thugs, we might get them to name Sontag," offered Chad.

"Maybe, maybe not. Wilson is a crafty no good guy who's parlayed his saloon contacts into a list of who's who in Juneau. He makes no secret of his illegal activities, rather he advertises them and makes sure to offer special deals to the local power brokers. He probably has a book on every man in town but especially focuses his attention on the big owners and managers. Like Sontag, they hire him to do the jobs that they don't want to dirty their own hands with. He's smart enough to know that if he turned on any one of them, he would be fed to the fishes in Chatham Straight."

Their steaks arrived, along with a second bottle of cabernet. The grass-fed beef from local farms was always a special offering at the Romanoff, as was the fresh salad that had started the meal. Even at eight in the evening, the restaurant was more than half full and the adjoining bar was packed.

"Miss Post," smiled Chad, "I have no standing in anything that we can go after either Wilson or Sontag over. Strom Johanson, however, is convinced that Wilson started the fire at his cannery and that Sontag put him up to it. Belinda Medev knows that the North Pacific crew is responsible for her grandfather's death. I'll chip in the first thousand dollars if you think that you can make either case stick."

"Chad Gritt, in the four years that I have known you, going back to when your sister introduced us in Boston, I have never once called you Mr. Gritt. Why do you persist in calling me Miss Post?"

"All right Danielle, I will try to remember to forget everything my formal Spanish mother taught me about etiquette. You know, people already talk about you and me. Belinda Medev thinks that you came to Juneau only because I was back in Alaska."

"How is Belle? I haven't seen her since I sat in on a luncheon at the education department at the University. I was in Oregon to get a quick course in Oregon law since those idiots in Congress decided to make it Alaska's law as well."

"Belle is well, except for the loss of her grandfather. She is all grown up now; chomping at the bit to get her school opened and her ministry started."

"Belle was grown up at twenty. I swear the education department had a dozen male students just so that they could go to class with her."

"She is a looker, that one," responded Chad.

"I'll have you know that I still turn a head or two Mr. Gritt."

Sweat dotted Chad's forehead. "You said that you never call me Mr. Gritt."

"Just drop it. Let's get back to the problem at hand. If Johanson will come up with a $2,000 retainer, I will get my researcher on the connection between Sontag and Rattler Wilson. Perhaps there is a thread that we can pull to unravel the truth."

"I'll drop the retainer off tomorrow. I can take your engagement letter to Johanson when I see him in a couple of weeks. Johanson will pay me back. Both Tex Walker and I believe that if we don't head off this conflict between the small canneries and North Pacific and even more urgently, the hatred for North Pacific in the villages there will be trouble."

"Do you really want to take on Sontag, with all of his backing in San Francisco and D.C.?"

"It's an old family business. Besides, as long as Sontag

operates his own shipping, there's not much chance of getting any business from him. The small operators and the villagers are my customers. With six more gold strikes in Alaska in the last five years and the rumors of something big in the Yukon we are going to attract every kind of get rich quick scheme and every type of crook. In the thirty years since the Alaska purchase, we have had a military government, treasury department administration, total neglect and now a weak civil administration with no authority. During that time Alaskans have taken care of themselves. This is just the next step in that process."

"Ok, I'll get involved, but only if you are going to stay here through Saturday and if you offer to take me to the commerce dinner and dance."

"Did you just ask me out?"

"I get tired of waiting for you to ask me. Besides the governor is going to be there along with Malcom Crier one of his old east coast pals. He is touring Alaska on a private yacht along with Abraham Guildham the head of Mining Capital Development Company. They are looking at investment opportunities. No one has a better understanding of the potential of the territory than the man who shares the name of our oldest business founders; a century of Gritt knowledge."

"I would be pleased to take you to the dinner, but none of that one-hundred year talk. Danielle, the reason I came back to Alaska is to get away from all the politics. Katarina and Fess are great at it, I'm not."

"Then just talk about business, I will stand daintily at your side, and smile. I'll even wear something low-cut to stimulate the conversation. I just want to listen to what they have to say.

CHAPTER 5

Juneau, Alaska

THE SMALL APARTMENT above the Russ-Am warehouse in Juneau was a strange place for a meeting between Governor Karp, Marshal Walker and Chad Gritt, but it was private. The Governor had arrived on the *General Mead*, the second of the inland passage ships owned by Russ-Am.

"I'll have to get to the hotel fairly soon to get on my formal politicking suit," said Karp. "Those big city boys will want to show their power by a formal lunch this afternoon."

"This situation with the North Pacific Canneries is going to blow up Lyman," offered Chad. "This shooting is really putting the villagers on edge. It's going to become the villages and the small cannery owners versus North Pacific."

"That and the fact that your administration is going to have to get a special appropriation from congress to feed people in at least a dozen villages by next winter," added Walker.

"I have already asked for ten tons of flour and five hundred cases of tinned beef. I included a report explaining that the fish traps were the cause of the emergency appropriation. I haven't received any word from the president's office," explained Karp.

"Why don't you ask for an appropriation to purchase canned fish right here in Alaska," asked Chad. "The people in the villages have never developed much of a taste for beef, and the cost would be a lot less."

"Chad, the President and some of the biggest names in congress are all connected to the big beef packers in one way or another. There's a better chance of getting the funds if it supports one of their big donors."

"What are the chances of getting the money?" asked Chad.

"Somewhere between a little and none. With the collapse of the fur seal harvest in the Seal Islands, there is little in tax revenues coming from Alaska. If congress decides to tax the big gold companies it will help, but I doubt that congress is going to fund anything beyond the bare bones budget that we already have."

"Then how do we feed the villagers?" asked Walker. "More importantly, how do we keep hungry men from burning down the canneries?"

"Marshal, there is nothing I can do. I have tried to get some form of home-rule legislation. I have asked for the Customs Department to regulate the fish traps. The President knows how I feel as do a number of those in Congress not connected to commercial fishing interests, but the committee chairmen are on the other side. That's one reason that I invited Malcom Crier and Abraham Guildham to tour Alaska."

"Ain't that a bit like lettin' the fox tour the henhouse?" asked Walker.

"Marshal, I have known Crier for more than a dozen years. I believe that he's honest. When he sees the trouble building here, Malcom will take his concerns to the committee heads. He is very influential."

"What about Guildham?" asked Chad. "His passion is mining and as a partner in the Alaska Investors Group, he isn't likely to support more taxes on the mines."

"My message to both of these men is that the development of Alaska with a stable tax base and skilled work force will be more profitable. Now is the time that they can influence how that is accomplished. If they wait, it's likely that when Alaska becomes a state, their treatment by a local legislature will be far harsher."

"Statehood, hell, we can't even legally found a town."

"It will happen Chad," continued the governor. "Maybe not in the next couple of decades, but it will happen. There is too much potential here. As the population grows, the people are going to be more and more trouble to congress. There will come a time when they get tired of listening to us and just cut us loose."

"In the interim, what do we do?" asked Walker.

"Keep the peace and do our best to help the people take care of themselves. We will interpret the law in ways that give us the most latitude."

"Governor, the judges here may not agree with your interpretation of the law," commented Chad.

"The magistrates and the judges have a job to do. If they honestly interpret the law, that's all that we can hope for. If they spend a few years here, they will become one of us, looking for ways to help."

"The hired legal help are all political appointees," interjected Walker. "They all have a constituency outside. I don't mean to imply that they are crooked or nothin' Governor, it's just that they seem to favor the big companies."

Governor Karp picked up his pipe and began filling it with tobacco from a leather pouch. He struck a match and sucked the flame through the packed tobacco. When he had a steady stream of smoke flowing, he looked up at the marshal. "Tony, this territory is desperately short of capital. We don't have the cash reserves to develop industry or schools or hospitals ourselves." Karp paused to enjoy his pipe. The leather padding of his chair creaked as he repositioned closer to the desk and ashtray.

"The system may favor the big business interests today, but maybe the opposite might be a lot worse. If the courts drive them away, we never develop; we never have the industrial base to become self-sufficient."

"Lyman, any businessman can see that," replied Chad. "A judge that constantly attacked business could set us back decades, especially if he got the ear of congress. Still, it's hard to look the small owners and villagers in the eye when they are getting screwed and they know it."

"It's up to those of us who care, here and along the gulf coast and throughout the Yukon country, it's up to us to make a difference. Let's start tonight at the chamber of commerce dance. Take the time, both of you, to talk to Crier and Guildham, make your case. Tell them about your concerns over the killing at Kukwa and the arson at Johansons. Let them help us make the case in Washington. Just don't rip into big business. We need them. Now, I have to get moving, my wife will be waiting in the room dressed for lunch. When she gets angry the Iroquois comes out in her, and she starts sharpening her skinning knife."

The laughter continued as all three men raced down the stairs and out into the drizzle on First Street. The Governor went up the hill toward the Romanoff Hotel and Marshal Walker headed for The Golden Goose to collect a fine from Rattler Wilson. Chad turned back into the warehouse to find his foreman. He needed two or three boats for Johanson's Cannery and his Juneau foreman, a supply non-com in the Navy in a different life, was just the man to start the search. Chad would offer him twenty dollars for each boat that he could have ready to ship within three days. Johanson would gladly pay the extra.

Danielle Post was ready when Chad reigned in the company supply buggy in front of her rooming house. The age of modern transportation meant that a woman of means in Juneau, Alaska could dress in the same fashionable way that a woman of means dressed in New York or San Francisco. She had her long auburn hair piled on top of her head accentuating her long neck. The red feathered wide brimmed hat contrasted with her pale blue eyes and pure white skin. All of this was missed by Chad as he helped her into the wool cloak that was to keep the light rain from ruining her matching red silk gown. "I am assuming that you like the dress Captain Gritt, or do your eyes normally sweep from a woman's shoes and stop at the bottom of her chin?"

"I am sorry, Danny. I don't think that I have ever seen you in anything that didn't button to the top of your neck before," he stammered.

"So, you approve of my neck."

"There will not be a man in the house tonight that will not be in trouble by tomorrow morning."

"Why? I don't understand."

"They will be mumbling in their sleep tonight about the 'woman in red' which cannot be healthy for their marriages," he laughed. "Will you take my arm Miss Post and allow me to escort the princess to her ball?"

"Once again Chad Gritt the third, that charming and handsome gentleman that I met in Boston has noticed that I am a woman. I'll see if I can hold your attention all night."

The Romanoff ballroom was a dark place. The four windows along the western wall added little light on a drizzly overcast evening and the chandeliers hanging from the high ceiling offered adequate light, but no more. The room was set with a lectern and a head table at one end of the room and a small bandstand and dance floor at the other. In between fifteen round tables topped with crisp white linen and sparkling crystal offered seating for more than one hundred. On the stage a pianist dressed in coat and long tails worked through a program of classics.

The receiving line of local dignitaries outside of the huge double doors was just wrapping up when Chad and Danielle reached the top of the stairs. A middle aged man with a trimmed black beard in an ill-fitting tuxedo extended his hand to Chad.

"Nice to see you here Captain Gritt, and you too Miss Post," offered Paul Tennant, "you both know my wife Florence I believe."

Florence Tennant was an impish woman with bright red hair and a face full of freckles that gave away her heritage. Dressed in a high necked purple gown that could not have clashed more with Danielle's red dress, she forced a smile while her glaring green eyes locked onto her husband whose own eyes never left Danielle. "The Governor changed the seating arrangements this afternoon, you two will be at his table along with our out of town guests."

Karp and his wife Kate were seated next to a graying man of at least sixty and his wife, both dressed as if they were at royal affair in Austria. "Danielle, Chad, allow me to introduce Mr. Abraham Guildham and his wife Gilda," said Karp. "You know my wife, and Marshal Walker, and next to the marshal, an old family friend, Malcom Crier."

The Guildhams worked hard to be the epitome of Jewish American aristocracy. His perfectly trimmed full beard and jet black eyes fit perfectly with his black tie and monocle. Gilda's salt and pepper hair was cut shorter than the current style and her smile scarcely hid a lifetime of experiences and secrets.

Malcom Crier on the other hand was not at all what either Chad or Danielle had imagined. A tall man, he wore a simple brown wool suit with a Scottish clan tie. He was only in his mid-thirties and would have been perfectly at home sipping a gin and tonic after a polo game in England, something that he had done dozens of times in his life. His years of discipline allowed him one brief smile at Danielle, where he took in everything there was to see. He extended his hand to Chad. "Mr. Gritt, I here that your family is among the American founders of everything western here in Alaska; it is an honor to meet you."

Chad made an appropriate comment about Crier's family and their generations of investment in North America and he and Danielle moved around the table to where the Guildhams were seated. Abraham stood and extended his hand to Chad but made no comment. His wife on the other hand extended her hand to Danielle first and Chad second and smiled. "Mr. Gritt, I hope you are well armed, for I fear that more than one of the ruffians in this room already has designs on Miss Post here."

Chad and Danielle seated themselves next to the Guildhams and a waiter rushed forward to pour a glass of wine for the late arrivers.

"My dear," asked Guilda," is that a Ponce Pickard fashion? It is just stunning."

"It is," replied a surprised Danielle," how did you know?"

"He is my daughter's favorite New York designer. I would love to wear his fashions, but five children and five decades has made it mandatory that I use a Paris designer who also drapes statues for museums."

Her own giggle allowed the table to join her. "Mrs. Guildham," commented Tex Walker, "back home in Texas, every young cowhand would be tapping his date at the dance on the shoulder and pointing toward you. Now that's a lady, he would say."

"Thank you, Marshal Walker, for the very nice compliment."

Over dinner, prompted by the governor, Chad and Walker voiced their concerns over the troubles brewing in Alaska. The Guildhams and Crier were courteous and engaged.

"Gentlemen," offered Crier, "the transition of industry from small cottage workshops to factories will create a living standard beyond what the masses ever dreamed possible. What is going on in the fisheries is the natural evolution of capital on a needed resource. In mining, the same thing is taking place. Look at the mines here in Juneau, they are all large industrial operations with hundreds of workers and shops filled with hundreds of thousands of dollars' worth of technology."

Abraham sat quietly, taking it all in, but his wife filled the silence. "Now Malcom, that's not what these gentlemen and the Governor are discussing. No one here wants to stop progress, they just want to make sure that it doesn't arrive over the graves of people who have been here for centuries."

"Your right of course, Guilda," replied Crier. "When we take a look at the North Pacific Fisheries facility tomorrow, we can ask about the fish traps. It's too bad that Patrick Sontag is in San Francisco, we could discuss it with him personally."

"Don't you placate me Malcom Crier," snapped Guilda, "both Abraham and you are part of the Alaska Investors Group, and I know that you have funded part of Sontag's growth. You can do more than talk to the man."

"Of course, Guilda, when we get back to Seattle, I will cable Alfred and have him track down Sontag. I will share your concerns with him. My family is the largest investor in Alfred's Marathon Bank."

Turning toward Governor Karp, Crier continued, "Lyman, what do you want done? The fish traps reduce the cost at the canneries by almost a third, so we aren't going to ask Sontag to do away with them."

Abraham placed his hand over that of his wife, a slight smile crossed his face. Guilda had seen the same signal from her husband for years. She returned his smile and quietly slid back in her chair.

"Malcom, I have known you and your father for years. I sit at the governor's desk only because you personally helped raise the money for my congressional campaigns a dozen years ago. We welcome the Alaska Investors Group's efforts to help us develop. As to the fish traps, the answer is simple, build them so that they can be left open two or three days a week to allow a third of the fish to reach their rivers."

"The reason Sontag wanted a third cannery was to process the extra fish that he was catching. He couldn't handle the fish from the traps in two canneries," offered Abraham finally.

"That is partially true, Mr. Guildham," offered Chad. "The way North Pacific's traps are built, they catch more fish than the lines in the cannery can handle. Instead of releasing the extra fish, they die and rot on the bottom of the pen. When Sontag built the third cannery, he built more traps."

"Ah, I see," said Guildham.

"As to the mining issues, the proxy staking and all," interjected Crier, "I will be happy to talk to the Division of Mines and point out the problem when I get back to Washington. I believe that the law is clear that mines must be staked in person is it not."

"It says that," replied Danielle, "but the Oregon law does not offer any penalties for violators. The law also assures that no entity will infringe on or harm any of the villages, but again the legal interpretation from the Oregon law gives us no penalties for someone or group who starves an entire village."

Up until that time Danielle had been good to her word and had practiced being a great listener.

"You are well read in the law Miss Post?" asked Guilda.

"I studied law at Harvard College Mrs. Guildham. With no Bar Association in Alaska, it is one of the few places where I do not have to fight the old boys network."

"Good for you, dear. Can we help here Abraham. Malcom, can you get your father and grandfather to try to help?"

Both men smiled at Guilda Guildham, a gesture that meant something to the woman, but that was hard to interpret by the others at the table.

"Mr. Gritt, you have not asked the young lady at your right to dance. If you do not soon, someone else certainly will," offered Guilda. "Abraham and I will join you for the next dance. How about it, Kate, can Lyman still toddle around a dance floor?"

Chad and Danielle headed for the dance floor, followed by the governor and his wife. Marshal Walker excused himself and headed downstairs to the bar, leaving only the Guildhams and Crier at the table. "Malcom," said Guilda Guildham, "that is the kind of woman you need in your life. Not the trollop like the one on the yacht or the society women that your father picks out for you. That woman will someday be part of a powerful team."

Guilda rose and gently pulled her husband to his feet. "It's been months since we danced, Abraham."

"Malcom, ask Miss Post for the next dance. Chad is a gentleman and will not object."

The yacht had been anchored in the channel for a week but was gone the next morning when Chad finally hauled his body from the bunk in the warehouse apartment. The night had only been winding up when the Chamber dance broke up at midnight. He had finally arrived home just when the short spring night was giving way to morning. Chad had dumped two large spoonsful of headache powder into a glass of warm water and pulled the covers up over his head to block out the light. Five hours later he picked up the formal clothes strewn around the apartment and began looking for the long wool coat that he remembered wearing the night before. He quickly shaved and dug out some canvas work pants from his sea bag and pulled a green flannel shirt from the closet. He gulped down a glass of warm water laced with more headache powder as he raced down the stairs to the warehouse floor.

The horse was in its stall, and the buggy pushed into the corner where it belonged. He remembered giving the reins to one of the young Native men that he employed when he left the Romanoff. The young man had been at the front door of the Hotel picking up tips bringing peoples buggies from the livery to the door. The Sunday early services were just letting out as Chad made his way up the street to the Palace Restaurant for his planned breakfast with the governor and the marshal.

"Coffee and keep it coming," requested Chad. He had asked for a table in the back of the restaurant where their conversation would not be overheard. "Please send the marshal and the governor back when they arrive. By ten past eleven the order was in the kitchen, and all three coffee cups had been topped off.

Karp scowled. "It is what I didn't hear that bothers me. Malcom danced around the issues all evening. I have always known that the real power behind the Criers is the grandfather in London, that's where the money is. Sir Rodney's reach is worldwide. From that oak paneled office on Lombard Street, he controls industry on three continents. His son, Richard moved his offices to Montreal about a dozen years ago when Malcom moved to the US to take over Business Development Partners. Even he defers many decisions to the old man."

"What do you know about this Sir Rodney?" asked Marshal Walker.

"He has a ruthless reputation. He has owned a major interest in the diamond mines in South Africa since the 1870s. He started as an Army Major who left the service to become a partner of the men who first discovered diamonds. One night over far too much scotch, his son, Richard, commented that he supported the British Army in the Transvaal while he sold arms to the Boers during the Boer War. Either way he would win. He has made it a family business, with agents reporting to Richard, Malcom or directly to him from all over the world. The Criers are the only men I know with a telegraph right in their offices, a bonus for their investment in the cable companies. No one knows who his agents are, but they scour the world looking for opportunities in mining and other resource industries. Last night was the first time that I learned of their interest in fishing."

"That would mean that he has agents in Alaska, wouldn't it?" asked Chad. "How would they keep in touch? The mail to Seattle would take at least three weeks. From there it could go on the wire, but they certainly wouldn't want their business moves sent in a way that others would know what they are doing."

"They would send it coded," offered Walker. "Both sides in the war between the states developed very sophisticated codes and employed teams of code breakers. In the business world it would be easy to say anything privately."

Their waitress brought three heavy, fried breakfasts and placed them in front of the men.

"You know, there is a telegraph station in Telegraph Creek, Canada, just up the Stikine River from Wrangell. It's the starting place for the system proposed for Alaska. With steamers between Telegraph Creek and Wrangell and the boat service that Russ-Am and your competitors operate on the inside passage, a message from London could be in Juneau in three or four days," said the governor.

"Were off the track," interjected Walker. "The question is, will Crier and Guildham help with congress?"

"I know the Criers," replied Karp. "If they think they can corner the fishing or mining industry in Alaska and close out all competitors they will. They may help if they see that they are destroying an industry that they control, like killing off all the fish, but they won't care about their competitors." Karp stopped to ponder the spoon full of sugar he held above his coffee. "Above all else, they avoid bad publicity."

"Walker thought a moment, and then asked, "would they commit murder to get what they want?"

"Malcom and his father may play the game very hard, but I would never believe that they would break the law."

"They might take advantage of poorly written laws and our inability to enforce it," mused Chad.

"They will be back here on Wednesday," offered the governor. "Kate and I are hitching a ride back to Sitka with them on Thursday. I will have another talk with them while we travel, maybe they will help."

"If that Guilda Guildham has anything to say about it they will, she's a pistol," observed Walker.

"I got the impression that she may be an equal partner in Guildham's operations," said Chad. "And she deals with Malcom Crier like a grandmother."

"Very good, Chad, she's his aunt. Guilda is Richard's wife's sister. I don't know how close the Guildhams and the Criers really are on business matters, but I know that the sisters remain close in spite of the fact that Malcom's mother left her faith to marry her husband," finished Karp.

"I have to get the *Miles Pierce* up to Haines this afternoon and back to Sitka by the end of the week," offered Chad. "Guilda invited both Danielle and me to dine with them on Wednesday evening. I can't make it, but I will talk to Danny and see if she can. One more appeal cannot hurt us, and maybe she can learn something about how they look at Alaska."

"Your date was the talk of the affair last night my friend," observed Walker. "After seeing Miss Post in that dress, I don't know how you can leave town. Your willpower is to be commended."

"I've got to run if I am going to make a three o'clock departure," said Chad. scooting his chair back and stacking five silver dollars next to his plate. "I'm going to run up to Danny's to say goodbye. I will suggest that she take Guilda up on her invitation."

The walk on a beautiful Sunday morning took about twenty minutes. Chad felt like a human being again after breakfast and he had a huge smile on his face as he knocked on the door of Danielle Post's third floor apartment.

"You forgot your coat here when you left this morning," Danielle said.

CHAPTER 6

Northern Lynn Canal, Alaska

THE DALTON TRAIL led across a narrow peninsula between the mouth of the Chilkat River and a deep-water port at the northern end of the Inside Passage. Used by the Tlingit Indians for centuries to shorten the trading trips between salt water and the interior, it had been the location of a small trading stockade built by Chad's grandparents seventy-five years before. Ten years later, that post had been abandoned in favor of a more centralized post to the south, once again leaving trade over the mountains to the Tlingit.

In 1880 a new trading post was built close to where the long abandoned structures had faded away to nothing, destroyed by the constant rain of the summers and the freezing and thawing of winters. Soon after a mission school was built, at the request of the local Indians and a small community had taken root, with the mission and the Native village at its center. The old Indian trail was slowly upgraded and served trade and mail travel between the new mines on the Upper Yukon during the winter when the steamboats were sitting on blocks on the banks of the frozen river. The *Miles Pierce* slid up against the rough dock below the mission just as the sun settled below the western mountains. The trip north from Juneau had taken eight hours.

The trading post was served by boats belonging to its owners, and except for the incidental shipment, Russ-Am seldom moved freight for them. The local Tlingit people, the mission and the few settlers around the mission however were important customers. The crew set to work unloading cans of fuel and other supplies aided by the dozens of local citizens who greeted the ship every time it arrived, looking for mail and newspapers. Chad tossed five bags of mail into a small pony-cart at the end of the dock. He followed the young Native girl leading the cart up to the mission office on the hillside about a quarter mile from the ship.

"The three bags on the bottom are for the Yukon," offered Chad, "the two on top are all for locals."

He was talking to the Reverend Old, headmaster of the mission school and the minister of the Presbyterian Church. "Samuel, I have four crates of school supplies and used clothing for you on the dock," said Chad. He watched as the silver haired missionary sorted through the mail looking for a letter from his daughter.

"Can you arrange with the village head for some packers to move the mail and the three or four hundred pounds of other supplies to the Yukon? I am paying for the trip north in advance," continued Chad.

"That will be no problem," replied Reverend Old. "They love it when the trip is paid for, that way they are guaranteed a profit on their own goods added to the shipment."

"I'll pay six men ten dollars each for the trip," offered Chad. "That rate is the same as last winter when they could use dogs.

It will be more work by canoe and pack frame, but it's what we quoted the shippers."

"I'm sure that the ten dollars will be acceptable; I am assuming that you will throw in the normal bonus."

"A box of 30-30 cartridges is built into the rates," laughed Chad. "What do these men do with two or three boxes of ammunition a year? Most of these men can feed their families on two or three bullets."

"They trade them to the Natives on the upper river. One box of shells goes for twenty mink pelts. The tobacco that they will take is worth two or three martin or otter skins a pound. By the time the miners pay them to bring back mail, each of these men will net close to fifty dollars for a round trip."

"These people have always been good businessmen. My grandfather told a story of canoe loads of local Natives coming to the old stockade to trade before the walls were even erected."

"If it weren't for the liquor that the trading post sells, these families could be rich by their standards," continued Samuel Old. "And I fear that it's about to get a lot worse."

Chad reached into his pocket for his pipe and a pouch of tobacco. He filled his pipe and then passed the pouch to his friend. "Oh?"

"There're rumors of a strike on the Yukon just upriver from Fort Reliance. The local people stripped the village of everything they could spare last winter and packed it over the pass. They came home with pokes of gold. You will want to spend an hour with the chief before you go. He wants to set up a store of his own."

"If you can set up the meeting, I will take the time," responded Chad. "Now what about the four passengers that you have for me?"

"Two of them are the railroad engineers that came in with you last January. They have finished their evaluation of a route up the Chilkat River. The other two are miners from the Fort Reliance area, determined to get home and back by next summer."

"Samuel, if the rumors of this gold strike are true, Haines mission and the village of Dtehshuh are going to be awash in stampeders by next year.

"I know that, Chad. Your company will do really well and anyone who is prepared could make a fortune. But the community will be torn apart. The couple of hundred of us on the North End of the Inside Passage will be swallowed up. The chief is right, if he can make this really valuable to all his people they might come out of a boom just fine. I have my doubts."

A meeting with the tribal chief ended with an order for more than a thousand dollars in trade goods, all paid for in gold dust. Chad met the four new passengers and showed them to their bunks. "We're not leaving until morning," he said. "Get some sleep. I'll arrange for breakfast at the mission at four. It will cost you a dollar each. I need to give them a head count." No one seemed interested.

Chad watched a beautiful sunrise as he walked to the mission. He was surprised to find the Reverend and the tribal chief along with two others waiting for him when he arrived at four o'clock. "A bit early, isn't it?" he asked.

"We wanted your ideas on how to take advantage of this," offered Samuel. "What should we do to get ready?"

Over breakfast, Chad saw excitement in the eyes of three of the men but only dread in those of the Reverend. "You will need a dock large enough for ocean going ships and a couple of warehouses. You will need to figure out how you will manage the lands in the area. If you don't have a town layout planned and some way to control who uses which piece you are going to end up like early Juneau, with stampeders taking whatever they need wherever they want. More than anything you will need to find some way to give the people some say in what is happening. You are wise to think this through early."

"This may be rumors," offered the chief. "Nobody talks about miners in the Yu-kan-ah. When we go there in winter we find few white people on the river, they were mostly up the Choindike River. But the ones there need everything, and the Gwitchin people say the miners are running off all the game and cutting down all the trees."

"I'll talk to the two miners who will be traveling with us and see what I can find out. I'll be back in a month or so and will fill you in. In the interim, I suggest that you start to plan. If this is real, charging a fee for using the dock or for land use may give you the funds to control this, at least for a while."

The *Miles Pierce* pushed off for its journey to two small canneries and Sitka, in a driving rainstorm. *It takes only moments for everything to change in Alaska,* thought Chad, as he spun the small ship in the harbor and turned south.

With Macky at the wheel, Chad headed to the salon where his passengers would be drinking coffee, trying to ride out the rolling seas without feeding the fish. He found the two railroad engineers, William Fischel and his assistant Malcom McKerlain in the corner away from the coal stove, each lounging in one of the over-stuffed leather chairs with a book in his hand.

"Bill, Malcom, how was your trip up the Chilkat River?" asked Chad.

"Just fine Captain, but we won't be building a railroad along that route. It would be possible to build a narrow gauge railroad through those canyons, but the cost would be enormous. Maybe with the rumors of a major strike in the Yukon we could raise the money, but a narrow gauge isn't what we need to serve the interior of Alaska, especially the planned army presence."

Bill Fischel dog eared his book and laid it on the table. The title caught Chad's attention. THE BUILDING OF THE CONTINENTAL RAILROADS AND THE ASSOCIATED LAND GRANTS. Fishel smiled at Chad. "The biggest problem in building from Haines Mission north will be the crossing of an unsettled border into Canada and the handling of military freight for the US Army through Canadian territory."

"What's your plan then?" asked Chad.

"We spend a week with you in Sitka and then head north to Puerto Valdez and Puerto Cordova and explore the trails over the mountains and up the Big River from tidewater to the Yukon along that route," answered McKerlain.

"You know that the Alaska Investors Group already has a railroad engineering party looking at a route up the Big River." advised Chad.

"We know of two parties, ours, and one from the Great Northern with exploration lease agreements with the government. The Great Northern folks are looking at the route from Resurection Bay to the Yukon River. The company that finishes a design and begins to build first will be the only one to get Federal Transportation funds and a right of way land grant. Our investors are counting on our expertise building in the Rocky Mountains. We will need a crew of at least eight and a new outfit to explore the route. The Alaska Investors Group has a head start, but I don't know of an exploration lease. If the route is viable, we can start building faster than they can."

"The Big River is a mile wide and braided like a fish net according to the Army survey reports. It settles down north of Valdez and runs through a huge valley almost all the way to the Yukon River. We think that it will be less expensive to build through Thompson Pass and pick up the Big River on the other side of the mountains than to build straight up the river from its mouth," added McKerlain.

"The Alaska Investors Group probably has parties looking at both the river route and the Thompson Pass routes," observed Chad.

"So far, it's a free country," said Fischel. "We have the right to look at the route."

"Bill, just be careful up there, the AIG has been investing in Fisheries here in Southeast and some of their partner companies are playing pretty rough."

"We engineers are a civilized lot," said Fischel, "we tend to work out our differences over drinks."

"Let me change the subject. How real do you think the rumors of a major strike upriver from Fort Reliance are?"

"Oh, there is a strike there, but I don't know how large it is," observed McKerlain. "We hired a man in Haines to keep his eyes and ears open. If the strike turns out to be huge, and if we can get Canadian authorization, we could start to build a railroad within three years. There is plenty of quality timber for trestles and bridges and the rest is all about manpower and dynamite."

"Why don't you talk to those two miners," suggested Fischel, pointing at two bearded men sitting next to the coal stove, their eyes closed, and feet propped up on chairs.

"We have tried, but they are not very talkative."

Chad thanked the two men, who had been winter customers, and assured them that his company would be happy to outfit them and help them recruit for their Big River venture. "We will spend the night at a cannery at Port Frederick. If I can find a couple of fishing poles for you two, maybe you can catch a King Salmon once we turn into Icy Straight. We can discuss how to get you to Cordova over a fresh salmon dinner."

Chad shook each man's hand and walked over to the coffee

pot on the oil stove. He released the spring clamp that kept it from tumbling off from the stove in heavy weather and refilled his cup. Picking two more cups from the rack next to the stove he carried the pot over to where the two miners slouched in their huge leather chairs. "Buy you gentlemen a cup of coffee?" he asked.

"The names Sprint, Ed Sprint and this here is my brother Bob," said one of the miners reaching up for Chad's hand. "We wanted to talk to you too."

Bob Sprint was in his early thirties, and his brother was a few years younger. "We went to St. Michael on one of your Russ-Am boats a couple of years ago and up the river on your steamboat *Denali,*" offered Bob. We paid for passage all the way to Fort Reliance."

"We both come from a mining family in Nevada, this was our adventure before heading home to work for the old man in the silver mines," continued Ed. "But it don't look like that is a going to happen."

Chad kept his mouth shut.

"Is there somewhere we can talk in private, Captain?" asked Ed.

"We can use your cabin, it's a lot larger than my sleeping room on the bridge," offered Chad.

"You wouldn't happen to have a bottle of rye and three glasses?" asked Bob.

Minutes later, Chad arrived with an uncorked bottle of rye whiskey, a pitcher of water and three glasses. His knock on the door was met instantly by Ed Sprint who invited Chad to take a seat on the only chair in the cabin. Ed plunked down on one of the bunks. "Brother Bob is down in the little house overhanging the water," he said. A minute later Bob Sprint slipped into the cabin after checking both directions for anyone loitering on deck within ear shot.

"Thanks for the drink, Captain Gritt, it's been over a year since we shared a nip. Me and Ed made a pact that we would not have a drink until we could do it where we could not be overheard."

"Brother Bob gets all friendly when he drinks more than a couple, and tends to talk too much," laughed Ed. "What we want to talk about is just between you and us; alright Captain?"

Chad looked at both men. "You have my word that whatever you tell me will be shared with no one that you don't approve of. Is that satisfactory?

The two miners looked at each other and then both nodded. The story that came out over two drinks and two hours was one of pure luck backed by true wisdom.

"We hooked up with three men from the prairies of western Canada. They knew a man by the name of Carmach who found a lot of placer gold on a stream about thirty miles from Fort Reliance. The five of us headed out the third day after we arrived, and within three days were finding good showings in another stream only a few miles away."

"We built a cabin and pooled our resources and began a systematic search of the stream. We found gold in the water and when Ed and I started to tunnel into the bank above the stream, even more."

"What Bob is saying Captain Gritt, is that we and our partners filed on a claim that will make us all rich."

"We wintered over and spent the next summer expanding our search. We filed on four more claims, one in each of our names, but formed a company where we all own all five claims."

"One of our partners went east to find a magistrate to file as a corporation and by the time he got back, we had a sluice built on the first claim. We cleaned almost ten pounds of color from that one sluice before it froze up. We spent last winter cutting lumber and proving up on all five claims."

"Why are you leaving now?" asked Chad.

Bob sipped his second glass of whiskey and scowled. "Early this spring we began getting visitors. In March we checked one of our other claims and found three men building a cabin near our workings. We decided that Ed and I would head for California as fast as we could get there and offer shares in three of the claims to some mining men we know. We decided we needed some big money to develop the properties and to hire enough men to protect them. Captain, when word of this gets out, we want fifty tough miners on those claims."

"I toast your success," offered Chad. "I hope that Russ-Am can be of help."

"That is what we wanted to talk about," offered Ed. "We are carrying enough gold to buy a lot of supplies and equipment. We can buy it used in Nevada where a lot of the mines are playing out and ship it by rail to California. But we need to get it from the dock in California to St Michaels and then up the Yukon as early next year as we can."

"And," smiled Bob Sprint, "we need to do it quietly. We need another year to protect our interests before the entire territory busts wide open."

"We need to move fifty men and about twenty-five tons of equipment, plus food and supplies for the men. Can you do it, and what will it cost?" asked Ed.

"I will have to work on the transport costs for the men, probably about forty dollars apiece. On the freight, the cost from California to Fort Reliance will be in the range of one-hundred dollars a ton. We can get it all to St Michaels on one ship, but it will take two trips to get all the men and supplies up the Yukon. I don't know about getting them up the Choindike, I don't know the river."

"That river is too shallow for a big riverboat. Have you got any ideas Captain?"

"It's either horses and wagons or a smaller boat, it seems to me."

"What about a smaller boat, what do you mean?"

"You could stop off in Seattle and see if you can find a very shallow draft paddle boat. The Mosquito fleet in Puget Sound has dozens of boats and they are constantly upgrading. There may be a boat that we could tow north for you. I wouldn't try to run a small boat through the Aleutians, it would be suicide. The safest bet would be to ship horses and try to find a flat bottom boat, that would cover you," concluded Chad.

"How do we arrange all of this?" asked Ed.

"I will provide a letter to our manager in Seattle, authorizing him to make all necessary arrangements and to reschedule the ships to take care of you. That will suffice I think."

"Thank you, Captain Gritt," said Ed extending his hand.

"There is one more thing, we will need to move your Yukon freight over several months. We have other long time customers to consider. We can move your men and building supplies and maybe horses and wagons first. The heavy equipment is of no use to you until you figure out how to move it to your claim anyway, so we can move it later in the summer. Next year we will operate two riverboats."

"You were the man we needed to find," smiled Bob Sprint. "Now let's have another drink to celebrate."

Ed Sprint picked up the half empty bottle and pushed the cork into the neck. He handed the bottle to Chad. "Bob, the agreement is two drinks until we sell out and become men of leisure."

Their arrival two days later in Sitka was as routine as could be expected with half of the crew joining the four passengers hanging over the rail in the booming swell the last hundred miles to Sitka Sound. The harbor was empty except for the *Juarez*, one of the Russ-Am ocean steamers. The *Denali* slipped in behind the much larger ship.

Chad quickly shook hands with his pasty passengers and bounded up the stairs to the office above the Sitka warehouse. The captain of the larger vessel sat at the transient captain's desk with a pile of papers scattered in front of him. "Hello there, boss," said Captain Scott Richmond.

"Scott, you old sea serpent, you aren't supposed to be here until the weekend," replied Chad.

"We combined our regular run with a charter for two canneries up in Prince William Sound," said Richmond.

"Going or coming from the sound?"

"Going," offered Richmond. "We unloaded twenty-two tons here yesterday and the cannery guys are off trying to line up a pile of lumber that was supposed to be waiting on the dock. Those guys at the mill swore that they would have it done by now but appear to be on wintertime."

"There was a North Pacific ship at the sawmill dock the day before yesterday," offered a clerk.

"You don't suppose that they sold our customers lumber to Sontag, do you?" asked Chad.

"Maybe, all I know is that the mill went from working a couple of days last week to twenty hour shifts after they left," replied the clerk.

Turning back to Scott Richmond, Chad asked, "How long before you head north then?"

"Probably another four days."

"Have you cabin space for six or eight more men and three tons of supplies, nothing big?"

"I'll have to check with the customer, but we can make it work if they are willing to share the charter."

"I just brought a couple of Railroad guys over from Haines who are putting together a small crew and then heading for Puerto Valdez to do a survey. They said they need a week, but if you're going up into the sound anyway, it would work out well for them," replied Chad.

"Let's go see if they can make do with only four days before we bother our cannery customer," suggested Scott.

"Let's wait until tomorrow, Scott. Fischel and McKerlain spent the last ten hours so sea-sick that they could barely walk down the gangway."

"I hauled their landlubbing arses up from Seattle last winter," laughed Richmond. "How are they and how was their trip up the Chilkat River."

"Until this morning they were just fine," replied Chad. "They aren't going to build out of Haines, at least not now. They need to find five or six men willing to spend four months hiking from either Puerto Cordora of Puerto Valdez to the Yukon and back to survey that route."

The clerk, a half Indian youth of twenty slid his chair back across the rough wooden floor. The sound, not unlike that of fingernails running down a chalkboard, raised the hair on the backs of the two captain's necks. "Captain Gritt," said Earl Molotov, "I would sure like to make that trip. I haven't been back to Eyak to see my family since I graduated from boarding school."

"I'll make you a deal Earl," replied Chad, "if you can help find five more reliable men to help out the railroad on their safari up the Big River and find someone at the school to replace you here for the summer, I will give you a leave of absence for six months. That gives you four months to help with the survey and a couple of months at home to help with the subsistence harvest."

"I'll have someone here tomorrow morning to interview for my position," offered Molotov.

"They will have to be reliable and as good at ciphers and the written word as you," replied Chad.

"I have in mind Belinda Medev's brother, John Jr. He finished his courses last December and went home. He just got back to Sitka yesterday after hiking hot springs trail from the eastern side of the island. His father told him to stay here until the troubles in Kukwa are over."

"Well, he can do the job, that's for sure. Is there more trouble in Kukwa, I mean after his grandfather's death?"

"I don't know Captain, you will have to ask him. I will put out word on the street tonight that there are five real paying jobs for the summer. I will bet that we can have a dozen men for the railroad gentlemen to interview by tomorrow."

"One more thing Earl, I will have a boat at the Eyak village two months after you finish the survey to bring you back here. I expect you to finish your two year contract and then go south to finish your education. I promised your mother that when you came back to Sitka."

"You have my word, Captain Gritt, and with the survey pay I will have some money of my own when I leave."

CHAPTER 7

Sitka, Alaska

MARSHAL WALKER SAT next to Judge Dischner. Magistrate Jorge Tome from Juneau sat in the chair next to the Governor. The late June weather in Sitka was terrible, and the governor's mood was worse.

"The magistrate here informs me that there are four new fish traps in Frederick Sound, all blocking the salmon runs so completely that there are virtually no early run fish getting to the rivers," snapped Karp. "When Malcom Crier left Alaska, he sent me a letter that the North Pacific Cannery folks had agreed to open the traps every third day to assure escapement. That isn't happening. Last week someone on shore started sniping at the workers on the trap at Kukwa, hell we're lucky that nobody was killed."

Marshal Walker shifted in his seat uneasily but said nothing. Judge Dischner placed his huge cigar in the ashtray. "Now Lyman, don't go getting too riled up over some missing fish."

"It's not the missing fish, Al, it's the hunger in the villages and the risk of a shooting war that has me riled up."

"Lyman, the Marshal here went over to visit the North Pacific folks just a couple of weeks ago. Sontag himself said that he never made any such commitment to open the traps, but as a gesture of good faith he was releasing all the fish that his cannery could not handle each week."

"Marshal, is that true?" asked the governor.

"That's what the son of a bitch said," snapped Walker. His statement was met by a hardened smile from the Judge and a finger point.

"Marshal Walker, need I remind you that our job is to enforce the law as it is written, not to judge a man for taking advantage of the openings that that law intentionally creates," growled Dischner.

"Judge Dischner," replied Walker, "I never quite got used to folks lying to me. I'm worried about the guards from the cannery and the villagers deciding to settle their differences with lead."

"Then Marshal, you will have to arrest the Indians who are threatening the traps. The law makes it clear that the property on which the traps are built is cannery property, sealed with a deed. No one has the right to threaten commerce in the territory," replied Dischner, his frozen smile barely allowing the words to slip from his mouth.

Magistrate Tome leaned across the table, the long legal pad in front of him extended toward the judge. "Al, here are a dozen different chapters and verses from the Oregon legal code that spell out different interpretations of what is right and legal here."

The judge pulled the huge cigar from his lips. This time he deliberately smashed it out on the legal pad in front of him. "Mr. Tome, you and the marshal here operate under the jurisdiction of my court, with your continued employment at least partially controlled by the monthly reports I send to Washington. I have made it clear which legal position takes precedence here. If anything other than that gets to my courtroom, I will throw it out."

Karp lost it. "Alouishes, no court in these United States has the right to deny justice."

"Two things for you to remember Governor," replied Dischner; "first this is a territory and not one of the states. Second, the separation of the judicial from the executive means that when it comes to the law, you play second fiddle."

The judge lifted his five-foot six-inch frame from the chair, pushing it off from his hips. "I am not looking for a fight with any of you, but you know my feelings on this issue. My marching orders are to protect the business investors and by God I will." He spun on his heels and marched for the door, his two hundred plus pounds wiggling like jelly underneath his blue pin-stripe suit. He turned at the door and continued, "Mr. Tome I suggest that you get your butt back to Juneau and next time send me a request before you leave to do any politicking. That's not allowed in the judiciary. And Marshal Walker, under the circumstances you had better send a clear message to the villages, that you won't tolerate any violence."

The other three men watched Dischner leave. Picking up their notes, they retired to their favorite watering hole to lick their wounds. With Alaska still legally a dry territory that watering hole was the private bar in the VIP room in the Russ-Am passengers' terminal only a ten minute walk away.

Chad watched the three men enter the terminal from his office upstairs and closed the journal book that he had been auditing and reached for his leather jacket. Except for the three new arrivals the terminal was empty. Walker emerged from behind the bar with a bottle of bourbon and a bottle of scotch and three glasses. Seeing Chad on the stairs he grabbed a fourth glass and headed to the table where other men seated themselves.

"Buy you gents a drink," laughed Chad.

"You already have Captain Gritt," replied Tome. "We just needed a private place to continue a very unsatisfactory conversation."

The impromptu meeting continued for an hour with all three men from the meeting bringing Chad up to speed. "Are you going back to Juneau on the *General Mead* in the morning?" Chad asked Tome.

"Dischner all but ordered me to."

"That's too bad, the salmon fishing just around the point has been incredible," offered Chad. "I would love to take you out tomorrow afternoon, but I am tied up this evening."

"Chad, if you will loan me your boat, I can take Jorge out this evening," offered Walker. "I could use a little away time myself," he paused looking out the window at a seagull scream-ing from the top of a piling, "after today."

"You know that you have a standing invitation to use the boat," replied Chad. "Just make sure you clean up any fish slime in the bottom. We still get the occasional bear on the docks, and they can really tear up a boat."

"How about it, Mr. Magistrate, do you trust a Texas cowboy on the water?"

"Lead on, you old bull buster," replied Tome rising. "I am going to steal this bottle of bourbon from a friend and take it with us."

Chad worked on his bourbon. Karp refreshed his Scotch. "We need to go talk to the people in all the villages. If Kukwa starts shooting, they all will."

"I am heading out in a couple of days; I'll see what might be done," answered Chad.

"What do you mean, be done?"

"This problem needs a solution, at least for this year while your letters get kicked around in Congress. The long term solution is in some action in Washington, but if we don't find some relief right away it will take the army to put the lid back on things," continued Chad.

"What do you have in mind?" asked Karp.

"Nothing yet, but I am working on it. Now does that invitation from Kate still stand for dinner. Danielle sent me a letter, some of which I should share with you."

Katherine Karp set a fine table, and after a dinner she excused herself and pulled her wrap around her shoulders. "Lyman, I have my bridge club tonight so you two just make yourself comfortable."

"What's Danielle got to report?" asked Karp. He placed a bottle of brandy on the small table and a humidor of pipe tobacco. "Here, let me get the windows open before you light that pipe. Kate has been known to sneak a pipe-full herself, but she will not tolerate stale smoke in the house at night."

The huge windows overlooking the harbor swung outward to the left and the right. An orange glow lit the tall, pot-bellied stove. The cool, moist air felt good in the stifling heat of the parlor.

"Your friend Malcom made a very good impression on Danielle," started Chad. "He was the perfect gentleman even after Gilda and Abraham retired to their cabin for the night. When Danny pressed him over the behavior of North Pacific Fisheries, he seemed genuinely surprised and assured her that he would help if he could."

"What kind of help did he offer?"

"He had already talked to the plant manager of the northern cannery. The same commitment that he sent you in his letter was made to Danielle. He offered to hand carry a letter from her to Washington and to use his influence to get some change in the laws protecting the fish."

"That sounds like the Malcom I know," responded Karp. "He is a master at using his influence to get things done in D.C. He can gin up a committee hearing faster than anybody I know."

"He pretty much said that to Danielle as well; invited her to attend when he got it all set up."

Karp laughed as he splashed a bit more brandy into his snifter. "Better watch that young lady. She really impressed Gilda Guildham, and you know what they say about the influence of Jewish aunties."

"You mean the old stories about their controlling behavior or about their cooking?" laughed Chad.

"Oh, they can cook alright. Given the opportunity they will cook up an entire plan for your life."

"Lyman, someday I may have some hold over Danny, but for now I think I'm just along for the ride. She has a real sense of right and wrong, and this fisheries thing is becoming a crusade for her. She was really impressed with Malcom's statements. He even called the boat's owner into the conversation and asked for his help."

"I thought that the boat belonged to the Guildhams," replied a surprised Karp.

"No, the boat belongs to a man by the name of Samuel Maples. He is from the east somewhere, Danny says he has a British accent. He bought the boat to keep an eye on business prospects in Alaska."

"I know Maples, he has been to Juneau four or five times in the last couple of years, usually in the spring and late fall. When I met him, he was on his way to the Yukon to look at mining prospects. Not a very talkative, almost creepy. He never socializes much when he is in Juneau. I've been told that he keeps an office upstairs in the Golden Goose Saloon."

"Danny didn't like him very much. Crier talked to him like he was a junior partner, but she wasn't quite sure who was really the top hand between the two. Still, when Crier asked him to check on the fish traps when he returns from the North, he said he would."

"I thought that the Guildhams and Crier were heading back south this week, not goin' up to Saint Michael," observed Karp.

"They are," replied Chad. "This Maples guy is taking a small expedition over Chilkoot Pass next month and then down the Yukon. His boat is taking Crier and the Guildhams south while he makes that trip, then turn north to pick him up in Saint Michael in October. He postponed his trip north to take a look at some properties up the Stikine, near Telegraph Creek."

"Alright, so we have Malcom trying to help, and Maples acting as his eyes next fall; that doesn't help us this summer," observed Karp.

"I will be in Kukwa in two days, let me see if I can help keep a lid on things. It might help if I had a copy of a letter from you to Congress or the President explaining the problem and asking for relief."

Karp poured himself a third brandy and repacked his pipe. "You will have it tomorrow. Could I impose on you to send the original with one of your captains on their next run south."

The morning was bright and pushing seventy degrees as Chad walked the beach from the house on the outskirts of town to the warehouse. The original house had been modernized by his parents twenty years before, and while it still held its rural charm, the dozen or more newer homes, built around it had changed the character from a cottage in the woods to a nice home in town. As he climbed the path to the road, he gazed longingly toward the far side of the bay, where the heavy spruce forest still stretched to the edge of the beach.

The passenger lounge was as empty as it had been the evening before. On the dock, four of the company's warehousemen were loading the last of fifteen tons of supplies for the canneries and villages for the mid-month trip. As Chad tossed his seabag onto the deck, a wagon from the Gritt Mercantile trundled onto the dock. The driver enlisted the help of one of the dock workers to unload a wooden case from the Winchester Repeating Arms Company. "What have you got there, Benny?" called Chad.

"One case of ten Winchester model 94 rifles and twenty boxes of cartridges," replied the driver. "They are consigned to Chief Medev at Kukwa." Benny returned to the wagon and removed two more smaller wooden cases and a package wrapped in kraft paper from behind the seat. "He also ordered these two Lee Navy rifles with telescope sights and four boxes of shells."

Not good, not good at all, thought Chad. The trading company had ordered a dozen custom built model 1895 straight bolt rifles with the new telescope sights the previous winter. With the last two going out to Kukwa, all twelve had sold by mid-summer. The modified rifle replaced the military adjustable rear ramp sites with a four-power telescope sight which gave the rifle the ability to deliver its 112 grain bullet accurately out to five-hundred yards. The other ten rifles had been sold to a stranger who had stopped by the mercantile in April. It slowly occurred to Chad that the rifles carried by the fish trap guards had been Lee Navy rifles with telescopes. "Damn," he said to himself.

"Benny, run back to the store and bring me six two-man cross-cut saws and a half-dozen pairs of wire cutters. Put them on my personal account."

"Aye, Aye Captain Gritt," replied the driver, snapping a sloppy salute.

With no passengers to worry about, Chad had the dock hands load as much freight as they could including a hundred cases of deck freight for Strom Johanson's cannery. Almost as an afterthought he had the crew retrieve his motor launch from the offshore buoy where it was moored. Using the boom, they swung it onto the rear deck of the *Miles Pierce* covering it with a tarp. The ship was underway before seven.

At Johansons they unloaded two-thirds of their freight. "Thanks for sending me those three boats from Juneau last month," said Johanson. "We have had to cover a lot of ground to keep the slime lines full. Those bastards from North Pacific go out of their way to run those power tenders over our nets if we are anywhere close to their traps, so we just stay away."

"Glad to help," replied Chad, "we can settle up at the end of your season as usual."

"While you are down toward Kukwa, would you keep an eye out for one of our twenty-four foot double-ended sailboats. They went out the day before yesterday and should have been back by this afternoon. If you see them, remind them that we won't can fish that are out of the water for more than two days."

"Sure will," replied Chad. "Any other trouble with the North Pacific Folks?"

"They took a run at recruiting a couple of boat crews, but with all local crews hating the traps, they didn't get very far. That's about it. When will you be ready to start hauling out my pack?" asked Johanson.

"The *General Mead* is on its way up from Wrangell and Petersburg. I asked them to stop by to see if you have outbound freight. You should see them about the end of the week. I'll be back in a couple of weeks."

The lack of passengers meant that the *Denali* had sailed with minimum crew. Second officer Macky was also acting as the boat's engineer, and the only other crewman was a young Indian boy from a village at the southern end of Admiralty Island. Ivan stood on the starboard deck as the small ship slipped past the fish trap near Kukwa. While a large steam tender loaded baskets of King Salmon from the center of the trap, three guards stood next to a small shack on the shore-side of the trap.

The trap started with a long fence extending out into the inlet. That fence ran toward the shore and then began to curl into a narrow channel that coiled into a holding pen at its center. A fish entering the trap would follow around the fence made up of chicken wire nailed to posts pounded into the gravel bottom until they found themselves trapped by their own homing instincts in the center. The spiral was about thirty yards across with the holding pen no more than twenty by twenty feet.

This day it boiled with large king salmon the color of new silver dollars. A wooden walkway crossed the top of the trap from the guard shack near shore to the holding pen and then made a ninety-degree turn to the heavy pilings where a tender was moored. A huge upright tree trunk set halfway between the tender and the holding pen allowed a scoop-net hung from a cross boom to ladle fish from the pen and dump them onto the deck of the tender.

The workers ignored the ships passing, but the guards followed its progress, one even studying the ship and the visible men through a telescope. Ivan climbed the ladder to the bridge and sat down on a stool at the chart table behind his captain. "That is not right Captain. They catch all the fish. I do not know how those men in the shack can stand the smell. The bottom of the pen must be full of rotting fish."

"That's the problem with traps," replied Chad. "When the tender is full, the remaining fish just sit in the pen. As new fish flow to the center they can pack the pen so tight that the fish cannot swim and they suffocate."

"The people in my village do not want trouble with the law or the Navy, but they aren't going to allow a trap to be built on our river," said Ivan. "Those of us at Mount Edgcumbe school talk about it all the time. It is not right, like the King of England taxing tea in Boston was not right. We have all sent letters home offering to help with whatever our villages decide to do about the traps."

As usual the entire village of Kukwa was at the dock when the *Miles Pierce* backed against the mooring piling and tied up. Ivan enlisted a half dozen young men to help unload the freight for the village. Chief Medev waited until the lamp oil and sacks of flour and barrels of sugar and molasses were safely ashore before he and Belinda stepped over the rail.

Chief John Medev was a barrel chested man in his mid-forties. No more than five feet six-inches tall. His years of hard physical work had left his body with the tautness of a coiled spring. "You got my rifles?" he asked.

"They are just inside the door to the cabin," said Chad. "I also brought a present for the prettiest schoolteacher in Alaska."

"You eat dinner at Belle's house," continued Medev. "Belle will make chicken with dumpling, my favorite new food. She learned cook it in Oregon."

"If it is alright with you John, we would like to tie up here for the night. We have been on our feet for eighteen straight hours."

"You stay for sure," responded the Chief. "But you go tomorrow before we go fish trap. We do not want our old friend to have trouble, but we must have trouble."

Chad grabbed one end of the case of rifles while Chief Medev took the other. In their other hand each carried one of the scoped rifles while Belinda cradled the ammunition in her arms.

"Are the rifles for use at the fish trap?" asked Chad.

"My friend, do not ask many questions and I will not have to go against God's word and lie."

"I know it's late," commented Chad, "but I would like to talk to the elders about the fish trap tonight. Maybe we can have chicken tomorrow. We are ahead of schedule, and I can stay two nights."

"No, we have chicken with dumpling tonight. Belle already cut chicken, and you bring flour. We all talk tomorrow. We shoot rifles tomorrow and go to fish trap next day."

While Belinda was away at school the Society of Mission Friends had built a small church in the village. The church became the schoolhouse during the week, and a presbyterian place of worship on Sundays. The teacher's residence was in the back of the building and although small was the most modern house in Kukwa. A hand driven sand point well brought water inside the house and a large cast iron stove and oven provided both heat for the house and a place to cook.

Dinner that night might have been found in any farm in the Willamette valley. Chicken and dumplings with a salad of local greens, served on China plates with linen napkins. After dinner John pulled on his old wool jacket and lit his pipe. "Belle not let me smoke in her house. We talk tomorrow, you and whole village. Belinda ring school belle and we all come.

With a twinkle in his eye, he smiled at his daughter and reached out for Chad's hand. "I go now."

Belinda cleared the table and poured steaming water from a kettle into a porcelain tea pot and set it on the table. "It is very nice to cook for you Mr. Gritt." Belinda's smile lit up her whole face. "You have already figured out that tomorrow or the next day there will be real trouble at that fish trap."

"I know, but somehow we need to find a way to stop this before someone gets killed." Chad went on to explain the policy of Judge Dischner. "So, you see, if someone gets killed, the judge will send the marshal to the village. He will need proof to make a case, but the judge will accept almost anything. He will hang someone just to send a message."

"Mr. Gritt, we will talk about this tomorrow. For tonight we will drink a cup of tea, and you can tell me what is going on outside."

"First, open your present," directed Chad, pointing at a bundle wrapped in butcher paper and tied with a cotton string.

Belle gently untied the string and neatly rolled it and placed it in a cigar box. "We do not waste anything here where supplies are so hard to get," she said. "She gently unfolded the paper and folded it and placed it beneath the cigar box. She then stood beaming as she pulled a new yellow print dress against her body and spun around. "It is very pretty. It is the first dress that a man has ever given me."

"Your friend Irma picked it out," stammered Chad, his cheeks more than a little red. "It's hard to be part of the outside world in the village. Anyway, I'm just the delivery boy."

"If you will excuse me for a moment, I will go try it on." Belle shut the door to her small bedroom for more than ten minutes and then emerged. She wore the bright yellow dress with lace around the sleeves and neck with the pride Danielle had worn her gown at the ball in Juneau. Belle had brushed out her hair and left it long and flowing over one shoulder.

Chad sat very still, not a word came to him.

"You do not like it?" asked Belle.

"You are beautiful, I mean it is very beautiful," he managed. "Is the tea ready yet."

An hour later, after Belle had entertained with three or four pieces on the pump organ in the school, Chad excused himself made his way back to the ship.

There were too many people at the morning meeting to fit into the school, so the meeting moved to the community house, a traditional Tlingit longhouse carefully cared for by a people with a proud heritage. Most of the smoke from a small fire trailed up through a hole in the ceiling with just enough circulating through the structure to ward off the biting black flies that swarmed the village.

"You talk now," directed the Chief, pointing at Chad.

Chad rose and pointed in the direction of the hated fish trap. "I know and the Governor knows that the fish trap is destroying the fish in your river. We all know that if something is not done soon, the people of Kukwa will have a hungry winter. We also know that if you kill the men at the trap the law will come, probably with the navy and they will arrest many of you and they will hang some of you."

A young man stood up on the other side of the fire. Chad recognized him as a former student in Sitka, but he now wore the ceremonial robe of a village shaman. Obviously, the village had made their selection to replace Old Joe. "Captain Gritt, you and your family have been friends with our people for almost a century. This is not your fight. But there will be a fight. We have already discussed who will be arrested by the marshal and we know that they will probably never come back to the village. We will miss them."

"You are Peter, do I remember your name correctly?" asked Chad.

Peter smiled and nodded his head.

"Peter, if no one dies at the fish trap, then no one will be hanged."

"Chad," said Peter using Chad's first name indicating that they were now equals, "we will kill the men at the trap quickly and then we will tear down the trap. It is better that we kill them quickly instead of waiting for them to kill us slowly. The elders have decided."

Chad pointed at his crewman, standing at the back of the room. "Ivan, tell these people what you told me yesterday, about Boston."

Ivan waited until Chief Medev nodded his approval. "The history books about the United States talk about the King of England making unfair taxes on the people in Boston. Those people were very angry and had the Boston Tea Party."

Watching the confused faces, Chad was about to ask Ivan to explain, but he was stopped by Belle Medev holding up her hand. She stood and looked at her father, who nodded.

"What Ivan is explaining is that in the United States there is a long history of the people opposing bad things, unjust things. In Boston, the men dressed up like Indians and went to the docks and went aboard the ships that carried the tea from England. Rather than pay the tax on the tea, they dumped it all into the harbor to show the King that the tax was unjust and that they would not pay it."

"Did they kill the men on the ships?" asked the Chief.

"No, they only destroyed what was hated. They dressed up so that the Boston marshal would not know who threw away the tea," responded Ivan with a smile on his face.

This gave Chad the opening that he hoped for. "If you kill the men at the fish trap there will be very bad trouble for the people of Kukwa. If you kill the fish trap there will still be trouble, but it will be much better for all of you."

"How do we kill the fish trap?" asked the Shamen. "The guards on the trap point guns at us every time we walk or paddle our canoes past the trap. Sometimes our young men get angry and shoot at the building or the tender boat."

"Peter, that is what we must figure out. We must get the guards away from the trap, long enough to destroy it." Chad smiled at Belle who was smiling at him.

"I brought six large two man saws like the loggers use to cut trees. I brought wire cutters to cut the wire from the logs to open up the trap. The boat that was used to drive the piles into the bottom of the bay hit a rock two months ago and sank. If we can destroy the trap, it will be at least a year before North Pacific could try to rebuild it. If no one knows who destroyed the trap, then the judge cannot put anyone in jail. He will try. He may have some people arrested, but without witnesses willing to testify, he has no case."

Chief Medev stood again. The room was silent for ten minutes as they waited for his decision. "We have tea party at fish trap," he said. "Good thing that we not have to dress up like Indian."

The entire room erupted in laughter. The chief continued. "We must cut down the trap at night when only guards are there. We shoot a couple of times from shore and run, guards always chase, shooting guns. Then we capture guards like in the old days, we catch great bears. When the guards are gone, we work all night to cut trap and burn dock and small house. We go tonight. Now we shoot new guns."

Blocks of firewood were set against the hillside next to the village, and ten men including the shamans were selected to receive, sight, and shoot the Winchester repeating rifles. Chief Medev unpacked one of the Lee Navy rifles and asked Chad for his help in learning to use the rifle and the telescope sight.

Having never used one himself, it took the two men an hour to hit a block of wood set up two-hundred yards away. The Chief handed the second rifle to his daughter.

The move surprised Chad, but no one else in the group. "Belle shoot gun better than all men in village," explained the Chief. Belle, unlike Chad, took the time to read the manual that came in the box. She set up a block at only thirty yards and shot three times. Using a screwdriver that came with the rifle, she adjusted the mounts on the scope and fired one more time. Satisfied, she then aimed at one of the blocks set at two-hundred yards.

"You may have to help me hold this rifle steady," she said to Chad. "Maybe I can just lean against you and have you support my left elbow."

She turned to look at Chad, finding him bright red. "It would not be proper for me to put my arm around you."

"Alright, I will do it on my own." Belle raised the ten pound rifle and splintered the target block.

"Nice shooting Annie Oakley," complimented Chad.

Two hours later, The village helped Chad unload and anchor his fishing boat in a cove just down the beach from the village. Belle Medev was singing as she paddled a canoe up next to the boat waiting for Chad to join her. "Isn't that Shenandoah?" asked Chad, lowering himself into the canoe.

"It is. It's one of my favorite songs. It seems appropriate with what we are setting out to do."

"You know that the South lost in the end," advised Chad.

"My people will probably also lose in the end," replied Belle, "but not tonight. A song from a people fighting overwhelming odds because they thought that they were right seems appropriate. Where to Captain?"

"Back to the ship, I want it out of here this afternoon while all of those at the fish trap can watch."

"Both Macky and Ivan have bigger dogs in this fight than you. Yet you stay while they go, why?"

"I promised the governor to try to keep a lid on this."

CHAPTER 8

Kukwa Inlet, Alaska

THE RAIN MEANT that it would be dark before midnight. That gave the Kukwa Tea Party, as they had started calling themselves, four hours to complete their work.

The *Miles Pierce* would wait across the sound at a cove just north of Johansons.

As he loaded his Colt pistol, Chad watched twenty men and women traipse silently back into the village. They looked exhausted, shovels, hatchets and baskets slung over stooped shoulders. Belle greeted the work party from the steps of the school.

"They look like they have walked for miles," whispered Chad.

"They have been digging a bear pit and covering it with sticks and moss. Peter has volunteered to fire a few shots at the guard shack and then run down the trail with a small lantern. We hope the guards will follow and fall into the pit. They dug it so that the guards can't get out until we help. It is how my people hunted grizzly bears in the old days when we only had spears."

"You talk about your people. Both your mother and father are both Russian and Tlingit," observed Chad. "You went to a mission school and then a university."

"I am both, but tonight the Tlingit part of me reminds me of how great our warrior ancestors were. We were feared from Cooks Inlet to the San Juan Islands. With your help, we will make a new legend tonight."

"You aren't going tonight, are you?" asked Chad.

"I am the closest thing we have to a doctor, Mr. Gritt."

Her move from formal to informal and back to formal puzzled Chad, but he ignored the thought. "This may be very dangerous. What if one or more of the guards doesn't feel like a bear tonight?"

"That is where my father and you and I come in. We will wait near the pit to make sure that all the guards are in the trap. I will have a storm lantern with the sides covered. You have a pistol, and my father will take his old fowling gun. We must be very persuasive."

"The guards cannot know for sure that the attackers are from the village. I should do all the talking," said Chad.

Belle nodded her head. "Do you think that a new legend will be born tonight?"

"I think that we will prevail, but I pray that you don't turn this into a legend. We want to leave as few tracks that point to the village as possible," replied Chad.

"I agree, but legends do not become legends for decades or more," replied Belle. She leaned over and kissed his cheek. "Then before the tender boat comes in the morning you must take your small boat and leave. If the cannery guards come here, I do not want you to be found. There will be fighting if they come to the village. I am the best shot in the village. I don't want you to think of me that way."

❧

"I can take the entire work crew. We will hide the boat in the small cove where we found your grandfather. We need a couple of men with a canoe to take you, your father and me to shore so that I can leave the boat anchored.

"Peter and five men already took canoes to the cove. They are watching the guards."

The soft puff, puff, puff of the steam engine was the only sound from the small power launch as it set off from the village. Fourteen people crowded the deck pushing the boat deep into the water until only inches of freeboard remained. The branches overhanging the inlet were only shadows where the moonless light of the summer night made the inlet slightly lighter than the dark of the surrounding forest. Chad had applied a heavy layer of grease to all the moving parts of the boat and removed the chain between the anchor and the anchor line in order to make the operation as silent as possible.

The boat crept along the shore just far enough from the beach to avoid hitting an unseen rock. It was half-past eleven when the anchor was carefully lowered into the brine. Chad waited until a dozen armlengths of line was played out into the water and then he slowly backed the boat away from where the anchor lay on the bottom. The moment that he felt the anchor bite and slow the boats motion he pushed the long steel gear-box control lever into neutral and stepped from the wheel.

"It's time," he said. He turned to the waiting work crew. "I will be back just as soon as we know that the guards are all accounted for." Belinda translated for those who only spoke Tlingit.

A canoe slid up next to the boat and Belle, her father and Chad stepped easily from the overloaded boat into the canoe.

Within minutes they were creeping along a moss covered trail led by Peter who carried a small candle lamp. Belle, Peter and Chief John moved silently, somehow anticipating every rock and fallen branch. Chad moved like a white man.

They stopped at a small opening in the dark forest. Two men armed with new Winchester repeaters stepped from the forest and guided the party around the edge of a mossy meadow, stopping at the other side. "We walk past bear trap," said the chief, pointing back down the trail that they had just skirted.

Belle pointed out a dozen small trees on each side of the trail that jutted from the forest into the meadow. "They cut trees and pushed them into the moss to make a funnel that runs directly to the trap." She lifted the metal shade from one side of her storm lantern, illuminating the trail beyond the trees. There was no evidence of where the trail had been disturbed by digging. "We will wait here, just behind that large fallen tree. The other two men will go back to the other side of the trap just in case one of the guards gets past here. They have been told to stop anyone with clubs not their rifles. No investigator can tell if the bump on the head comes from a fall on a dark trail or one of us."

"We make sure three guards go to trap," directed Chief Medev. "Only you talk," he said, tapping Chad on his chest with his finger. "Peter, you go now."

The log that concealed them was from an ancient tree, the kind that only grew in the rainforests of the Pacific northwest. It was more than ten feet across at its base, too large to see over. Belinda climbed to the top of the log where she could watch the path below her, silhouetted against a pool of rainwater on the other side of the trail. "I will count the guards," she said. Hold my foot in your hand. I will flex my ankle as each run by."

Five minutes later two rifle shots spaced about thirty seconds apart boomed through the forest, followed by a third a minute later. Those shots were answered by a half-dozen shots from different rifles. A few seconds later a voice in clear English called out, "You shot me, oh God, I am shot."

Chad picked up his rifle and started toward the trail but was stopped by Chief Medev. "It is plan."

Moments later a faint light could be seen running through the forest, then it stopped. Peter screamed, "when they find my body, you all will hang!"

In less than a minute a man could be heard running past the log. "They are coming," he hissed as he passed.

Less than a minute later the thunk of heavy boots told the story of his pursuers. Belle's foot twitched once and only a second or two later a second time. "God Damn," bellowed out through the forest. A second voice followed with a scream just as Belle's foot twitched for the third time. Chief John and Chad slipped from behind the log and blocked the trail.

"What's going on boys?" came a voice. "I can still see that lantern light farther down the trail, but other than that it's darker than midnight in a coal bin."

"Both Stanley and me fell in a big old hole. Come help us out!"

Chad carried the lantern, still blacked out, in one hand and in the other his old Colt. He and Chief John crept toward the voices.

"You damn fools, that boy ran you right into a pit trap," laughed a voice.

"Reed, get us out of here!"

Chad and John slipped up close enough to see the silhouette of a man in the trail only a few feet in front of them.

"You hold on, boys. I need to make sure that there ain't bushwhackers waiting to shoot us all."

"Reed, that shooter dropped that old rusty match-block rifle right where we shot at him. He ain't armed. Now get us out, I mean right now."

"You two cover the edges of the pit with your rifles while I go back to the shack for a rope. I'll be back in ten minutes," came the reply.

Chad held the lantern out and dropped the shade from the side facing the pit. "I think not, drop that rifle."

The guard swung his rifle upward as he turned and pulled the trigger. The bullet shattered the lantern glass and ripped the top off from the lamp oil tank splashing the fluid back toward its holder. The oil began to ignite, first down Chad's bleeding arm and then down his side onto his pants.

The shooter, now rattled and shaking with rage, stumbled trying to work the bolt in his rifle. He turned toward the chief, silhouetted by the fire. Chad sprang swinging his pistol like a club, he hit the man across his nose. The guard stumbled back two steps and fell into the pit.

At almost the same moment a blur from Chad's right caused him to turn just as Belle leaped from the top of the log, knocking the burning man sideways into the pool of rainwater. Belle pushed his burning arm, side and leg into the pool. The pool hissed as Chad's burning clothing turned the water to steam.

Chad rolled into a sitting position. "Are you alright?" she whispered.

"The glass cut my hand and arm, but I don't think I'm badly burned."

"We need to disarm those men in the pit, and then I need to get you back to the boat where I can get a light on you. Can you talk to those men?"

Chad stood up, the burned fabric of his jacket, shirt and pants hanging at his side. He started for the pit stopping where he could not be seen.

"You surprised me with that shot, lucky for you or I would have gut shot you and left you for the bears. Now I want to see three rifles thrown out of that pit and three knives and I mean now."

"You ain't no savage, why is this your fight?" came a snarl from the pit.

"I don't think that is a very important question right now, do you? If I were you, I would throw your rifles out before I have my friend John lean out and cut loose with the shotgun that he carries."

"Looks to me like with three rifles down here and only two guns up there we have a standoff."

"John, sweep the edge of the pit," snapped Chad.

A boom and then a second exploded through the forest. Dirt and rocks showered the men cowering in the hole.

After the echo died, Chad continued, "he just reloaded and in one minute he is going to walk around the edge of this pit and let fly with buckshot until he runs out of shells. If any of you are still alive, we will leave you for the bears."

A rifle flew up and out of the pit. "What the hell are you doing?"

A match flamed from the pit. "Reed, one of us is out cold from the fall, and you are bleeding like a stuck pig from that broken nose. We can't get at them and they sure as hell can get at us. Besides, if they don't show mercy we maybe sit here until the bears figure out how to finish us off."

Two more rifles and then three knives soared out of the pit. "Can you get us a rag or something to work on my busted nose?"

"I am sad to say, that we are fresh out of rags and patience. I am going to leave two men behind to keep an eye on you until we are done at the trap. When we leave, one of them will slide a log down there to give you something to crawl out on."

"I will find out who you are," came a voice, "and when I do, I will finish what I started with that shot."

"I have the advantage, I know your name is Reed, and where you work. If I ever see you again, I will shoot you so full of holes that your friends will think you are a piece of ladies' lace. I think that all three of you had better find a way to head toward Wrangell or Ketchikan and then find a way out of the territory."

"I ain't afraid of no one who wouldn't shoot after I set him afire."

"Do not take my mercy for anything but my not wanting to have to explain your blood to my maker. That would be a mistake. My associates from the logging camp here are worried about the trouble you and your cannery friends are stirring up. When they tell Rattler Wilson that you just ran away and let them burn the fish trap, I won't need to find you."

There was silence from inside the pit. A third voice joined the discussion. "Reed, my head hurts but I ain't crazy. I do not want to tangle with Rattler. How the hell are we going to get away from him?"

Chad chuckled through clinched teeth, the burns now beginning to hurt. "Once you get out of that pit, I would go hat in hand to the village down the bay and tell them that you helped burn that trap and see if they will smuggle you down to Wrangell. They will probably be willing to help anybody that got rid of that monstrosity."

Ten minutes later Chad, with the help of the villagers, had the anchor up and the boat on its way to the trap. Belle had a lantern lit and was working on cleaning the cuts in his left hand and arm. The cold salt water from the bay stung in the cuts but cooled and soothed the burns. She waited as he nosed the bow of the boat onto the beach and the Kukwa Tea Partiers leaped to the beach. With the boat right at the trap, Chad tugged on the cord sounding the steam whistle three times as a signal to the village that the destruction was under way. They needed to bring the two large canoes to take the villagers home after their work. He also meant it to send a message to the men in the pit that whoever was destroying the trap came in a powered boat.

Six crews began working on the edge of the falling tide, cutting down the posts that supported the wire mesh of the trap. The posts were cut near to the ground to keep them from being used as foundations to quickly rebuild the trap. As the first six posts began to fall, another crew began to cut the chicken wire from the posts and roll it up.

In three hours, they had cut more than thirty-five posts, working in dim light on the rain slick beach. They waded into the incoming tide to continue cutting. They left some pilings standing where it was too difficult to cut them but cut away as much wire as they could reach. As they opened an escape route, hundreds of salmon flooded out of the trap, heading for the Kukwa River. At the bottom of the trap, a layer of dead and decaying salmon made the footing slippery and the stench almost overwhelming.

The boat remained offshore, tethered to a piling. Belinda worked to clean the charred cloth from Chad's burned leg and side. The blackened skin made picking the scorched fabric from the cuts difficult in the dim light. She poured water over the wounds until she had to stop to bail the boat. Belle dug through the chest at the back of the boat and recovered the bucket of tallow that Chad used to grease the gear box.

She looked back as Chad slowly melted to the deck, his burns becoming excruciating. "I can't get to the worst of the burns with you lying down," she said. She helped her patient sit on the box in the middle of the deck. Slipping the Captain's knife from its sheath she cut away half his shirt and the remaining shreds of his pants leg.

She carefully rubbed the grease into his burns until all were covered with a thick layer. "It will keep the air out which should lessen the pain, and it will help protect against infection. Chad lay back on the cover over the propeller shaft and moaned the pain evident on his twisted face. Belle rummaged through the tool chest and recovered the partial bottle of whiskey that the marshal and magistrate had left. She pressed it to Chad's lips. "Here this will help with the pain."

Chad took her hand in his, pushing the bottle away. "Thank you for all of your help, but I have to navigate out of here in the next hour."

"Captain Gritt, you have helped all of us more than you will ever know. We are no longer powerless. We are not going to let you try to run this boat across the sound alone, not in the condition you are in. Now drink this while I recruit some help."

As the work crews finished their work, Chad's boat was pulled to shore, and the rolls of cut chicken wire were stacked on the deck. The huge two man saws and the wire cutters were lashed to the side of the boat where they could be discarded in a hurry if necessary. Then the tea partiers pushed the boat out from the beach. With Peter at the wheel, they started out across the narrow bay toward the open sound. "The walkways and the building are burning," said Belle. "All of the canoes are heading home."

Peter tugged on the boat whistle three times to signal the men watching the pit that the time to head home was at hand. As the boat cleared the bay into deep water, Peter tied off the wheel and began dumping the wire bundles over the side where they could never be recovered.

Five hours later they pushed up against the dock at Johansons cannery. Belinda ran up the dock, turning toward the manager's office. In minutes, Strom was aboard the small boat with a first aid kit. Peter headed for the *Miles Pierce* anchored only five miles away. "He needs a doctor," said Belle, "but one who won't talk."

Johansen and Belle helped Chad onto the deck of the ship as Ivan and Macky made preparations to get under way.

Johanson nodded, "take him to old Doc Ginder, he was an army surgeon in the war, he will know about burns. He is one of the biggest critics of the way some of the big businesspeople and the politicians are treating Alaska. Tell Chad that I'll take good care of his boat and make sure that Peter gets home. Now you take good care of your patient young lady."

It was dusk when the small ship pushed up against the dock in Juneau. While Belle and Macky helped Chad into the wagon, they sent a runner to find Doc Ginder, at his usual table in the bar at the Romanoff.

The doctor arrived at Danielle Post's apartment to find Chad sitting on a chair in the kitchen. Both Danielle and Belle were helping to remove the old cotton shirt that Johanson had given to the patient.

An hour later the doctor pronounced his diagnosis. "That man will fully recover, but it will take three or four weeks for those burns to heal." Doc Ginder smiled at Belle Medev. "Young lady, you did a really fine job in cleaning those cuts and dressing the burns. One of you will have to help keep them oiled for another week and then he should be back on his own."

"I will be happy to take care of Captain Gritt," volunteered Danielle." Turning to Belle she continued, "I am assuming that is why you brought him here."

"It is," replied Belle. She hoped that no one noticed tears in the corner of her eyes. "I must get back to Kukwa before there is more trouble."

Macky, Doc Ginder and Danielle all started to speak. Belle lifted her hand, silencing them. "The Captain was burned trying to help the village, and I must get back to finish his work. No one can know about his burns."

Macky picked up his heavy oilskin jacket and opened the door. "There won't be a Russ-Am boat going that direction for ten days."

"I must get back."

The doctor picked up his black bag and flopped his old campaign hat on his bald head. "You are in luck young lady. I sewed up one of the cannery workers from Johansons yesterday; sliced wide open in an accident on the line. He is spending the night at my office, but he will be ready to travel tomorrow. The boat that brought him up here is still in town."

"Can you take me to him?" asked Belle. "I need to ask him for a ride."

"Not tonight, Miss, I have given him a touch of opium, and I want him to sleep. Doc Ginder handed a small bottle to Danielle. "Give the good Captain one teaspoon of this to help him sleep. He should only have a dose every four or five hours."

The doctor turned back to Belinda. "Have you a place to stay tonight?" he asked.

"No," replied Belle.

"When was the last time you ate?" asked the doctor.

"Late last night."

Then let's get back to the Romanoff before it closes. I can use a nightcap, and we can get you something to eat. Then you can spend the night with my wife and me."

Danielle placed her hand on Belle's arm and smiled. "Doc, the Romanoff doesn't allow Natives in the bar," she said. "They especially won't appreciate a girl in rough wool pants and a flannel shirt."

"I am somewhat of a regular. They will make an exception for me."

"Just a minute Doc, let me get Belinda a quick change of clothes, maybe they won't even ask."

Ten minutes later Belle and Doc Ginder followed Macky down the stairs, out into the rain. Belle was wearing a simple blue dress and carried her village clothes in a cloth shopping bag. She turned to Danielle, "You will take good care of him?"

"I will," replied Danielle, "and I will make sure that he knows who gave him all the help getting him here. And if you find that you need a lawyer to help with the troubles in Kukwa, look me up."

The tears on Belle's cheeks mixed with rain were impossible to hide as she turned into the street.

"Damn," was all Danielle said.

CHAPTER 9

Juneau, Alaska

THE CUTS FROM the flying glass had healed to the point where even the rubbing of his shirt no longer opened the wounds. The burns stung with the sweat that came from unloading freight on the only day that summer where the temperature in Juneau pushed past eighty degrees. Like all four men working to unload the ship *Maximilian* that afternoon, Chad was stripped down to his sleeveless undershirt. Unlike the others, his arms were mottled, some white, some a light red and other places a soft tan. He had turned the clipboard over to his foreman, the lasting effects of the opium leaving him with no interest in bookkeeping.

"Take a break boss," suggested the ship's captain. "I have a note for you from an Ed Sprint.

He passed me a letter just before we cast off from the dock in Seattle, asked for me to get it to you."

Chad sat down on a stack of boxes and ripped the end off from the envelope. The note took only a minute to read. Chad folded the note and placed it back into the envelope. "Hey anybody know about North Pacific losing a passenger between here and Ketchikan in the last month?"

Thankful for the excuse to take a break, the dock crew crowded around. The foreman pulled a dollar from his pocket and handed it to the youngest hand. "Run over to the Golden Goose and fetch us a pail of cold beer Tommy boy and keep the change."

Turning to Chad, he handed his boss a folded red bandana. Chad used it to wipe the sweat from his face and burned arm. "We heard-tell of a Yukon miner who fell overboard somewhere just north of Wrangell. The ship wasn't even supposed to be stopping there, but some big wig pulled some strings. Rumor has it that the guy had been drunk since before he left Juneau. No one will find that body Chad. Why, was he a friend of yours?"

Chad carefully folded the bandana with the damp side in and handed it back to his foreman. "I picked the miner and his brother up in Haines and then put him on the *General Mead* to Juneau where they could get a berth south. His brother and I put together a plan to help them next summer, up on the Yukon. This note says that the older brother started shooting his mouth about their mine over too much drink at the Golden Goose and the next night went missing from his stateroom on the way south."

Pat James, the skipper of the *Max* rolled a keg of flour over next to Chad and seated himself. "I am sorry about the loss of a customer, hell every man of the sea hurts when the sea gods take one of ours."

"His brother isn't sure he is drowned," replied Chad tapping the envelope."

"What's that supposed to mean?" asked one of the dock crew.

"The brothers were part of a small company that was

prospecting on the Upper Yukon. They thought that they might have found something worthwhile and were going outside to find a grubstake," replied Chad, shading the truth a bit in order to keep his promise of discretion. He paused, looking for just the right words. He'd seen too many workers disappear when rumors of a gold strike swept through town.

"Bob always had trouble with drink, and he apparently made some new friends in the couple of hours that he spent at the Golden Goose. Those men arranged for passage on the North Pacific supply ship the next day. Bob and his friends were in their cabin drinking the night before. Ed, that's the brother who wrote me, couldn't find any of the three when they docked in Wrangell the next morning. Only Bob's disappearance was reported. Ed wanted to organize a search, but the crew of the ship insisted that he go on south with them."

The beer arrived, and the men retreated to the warehouse to find cups and glasses. Each dipped a mug and sat down on the edge of the dock, their legs hanging out over the water. Pat James rolled his barrel over to the seated men, his bad back making it impossible to get up without help if he had joined them. "Why in the hell wouldn't the brother just get off the ship?"

"His note says that he was almost a prisoner. The North Pacific agent in Ketchikan told him that there wouldn't be a ship either north or southbound for at least two weeks. The agent agreed to send word north and from what you say, he did. Ed went on to Seattle alone and then sent the note to me asking me to check with the authorities. Is the marshal in Juneau?"

"Yup. What would someone want with a drunk miner?" asked the foreman.

"He knew a lot about their supposed strike," replied Chad. "From Wrangell, it's only a day up to Telegraph Creek by steamboat and from there only a couple of weeks travel to the head of the Yukon. A couple of claim jumpers could be walking the Sprint brothers claim already." Chad swung his legs around and rose. "I think that I will wander up to Magistrate Tome's office and see the marshal. He should read Ed Sprints letter. The rest of you finish that beer before it gets warm then get back to what I pay you for."

On the way to the magistrate's office, Chad found himself in front of the Golden Goose. The noise from the half-filled saloon echoed out into the street through the open front doors. Chad painfully pulled his long sleeved shirt on over his burns and headed for the bar. He ordered another chilled beer and reached for the coin poke in his canvas pants.

"This ones on me, Captain Gritt."

Chad turned to find Rattler Wilson walking across the floor from his office at the back of the room. "I wanted to find out what you knew about the fire at the Kukwa fish trap and the disappearance of two guards down there. The marshal and me are taking a little trip to Kukwa in the morning," said Rattler.

Chad gulped down the first third of his beer. "Thanks," he responded. "As to the fish trap, hell I'm glad it's gone, but I can't give you any information on it or your men."

"The head guard, I think you know him, Reed, was waiting for the work boat the next morning with some bull story about some loggers dumping him and the other guards in a hole in the ground while they burned the trap."

"The loggers are really upset at the cannery folks for stirring up trouble with the Natives. Some of their work crews have gone back to the villages to protect their fisheries."

Wilson poured himself a beer. Leaning on the bar next to Chad, he continued. "Sounds like what Reed described alright. The pilings were cut off clean like with crosscut saws and the wire was all hauled away. The walkway and the guard house were doused with lamp oil and burned. While in the pit, the guards heard the whistle of a workboat."

"There you go then, all you need to do is start to canvass the logging camps," replied Chad, downing the next third of his beer.

"Maybe, but I don't think so. I think that the loggers couldn't have sneaked up between the village and the fish trap and dug a pit. I think it's your friends in Kukwa. We will find out, you can count on that." Wilson smiled, gripping Chad's burned arm in his hand as he turned away.

It was all Chad could do to hide the pain. He picked up his glass and drained it to mask his face. "Is Samuel Maples still in town?" he asked. "I heard that he went down to Wrangell but was going to come back through on his way to Haines and the Yukon."

"Sam changed his mind after he sent your pals Crier and Guildham on their way. He hitched a ride to Wrangell on one of the North Pacific boats and was planning to go up the Stikine and then overland to the head of the Yukon. I suspect that he won't be back in Juneau until early winter. Why do you ask?"

"Oh, Danielle Post suggested that he might be a possible investor in a mine that some friends are developing. I'll catch him in the fall."

Magistrate Tome and Marshal Walker were just closing their office for lunch as Chad arrived. "Where you boys heading?" he asked.

"Somewhere that we can get a real meal for lunch," answered Walker.

"I have a date with Danielle for lunch down at the Crossing Café in an hour," offered Chad. "Why don't you two join us?"

"I shouldn't take an hour away from work," replied Walker

with a smile. "The magistrate has me really loaded up and I am heading south on the government boat tomorrow."

Chad pulled the envelope from his pocket and handed it to Walker. "We will make the first forty-five minutes a working meeting then."

Walker and Tome nodded as Chad started toward the small boat dock just across the channel from Douglas Island. As they walked, Chad offered the background on his relationship with the Sprint brothers. At the small working man's café, they asked for a table to be moved out onto the dock and when the owner learned that Danielle would be joining them, he found a tablecloth.

"Is that Miss Post your lady?" the owner asked Chad.

Chad fought off his red face. "Danny and I see each other, but she's not anybody's gal."

"Too bad. She the best catch in Juneau. She help me a lot with plenty of trouble in last two year. Chinaman still not welcome by all people in Juneau. Still, much better than ten year ago. You want fresh lemonade? We just get plenty lemons from California."

Tome and Walker looked at Chad with puzzled expressions. "Ten years ago, the mine owners were bringing Chinese workers to Juneau. They worked hard and some say for less pay. Anyway, the Irish and the Polish workers felt threatened and began to raise hell about the new workers. It turned into several days of all-out riots. Most of the Chinese were herded onto ships and sent south."

"That happened in a lot of cities," replied Tome. "Most of the Chinese ended up in enclaves in the big cities where they stick to themselves. Those that connect with the white population do so almost exclusively through commerce, and they are damned good at it."

After the lemonade was served, Walker diverted the conversation. "I don't suppose you know what really happened down by Kukwa?" he asked.

"I stopped by the Golden Goose for a beer on the way to meet you. Rattler Wilson told me that the piles had been cut cleanly off, and the wire had disappeared. The walkway and the guard shack had been burned. He said that the guard thought that it was some pissed off loggers," offered Chad factually.

Tome smiled at Chad, "I don't think that you answered the marshal's question Captain."

"The *Miles Pierce* left Kukwa the day before the trouble at the fish trap," answered Chad. "I don't think that I can help you Tex."

"Well Sontag is madder than a wet hen and Wilson is threatening a war. I need to go down there and see if I can come up with something. While none of us feel much regret for the destruction of that trap, the Judge is going to demand some answers. His one-sided attitude on the rights of the commercial operators will demand that."

"Walker is right," interjected Tome. "The judge will demand a full investigation. That guard, Reed, said that his two companions took off for the south rather than face Wilson. If they can be intimidated by Rattler, then our fearless judicial leader will be too."

Chad smiled at the two men across the table from him. "Well then you will have to just go search Kukwa for saws and wire cutters. If you ask Chief John for permission, he won't object. He knows that its part of your job, Marshal. If you can't find any evidence in the village then you will have to go on south and start talking to the loggers."

Tex Walker pulled the small pad of paper and a pencil from his shirt pocket and made some notes. He finished, smiled, and then slid his chair out and rose. The other two men looked over their shoulders to find Danielle being escorted toward their table.

The lunch was just what Walker was looking for. Huge slabs of pot roast and mashed potatoes covered in brown gravy, arrived only a few minutes after Danielle's arrival. The conversation turned to the Sprint brothers and the letter.

"It appears, Marshal that you are going to have to go south of Kukwa to check out the logging camps anyway," said Danielle. "Why don't you make a stop in Wrangell and check out this missing man report?"

"Danny, tell the magistrate and the marshal what your impressions were of this Samuel Maples guy," suggested Chad.

"He owned the yacht that Malcom and the Guildhams were traveling on. He seemed to intimidate both of them, which I found quite strange. He is cordial, but volunteers nothing in a conversation. He told me that he was an officer in the British army in South Africa, something to do with intelligence. He seems to be a good businessman, and I got the impression that he has a lot of money. But he made me very uncomfortable. While we talked, I noticed a small revolver in a holster under his left arm and one of those hide-away two shot guns in his sleeve. Now why would a man need to carry two guns on his own boat?"

Tome wiped his mouth. "And the thing that I don't understand is his connection with Rattler Wilson and the Golden Goose."

"Right, I have seen him going in and out of the saloon every time he is in town," said Walker. "All that I could get out of Rattler was that he rents a room above the saloon."

"You may have to hitch a ride up the Stikine and see what the Mounties in Telegraph creek know about Maples and our missing miner," suggested Chad.

"It would be good for you to get to know the police in the

next town anyway," offered Tome with a laugh. "I will sign off on any expenses as part of the investigation of the fish trap problem. If we need a little more to cover your expenses, I will just fine the Golden Goose a little more for violating prohibition," laughed Tome.

"Hell," offered Chad, "maybe our missing miner has decided that Maples is the person that they need to help develop their mine and the Mounties will tell us that he is leading the party north."

Danielle shook her head. "That is not very likely from what you told me about those two brothers. Somehow this Maples is involved in a lot of the troubles in Alaska. Even Malcom Crier whose family fortune seems to be bankrolling a lot of the development didn't seem to like or trust his yachting host."

❧

With Belle Medev guiding Rattler Wilson and the marshal around the village and only a handful of tribal members remembering how to speak English the investigation in Kukwa took less than two hours. While they were at the village a dozen men were seen with new Winchester repeating rifles.

The government boat passed the destroyed fish trap two hours before high tide. There was little to see where the trap used to stand. Wilsons mood was bitter but even he had to admit that there was no evidence. "Me and the boys could grab one of those savages and beat the truth out of them," he said.

"I don't think that a dozen of you could do anything in that village except get yourselves dead. And I wouldn't recommend you making any trouble outside the village. Mr. Wilson, the territorial law protects commercial interests, but the federal statutes that pre-date the adoption of Oregon law protect the villages and their people from any harassment. If I hear of any problems with the Kukwa people, I will come looking for you personally."

"You know Marshal, its damned easy for one man to go missing in this country," said Wilson.

"If you mean that as a threat to me, you better bring an army. If you mean somebody from the village, I meant what I just said."

The marshal directed the skipper of the government boat toward the North Pacific cannery. As the boat slid up against the dock the marshal handed Wilson's rifle and pack to him.

"I thought that we were going to start canvassing the logging camps," said Wilson.

"I am going to do just that, but I can't say that I find you a very objective investigator. You can catch a ride back to Juneau from your friends at the cannery. I need to get down to Wrangell and check out the villagers claim that they smuggled your two missing guards to where they could catch a boat south. Besides I think that I would feel better watching my own back; now git."

Wrangell wore its mantle as one of Alaska's oldest towns as a badge of pride.

Founded by the Russians as a trading post, for years it was part of the Hudson's Bay trading group. Before the Russians and the British, two powerful Tlingit clans made the area home and after the purchase of Alaska, Americans had made it a center of Presbyterian religion and education. When the gold fields up the Stikine, in the Cassiar region of Canada, began to draw hundreds of stampeders in the 1870's, Wrangell became a boom town and the center of commerce for the new mining camps. Walker had never been to Wrangell because there had never been a need.

As the government boat slipped past the remnants of the old fort on the island that guarded Wrangell harbor, the first thing that Walker noticed was how the small town resembled a community around Puget Sound or on San Francisco Bay and not one of the instant towns of Alaska. The second thing he noticed was that there was no one on the docks to greet them. As he walked up the hill, he could see people standing around the open doors to a large building with a sign that read THE WRANGELL INSTITUTE.

Walker pulled his coat aside revealing his badge. "What's going on," he asked?

One of the men watching the proceedings inside the building turned as if to object to the interruption. Seeing the badge he instead grabbed Walker's arm and pulled him through the crowd. "It's a town meeting. One of the fishermen found a body on the beach only five miles out of town yesterday. His throat's been cut. We never had something like this happen here before and we were meeting to figure out what to do. With you here, well, we probably should let you figure it out."

Within minutes the meeting broke up and the members of the Home Rule Committee led Walker to a rough wooden net shed on the wharf. The body had been packed in ice, but the smell of a body that had been riding the tides for weeks met the group at the door. It was not the gut wrenching stench a hot battlefield, but rather a sickly sweet smell somewhat like rotting apples.

"I think it's the man that disappeared off from that ship," offered one of his guides. "He carried no wallet, no watch, nothing that will tell us who he was."

Marshal Walker carefully ran his hands through the man's clothing, checking every pocket and even the inside of his belt. He found nothing. Moving to the man's boots he slipped his finger inside the boot tops thankful that the post-mortem swelling was gone. He pulled a thin knife from a sheath on the inside of the left boot and handed it to the guide while he checked the other boot.

"To Bob Sprint in appreciation of your help saving our son, September 7, 1885," read the holder.

"That's him," replied Walker. Looking at the man's neck, it was difficult to see the slash due to the decomposition and disfigurement from weeks in the water. Carefully lifting the man's chin, the cut from almost one ear to the other became evident.

"Was this the only man found?" asked Walker.

"Were there more men missing?" asked someone from the crowd.

"Not necessarily," replied the marshal, "but he was seen with two other men who were not on the ship when it reached Ketchikan. Did anyone else leave the ship here in Wrangell?"

"The only ones who got off from the North Pacific ship were my partner and a couple of his hands," offered one of the bystanders. "They didn't say nothing about any other missing men."

"And who might your partner be?" asked Walker.

"His name is Samuel Maples. He's a big time miner who has interests in British Columbia and in Alaska."

"What do you do for Mr. Maples?"

"Mostly I relay messages from his folks up north to the telegraph operator and then forward the answers back. Maples has a part-time man in Telegraph Creek."

For a man raised in the deep south where luxurious steamboats were part of life, the tiny boat that Walker found the next morning was a shock. The cabin had two wooden benches along the walls, each capable of seating four normal people. The captain's station was at the bow end of the cabin, the deck along the side of the cabin was no more than three feet wide. Overall, the length of the boat was at most fifty feet, with most of the aft portion of the deck dedicated to freight.

Crammed into the tiny cabin were twelve other men including the captain. Being new to the trip, Walker didn't know that in order to get a seat he needed to be at the dock two hours before sailing. As the day warmed, the heat from the steam boiler, shielded from the cabin by only a thin panel, made the cabin unbearable. Even with both doors open, the air inside was suffocating. The passengers had a choice, sit out on one of the crates in the rain or to risk cremation.

The Stikine was a large river that cut through a range of coastal mountains, the first half of the trip following a deep steady gorge and the second cutting through a wide plain surrounded by more mountains. How the captain determined which channel to follow, Walker couldn't figure out.

The first night they stopped at a roadhouse, where the men were fed a hearty meat soup and bread. They spent the night in a bunk house in narrow bunks stacked from floor to ceiling. The five o'clock wakeup call was welcome to Walker, whose huge frame spilled out of his bunk making sleep almost impossible. After a breakfast of sourdough pancakes, they were back on the river.

The weather on the eastern side of the mountains was much improved and within ten minutes Walker found a place on top of the cabin for some much needed sleep. He was startled awake by a hand shaking his shoulder four hours later. "You going to pitch in with loading the firewood, came a voice from below him? The Captain says that if we all pitch in, we will be on our way again in fifteen minutes."

There was not much to telegraph creek. It took only ten minutes to find the small log house, with the Canadian Maple leaf flying from a pole attached to the side of the building. In front of the cabin, two red coated Canadian Mounties lounged in wooden chairs that would have been right in place at a beach resort along the Texas gulf coast. Neither the sergeant or the corporal stood as Walker approached or even after he introduced himself.

"Pull up a chair and sit a spell, Marshal," offered the corporal, in his best southern drawl.

"We really are working here," he laughed after Walker had pulled a chair over next to the men. "We watch every boat that comes in and make note of who is coming and going."

"Happy to hear that," replied Walker. "I am investigating the murder of a miner who was traveling from the Choindike back to the states. Managed to get his throat cut just north of Wrangell. He was last seen with some men who may have come this way."

"How long ago might they have passed through?" asked the corporal.

"Maybe three weeks or a bit more; they may have been making tracks for the Upper Yukon."

"That's not much to go on Marshal. We only get about three boats a week now with the rush to the Cassiar over. Most of our traffic is just resupplying mines that have been operating for years. Still, that's a couple of dozen folks every week coming up from the tidewater."

"I don't even have descriptions," replied Walker honestly. "If they came this way they would be hot footing it for the dead man's workings."

"If they were Americans we will have some names in the daily log. If they are Canadian, we just let them pass. Do you know their nationality?"

"Nope. It don't sound like very good police work, does it?" laughed Walker.

"On the contrary," snarled the sergeant speaking for the first time. "Out here, and I would guess in the Alaska territory as well, there isn't much history to work with and damned few witnesses to the troubles that we all see. The few crimes where we actually have a clear picture of what and who, are pretty easy to work since everyone leaves a trail. It's not like in a city where you can hide in the crowd. Here and in the Yukon it's just a matter of tracking the culprit and moving just a little bit faster. There must be a bit more in your suspicious brain that we can work with."

Walker took a sip from a coffee that the corporal brought from the cabin. "Tastes like afternoon police coffee anywhere in the world. Mornin' coffee gets us all in motion and keeps us in motion. Afternoon coffee sits until you can tar a boat with it or until someone either closes the office or starts the night coffee. Thanks."

Walker took another sip. "They may have been traveling with a man by the name of Maples."

The two Mounties looked at one another, but neither spoke right away. Then the corporal got up and took the two steps to the door of the constabulary. A moment later he returned with a bound logbook and began fumbling through the pages. "Twenty-four days ago, Samuel Maples arrived on the same boat that you just came in on. He was traveling with two Americans, Bush and Kline. Maples is British and as a citizen of the commonwealth would not have had to give us any information. He did vouch for the two Americans however and said he would be financially responsible for them while in Canada."

"He has an agent in Wrangell, that man said that he had another one here. They work together to shorten the communications link using your telegraph. Maybe that man can give us a bit more information," suggested Walker.

"Right after Maples cleared his two men, he went up to the telegraph office," offered the corporal. "It's in the same building as claims registration. There is another office in the building, in fact the man who owns the building has his office there. His name's Burger, and he is the closest thing we have to a lawyer in town. He even has a telegraph set in his office, I have never seen that before."

"Burger is from Montreal. He showed up here three years ago. I always wondered how he makes a living," replied the sergeant. "He's always got money, but he sure doesn't make much doing the few legal jobs around here. I assumed that he was an agent for some of the miners up the river."

"Seems about the same deal as the agent in Wrangell," offered Walker. This Maples guy is reportedly a rich mining financier. Not the kind that sits at his desk in San Francisco or Winnipeg. The kind that spends his time following the mining booms."

"How long are you in town for, Marshal?" asked the sergeant.

"The boat is going upriver a bit to drop off freight. The captain said he would be back here early in the morning the day after tomorrow. I will need to be on it unless we come up with a reason for me to stay."

"One day should be enough. The telegraph office and Burger's office are closed until tomorrow morning. We can take a walk over there in the morning."

"Name's Trudeau," offered the sergeant finally. "This here's Wilton Bates. We have an extra bunk in the constable's house if you need a place to stay."

"Happy to take you up on your offer sergeant. I just happen to have a bottle of Kentucky bourbon in my pack down on the dock, that is if you gentlemen are off duty," replied Walker. "And the name's Tony but most folks call me Tex."

"Well, since you are buying the drinks later, and since this is legal business, the government of Canada will spring for dinner down at the Pub."

"You have an Irish Pub in Telegraph Creek?" asked an astonished Walker.

"That we do," replied the corporal. At least a third of the men who work in the mines are Irish. You can get a good black beer with your stew."

The next morning the three men were at the telegraph office when it opened. "Is Burger around or is he sleeping in?" the sergeant asked the young telegraph operator.

"Burger is having me handle all his telegraph work for a month or two. I'm just taking notes until he gets back."

"Where did he go?" asked the corporal. "We didn't see him down at the landing."

"He went the other way. Some man came in and Burger dropped everything he was doing and helped that man organize six men to go up the river and then over to Teslin Lake. From there they were heading for the Yukon. Burger and his client stayed a week exchanging messages with Montreal and London."

"How long have they been gone?"

"Couple of weeks."

As the three law men retreated down the hill toward the Mounties office, the corporal looked at his sergeant sheepishly. "You were off chasing down that drunk Indian kid who stole the minister's horse, and it got real busy around here. I just never noticed that Burger was gone."

Turning to Walker the sergeant laughed. "Can't get good help in this city."

"Well, we know a bit more than we did yesterday," replied Walker.

"Not enough for us to chase down Maples or his party," offered the sergeant. "So far, they aren't suspects, even in your crime. Even if we had some evidence, we couldn't arrest anyone since the crime was in Alaska. All we could do is see if somehow the bad guy accidentally ended up in a wooden toolbox all trussed up. You would have to check the freight very carefully when you got back to Wrangell."

"Thanks for the thought," offered Walker. "Sometimes we all have to be a little creative. I'll be heading back early in the morning. In the interim, I would check on this Maples guy if this was my jurisdiction. He just keeps turning up in situations that I am sent to check on; if you know what I mean."

"We will send a couple of telegrams this afternoon." Turning to the corporal the sergeant continued, "Wilton it may just be a good idea for you to call one of your trackers and set up a trip to the Choindike area to keep an eye on things. Something here makes me nervous."

"I'll plan on leaving in a couple of days. For tonight I plan on helping the marshal here lighten his luggage by doing my part to finish that bottle we started last night. Besides, by morning we may have some answers to the telegrams we sent."

CHAPTER 10

The Bering Sea, Alaska

AT 190 FEET, the steam ship *Juarez* was a bit larger than most of the ships that made the run to the mouth of the Yukon. She could push across the Pacific at a steady fifteen knots, if the weather cooperated. In the north Pacific and the Berring Sea, it never did. A trip that could conceptually be made in just more than a week usually took twice as long.

Over the past two years, the last trip of the year carried more than two-hundred broke prospectors, fisheries workers and lumberjacks south, based on a promise to pay someday. Virtually every one of those passengers had made good on the debts. Starting a midsummer southbound passage with seven passengers who paid cash in advance was a new experience for Captain Richmond who also acted as the ship's purser.

They would have been in Sitka in ten days were it not for the two days lost as they anchored just north of Unimak Pass to wait out a fog bank that seemed to stretch on forever. By the time the ship sighted Mount Edgecumbe, the sentinel overlooking Sitka

Sound, they had been at sea for a dozen days and the railroad surveyors who had been seasick within hours of their departure from St Michael were seasoned ocean travelers.

"How was the trip?" asked Chad, shaking hands with Fischel and McKerlain.

"Just fine. A bit rough in places. That ship is the lap of luxury," replied McKerlain. "I can't even imagine making that trip in one of those old sailing ships that we saw scattered all over the ocean. I thought that they were obsolete."

"The fisheries companies use them for hauling workers and freight. Canned salmon is more than a penny a can less expensive landed on a dock in Seattle if you don't have to buy fuel."

"I would think that the canneries run a far greater risk of losing a whole shipment in one of those old ships," added Fischel.

"We make that case to them every year, but with the shipping industry moving to power, they can buy those old boats for a song and there are a lot of old salts who will ship aboard them just to feel the joy of sailing. Most of the fisheries companies we serve come to us after they have lost friends and inventory when one of those ships is lost."

"Anyway, Captain Gritt, we need to set up a meeting with the governor," continued Fischel. "I have taken statements from all my crew about some troubles on our trip out of Porto Valdez. Your young man, Molotov prepared them on our trip here. He also has two important letters from your brother and a marshal up the Yukon. I am sorry that he didn't have time to visit his village."

"The governor is down in Wrangell, visiting with the council. There was a miner from the Yukon murdered on the way to Seattle. The marshal from Juneau wanted the governor to interview the men who found the body."

"We will have to wait then," offered McKerlain.

"We are on our way to pick up the marshal and governor in a couple of days. If you can handle a few more days on the water, it would give you a full day with the governor to discuss your problem on the run to Juneau. I have a couple of other stops on the way, but you would still be back in Sitka in time to catch the *Maximilian* south in ten days."

The two railroad men looked at each other with the same joy that they would have exhibited if they were on the way to the dentist.

"Besides," continued Chad, "I want you to meet a couple of other folks who are having trouble that the governor is concerned about. One of them is an attorney who is documenting trouble with one investment group."

"Put us on your manifest then Captain. We will need some new books to get us through the trip. Between us, we worked our way through half of the library on the *Juarez*."

The *Miles Pierce* rounded the southern tip of Baranof Island and turned east toward Sumner Straight, the most direct route through hundreds of islands to Wrangell. The seas were flat except where the currents from the huge tides collided with one another. There eddies and whirlpools forced the captain to carefully maneuver around dangerous conditions. It was in one of those places that one of the crew spotted a white painted sailboat wedged between two rocks on a sandy beach.

While the second officer battled the tide run to hold the ship offshore, Chad, Fischel and one of the crew rowed the small ships skiff to shore to investigate.

"The whole side of that overturned boat is smashed in," observed Fischel. The men carefully skirted the damaged craft. "My God, is that a man's foot?"

Bleached bones extended up from a boot to a skeleton still tied to the rail of the overturned boat. Chad slipped his knife from its sheath and sliced through the light line that held the corpse. With Fischel's help, he carefully slid the body from underneath the boat and out onto the sand. "Red," ordered Chad, "Climb up under there and make sure that there aren't any more."

"This must be the gill net boat that went missing from Strom Johanson's cannery a couple of months ago," mused Chad. "He has been looking for it about a hundred miles north of here."

"The way those tides roar through these islands, it could easily have drifted this far," observed Fischel. "I am surprised that it doesn't have the canneries name on it. There's nothing but the number 29 on the bow."

"Theres no one else under here captain," came the voice from under the boat.

"See if you can find something that will give us a name. Also, something that we can wrap him in."

Chad and Fischel went through the pockets of the ripped pants and coat clothing what little was left of the man, finding nothing that helped. Red began tossing what he found from under the boat. First was a folded spare sail that he found wedged under a seat, and then a coil of light rope.

"The body was never submerged," observed Chad.

"How do you know?" said Fischel.

"The ligaments and cartilage are still holding the bones together and there is still flesh on the face. If this body had been under water, sea lice and crabs would have eaten everything that was not rock hard. Besides, look at those leg bones. The foxes got to this man after he floated ashore. The bears couldn't reach him under the boat."

"God, I hope he was dead before they found him. Can you imagine being eaten alive?"

"Look at the spine just above his hips, the vertebrae are crushed and out of alignment. Not the kind of injury the body would get in an accident on the boat or drifting ashore. Unless whatever happened to him was within a few miles of here, our dead friend was gone long before the animals got to him. But how could this injury occur on a sail powered fishing boat?" continued Chad.

"Captain, can I borrow your knife?" came a call from under the boat.

A moment later a small net with a Nestles Cocoa can landed on the sand next to the body.

"I found that tied under the seat," offered the crewman emerging from under the boat. "There ain't much else under there."

Fischel picked up the net and pulled the tightly sealed can from the web. He opened his pocketknife and pried off the lid. Inside was a pencil and a small note pad, folded open to reveal a short message.

"Rammed by a large motor scow that came up on us while we had our net out. Mickey went over the side and my back is broke. The boat is crushed. If you find this, tell Minella and little Marcos that I loved them. Ronald Aluvia."

"Filipino, a number of Johansons workers are. Most of them are now second generation, their parents recruited to work in the canneries years ago."

Within an hour the body, now wrapped in the sail, was aboard and the boat was underway. The height of the tidal run was past, and the seas had smoothed.

In Wrangell, a couple of tons of freight were offloaded and the only two passengers going north came aboard. Walker was animated and the governor stoic as they continued their discussion on the way to the salon. "The evidence points at one of those men who Bob Sprint was drinking with. Maybe even implicates that Maples guy," said Walker.

"There may be a connection," replied the governor, "but you can't prove it."

"You are right Lyman, I have just enough evidence in a half-dozen cases to point a finger, but not enough in any of them to make a case. It gets damned frustrating."

Chad greeted the two men and introduced Fischel and McKerlain. "I couldn't help but overhear you two. I think we have another of those on our hands and Mr. Fischel here also has an interesting story."

"Well, aren't you just a bundle of good news Captain Gritt," responded Walker. "I was looking forward to a full day to just look at the scenery and read a book."

"We're going to swing by Kukwa to drop off some freight and then we have to stop at Johansons. We think we have the body of one of his fishermen stored in our skiff." Chad handed the cocoa container to Walker.

"What's this?" he asked.

"Look inside Marshal," directed Fischel. "My conversation is really for the governor here, and it looks like you are going to be busy."

The *Miles Pierce* skirted what was left of the fish trap and swung around in front of the village of Kukwa. Belinda Medev tied her small canoe to the rail and scampered over the side of the boat looking for the captain. She barged through the door of the salon, knocking Governor Karp flat on his back, the young woman landing on top of him.

"In Texas, that would be written up in the history books," said Walker. "Indian girl captures the governor, not a shot fired."

Dusting herself off, Belle couldn't hide the bright scarlet of her face. "I am so sorry."

"No damage done young lady," replied Karp. Not wanting to let her off the hook to easily, he continued, "it's been years since a twenty something girl came after me with that kind of gusto."

"What have I done," moaned Belle. "I was just anxious to find Captain Gritt."

"You will find him in the wheelhouse miss," laughed Walker. "If you give me a minute, I will run up there and position him just inside the door. He would probably appreciate how you meet and greet folks."

Belle covered her face with her hands, tears running between her fingers. "It really is alright, there was no damage done. I am Governor Karp, and you must be Belinda Medev, I have heard a great deal about you," he said extending his hand.

"Oh my, you *are* the governor aren't you," observed Belle.

"I am, young woman, and since I have never been in Kukwa before, I was hoping to recruit the schoolteacher to show me around, and to introduce me."

"I would be honored sir," proclaimed Belle, finally gaining her composure. "I came aboard to tell Chad, I'm sorry, Captain Gritt of the problems that we continue to have with the North Pacific folks."

"Perhaps you can discuss it with the marshal and me as you act as our guide," offered Karp.

"I'll be right back," offered Belinda. She quietly exited the cabin and then vaulted up the ladder to the wheelhouse.

"There you are captain. Are you staying the night?" she asked.

Chad instinctively gave the girl a huge hug. "Oh, I am so sorry Belle, that was very uncalled for and not the way a gentle-man greets a lady friend."

"I am not offended Chad, besides my meeting with the governor would probably require a session in a confessional, if I were Catholic."

Chad could not hide the puzzlement from his face. "I will let him tell you about it," added Belle.

"No, we won't be staying the night, I just have some supplies to drop off, and I wanted to invite you to tell the official story of what happened at the fish trap directly to the governor. It might help if he also understood what that trap was doing to the people of the village."

Belle forced a smile. "What would we do without you? I have wanted an audience with the governor for months. It has gotten worse, Chad. The North Pacific folks have been sending their net boats right into the mouth of the river netting the silver salmon. When we object, they shoot at our canoes, not to kill anyone, but to chase us away. I wanted you to tell the marshal and the governor."

"You can tell him yourself, we are going to be here for a couple of hours lightering the freight to shore. What happened to your dock?"

"Three weeks ago, the village was awakened by a series of large explosions. There is nothing here that is explosive. It terrified most of us. When we crept out of our houses, the dock was sagging in the center. Someone put dynamite on the three center pilings and blew them up. Since then, my father and the other men have taken turns guarding the entrance to the bay every night."

"You need to tell the governor what you just told me Belle."

"I am taking him on a tour of the village. I will wake my father and let him tell the story, one chief to another."

"Good, that is the way it should be," offered Chad.

Belle's smile faded. "I would like to fix you dinner again

Captain Gritt. I found it very pleasant just sitting on the porch of the school with you the last time you were here."

"I enjoyed it too, but don't discuss that with either the marshal or the governor, they thought I was on the ship the night that the fish trap was destroyed. I choose to let them believe that."

Belle smiled a sly smile. "I am as clever as any spy trying to save her people."

The tour took a couple of hours and when the marshal and the governor returned, they got busy writing in their journals. Belle left them and joined Chad on the stern of the boat as the last load of tinned beef was lowered into a waiting canoe. Belle reached out and squeezed Chad's hand and held it. "I go now. You come back soon."

Before he could respond, Belle slipped over the side, seating herself in the canoe.

"I will," called Chad, but Belle refused to look up.

Four hours later the ship swung into the dock at Johansons cannery. The body of the deceased fisherman was recovered from the skiff hanging from davits on the side of the ship. Johanson stood quietly as did a few of his workers. The marshal handed him the letter from the cocoa can and Johanson read it and then wiped a tear from his eye. He knelt to untie the canvas in front of him.

"I wouldn't do that," advised Walker. "There isn't much left and what there is won't give you any evidence of who this was. When I examined the body, I took the liberty of taking all the clothes and putting them in this bag." Walker handed a canvas bag to the cannery owner, who carefully pulled the tattered coat from the bag.

"This is Aluvia's coat," whispered Strom. "His wife is on the line now, and his mother is taking care of the children, including

Ro's baby son. His father and mother were the first Filipino workers here. Ro has been my winter watchman for the last two years. I watched Ro grow up, he's only a few years younger than my own son."

"I will try to get to the bottom of this Mr. Johanson," said Walker. "It's good to have the governor here. This ain't some Asian foreigner here to take some Polish foreigner's job. This was a citizen of the territory. I just pray that I can get to the truth." Walker looked over at the governor who was standing quietly next to Chad.

"Marshal, it would be good for Ro's wife and mother to hear that from you." Johanson sent his foreman to find the two women. "I will give them the bad news myself, that's the decent thing to do. I would appreciate you making it clear that there will be an investigation." Then he turned to all of those watching. "Listen up. I will read them the note. We will leave justice to the marshal. I'll tolerate no revenge."

Chad waited until the body had been claimed by the family before starting to unload the supplies. An hour later the workers began to load cases of canned salmon for their trip south. The four men moving fish from the warehouse to the dock picked up their pace, singing a snappy chant as they worked.

"I think your men are handling the loss of their friend really well," offered Karp.

"Governor, what those men are repeating over and over again in Tagalog is 'an eye for an eye, a tooth for a tooth.' This is a long way from finished I am afraid, said Johanson.

The trip to Juneau was filled with conversation about what was going on in Alaska. Chad shared a letter from his brother about trouble on the Yukon and advised the governor that he was sending a confidential letter from Falcon on to Washington. Fischel and McKerlain passed on their reports and personal statements about the incident on the Big River. All the men agreed that they would sit down with Danielle Post when they got to Juneau to discuss her research.

⌘

Payday in the mines was not much different than payday in any industrial town. The workers coming off from their twelve hour shifts walked through a hallway in the administration building and past a long desk where they signed for cash. Most set aside a large portion to be collected later when the bank was open. That money would be sent home to waiting wives and families. The rest went into worn pockets and headed into town.

The *Miles Pierce* reached the dock just as it got dark. The newly paid miners wandering the bars on first and front streets stopped along the docks long enough to see who was arriving, hoping that at least some of the passengers would be women. Men outnumbered women in town by a factor of four, and the vast majority of the women who made Juneau home were married. That made Danielle's presence on the docks a minor event, one of courtesy and respect.

In many places seeing the governor arriving would at least start a conversation or two, but without a skirt he attracted little notice until Danielle stepped forward and extended her hand.

"It's always the blokes in suits and ties that gets the girl," came a comment in an Irish drawl.

"Not that one, she isn't interested in the governor, she prefers captain's caps to bowlers."

Seeing only four passengers leave the ship, none of them women, the crowd broke up. Most headed for one of the illegal saloons where the only available female company in town served drinks and otherwise entertained the men. Danielle waited for

Chad to close out his captain's log, quietly chatting with the governor, the marshal and the two railroad men.

"Gentlemen, it is late, and I am starving, so if you will excuse us until tomorrow, I intend to use what charms this rough town has not worn away to entice Captain Gritt to take me to dinner."

The group gathered their bags and followed Danielle and Chad uphill toward the Romanoff where all but the marshal hoped there would be rooms. On a payday night, all the other places to stay would be noisy and rowdy.

"Are you going to try to get some sleep, Tex?" asked Danielle. "You know that someone will come find you later tonight."

"That's the problem with working for the law, you are never really off duty. Good thing that I got a nap on the trip."

"We can meet in my office tomorrow morning, say about ten. See you then."

With the *Miles Pierce* only at the dock for thirty hours, all agreed to the meeting and the marshal left the group for his rented room and what he knew would be a short sleep. The governor pulled some strings to get the two railroad men a double room in the crowded hotel and his own favorite room on the quiet side of the hotel, then all went their separate ways.

"What's so special about today?" asked Danielle. "You never buy champagne."

Chad smiled as he took Danielle's hand for the walk to her apartment. "I just figured that if I didn't buy you champagne, someone else would." He squeezed her hand. "Besides, after days of bad news, I see a light at the end of the tunnel. The governor saw the troubles here with his own eyes. His ears had to be ringing after what the railroad folks and those at Johansons had to say. Maybe this will be enough to force some changes."

"Just like a Gritt, can't separate work from play." Danielle lifted Chad's hand with hers and kissed his fingers. "I received a very nice letter from Malcom Crier the other day. He has invited me to meet him in Montreal to discuss our concerns with his father, Richard. What do you think? Would it do any good?" she asked.

"After tomorrow's meeting, I think that we all will be looking for some help. Something ugly is happening in the territory. But I'm not sure that I trust Crier. Somehow, he is involved in this."

"Malcom is a gentleman, and I believe that he is disturbed by what we discussed. If his family is part of this, I don't think that he knows that."

"You got a better read on him than I did," responded Chad. "Maybe he can help, but I wouldn't commit a two month trip just on speculation."

"Oh, I am not considering traveling until late fall. I could swing through Montreal on my way to Boston to see my folks."

"Probably worth a try, but I'm sure not very comfortable with the idea."

"You silly man, we are on the way to my home together, you will be spending the night, and you aren't comfortable with the idea?"

"Are you inviting me?" asked Chad.

Danielle grabbed Chad's ear and pulled his head down, kissing his cheek, "I didn't think that I had to."

CHAPTER 11

Southeast Alaska

Patrick Sontag sat on the dock of the North Pacific Cannery. The steamship in front of him was loading canned salmon from the first half of the season and the plant manager was not happy. After the incident at Kukwa, two of the other fish traps that he had been counting on had been sabotaged.

The trap just north of Kukwa was damaged one week after the Kukwa incident. The guards had been locked in their shack. They had been playing cards, trying to stay out of a roaring storm. Someone wrapped three loops of rope all the way around the shack and knotted it, effectively keeping those inside from opening the heavy timbered door. When they finally carved a hole through the door, using only their knives, they found huge holes in the wire fences of the trap where someone had ripped it from the pilings.

At the other trap the same storm brought dozens of logs roaring down a river ripping one of the new floating traps apart.

It might have been natural except that many of the logs had been cut cleanly and there was no logging upriver. The bottom line to Sontag was that the salmon pack being loaded on the ship would not pay for the expenses of the cannery let alone show a profit.

Sontag pulled the dog-eared letter from Samuel Maples from his pocket and reread it. The letter reminded Sontag that his twenty-five percent ownership of the canneries was based on their profitability. "You will do what needs to be done to achieve your financial goals," ended the letter. Sontag had tried hard to make up the shortfall by pressing his net boats. His crews were working twenty hour days, but they found more experienced boats from other canneries were always where the fish were before them. The nets of his competitors boats took the hearts out of the fish schools while his boats seemed to clean up the strays.

It took more than a month to get new wire for the traps from Seattle. The runs of king salmon were over, and the sockeye salmon runs were reaching their end. The early silver salmon were moving up the rivers which left the late silvers and the less valuable pink and chum salmon to make up the shortfall. As Sontag sat, his stormy mood barely subdued, a motor launch from Juneau rounded the point at the head of the bay. For the first time in days Sontag smiled. Tomorrow his men would go out to begin repairing the traps, but today he had a higher priority.

Rattler Wilson leaped from the boat, dock line in hand and wrapped it around a cleat on the floating dock. A moment later another man tossed Rattler the stern line which he used that to pull the boat tight. Six graying, hard faced men joined Wilson on the dock, then shouldering light packs and rifle cases they trudged up the steeply sloping walkway to where Sontag sat rolling a cigarette.

"These are the men we discussed," said Wilson. "They were

up on the Big River earlier working on a railroad survey. Sam Maples recruited all of them mostly because they were veterans who had put their skills to use outside the law at one time or another. They jumped at the chance to earn another thousand before they head south."

Sontag extended his hand to each of the men. "It will be ugly work men, but it needs to be done."

That afternoon the two small steam launches that had arrived strapped to the deck of the steamship were moved to the small boat landing. A steel blade fashioned in the cannery machine shop was bolted to the bow of each boat. The blades extended from a foot above the water line to just above the line of the keel. Each blade had been sharpened to a razer edge.

"Your job, gentlemen, is to clear the waters for my drift boats and make sure that no one gets in their way. If there is another boat where they want to fish, you will run your powered boat along just behind the competitor and cut his net loose. While one of you runs the boat, two others will stand by with rifles to ensure that there is no interference. I don't want to see any bloodshed." Sontag flipped his cigarette butt off the dock. "But even more than that, I want the competitors boats gone. They can fish the other side of the damned channel."

"If any of you have to use your rifles, don't leave any witnesses for the marshal," added Rattler, shouldering his pack.

Late that evening, a boat from Johansons had just set a net when they saw a powered launch round a point of land a half mile away and head straight for them. "What do you think they want?" asked one of the fishermen to no one in particular. His partner began taking down the sail, allowing the boat to stay in the middle of the small school of salmon that they had found. Within a half hour the floats on the net were dancing as one fish after another became tangled in the web. Neither man paid attention to the steam launch until it was almost on them.

"It looks like they are going to ram us!" screamed his partner. "Saints be with us."

At the last moment the powered boat swept just around the stern. Two gruff men with scarfs concealing their faces stood in the boat pointing rifles at the fishermen as their net was cleanly severed from their boat. "Now get that sail up and get the hell out of here," ordered one of the men holding a rifle. "Tell whoever your owner is that we'll tolerate none of his boats on this side of the sound."

The next morning two more Johanson boats received the same treatment.

"Your idea of preventative medicine was a good one," remarked Sontag to Rattler. "Our six boats are out this afternoon working those bays with no competition."

"We will stay another few days to make sure that the message has been received. So far nobody has been shot," replied Wilson. "We'll go out tomorrow to police the fishing grounds. Easiest two grand I have ever made."

At Johansons docks the mood was somber and angry. "Mr. Johanson," offered his foreman, "it will take until tomorrow to rig three new nets, but that's not the real problem. The majority of fish are on the other side of the sound. We need to be out there."

"Your right Marco, but I won't risk any lives. I am taking the launch to Juneau this afternoon to see the marshal. I will be back in three days. Until then we fish where it is safe."

Before the cannery launch was out of sight, a meeting of the cannery's fishermen was underway. All were friends of the dead fisherman Ro. They had no plans to do what Johanson had asked. Two hours later the largest of the cannery boats had been fitted with an extra foot of heavy freeboard fashioned from oak. It headed out to fish the "far side."

The two men running the boat completed two sets, dumping the flopping salmon from their net into compartments in the front and rear of the boat. They had just reset their net when a steam launch rounded a point and headed straight for them. "They come," a fisherman nervously blurted. "That boat will be here in twenty minutes."

"We told you not to come back and we mean it." One of Rattler's thugs pointed his Winchester at the center of the drifting boat. His partner cradled his rifle in his arms.

The fisherman standing at the mast reached into the bottom of the boat and came up with a rifle. He aimed it at one of the men in the launch and pulled the trigger. Nothing happened. He'd forgotten to chamber a bullet. He desperately worked the lever.

He was flung out of the boat by two bullets that hit him simultaneously. Seconds later his seated companion lifted a rifle, that he had been cradling in his lap and fired, joined instantly by three more rifles resting on the side of the boat. The four men continued firing as the launch lurched from its course and hit the middle of the floating gill net tangling its propeller in the mesh. Movement in the launch was met by more bullets and then there was silence.

"Grab Marco with the boat hook." Two men pulled the wounded man back into the boat. "How is he?"

"Hurt bad. He needs a doctor."

"There are no doctors for a hundred miles, but we can take him to Kukwa. The schoolteacher knows how to treat wounds, remember when she came in with Captain Gritt."

"That's a good idea. We can be there in a couple of hours."

"First, directed the foreman, we sink that boat." He pointed at the steam launch which had now drifted away. "Put the oars over and pull. We will salvage our net and then burn her."

The bodies of the three dead men were tied securely into the bottom of the boat. Everything that would keep the boat afloat was thrown over the side. Two gallons of lamp oil was poured over the gunnels of the boat and over the seats and the bodies. Then a burning ember from the firebox was raked into a pool of oil. The launch began to burn fiercely. It would burn to the waterline and then sink just as hoped.

Just at dark the boat ran up onto the beach at Kukwa.

"What happened to this man?" asked Belle.

"Miss Medev, he was wounded in a battle with a North Pacific boat. He must not come back to the cannery, and no one must know," replied the foreman.

"What of the other boat?" asked Belle pulling away the rough bandages of torn shirts covering the wounds.

"It sunk."

"We want no part of a war," responded Belle.

"Your people are part of this," replied the foreman. "We defend our lives and families just as those who attacked the fish traps have done."

Belle frowned, but shook her head, yes. "You can leave him here. He will live."

"He fell overboard while we were fishing. You found him on shore. That is the truth," continued the foreman. "Now we must get back before morning. Thank You."

❧

Sontag passed a bottle of whiskey across the table to Rattler Wilson. Don't worry my friend, the cannery boats go out unarmed and the villagers have been put in their place by the marshal. They probably are having boat trouble. We will go out tomorrow and find them.

The following morning a search started with the cannery launch out looking and Wilson and the remaining three enforcers out in the remaining cutter boat. No sign of the missing boat was found.

The search continued the next day, with a new sense of urgency. Shortly after two in the afternoon, the government boat was observed making a direct course for Wilson's boat. "Hand me the wrenches fast, and steer away from that boat," he ordered, pointing.

Rattler went to work removing the nuts from the bolts that held the cutter bar, thankful that they had only been in place a couple of days. The boat was a quarter mile away when the last bolt came free and Rattler allowed the cutter bar to drop into the water. The holes below the water line were stuffed with cloth, but there was no filling the holes higher up without calling attention to them.

As the government boat came along side, Wilson was not surprised to find Marshal Walker glaring down at him. "What are you and these men doing out here Rattler?"

"We were at the North Pacific Cannery. The cannery has a boat missing and we came out to look for it. I was giving these men a tour of a working cannery before they go back south next week," replied Wilson.

"Johanson says someone's out here trying to ram his fishing boats and cutting their nets. You know anything about that Rattler?"

"Nothing, marshal. Sontag had this launch shipped up on one of his supply ships. We're going to take it to Juneau. I can use it to change out the cannery guards."

"I don't want a war between the canneries, Rattler. I have

made that clear to Johanson and I will swing by the North Pacific docks to have that same conversation with Sontag. We will keep an eye out for your missing boat on the way. What does it look like?"

"Almost the spittin' twin of this one," replied Wilson.

"Well, it might have some structural problem. Power boats don't just go missing unless the boiler blows. Maybe you and those three men should head for Juneau first thing tomorrow and get a boiler maker to check it out." The tone of the marshal's voice made it clear that he was not asking.

"Sounds like good council," responded Rattler. We have been looking for the missing boat for a couple of days and we know that it was in this general area."

"Rattler, Johanson lost a gill net boat at the beginning of the summer, and it was found two months later on a beach seventy miles south of where it was last seen. Like I said, I will keep an eye out for it. Maybe the men aboard that boat will get lucky."

"Thanks, marshal, we will see you at the North Pacific dock later," replied Rattler.

"And Rattler, you had better get that boat thoroughly checked out, it looks like something has already fallen off from the bow." The marshal's smile had no warmth in it.

The look on Patrick Sontag's face reflected the anger that seethed just below the surface. "The three missing men were all new guards. We were letting them get the lay of the land before starting work," he responded, staring at the Marshal.

"I talked to Rattler Wilson in Pleasant Cove earlier. He says that he is taking that boat into Juneau tomorrow. I told him that he should get it looked at by a boiler maker. I don't want to see three more men disappear. Sontag understood him even if he didn't like the words.

"I want you to report any efforts to disrupt your boats, just as Johanson is doing."

"We will," said Sontag, his lips pressed so tightly the words barely escaped.

"How are you doing repairing the fish traps that were damaged?" asked Walker.

"We got a shipment of wire four days ago, and one of the traps is operational again. How are you doing in arresting the men responsible for damaging them?"

"There isn't a trace of the men your guards described anywhere. None of the villages have seen them. None of the logging camps are missing a skiff and I have yet to meet a single worker who fits their description in my investigation."

"Hard to believe," argued Sontag.

Walker laughed. "Lot of that going around right now."

"Now, Patrick I want to make it clear that there will be no war between the canneries in Frederick Sound. I told Johanson the same thing. Governor Karp will order your permits canceled if anything starts to get out of hand."

"Marshal, the governor doesn't have the authority to do that," snarled Sontag.

"Maybe not, but I will enforce his order and let the courts sort it out. They should get you a decision by next summer. Am I making this clear."

"You won't hear about trouble from us, Marshal, just make sure that everyone is playing with the same rules. Now I have to get back to work, I need to write letters to the families of the missing men, I am sure that Rattler Wilson won't do that."

CHAPTER 12

The Bering Sea, Alaska

THE STEAMBOAT *DENALI* sat on a crib of logs. Her crew had moored her in a Yukon backwater, just above the tidal surge. The falling water level as the river froze would leave her high and dry until the spring floods. The families that wintered in St. Michael, laborers and warehousemen in the summer, and watchmen in the winter, would pack a hard trail between the town and the boat and keep an eye on her. Those same people would spend a week or more living aboard the marooned boat in the spring painting and doing other maintenance before Parker and Al Naise led the summer crews back north in the spring.

The second Russ-Am riverboat, a twin of the *Denali* would take shape over the winter in St. Michael, the hull and upper structure already standing as tall as any building in town. Her boiler and much of the running gear had come in on the *Maria Gritt* and the last thing that Parker had done was to supervise the complex task of lowering the engine through the gaping hole in the hull. Al Naise would spend the winter completing what everyone referred to as Al's boat.

Hopefully the sea ice of Norton Sound would hold off, allowing two more steamships to dock that fall, offloading cargos that would allow the Russ Am boats to push their first load of freight upriver the minute the river opened. The *Maximilian* and the *Juarez* were already heading north. The *Maria Gritt* would pass the *Max* on its way south with its outbound Yukon passengers and Parker and Annalee Gritt.

The ships port schedule included the cannery community at the mouth of the Nushagak River, then Kodiak Island, Porto Valdez and Sitka, before a stop in Juneau and Ketchikan. Many of the Yukon passengers were headed for Seattle, and then to their homes all over the country. Their stories of rich Yukon River gold strikes on both sides of the border would lead hundreds of men to leave their homes the next spring to try their hand at prospecting.

The ship slid up to the dock in Sitka in a torrential October downpour. On the dock to meet the ship was Parker's brother, Chad. "Good afternoon little brother." Chad took Annalee's hand and kissed her on the cheek. "You look just plain beautiful."

"Many men say that about women with child. It must be something passed down through the ages."

"Well, congratulations you two," replied Chad. I know that you are anxious to head home, but I was hoping that you could stay a couple of weeks."

"We are waiting for the *Maximilian* before heading on to Boston. That will give us most of two weeks," answered Parker. "We need to talk for sure. There is real opportunity and trouble up on the Yukon, and from your letters here as well."

"That there is, but it'll wait until tomorrow. Tonight, we

have a family dinner planned at the old house. I have a guest that I think you both know, Danielle Post."

It was almost dark when the *Maria Gritt* slipped her mooring lines and turned north, Juneau bound. The dinner patrons, at the old house by the bay carried their wine glasses out into the fine mist that had replaced the hard rain of the afternoon. "I still make it a habit to watch the company ships whenever they arrive or depart," commented Chad. "It's like part of me wants to be aboard every single one. The bridge of a ship or even a boat is more like home than this house."

"Me too," offered Parker, "but I find that I miss home more knowing that my beautiful wife is there waiting." He pulled Annalee close and covered her shoulders with his arm.

"Perhaps I will feel the same someday. One thing I know for sure is that this is home. I am not cut out for Seattle or Boston." Chad smiled at Danielle and touched her cheek.

"Any woman in your life will have to accept that." Danielle looked up into Chad's eyes, tracking the ship. "Five people with instruments will always be your orchestra." Danielle kissed him on the cheek. "I'm hungry, and you shouldn't overcook crab." She turned and stepped out of the rain.

Word spread quickly that a Gritt woman was visiting town and that she was carrying a Gritt baby. By nine the next morning a half dozen women, most with Russian names had arrived with pastries and tea and had settled into the house like they belonged there. Most had grown up with the stories of grand dinners and music and dancing that surrounded the Gritt family. Annalee had heard many of the old stories, but the retelling from old family friends made them real.

Danielle, Parker and Chad were spending the morning at the governor's office. "I have never been up on the Yukon," observed Governor Karp. "I will plan on joining you sometime next summer. That country is going to play a larger role in the economy and the growth of Alaska. The governor should at least know where all those places are."

The story of the Klondike and the area around Falcon rushed from Parker like a torrent. The problems with the claims and the questionable judicial decisions didn't seem to surprise Karp. The tales of rough and tumble miners, and even the handful of unsolved deaths of miners brought the only comment. "We are stretched so thin, it's wrong, but we don't have the resources to do much about it. It's almost like Congress and the administration want it this way. With the revenues from the fur seal trade collapsing, I sometimes think they are willing to allow almost anything that will add a bit to the treasury."

"The treasury isn't going to get much from the mines around Falcon," commented Parker. "The only revenues are a small filling fee which all goes to keeping the offices of the judge and the marshal operating."

"That's not quite correct Mr. Gritt. The customs fees on everything imported represent a substantial sum anymore. The taxes on transportation and fuel are becoming substantial. That's especially true of coal and alcohol from Canada. The U.S. government seems to favor those products over our own. Liquor is illegal in the territory, but we tax the stuff and there is no penalty for shipping it."

"Still, it isn't right that we have judges who clearly favor one group over everybody else," said Danielle.

"Be a bit careful young lady, even our misplaced Oregon law creates a low threshold for slander."

"Governor Karp," offered Chad," there is something terribly wrong in the fisheries business here in southeast and in mining up north. Now it has spread into the quest to build a railroad. The Criers and their henchmen headed by this Maples guy are involved. In every case the interpretation of the law is helping them."

"To all of you, let me say that I am concerned. I am also concerned about the lack of response to my dozens of letters and reports to the Secretary and Congress. The financial powers in San Francisco and on the east coast have a strong lobby. It only takes a couple of dozen congressmen or a handful of senators to bottle up legislation. That is a fact of life, one that a territory with no voting rights will have to suffer until we are granted some self-rule."

Danielle straightened her wool skirt and arched her back. "Congress is the long-term solution, but the short term problem is with the regulators and quite frankly a very strange relationship between the appointed judges and a handful of big time investors."

"Danny is right," echoed Parker. "The marshal in Falcon has sent two or three letters to the Department of Law, documenting some shady dealing on the Yukon. I personally have seen enforcement of laws that don't even exist, used to steal from the very men who will build our territory. I watched a man get shot just for warning me that I was a target of one of those dealings."

"Young man, walk softly. Those types of accusations can lead to real legal trouble, especially if they are tried in the very courts that you object to," replied Karp.

"Governor, neither my brother nor me were raised to shy away from a fight," replied Chad. "We were taught to use our heads, and to never take a knife to a gun fight. Still, the golden rule was proudly displayed in the parlor of our homes, both here in Sitka and in Boston. We could read the Constitution before we were ten and Lincoln's speech at Gettysburg."

"To you two gentlemen and your family, this territory owes a deep debt. You too young lady; you could have chosen to practice your trade in a much more gentile location. But the power over the lives of our small population is in the hands of men who will probably never see this great land. America didn't buy Alaska because it wanted to expand into the north. This decision was made to stop the British from expanding into more of North America. That, and to appease the expansionists at the end of the Civil War. Someone convinced Secretary Seward and Congress that Alaska could pay handsome profits to the treasury."

"You know Governor, the process of how that all happened is part of our family's folklore," added Chad.

"I suspected that," replied Karp.

"And Governor," added Danielle, a strange smile on her face, "I doubt that anyone in Congress is ready to hand the whole place back to an English mogul."

After lunch, the Gritts and Danielle strolled down the hill to the Russ-Am Warf and warehouse. The sun pushed the morning fog up the mountains displaying the first new snow. Chad dragged a huge old oak chair from the office out for Danielle and then he and his brother parked themselves on the dock, their feet dangling above the blue-green water a dozen feet below them.

"That was a waste of time," observed Parker. "The governor is a nice guy and all, but he isn't going to rock his cushy boat."

Chad just smiled at his brother. He didn't say a word.

"Don't judge the man by the lack of progress," offered Danielle. "That man is fighting the battle the way he knows how, inside the system. He has a reputation for stubborn resolve. He gets his reward from small, almost imperceivable steps forward."

Parker began packing his pipe, striking a match on his trouser button. "I remember you telling me that you weren't a politician big brother. That was why you needed to come back to Alaska. I may not be much better than you."

"Let men like Karp be the politicians. Let him fight the

inside battles. We need to think about how to find allies who will help fight the local battle. Taking care of each other is good business."

"You two do that. I am going to see if I can find an ally in the enemy's camp and then sit down with your sister and her husband," said Danielle. "I have never asked my best friend for a favor, and I am not starting now. But there's nothing like uncovering a big scandal to help a Senators career." She turned toward Parker. "I will be going with you and Annalee as far as Chicago."

"So, you are really going to take Malcom Crier up on his offer to stop in Montreal?" asked Chad.

"Who is Malcom Crier?" asked Parker.

"We have been listening to you and your stories of the Yukon for a full day now little brother. We have a story or two for you about the old homestead and the fights down here."

"I'm not sitting through that without alcohol," said Danielle. "I will relieve the Gritt brothers of any chivalrous responsibilities and buy the first round."

Many years before, Kuzanofs had been the only bar and restaurant in the former Russian-American capital. It had evolved into a fine small hotel. The downstairs saloon featured a thirty-foot bar made from the weathered wooden hatch covers from old Russian sailing ships. In front of the full-length mirror stood rows of bottles from around the world and separating two tall shelves of liquor was an old Russian four-pound cannon resting on a cabinet of clear yellow cedar. A dozen tables sat between the bar and the double front doors, just to the right of the cozy dining room.

Danielle ordered a full bottle of Southern Pine sour mash bourbon and three glasses from the bartender and a basket of peanuts. She carried the peanuts to the table. A minute later Marcello brought the whiskey along with a pitcher of rainwater.

Danielle and Chad touched their two fingers of whiskey with a finger of water. Parker preferred his neat. The three clinked glasses.

"Who is Malcom Crier?" asked Parker for the second time.

"The Crier family seems to be the real money behind the North Pacific Fishing and Transportation Company. They are the folks determined to corner the market on canned salmon. Somehow, they are also connected to that Maples man that seems to be on the edge of every major trouble in the territory. Malcom is the son of the head of London Capital in Montreal and the grandson of Sir Rodney Crier in London. He was here early this summer," continued Danielle.

"He invited Danny to meet him in Montreal for a visit with his father, Richard. Danny thinks that he really doesn't know what is going on here," added Chad.

"Maples isn't just some behind the scenes flunky," replied Parker sipping his bourbon. "He was directly involved in a shooting up on the Klondike, and I believe part of the group who killed Cobra Wilson right in front of Al Naise and me."

"Cobra Wilson—has to be a relation of Rattler Wilson in Juneau," responded Danielle.

"He is, and I now own his saloon in Falcon," replied Parker.

The story of how the Gritt family had gotten into the saloon business took just about the same amount of time it took the three to finish their first drink. "I promised Cobra that I would pay his brother a fair price for the saloon and get him the thousand dollars of dust and nuggets left over from his nest-egg," finished Parker.

"We can spend a couple of more days here to let Annalee rest up a bit and then take the *Miles Pierce* over to Juneau so you can meet Rattler," suggested Chad. "I want to warn you that he is not a nice man to deal with."

"Can we make it back in time to meet the *Max* headed south?" asked Parker.

"Little brother, we own the company. We'll order the *Max* to come to Juneau to pick you up."

"That works for me as well," replied Danielle. "I can get a traveling trunk ready for four months on the east coast."

"Trunk?"

"Alright, trunks," laughed Danielle.

"But not tonight," suggested Chad. "We will come back here for a late dinner. In the interim, I want to take Danny sailing. We have a nice breeze and a sunny day. Besides it's a tradition for Gritt men to take their lady friends sailing."

"Home then, older brother. I should save my bride from fifty years of Russian gossip. Besides, Danny will want to dress down for the occasion."

Danielle looked at Parker with arched eyebrows. "My grandmother's sailboat and my big brother have never gotten along very well," laughed Parker.

The small boat built more than fifty years before waited at the floating dock below the Russ Am warehouse. To cork life preservers in the bottom of the boat, Chad and Danielle added a bottle of white wine and a small basket of food for a beach picnic. The ten knots of breeze from the north sent the small red boat skimming across the ripples of Sitka Sound. It took only thirty minutes to reach the gravel beach across from the town where Chad sacrificed his dry boots to pull the tiny sailboat above the line of waves lapping at the beach.

"My Lord that is beautiful," commented Danielle as she seated herself on a drift log next to a fire. Across the bay the mostly white town sat in front of a huge forest of spruce and cedar that stretched halfway up the steep hillsides behind the town. There the dark green, almost black, forest gave way to a lighter green band of scrub alder and grasses. Topping the mountains were tiny caps of new snow, glistening in the afternoon sun. The high mountain backdrop was slashed with dozens of valleys and ravines, and every place that the gaps crossed a layer of harder rock the glitter of sun on falling water flashed through the surrounding trees. The sun, receding toward the ocean horizon, acted as a giant floodlight, highlighting a different spectacle every few minutes.

Chad pulled the cork from the wine bottle and poured a small amount into one of the antique crystal glasses from the basket and swirled it in his mouth. "I pronounce it the best wine on this beach. May I pour the young lady a glass?"

"Let me start with a small glass. My stomach didn't like the rolling and up and down of the boat over that huge ocean swell. I will try a bit of wine first before I even consider sausage or cheese."

Chad ripped the end from a flat round of bread and handed it to Danielle along with a half glass of wine. "Try some bread, it is an old sailors cure for an unseasoned stomach on the sea."

"I know that I get seasick. I probably should have suggested a walk instead of the boat ride."

"I would have been just fine with that."

"I didn't want to disappoint you captain. Your brother made it sound like a family coronation of some type."

"Parker can get a bit carried away with his old family stories."

"The bread and wine are helping, I think. Tell me more about the tradition."

"My grandfather took my grandmother sailing in that same small boat back in the eighteen-twenties. The boat then belonged to the daughter of the famous Governor Baranoff. She gave it to my parents as a wedding present. The rest is a long story, but one interesting part was that my grandfather almost fought a pistol duel right here on this beach. My grandmother convinced the acting governor to lock up the other man rather than see her future husband's blood in these very rocks."

"That is amazing, I mean that any woman would get between a Gritt and his honor."

"It turns out that she found out that the other man, a Spanish aristocrat, was a crack pistol shot. She intervened in a way that grandfather had no say in the matter."

"It takes a smart woman to save her man's life, and his honor."

"You would have liked Grandma Katrina. We Gritt men have been blessed to have many very intelligent and beautiful women in our lives."

"That doesn't surprise me. I am honored to be here, Chad. It is so very beautiful and like so much of this country a place to sit and let your worries and stresses drift away on the breeze."

"I am relieved to hear you say that, Danny. I know that you came to Alaska in part just because I moved back here. Sometimes I feel that you love the fight, but I am never too sure of how much you love the arena. You know, like we are right for each other except for how we want to spend our lives."

Danielle held out her glass. "I'll try a bit of that sausage and cheese with a bit more wine."

"Listen to the song of the gulls and the rumble of the waves on the ocean side of the beach," offered Chad. "It isn't a symphony, it's more like music from the creator." Chad sliced a slab of cheese from the small round on the log.

"I can imagine a single cello adding a melody," replied Danielle.

"Really, a cello? That's an interesting idea, adding music made by man to nature's song." Chad refilled the two wine glasses.

An hour later the two watched as the wine bottle began to melt in the white-hot coals of the fire. "I think that this is the first time we have ever had this much time to ourselves. You know, just water and wind and a fire," said Chad.

"This really is what makes you happy isn't it?" she asked.

"Danny, I function just fine in the towns or even in the city. I love a coat and tails at a concert in Boston or San Francisco."

Danielle watched Chad's face, sweeping the beech, then the bay, and then the mountains and the sky. Then he repeated the process, not really smiling as much as part of the whole. "You are part of this country, just like a tree or a bush or a great brown bear."

There was only the sound of the waves and the gulls and the rattle of the increasing breeze in the dried beach grass. Finally, Chad used a stick in the neck of the now twisted and flattened wine bottle to lift it from the coals. He carried it to the surf and slid it into the water, turning his head as he did. There was a crackling sound and a gush of steam from the submerged bottle. A few minutes later he returned to Danielle who was picking up after the picnic.

"Sometimes they explode when you put them into the water, that's why you turn your head, said Chad. But when the glass and the heat and the water are just right you get a cracked glass twisted vase that will hold just one flower from the one who brings you flowers."

"You picked me flowers the first time we walked on the James River Road."

"It's a bit late for most flowers here, but I'll take a look," replied Chad. He headed toward the edge of the tree line a hundred yards from where Danielle sat. Minutes later he returned with a tall spindle of Fireweed. Only the top three inches were still in bloom. The leaves below the blooms were dark green turning yellow and scarlet further down the stem. "Perfect for a new vase. We will have to get some fresh water when we get back to the dock."

Chad tied the small boat to the dock and reached into the boat for the basket, the new vase with flower, and the life preservers. Then he extended his hand to Danielle.

"I am so sorry Chad. I can't believe I did that." Danielle handed Chad the wool blanket that she had spread over her lap, carefully folding it in onto itself. Chad moved away from the boat and shook what was left of her lunch into the water.

"Do you feel you can walk up the ramp?" Chad asked.

"I can do anything that I want to do. For now, I just want to go home and crawl into bed for a while."

"I will pick some peppermint from the garden and make you some tea, it will settle your stomach," offered Chad.

"Chad, neither of us will ever make a good nurse, but I will accept your arm around me to the top of the ramp. Then you had better find a ride because I am not walking.

CHAPTER 13

Juneau, Alaska

THE TRIP FROM Sitka to the mining town of Juneau took hours longer than normal. The weather was excellent, and the seas as calm as any that summer. The length of the voyage was due purely to a tub of iced beer and two fishing rods dragging feathered lures through a wave of silver salmon moving toward the streams of Alaska's inside passage. The ladies sat in lounges that could have graced the patio of the finest resort in the Catskills. The men took turns reeling the feisty, ten-pound salmon, on stubby wooden fishing rods with simple direct drive reels.

"I know little brother, but neither of us has had much time to just enjoy the land this summer. I vote for a couple of dozen, they will all go into the smoke house when we reach Juneau."

Parker picked up a metal pail on a long rope and heaved it out into the saltwater. Retrieving the bucket, he washed away the salmon blood on the deck. "We haven't fished like this in years, and I don't remember how long ago I put up my own smoked salmon. How do you plan on curing these?"

"First, we rub the fillets with black pepper and then we soak them in brine for a day. Then into a cool smoke until they feel like leather," answered Chad.

"Cottonwood or alder?"

"I prefer cottonwood smoke with lots of fresh air to dry the fish as it smokes."

Parker paused, then turned to Chad. "There are some pretty bad things happening up on the Yukon. Two friends, a guy named Kelley and another named Dankescu, who fought in the Civil War, filed mining claims. They were cancelled by the judge in Falcon. He says that immigrants cannot be granted title to property. Marshal Hickox said that he can't find anything like that in the law books, but the judge ordered him to force my friends off from their claims. A half dozen other prospectors rumoured to have hit it big have just disappeared. The whole town is on edge.

Chad flipped his feathered jig back into the water and fed out fifty years of line so the lure would work well behind the wake of the boat. "We're having similar problems here. Is the judge that Jack Wildham we hauled up here eighteen months ago?"

"That's the guy. Marshal Hickox is keeping a file on what he considers stolen mining claims in the area. Every dishonest thing in the region somehow involves the group of thugs that seem to work out of Cobra Wilson's saloon in Falcon. Most of them showed up with some big wig mining engineer named Maples who also is damned friendly with Judge Wildham." Parker paused to reel in a salmon.

"We need to spend some time figuring out how we can stop this," added Parker. "It's like the kind of problems our father faced a generation ago. I just can't stop thinking about how wrong this is. But I guess this conversation can wait 'til later, when we can figure out how we can help."

Chad seated himself next to Danielle. She handed him back the beer he was working on before the fish struck.

Even after Parker's next fish was stolen from the end of the line by a seal that darted out from under the boat, it took only an hour to catch the last eight fish. The two beers apiece that paced the final hour of fishing were followed by a few more on the way around the northern tip of Admiralty Island and down the passage between Admiralty and Douglas Island. The wake behind the boat created a pattern of small waves all colored into a rainbow by the setting sun.

Danielle looked at Annalee. "I wish you would help me with this champagne."

"My mother had a rule when she carried me and my three sisters. No more than two glasses of wine in any one day, and I am saving room for a glass at the hotel later."

The boat turned north into Gastineau channel for the final ten miles. It was completely dark when the boat slipped up to the dock where four of the company warehousemen waited. "How did they know to be here?" asked Annalee.

Danielle pointed up to the bridge where four lanterns with alternating red and yellow lenses shown clearly from the dock. "Each of the Russ-Am boats lights four lanterns in that pattern when they head into the harbor. Anyone with a telescope can pick out the signal from miles away and gather up a crew."

The Romanoff was strangely silent when the group entered the lobby. "Good evening Mr. Gritt and Miss Post," greeted the man at the front desk. "Room for your friends there?"

"You have it right, Clarence," replied Chad. "This is my little brother Parker and his wife Annalee."

"The governor's suite is open, you can have it for the price of a regular room."

"We will take it. I know it's late, but is the dining room still open?"

"Word came round an hour ago, that you were in the channel, the chef stayed to see if he needed to feed any late-night customers. Just leave your bags in front of the desk, I'll see them to the room."

"That would be in the tradition of your fine service." Chad flipped a silver dollar to Clarence and the foursome headed toward the dining room. They seated themselves as the chef emerged from the kitchen. "I let everyone except for the busboy go, so your stuck with boarding house service this evening."

"Fine, Boris, that's just fine. We will start with a bottle of cabernet."

"In a minute, but first my late night for old customers menu. Steak with onions and some wild mushrooms that just came in this afternoon, or I can whip up a seafood rigatoni with smoked salmon."

While they waited for the wine Annalee's curiosity got the better of her. "What about your bags and the buggy out front?"

"The dock boy will take them on over to Danny's and set them inside the door for us," replied Chad.

Annalee's eyebrows almost disappeared into her scalp, but she managed a smile.

Parker came to his brother's rescue. "I am sure that the spare room in Danny's house is far more comfortable than the cot in the office apartment down on the dock.

"Oh," exclaimed Annalee, "and, what about those fish in that box on the boat?"

"That same young man will fillet them and put them in a brine in the warehouse," offered Chad. "I gave him instructions and a quarter apiece for taking care of the fish. With the two dollars for taking care of the buggy he will make two full days of pay for his evening's work."

"Is he Tlingit. He looks a bit different than the Natives on the Yukon?" she asked.

Parker took his wife's hand. "This is your fourth trip to Juneau dear. Most of the Natives here are Tlingit. I wish I could get you to visit a couple of the villages with us. You would really like the people. The word of the Lord is the law in most of them. You would feel right at home in a day or two."

"Your husband's company hires a number of Native kids. Part of the pay for hard work and loyalty is the opportunity to go outside for more education. Your family is well thought of in this country," said Danielle.

The wine arrived and twenty minutes later, dinner was served.

The fall morning made it too easy to sleep a bit longer than they planned. Danielle slowly swept Chad's face with her long hair until his eyes slowly opened. She smiled at his smile. "I wish you were going east with me," she said.

"Danny, I would love to, but this is our busiest time of year. We will be moving those miners who have made their grub steak, and are heading home, as well as those hired to replace them in the tunnels and stamp mills. We will be helping the canneries close, and the temporary workers will be going south. I can't get away until at least Thanksgiving."

"I know my captain; I am just ready for some city time. You know, a Broadway play, a real orchestra. I am looking forward to wearing a dress every day for a month. And I will buy new dresses and new shoes and go have high tea with old girlfriends."

"I hope you do all those things, Danny. I will come for the

holidays. Now, let's find something to occupy us until I meet Parker at The Golden Goose at noon."

Chad swung the door to Wilson's saloon closed and pointed his brother toward the end of the carved wooden bar. "Rattler around?" he asked the bartender.

The heavy-set man pointed at the door at the end of the counter. "He's smoking a cigar with one of Maples' men from up north. He should be done in a few minutes.

Parker and Chad exchanged glances. Chad pointed towards the street. "Would you have him stop by my office when his guest leaves? This man was entrusted with delivering a package to Rattler. The sender wanted it delivered in person."

"I would guess the man in the office is Link Bean," offered Parker. "He headed out with Maples on his private boat a few days before I got back to St. Michael."

"I know the name, but I can't connect a face," replied his brother.

"Small man, built solid, brown eyes and brown hair, walks everywhere like he is in the middle of a ten-mile march."

"I still can't place him," said Chad.

"You will when you see him. He was with Maples when the shooting on the Klondike took place. Cobra said that he was one of the men watching us the day someone tried to part Cobra's hair with a bullet but aimed too low. We don't want him around when we talk to the brother."

Like so many remote places, the people in Juneau often had big differences, even more than a little hostility toward one another. They were also forced to live close and even do business with each other. Chad and Parker were laying out a timeline and budget for the start-up of the Yukon routes the next summer when the bell on the door downstairs jingled. Chad rose from the old desk and leaned over the rail and motioned for Rattler to join them.

"Rattler, this is my brother Parker," introduced Chad. "Here, please take a seat; I think you may need it."

Rattler dropped his lanky frame into the overstuffed leather chair next to the door. "I understand you have a package for me."

Parker reached into the leather valise next to the desk and retrieved the canvas drawstring bag. "I think there is somewhere in the range of a thousand dollars in gold dust in this bag. Your brother wanted me to deliver it to you."

Rattler tugged at the drawstring and then licked the end of his index finger and pressed the finger against the contents. The finger came out dusted with gold. "I don't understand."

Parker took a deep breath. "I have some very bad news; your brother is dead."

Rattler said nothing, he just folded one leg over the other and stared first at Parker and then at Chad. "Is that so."

Parker handed Rattler an envelope. Inside was a sealed letter from Marshal Hickox in Falcon. "The marshal is investigating his death. He was murdered on the banks of the Yukon just below the Canadian border. I was there when someone shot him between the eyes. They tried to kill me and then shot up the *Denali*, I'm sorry, our steamboat for trying to come to his aid."

"Link Bean and Sam Maples told me that they had had some trouble with you up on the river," snapped Rattler. "They said the last time they saw my brother he was with you. They couldn't wait for his to return, they had to race the ice downriver."

"All of that is true, I guess. A week earlier I saved your brother's life when Bean and some guy by the name of Wolcott watched him fall out of a boat on the river and then sailed off and left him. After that Maples didn't trust your brother much. Maples and his group were traveling the river and forcing prospectors to sell their claims for pennies on the dollar. Sell, or get beaten half to death was the pitch."

"That still doesn't mean that you weren't the one who shot him," snarled Rattler.

Parker reached into the valise a third time and handed Rattler the note that Cobra had handed him on the *Denali* and the bill of sale for the saloon."

"The marshal who was visiting the Mounties up on the Klondike and my crew stopped where your brother was shot to recover his remains. I don't know if the marshal talks about that in his letter. There was nothing left after the bears found him but a few bones and his pistol and his wallet and coin purse." He handed the three items to Rattler.

"When we got back to Falcon the marshal went looking for Maples, your friend Link Bean and that man by Wolcott. Maples and Bean had headed down river."

Parker pulled another letter from the valise and handed it to Wilson. "Here is a note from the bartender at your brother's saloon and witnessed by two townsfolk. It explains that Maples claimed the right to sell your brothers saloon to the Wolcott man. But, as you can see, your brother had already sold it to me on the basis that I come here and pay you, a fair price."

"Where's Wolcott now?" asked Rattler.

"Your brother was on the wrong side of a lot of things up on the river," said Parker. "Still, he had some friends. Wolcott drowned body was found washed up on a bar downriver from Falcon the day after your brother's funeral. He may have just fallen out of a canoe, but the marshal thinks that some of your brothers' friends helped him into the water."

"This still could have been your work Parker Gritt," barked Wilson.

Chad leaned forward and gently took the letters from

Rattlers hand and quickly read each of them. "The timeline doesn't work for that to be the case. The marshal's note explains that your brother left Falcon with Maples and his crew. The way to stop a steamboat up on the river is to wave a flag from the shore. That explains how my brother and yours happened to be on this 'Fifty-Mile River.' Your brothers handwritten note makes it clear that he was worried about his life, and the copy of the buyout agreement for my brothers claim in the name of one of Maples' men, indicates why the boat was stopped. Besides, why would Parker come all the way down here to give you a bag full of gold?"

"Just how did you come to have my brother's gold?" snapped Rattler.

"Your brother told me where he had it hidden. It was under a rock in front of the fireplace in his cabin. The marshal and I found it the same evening that we brought your brothers remains back to Falcon. There was more, but I left enough with the marshal to pay off the note to Maples when he comes back next year."

"Who was in the trees when Cobra was killed?"

"I honestly saw no one, just heard voices challenging your brother when I refused to sell my claim. They may have seen him pass the other papers to me. Someone took a shot at me and missed. Your brother yelled at the shooter, then he and someone on shore exchanged some words and your brother showed a pistol that he had hidden behind his back. A moment later someone with a thirty-thirty or larger rifle shot Cobra in the head. Cobra told me that he thought Bean, Wolcott and Maples were watching us talk."

Rattler sat silently, the only indication of his mood a red blush on his neck and forehead. Finally, he spoke. "I need to get back to the Golden Goose."

"Would you like me to find the parson and have him meet you there," asked Chad?

"No."

"What about the payment for your brother's saloon?" asked Parker. "Or should we wait to discuss it tomorrow?"

Wilson was on his feet. He turned at the top of the stairs. "What's it worth?"

"Probably around two thousand or so, after the payment to Maples."

"A net of two thousand then," replied Wilson, "done. Can you have somone draft the appropriate receipt for my signature when you deliver the money?" There were no tears or indications of any emotion as Rattler walked away from the Russ-Am dock.

The Gritt brothers tried to return to their planning, but the intensity of the afternoon made that impossible. "You know, you never told him how much Maples claims he was owed on the note," observed Chad.

"I didn't have to. I'll bet that Maples has an identical note on the Golden Goose."

"Sounds about right to me," responded Chad.

The sale was done the next day. Three days later a letter signed by Link Bean admitting to being with Sam Maples when Cobra Wilson had been shot was delivered to the magistrate's office. The following day Links body was found. His arms and head had been tied above the water line of a discarded wooden vat previously used to cure salted cod. His feet were cinched to a ring in the bottom of the barrel. The vat was filled with seawater to Beans chest. Three dozen crabs lay dead in bottom of the tub. They had died of oxygen depletion, but not before they had eaten much of Link Bean below the belt.

That same afternoon, Marshal Walker arrived in Juneau after investigating the death of a missing cannery worker from

Johanson's who had been living in Kukwa. He had been sitting on the dock with the schoolteacher when someone with a high powered rifle shot him from four-hundred yards across the bay. The marshal found no evidence, and no one had seen a thing.

"Christ what a way to go," blurted Tex Walker looking at the vat full of dead crabs. Beans body had been removed the day it was found and had already been buried. The vat, hidden in a tumbled down old shack along the sand flats north of Juneau had been left alone for his investigation after a photographer had taken a series of photos of the body. "This has to be the work of Wilson based on what you have told me."

"That's probably true," replied Magistrate Tome. "But he has a damned good alibi. The Parson says that he has been living at the parsonage since the day after the Gritts met with him, praying three times a day and fasting."

"I'll just have to start interviewing his associates and put the word out that I want to talk to anyone who has seen Wilson in last five days."

Chad and Parker stood at the door to the shack. "We saw Wilson for breakfast this morning. He claims that he had nothing to do with this. But he wasn't very remorseful either."

"So now you and Rattler are best friends," shot Walker.

"Not quite," replied Chad. "We just wanted to know if there was anything more, he could tell us about Maples. Danny is going to meet Malcom Crier in Montreal in a month, and we didn't want her in danger."

The following morning dawned bright and colder. The constant hum of the mines that surrounded the town echoed off from the mountains. Danielle and Chad walked from her rooming house to her office downtown, both in a quiet mood. The ship south was due any day and neither felt good about the pending parting. The mood was not improved by the small crowd waiting at Danielle's door.

"What's going on?" she asked Paul Tennant.

"Went to the bank this morning and it was closed. There was a note from old Kinsman that he was on his way to Sitka to file bankruptcy. Within an hour there were ten of us standing on the sidewalk. I suggested that we needed to come talk to you."

" I am not a bankruptcy attorney, that's a rather special field of law," replied Danielle. "I don't know of anyone in the territory who is an expert, but if you would like to come in, I can stick my nose into the codes and see what I can find out."

"That's all we can ask for," replied Tennant."

Danielle turned to Chad and gave him a quick kiss on the cheek. "Come by when you are ready, and I will break for lunch."

Two hours later the men left her office with three pages of handwritten notes. "Let's go find the magistrate and get started on filing our claim," said one.

"Nope, we will have to wait until Kinsman files his bankruptcy in Sitka, and then we can file a claim," said another.

"Benny is right," confirmed Tennant, "that's what Miss Post told us."

"Hells bells Paul, she's just a girl. I think we should go talk to the Magistrate Tome," answered the first man.

Dannielle stood at her open window and watched the men walk slowly away. She shook her head, then turned back to her desk and began gathering files for the secretary that she had hired the week before. It would be up to the secretary to keep an eye on the ongoing cases and issues. If something was pressing, she would have to find someone else to handle it or take one of the twenty pre-signed requests for extension from an envelope on the desk and fill in the client's name and the date and get it to Magistrate Tome.

The last thing she did was review the bill of sale for the fledgling Juneau Electric Company. The founder of the company was selling it to a group of mining executives and another Juneau attorney. Danielle smiled as the seller and the buyers all walked into her office. "Any of you have money in the bank?" she asked as an ice breaker.

Fifteen minutes later the deal was done and the buyers headed out for lunch. "Now what are you going to do with yourself, I mean with the proceeds?" she asked the seller. He had been her first business client.

"I been thinking of buying a herd of beefs from some ranchers in eastern British Columbia and driving them north toward the Cassiar and the Upper Yukon. Men with new gold in their vest will pay almost anything for a beef steak."

Danielle just smiled. "Well, good luck with that. I guess you will be gone before I get back from Boston."

The man reached over and took Danielle's hand. "You really coming back?"

CHAPTER 14

Juneau, Alaska

THE SMELL OF creosote from the treated pilings hovered in the air like some kind of perverse perfume. The crowded dock creaked and shuddered as huge waves pushed the ship against its moorings. Chad and Danielle moved back toward the street where it was quieter.

"I'll take a break after the fall rush," said Chad, "head home and spend Christmas with the family. Will you be in Boston?"

"After my stop in Montreal I will be heading straight for my parents' home."

"I could be home by the third week of November," offered Chad.

"And just how long will you stay?

"Probably just through the new year. I need to get back to San Francisco and then Seattle. I have a whole season to set up."

"I was hoping that you would stay a bit longer." Danielle carefully wiped an unseen tear from her eye. "We used to have so much fun in New York. A week there to take in three or four plays or concerts wouldn't delay your spring startup."

"Danny, I hate winter in New England. Why don't you come to San Francisco with me? We can take on the town. I can stretch my visit a couple of weeks while we tour the shows and restaurants. The weather will be much more pleasant than New York in January."

"I promised my parents that I would spend most of my time with them. I promised myself that I would soak up enough of Boston and New York to get me through a couple more years up north. Besides, why would you swap a New England winter with parties and sleigh rides and dances at the club for the drizzle and wet snow of Juneau? I don't know how you avoid the cabin fever that takes over my body by January."

"I don't have an answer for that, but with my job I'm never shut in." He lifted Danielle's face and kissed her. She tasted salty. "If you give this country a chance, it will grow on you."

"It is beautiful country, and I came to be near you." "Sometimes though, I feel the only thing growing on me is mold." She squeezed Chad's hand and pulled away.

A minute later the gangway to the steamship clanged onto the wharf and the lines fore and aft dropped into the water. Parker and Annalee stood on the deck and waved as the ship slipped away from the dock. Thirty others joined them at the rail, but Danielle Post had disappeared into the bowels of the ship.

"I will keep an eye on her, Chad," yelled Annalee over the noise of the thrashing of the prop as the ship gained speed for its dash to Seattle.

Chad turned and headed to the office only a few steps away. *Sometimes it was lonely being away from friends and family,* he thought. *I don't blame Danny.*

He opened the door and greeted Governor Karp and Kate who had made the trip to Juneau on the ship that now carried his brother, sister-in-law and Danielle. Kate smiled at him, unwrapping the wool scarf that protected her from the damp wind. "Separation is to love what wind is to fire," she said. "Lyman and I are headed to the hotel for a brandy and coffee, care to join us?"

"I have a buggy waiting to take you two up the hill. I have some work to do, but if you are going to be there in an hour, I would be happy to join you."

Chad climbed the stairs and sat down at the huge rolltop desk that trapped him far too often in the office. He began entering the manifest and passenger list into the sailing report but found he had little interest in the paperwork. He crossed the office to the southern window and swung it open. He watched the ship disappear into the gathering mist and darkness until not even the running lights were visible. Closing the window, he brushed at the moisture on his wool shirt. It was soaked through from the damp wind. He stripped the shirt and found another in the small closet at the foot of his narrow cot.

Only in Alaska could a man wear a blue stripped cotton work shirt to the nicest hotel in town. Only in Alaska would not only the governor but also his wife find that to be appropriate attire for a drink in the nicest public house in the state. He quickened his pace as the rain changed from a mist to a downpour. *Damn,* he thought, *the very things that I love most about this place are the same things that Danny struggles with.*

The governor and his wife were at a small table in the corner when Chad slipped through the door from the hotel lobby. A half dozen locals had already found the couple. They were surrounded by chairs pulled from other tables.

"Gentlemen, the governor will be happy to meet with you

tomorrow. For now, we have committed to a special evening with an old friend, please excuse us," said Kate.

The governor and Chad had just ordered their second brandy when the waiter from the restaurant found them, announcing that their table was ready. "I didn't know we had one reserved," commented Karp.

"Mrs. Karp set up the reservation when you first arrived."

Katherine just smiled and waited until her husband rose to help her with her chair. She led off toward the dining room while Chad fumbled with the bill. Both men followed, meeting Marshal Walker coming in the door.

"Captain Gritt, are you up for a quick jaunt down to Kukwa after I meet with the governor in the morning?

"Why Kukwa so soon after you just were there?" asked Chad.

"A couple of men from the village came into town this afternoon. They dropped a cartridge case from a 6mm Navy rifle on my desk. They found it across the bay not far from where we searched while I was down there."

"Well, that gives you somewhere to start an investigation," replied Karp.

"As I recall, the North Pacific folks bought several 1895 Navy rifles with telescope sights from your firm in Sitka," said Walker, addressing Chad.

"If we had known who the buyer was, it would have never happened."

"We will deal with that as we can, for now I just need your help in getting some of the village hot heads to forget about burning down the North Pacific Cannery. There is only a winter watchman and a single guard there."

Karp smiled a huge smile as he approached the table where his wife waited with a very perturbed look on her face. "It is so unlike you to make me seat myself Lyman," she said.

"I am sorry my dear. I was watching 'Doctor' Tex Walker deliver a prescription for what ails our friend Captain Gritt. The two are on the way to Kukwa tomorrow to solve one of the worlds small problems."

It seemed strange to Chad to be a passenger on his second boat ride in just a few days. The government boat had been a harbor tug in logging camps on Puget Sound before the customs service had purchased it for use in Southeast Alaska. The boat had been modified by extending the small wheelhouse both forward and aft creating room for two facing seats. The backs of the seats folded up where straps at each end could be hooked to eye bolts set in the overhead, creating four bunks. The front of the wheelhouse now started only three feet behind the bow, giving the boat a stubby grotesqueness. What it lacked in appearance it made up for in speed, although the relatively flat bottom also gave the vessel a rough ride in choppy water. The man known as Skipper who had ferried the boat from Seattle had stayed and was now at the wheel.

On a flat day the trip to Kukwa could be as short as ten hours. But on a day when wind lashed the windows of the small cabin with sea spray, the trip could be twice as long. On the late October day that Walker and Chad were making the trip, they had a bit of both. A blustery northeast wind that slashed the boat from the mouth of the Taku River, slowed the small boat to a crawl for miles. "There's a storm coming from out in the ocean," commented Chad. "The high pressure over Canada is blasting through the valleys on our port beam on its way to fill in the low over the Pacific."

The mouth of every inlet was filled with a mist created by the venturi effect of the wind. Between inlets the boat could dash south at its top speed. The waves right on the side of the boat every time it crossed an opening in the mountains slowed them to a crawl as the boat turned toward the shore to take the wind on a quartering bow. While Skipper handled the wheel, Chad and Walker occupied themselves by playing chess with a board that used pieces with pegs in the bottom.

"That may be the first time that I have ever won two games in a row," laughed Walker. "You must be really distracted."

"I guess I am, just a bit," replied Chad.

"This country isn't for everyone," observed Walker. "You ever notice how many of the men who come to work the mines and bring their wives end up leaving after only a couple of years?"

"I don't much want to talk about it."

"All right, put it in your saddle bag and see if you can whip me just once before we turn toward the village."

"You going to play this game or practice writing a social advice column? It's your move."

"Just reading the sign along the trail Captain Gritt. Sometimes all the right moves don't help a man who's playing the wrong game."

Chad stood, his flushed face and tight lips telegraphing his response. "It's hot in here, I need a bit of air."

"Take your time young man. I predict that my next chess move may be the only one where I have any control. I'll just think it through."

The tide was full-in when the boat turned into Kukwa Inlet. The branches dripped. It had been raining, and raining hard, but above the boat the evening sky was clearing and at the head of the bay a bright light behind the mountains signaled the rising full moon. Chad had indeed won the final game. Now he and Walker sat in two folding chairs on the cabin roof.

The wake stretched out to both sides of the inlet as Skipper slowed the boat in the failing light. Off to one side a ball of sparks erupted from the water as three seals chased a ball of candlefish to the surface. And ahead of the boat the glare from the rising moon turned the water a strange pale silver. "Man will never create anything that holds a candle to this," observed Chad.

"I agree," replied Walker. "I once sat in a Catholic cathedral full of silver and gold and beautifully carved woodwork. It certainly helped you find a holy spirit. But here, on a night like this, you know where that spirit came from."

"That sounds a lot like poetry," came from an open window below.

"You old sea monkey," replied Walker, "there are a lot of cowboy poets."

Skipper laughed. "Not in Alaska, and not without a bottle in front of him."

In the distance the soft glow of oil lamps in windows announced the village. The skipper signaled their coming with three sharp tugs on the cord to the steam whistle. Walker handed the folding chairs down to Chad who stashed them under one of the seats in the cabin. As the boat turned at the head of the bay and began its approach to the dock a dozen lanterns started down the paths from the village.

"What you want this time, Marshal?" asked John Medev. "We figure you're gone until summer, you know, when the sun shines and the winds stop."

"You know why I came back," answered Walker. "Your son and two of his friends brought me the cartridge case and a wild story about an Indian uprising on the Kukwa River. I figured that you sent them."

"Nope," replied the chief. "I did tell em' that anyone who got in real trouble with the law would be banished from the village. A village without young men will be a ghost town in short time. I am just trying to protect my people. Who is that in the cabin? You bring the cavalry this time?"

"That's Chad Gritt. He was in Juneau so I asked him if he would like to take a ride with me."

"You two eat yet?"

"Only a piece of hard tack and some jelly."

Medev turned to one of the young boys who had just helped tie the boat to the floating dock. "Nathan, you go tell my daughter that she has guests coming for dinner. Tell her they are important people."

Chad threw a small duffle bag out of the cabin and turned the small oil lamp down. Stepping onto the deck of the boat he grabbed the duffle and jumped over the rail onto the dock. He extended his hand toward the chief and then to each of the four elders waiting. "The *Miles Pierce* will be coming through here in a couple of days, I thought that you might allow a gussuk to visit until it comes."

"You always welcome to this place," offered a graying woman with only a scattering of teeth in her mouth. "You and your family are part of this village, even if you are part of the Raven Clan."

"Mary, I am a Raven because they adopted my father. Your Clan was too wealthy, to many potlatches, too busy back then."

"It is true, we always held the biggest potlatches. You come by my house tomorrow morning and I make you some sour-dough donuts. We drink tea."

I was counting on that Mary." Chad reached into the bag at his feet and pulled out two small packages wrapped in paper. "For you, I brought some brown sugar and some of that white powdery sugar that you like for your donuts."

"Thank you, Captain Gritt." The old woman pointed at

Walker, Skipper, and Chad and then pointed up the hill toward the schoolhouse. "You go now and surprise Belinda."

Chad retrieved several other small gifts from his duffle and distributed them. Turning to the chief he presented a pair of reading glasses. "The marshal informs me that you and several other adults are learning to read from Belle, but that you are having trouble seeing the words."

"That lawman maybe talks to much," replied Chief John with a big smile. "We go now."

Belle Medev waited on the porch, her hair pulled back and tied with a soft blue ribbon which matched the blue skirt and white blouse that had become her teacher's uniform. She stood, wide eyed as she recognized the third man in line walking up toward the school, still talking to her father.

"Welcome Skipper, welcome Marshal Walker, welcome Captain Chad Gritt, please come inside."

The three guests and Belinda's father followed the young woman through the benches of the school room and into the small apartment in the back. Remembering that there were only four chairs in the kitchen, Chad carried the chair from the teacher's desk with him into the warm, dry air that only comes from a wood stove. A large silver samovar sat on the counter surrounded by cups and saucers.

Belle lifted the lid from a large kettle that rested on the wood cooking range, then poured most of the steaming water into the samovar. Chief John struck a match and lit the candle below. "You will have to be happy with tea for the hour it will take me to make dinner," she said. "My father doesn't allow strong spirits in the village."

While Belle sliced an onion and placed the rings atop a huge halibut fillet, Walker began to quiz her father. "How many of your young men want to burn the cannery?"

"Young men who have lost a friend sometimes talk," replied Medev.

"You mean that young cannery worker who was staying with you, the one who got shot? How did he happen to be here in the first place? You never answered my question when I was here last."

"He was on the beach," replied the chief.

"You said that last time, but what was he doing there and why didn't you send him back to Johansons?"

"Marco not want to go back."

"Well, that's part of an answer," replied Walker.

Belle slipped the roasting pan into the oven of the stove and made herself a cup of tea. She took the seat at the head of the table opposite her father and next to Chad. "Marco had been injured and fell out of his boat. Both his shoulder and leg were injured. We found him on a beach and allowed him to stay until his wounds were healed. He was very concerned about the trouble between the Johanson people and the gang that worked for the North Pacific Cannery. He didn't want to go back to the cannery until after the season ended."

Walker leaned across the table and smiled at Belinda. "What kind of wounds?"

Belle smiled back. "Puncture wounds like if you fell on a gaff hook."

Walker turned back to her father. "When I was here last you couldn't think of any reason the boy was shot."

John Medev sipped his tea and stared out the window at the glow of a full moon in the forest behind the village. Finally, Walker shifted back to Belinda.

"What about you Belle, do you have any idea why this Marco lad was killed?"

Belle rose to open a tin of green beans, one of only five cans of store-bought goods on the shelf next to the sink. She mixed them in with some diced onions and potatoes and set the pot on the stove.

"Marshal Walker, the North Pacific Cannery boats came up to the village at least a half dozen times looking for their boat that went missing. Each time they came they accused us of murdering those men and sinking their boat. More than once, they accused us of working with the Johanson men."

"So, you think that it was a revenge killing."

Belle joined her father in studying the shadows of the forest. Walker tried for another ten minutes to learn more, but as often happens in the village when there is nothing more to say, the people stop talking.

The halibut baked on a bed of seaweed and seasoned with only onions and salt and pepper would have won a grand prize in a chef's contest anywhere in the world. After dinner Walker and Skipper excused themselves and headed back to the boat. "We would like to talk to your young men in the morning if you can arrange it."

Chief Medev smiled as he turned off toward his own home. "You bring some real coffee and some sugar to my house in the morning, and I will have the young men there. Do not let the monster of Kukwa onto your boat tonight. You sleep good now."

Chad and Belle finally found themselves alone as they started doing the dishes. "I don't know how my father ate another meal."

"What do you mean? He ate like he hadn't eaten in a week," replied Chad.

"You still do not understand us very well Captain Gritt. He always eats dinner early and he is normally in bed by the time your boat arrived. He joined you in dinner to be polite. He also wanted the marshal to know that he had defused the crises."

Chad reached into the duffle at his feet and set a small bottle of Spanish Port on the table. "I know your father's rules, but as I recall you enjoy a small glass of port after a great meal."

Belle found two old chipped heavy coffee mugs and set them on the table. "Only if we can sit on the porch and sip them together. On a night like this, there will be others on their steps drinking tea."

"This is medicine. I brought it for the only nurse in a hundred miles, one who once saved my life."

Belle carried both mugs outside and sat down on the top step. She patted the seat next to her. Chad took the cup and sat. The faint light on the eastern horizon faded in minutes, but it didn't get dark. The full moon behind the village cut through air washed clean by the afternoon rains and lit up the inlet like afternoon on a stormy day. Unlike a stormy day the tops of the mountains behind the village sparkled with moonlight on fresh snow and the water dripping from the huge evergreen trees caught the moonlight creating sparkles in the dark trees.

"I really missed this while I lived in Oregon," said Belle. "It rained a lot like it does here, but even when it was clear, the land was tame, and the beauty subdued."

"I fully agree, Belle. I didn't see this country until I was five and my parents brought the whole family to Sitka for the summer. I knew then that this is where I wanted to live."

"But it's not for everyone, praise God. If it was it would look a lot like Puget Sound with towns in every bay and huge logging camps. I was amazed traveling around Oregon by the huge farms in every river valley, even on the San Juan Islands."

"My brother Parker and his wife have been spending the summers on the Yukon River, then moving back to the Boston area for the winter. They spend ten days or two weeks in Sitka coming or going but aren't going to cut their New England ties. Danielle Post went with them this year."

Belle smiled, but Chad couldn't see it. "I understand her feelings. I tried to cut my ties to this country when I went outside to school. I fully intended to write the Guildhams and the Society of Mission Friends when I graduated offering to pay them back for my education and advising them that I was going south not north. Instead, my senior year seemed three years long. This country is where I belong."

"Me too," replied Chad. "Can I get you another small cup of tea?"

Belle handed her empty cup to Chad as he rose. "Don't you miss your family?" she asked.

"I do, more in the winter when things are slower. But then I climb the ladder to the bridge of a boat and signal the engineer to get under way, and I am transported into the only place where I am truly happy."

"Maybe you can have a new family here someday so that you can have both."

"I think about that more this year than ever before," replied Chad. "Just this summer I have experienced more than a half-dozen deaths. If I died on the way back to Sitka, it would be months before anyone who really cared even knew."

"That is not true Chad," offered Belle. "You had better go now, I have a surprise for you tomorrow and you will need to be rested."

Chad took Belle's hand and squeezed it. Then he rose and started for the government boat where Skipper and Walker were already asleep on the seats without setting up the upper bunks.

"I'm sorry to see you back," offered a half-asleep Walker. "Hang on and I will help get a bunk set up. There's a blanket in the chest."

Belle found Chad at Mary Ivanofs house the next morning. He had joined the marshal for an early meeting with the young men of the village. The marshal and village chief seemed to have the situation under control as he slipped out the back. Mary had been a friend of the family for decades, and she made the best donuts in Alaska.

Belle crossed the room and took a seat next to the captain just as Mary put a heaping plate of donuts on the table. Belle reached out and wiped a streak of white powdered sugar from the side of Chad's mouth. Mary pushed a huge ceramic mug of tea across the table to Belle. "The young pretty girls always get the handsome ones," she said. "You eat some donuts, get fat, give Mary a chance."

A half hour later, the two stood on Mary's porch. "You go get your pack and rifle from the government boat and meet me at the schoolhouse," said Belle.

"I thought you had school this morning."

"I left a message on the door canceling school. Of the fourteen children, only three will be really upset, the others will be happy to start their weekend early. I left an extra-credit assignment that will keep my three best students busy."

"It doesn't seem fair that the students would all get ready and walk over to the school only to find it canceled," commented Chad.

"Just like last night, you really don't understand us well, Captain. I have the only watch in the village. No one even starts getting ready until I ring the bell. We are on village time."

After dropping his gear, Chad waited while Belle packed a small bag and then the two of them headed down the hill where Belle had her father's small canoe ready at the edge of the water. Chad slung a small duffel with a set of rain gear and a few survival items over one shoulder and his 30-30 Winchester over the other. Belle carried a small canvas bag with lunch and an old breach-block 45-70 carbine.

"Now that's quite a weapon."

Belle smiled. "This old rifle throws a bullet about the size of a fat-cats cigar. It will cut right through a six-inch alder tree and flatten anything behind it. It would be a perfect bear gun if it held more than one shell."

"Are we going bear hunting then?" asked Chad.

"No, Captain, I just want to show you a small cove where I am going to build a cabin next summer. There are still old salmon in the stream. Where there are fish there will be bears."

The two paddled out to the entrance to Kukwa inlet and turned south. The fall sun climbing in the eastern sky found only a handful of wispy high clouds. The air was cool but dry and most importantly there wasn't a ripple on the water. A half-hour later Belle turned into a small inlet only a hundred feet across. The short bay curved to the north making the small round harbor at its end impossible to see from the main passage. Even at low tide the passage and the bay would accommodate a fair-sized boat. At the head of the bay a grassy hill stood out from the dark forest all around it. Chad could see a small stream flowing around the hill from the north and emptying into the bay. They beached the canoe and together hauled it above the high tide line.

From where they left the canoe, a trail worn into the earth more than a foot deep wound toward the top of the hill. Belle led the way to a large rock cairn and four totems that were in the process of rotting away. Two large logs had been flattened into a bench behind the totems and between them a large fire pit was filling with leaves.

The hill sloped gently down behind the firepit to the shore of a clear round lake, about a mile across, by Chad's estimate. Small circles dotted the surface indicating plenty of feeding trout. The shore was surrounded by a dense stand of cedar trees, their branches hanging over still water. A small stream emptied the lake, flowing about a half mile around the edge of the hill before spilling into the saltwater bay.

"My God," exclaimed Chad, "what is this place?"

"For centuries it was the place where the spiritual leaders of my people came to cleanse their minds and to initiate new shaman. It hasn't been used for three generations, probably since the Russians came. My grandfather brought me here several times. He was considering restarting the tradition, but the Methodists were against the practices of the shamans. One day he brought me here and told me that the spirits wanted this place to belong to me."

Belle gathered some firewood by breaking the branches from underneath several fallen trees and by gathering huge pieces of bark from under the heavy canopy. "There is plenty of dry firewood even in a rainforest if you know where to look."

"What's for lunch?" asked Chad.

"Trout from the lake. Go catch four or five while I get the fire going."

"Now just how am I going to do that?"

"It is man's work, you will figure it out," laughed Belle. She scooped out the wet leaves from the fire pit and carefully laid dry moss and a few twigs into the bottom. In minutes she had a tiny flame going. "Where are those fish, Captain?"

Chad reached into his bag and pulled out a length of cutty-hunk cotton line. "I have line, but no hook or lure," he commented.

"Native fishhooks are just a tiny piece of wood or bone sharpened at both ends with a hole drilled in the middle. When a fish bites the fisherman pulls on the line and sometimes it will wedge into the fish's mouth."

Chad pulled his pocketknife and began carving a sliver of wood from a knot that he pried from a log. In a few minutes he had a small shaft about three-quarters of an inch long. He carefully drilled a hole through the center and tied it to his line. He found a small, rusted bolt and nut in his bag and backed the nut off. He tied the nut above the hook and began rummaging around for something to use for a lure. After ten minutes of trial and error he settled on a piece of red wool yarn from the top of his sock. "I'll be back in a few minutes."

The path had been mashed down more than a foot into the surrounding earth. The puddles had drained away leaving damp soil that cushioned every step. Every few feet a muddy spot was decorated with fresh footprints of the local bear population. In one particularly wet stretch there were the tracks of a half dozen different bruins including one that was two inches longer than Chad's boot.

"A lot of bears in the area," he called to Belle.

"That's why we brought the rifles."

"I left mine leaning against the bench behind you," called Chad. "I will keep my eyes open; if you need help, just yell, I'll come a running."

Except for the area along the grassy hill, the rest of the lake was heavily forested with a tangle of fallen logs. The grassy area stretched for more than fifty yards below the hill and along the shore a game trail the size of a city boardwalk stretched along the water line. Chad stopped right where the trail from the firepit touched the water and gathered his line into two-foot loops in his left hand. With his right hand he grasped the line above the makeshift sinker and began to twirl the line in easy loops. The line swung around, sky to land, sky to land, until Chad felt he had enough momentum to launch the hook with the red yarn above it out into the lake.

After the fifth swing he released the line with his right hand and opened his left hand pointing his fingers out toward the lake. The line shot out of his right hand and straight up into the air. Realizing the error Chad closed his left hand bringing the lure to a jarring stop right above him transferring the upward momentum into one straight down. The line collapsed around his shoulders, the nut he was using as a sinker bouncing off from his skull. His eyes filled with tears, but he worked to stifle any exclamation, preferring to suffer the pain in silence.

Sorting out the line again he refocused on the swinging sinker and this time made a perfect pitch, the red lure and sinker landing more than thirty feet out in the lake. He began to retrieve the lure rapidly pulling the line in using both hands and allowing the line to coil at his feet. On his third pitch he felt the tug of a strike and jerked the line hard but felt no fish on the other end. Three more casts brought the second strike which yielded the same result. "Damn," he mumbled.

Turning he noted a strong white smoke from the firepit and Belle sitting on one of the log benches watching him. The white smoke meant that she had a hot fire going. He returned to his fishing and for the next twenty minutes could feel the tug of a fish from time to time, but the sharp homemade hook never lodged in a mouth. He turned again to Belle. "If I had a real steel hook we would have lunch already."

"Next time you feel a fish, don't jerk, pull slowly. Let the fish hook themselves."

It worked, the next tug on the line producing a fat twelve-inch trout. Chad had caught hundreds of speckled Dolly Varden trout in salt water and in the streams of Southeast Alaska, but this fish was different. It was bright silver with a faint red blush along its sides. Turning the fish over he noticed scarlet slashes along the bottom of the jaw. He flipped the fish into the tall grass behind him and made another cast, this time losing a fish right at his feet. "Get the fire ready he called; lunch will be delivered in just a few minutes."

It took only another ten minutes to put four trout on the bank. Five minutes later he hung the cleaned fish on a small branch and was headed back to the fire.

"I don't know this particular fish," he observed as he approached Belle kneeling next to the fire.

"You find them in lots of the streams that drain lakes from here south. You would never remember the Indian name, but in Oregon they call them cutthroat trout. You are in for a real treat."

Belle lifted the frying pan and placed a glob of lard in the pan and set it on some coals that she had raked from the fire. When the lard had dissolved, she slipped one of the trout off from the carrying stick and laid it into the pan. "Too long," she observed, "we will have to take the heads off. Hand me your knife."

Chad reached into his pants pocket for his folding knife. "Damn, he said, I left it down where I cleaned the fish. I'll be right back."

In minutes he was back where he had been fishing and picked up his knife. Turning back for the trail he looked up and saw a huge bear emerge from the forest only fifty yards away. He stepped back toward the trail to the firepit just as the bear noticed him. The bears pace quickened.

"Belle, there's a bear down here, coming right at me!" he yelled.

Belle stood up on the bench where she could get a better look and flipped the trap door of the old 45-70 rifle open and slipped a shell into the breach. "Do not run, just slowly back up the trail and keep your eye on him."

The bear waddled no more than a hundred feet and stood on

its hind legs to get a better look at the creature in the trail above him. "Keep coming, and don't turn away from him."

By the time Chad reached the benches, the bear was only thirty feet from the firepit. He reached down without losing sight of the bear and picked up his rifle and levered a shell into the chamber. "That's the biggest bear that I have ever seen."

Belle sat down on the end of one bench with her rifle in her lap. "Sit down on the end of the other bench facing the bear," she commanded. "Don't raise your rifle."

Chad could hear the panting as it climbed the hill, its head the size of the end of a barrel. *If he comes now, I can only get one shot off*, he thought. "I am not about to sit down," he replied.

"Sit down," Belle ordered, "it will be alright."

Chad sat, but he hoped the bear wasn't attracted to the drumming sound that came from his chest.

"Oh Grandfather," said Belle, "I have just come to this special place with my friend to be with you and the spirits."

The bear stopped and looked toward Belle, noticing her for the first time.

"Did I know you before, from when my human grandfather used to bring me to this place? It has been a long time. If I knew you before, you were small. You have grown large and wise."

The bear swung his head back toward Chad and then tipped his nose high in the air and sniffed three long deep breaths.

"You smell the lunch that the white man has caught for me. They are trout from your lake. You do not try to catch trout this time of year, you have salmon. Look at how fat you are. We will not take any of your salmon, I promise."

The bear's ears were rotating like a flag on a day when the wind couldn't make up its mind. Then he sat down.

"Oh Grandfather, thank you for being a good host. We will take only what we need, and we will leave before sunset. I will come back next summer and if it is alright with you, I will build a small den here where we both can remember the old shaman together."

Belle sat quietly as the bear began to scratch at a worn place on its neck and another on its side. He gave every appearance of ignoring the people before him. Finally, the bear stood slowly and looked at Belle and replied to her with a muffled 'woof.' It looked at Chad and offered a faint snarl and then another woof. Then the old bear turned and ambled back down the trail.

"Thank you, Grandfather, for visiting us. Please tell your family and friends that we mean them no harm."

The bear reached the bottom of the hill and stopped where Chad had cleaned the fish to lick the blood off from the rocks. It then continued until it crossed the outlet from the lake and disappeared into the forest.

Belle snapped open the trapdoor of her rifle and removed the huge cartridge. "It's time for some lunch."

"That was amazing, Belle," offered Chad. "How did you know that he wouldn't charge?"

"I just knew. He was curious and he certainly didn't need to hunt us. He was so fat that he waddled. My grandfather believed that the great bears were warriors. Like all great warriors they do not need to prove that they are tough by taking on those weaker than themselves. Some believe that the greatest of the great bears are transformed from great Tlingit warriors who pass."

"Besides, with you between me and the bear, I could have never gotten off a clean shot if I had wanted to."

"Well, thank you Belinda Medev. I might well have done all the wrong things just now. I most likely would be visiting with St. Peter trying to explain some things on my resume. You probably just saved my life a second time."

"You are probably correct. Now let's build the fire back up

for a half hour, we need more coals if we don't want to eat those fish raw."

Chad rose and removed the cartridge from the chamber of his rifle, but he didn't put the rifle down. "I'll go get another armful of dry wood."

The canoe rounded the point that marked the southern entrance to Kukwa Inlet just as the government boat passed the destroyed fish trap. Belle waved at the boat. Skipper slowed the boat and allowed it to glide to a stop. Belle and Chad slipped the canoe up next to boat where Marshal Walker stood on the back deck.

"There isn't going to be a war down here this winter," offered Walker.

"I promised that I would stay on the case of young Marco's shooting and the young men of Kukwa agreed to leave the problems with North Pacific up to the governor and me. Now where have you two been?"

Chad smiled. "Belle just showed me a hidden bay with a lake full of trout and bears that speak human."

Walker looked at Chad like he had gone mad.

"I am telling you the truth Tex," continued Chad. "I thought we were going to get eaten for sure, but the biggest bear I have ever seen was just dropping by to have a chat with this young lady."

Walker watched the smile on Chad's face as he told his story. "Looks like I am not the only one who thinks Kukwa is a good place for a man to consider more education."

CHAPTER 15

Seattle, Washington

THE *MAXIMILIAN* FOUND perfect weather for a change, reaching Pier 5 in Seattle on schedule. The Russ-Am manager met the boat as the seventy passengers started down the gangway. "Welcome back cousin Parker," said Travis Gritt. "I trust that your voyage from the far north was pleasant."

"You remember the story about our father's trip from Cuba, well that's just how smooth the water was and how much we were looking forward to getting down here."

"Parker, I already have guests at the house. Camile's mother and father showed up a month ago and never left. I'll have to arrange for a hotel room for you and Annalee. You really don't need any time with my mother-in-law."

"Make it two rooms, Travis, we are traveling with Chad's lady friend. Do you remember Danielle Post?"

"I do. I remember when she went through here a couple of years ago. She was on the adventure of her life. I figured once she found cousin Chad, she would put a hook in him and haul him back to civilization. I take it that he is not with you?"

"No, Danny is on her way home for the winter with a stop in Montreal. Chad should be down in five or six weeks to spend the holiday in Boston. They will be together then, but my brother will not be staying very long."

"Will Miss Post be going back north with you in the spring?"

"Maybe, maybe not," replied Annalee, "but if she does, I think she has given herself only two more years to drag my brother-in-law out of Alaska."

Danielle emerged from the passageway and extended her hand to Travis. "Nice to see you again."

"I will have your things delivered to whichever hotel you want. There's not much going on right now so you can take your pick. How long will you be staying?"

"I am only going to be here long enough to buy some new clothes and send a couple of telegrams, then I will be on the next train east," replied Danielle.

"And you two?" asked Travis turning to Parker and Annalee.

"We have some banking to do, and then you and I have several days of planning for next year. You won't believe what is about to happen up north."

Annalee placed her hand on her husband's face. She then turned to Travis. "You two better keep a lid on this until next year or you will have every businessman on the west coast trying to get a piece of the business by spring."

"My wife's father was a merchant who made a fortune following the gold and silver strikes in California and Nevada."

Annalee smiled and began to giggle. "He wanted me to have a stable life, so he sent me to Boston to study before he and my mother retired there. Now look at me, I travel five-thousand miles between my summer and my winter homes."

"It sounds like your father was quite a businessman," said Danielle.

"He was, and he lived by three or four rules. The one that's appropriate here was, 'never tell a stranger about your best fishing hole,' and he lived the proof of that wisdom."

Travis sent two of his dock hands to bring the luggage for his friends. If you have no objection, I will put you at the Washington Hotel. It is almost new and offers the nicest rooms in town. If you need a coach from anywhere in town back to the hotel, tell the driver that you are at the Denny, that's what the locals call it." Travis scribbled a note on a pad on his clipboard and handed it to one of the schoolboys watching the boat unload along with a two-bit piece. "Here, take this up to the Denny and give it to the front desk."

"Camile and I can probably duck her parents for dinner if you want. We live only a couple of blocks from the hotel."

With dinner set, and the luggage on one of the companies Studebaker wagons, Travis waved for one of the coaches waiting across the street. "Take these folks up to the Denny."

"I need to send a telegram; can we stop at the Western Union office on the way?" asked Danielle.

"There will be a Western Union messenger at the hotel."

"And railroad reservations?"

"The hotel will make them for you. I understand that you are stopping in Montreal."

"That's what the telegram will confirm."

"I suggest taking the Northern Pacific to Grand Forks and then on to Winnipeg. There you can transfer to the Canadian Pacific. There are fewer stops on the Canadian route; you can shave a full day off from the trip," suggested Travis.

"Thank you, Travis, It's clear why this company is doing so

well. As long as the Gritt family keeps new generations coming it will prosper." Danielle patted Annalee's abdomen and laughed.

Danielle sent messages to her parents, Malcom Crier at his office in Alexandria and to Abraham and Gilda Guildham in New York. She then made arrangements to meet Annalee for afternoon tea and some shopping before retiring to her suite for a two hour soak in the bathtub.

"Look how out of date we are!" Danielle and Annalee rode in the hotel provided carriage. "The fall color is purple. The shoes are all buckled. The hats are round with small brims. I feel like I have been gone for a generation."

Annalee smiled at her companion. "We will take care of that shortly, although I am not about to spend a handful of my husband's money on clothes that I can only wear for a month or two. Maybe if the baby comes before we head north again, I could use an outfit or two, but there's no place to wear them up on the Yukon."

"You are really going back to that wilderness house on the north coast again next year?"

"Danny, if you could have seen the cabins and even tents that I grew up in you would consider a small five room house in St. Michael a palace. I wouldn't want to spend the winter some place where everything froze solid for months and the wind made everything so cold you can't tell man from woman, the way everyone is bundled up. But that country is amazing and wild and beautiful. And, we are pioneers there, bringing civilization and education just like the folks who pushed across the plains in covered wagons."

Danielle sat quietly. Finally, she reached over and took Annalee's hand. "I am not sure that I am cut out of the rough canvas cloth it takes to make a northern pioneer. I didn't grow up in that kind of life."

"I love Boston too," answered Annalee. "But we are going to have a boy, and I want him to grow up to be the kind of man his father is. You know, watchful and quiet, generous but tough, a man at home working on a steam engine or calculating how to get a quarter-million dollars' worth of freight to hungry miners five-thousand miles from home."

"How do you know it's a boy?"

Annalee just smiled. "The first born of every generation of Gritts is a boy. It's the same in my family."

"I didn't know that you had a brother."

"I had a brother. He hated the mining towns that we lived in, and the minute that he was old enough to leave, my father sent him and a bag of money to study at Yale college. He enrolled and decided medicine was his calling. When the flu epidemic hit New England, he volunteered to help. He moved to New York and worked with the immigrants being held in quarantine. He died of the flu."

"I am sorry, Annalee. I am sure you and your parents are very proud of him."

"We are. You know the last thing he did the day he died; he changed into a suit with a silk shirt and a tie. He didn't want to die with canvas pants and a flannel shirt. He never understood my father and what he stood for. But his nephew, who will be named for him will."

The carriage stopped at a large four-story building. "Ladies," said the coachman, "if you can't find what you are looking for within a block of this place it doesn't exist in Seattle. When do you want to be picked up?"

The evening was hosted by Travis Gritt and his wife Camile, a Rubenesque woman of Italian heritage and Latin temper. They had decided on the hotel dining room where more than twenty tables were filled with men in English tweed jackets and women in high collared dresses. The waiter, in a starched white jacket and bowtie, seated Danielle next to Camile. "May I take a drink order?" he asked.

Before anyone else could answer, Camile ordered two bottles of her favorite champagne. "It is so seldom that we get to entertain out of town guests we shall start with a toast."

"If you would not mind, I would prefer a cold beer," offered Danielle, "I am as thirsty as a Kansas field hand in August."

"After our toast, Miss Post," answered Camile. "We are not field hands or dock workers."

Her husband started to speak but swallowed his words as his wife shot a bitter glance across the table. The rest of dinner was dominated by endless questions about the trials of a "lady" in the wilds of Alaska and a fully detailed commentary on the lifestyle of Mr. and Mrs. Travis Gritt in Seattle.

Danielle was rescued by a hotel bellboy entering the dining room with a note board on a long handle. It read, *Telegram for Miss Danielle Post.* Parker waved to the messenger and pointed toward Danielle at the end of the table. As she opened the envelope, Travis flipped a quarter to the messenger who smiled and walked away wiping chalk from his board.

After a few minutes, Danielle folded the message and returned it to the envelope. "It's from Malcom Crier. Samuel Maples is in Seattle and will be traveling to Montreal this week. Malcom doesn't know where he is staying but expects to hear from him in the next couple of days. He wants to know if I would be interested in traveling with him."

"Who, pray tell, is Malcom Crier and this Mr. Maples?" asked Camile.

Parker looked around to determine whether anyone from the other tables were focused on their conversation. Lowering his voice, he explained the Crier's involvement in Alaska and his less than favorable perception of Samuel Maples. He left out the fact that Danielle carried a letter signed by both Marshal Tex Walker and Magistrate Tome in Juneau advising that Maples was wanted for the murder of Cobra Wilson. "Perhaps you should return Malcom's telegram tonight," he suggested.

"I agree," said Danielle. "If you excuse me, I will tend to that right-away."

"Travis and I need an hour or so, for me to bring him up to speed on some business issues," offered Parker as Danielle rose to find the telegraph office. "We will be in the bar with a cigar and a brandy if anyone would like to join us."

"Travis, I detest all of your business talk," replied Camile. "Perhaps Annalee would join me in the lobby for a glass of sherry."

"Camile, I am so sorry to have to decline your pleasant offer, but with the child and all, I need to turn in early. My doctor recommends at least ten hours of sleep every night," replied Annalee.

"Well, that's just fine, Travis," snapped his wife, "you invite me out for a night on the town and then abandon me to talk about ships and cargo and Seward's Icebox. I will see myself out. I will be at home with Mother. I expect you to be home early in case we need a fourth for cards."

"I will walk with you to the door, offered Annalee, it's on the way to the elevator."

Forty minutes later, Danielle stepped through the door into the bar attracting a lot of attention. Parker waved from a private table in the corner, just as the waiter started away from the table with a new order for Travis and himself. "One minute please," he uttered, "would you please add one of those sweet Havanna's and a glass of port for the lady."

About half of the bar's patrons stared in disbelief as the

proper lady who had just seated herself at the corner table, with two men, snipped the ends from a long thin cigar and, accepting a light from the steward, pulled a long puff of honey sweet smoke into her mouth. "How did you know that I am a cigar aficionado?" she asked Parker.

"My brother asked me to make sure you were well taken care of on the trip. That included a list of your likes and dislikes."

Danielle just smiled.

"This Maples guy sounds like real trouble," commented Travis, giving Danny a worried look. "I am assuming that you are not traveling with him."

"I am not, and I do not want to end up on the same train with him even by accident. I advised Malcom of the letter from Juneau and of our other concerns about the man. I also told him that I would be altering my travel plans to avoid any contact. He will be meeting me in Montreal."

Parker pulled the gold pocket watch from his vest and checked the time. "It's two in the morning in Washington D.C. I suspect you will not hear back from Malcom until morning. Perhaps you can flesh in some detail of the problems in Southeast for cousin Travis; I have given him a pretty clear picture of the trouble on the Yukon."

The three agreed to meet again in the morning. "Travis and I will be down at the office. Travis knows a small company that does assay and smelting work, friends that will keep their mouths closed. We need to convert some gold dust and nuggets to small bars before we can convert them to cash at the bank. We should be back at the wharf by eleven," offered Parker.

The skies had cleared as Danielle walked across the dock and turned the handle to the Gritt offices, barely catching the door as it tried to detach itself from the building in the brutal south wind. The bell attached to the door clattered and brought a short balding man from the shuttered pursers office to the counter. "May I help you young lady?"

"My name is Danielle Post, and I am here for a meeting with Travis and Parker."

"Ah, Miss Post, I knew your father, well back in the days when we both lived in Sitka. Welcome."

"And you are?"

"McGurk, Scottie McGurk is the name. I was one of the naval officers serving your father's customs work, that is, back in a different life. That was more than twenty years ago."

"Mr. McGurk, you would not recognize the place. The industry and the new residents have turned it into a magnet for both business and for every get rich quick artist on the West Coast."

"It was always a place where a large percentage of the white population lived on the edge. A lot of us had left everything we knew and held dear. Many of us believed that our best friend came in a bottle. It cost me a promising career. I will forever be grateful for the Gritt family's offer of work here in Seattle after I resigned my commission. The Gritts and the Catholic Church saved my life. Anyway, the two gentlemen you seek are not back yet, perhaps you would like a nice cup of black Russian tea. I still prefer it to the trash American companies pass off."

The hour that Danielle spent with McGurk filled in a lot of holes in her understanding of her family's early days in Alaska. Most importantly, she finally understood how her father, who had always spoken of his Alaskan experiences with great joy, had been dragged kicking and screaming back to the states by her mother, who refused to raise her family in the wilderness. "A lot of us would have been far better off chasing those wild dreams," offered McGurk as the Gritt cousins hurled their wind scoured bodies through the front door.

As Danielle joined the cousins in the large office upstairs, she took a seat and folded her hands in front of her, cradling a large cup of tea. Both Parker and Travis filled coffee cups from a huge pot that rested on an old pot-bellied coal stove in the corner.

"You are particularly quiet this day," commented Parker looking over at Danielle.

"I enjoyed my time with Mr. McGurk. That man can give a woman a lot to think about."

Travis looked at Parker and shrugged his shoulders. Then looking back to Danielle he asked, "have you heard from your friend Malcom?"

"I did, and he advises that his father has asked Maples to divert his trip to Denver to look at some mining properties on the eastern front. He isn't sure that Maples will comply, but they reset their meeting with him for three weeks from today. Somehow Maples already knew that Parker and I had arrived on the *Maximilian*."

"That doesn't sound particularly good, unless I misunderstand the situation," commented Travis.

"It isn't," replied Parker. "I really don't like the idea of Danny stumbling into the man on a train east."

"I feel the same way about you and Annalee on your trip back to Boston," interjected Danielle.

"Malcom has offered to send the family's private car to Vancouver to carry me to Montreal. It will take five days to reach the coast. How much trouble would it be to reach the Canadian Pacific station on Burrard Inlet?" she asked.

"The *Max* goes north at the end of the weekend. We could have her captain make an unscheduled stop right at the Canadian Pacific docks. You would be there in a day."

"I think that would be my best bet." She looked up at Parker, "you and Annalee could come along as far as Winnipeg and then cross the border to Grand Forks or go on to Montreal and then catch a train to Boston."

"How can we turn down a trip in a luxury car?" laughed Parker.

Travis picked up a pencil and began writing. "I would book passage east on the Northern Pacific for a couple of days after the train leaves Vancouver, just in case this Maples fellow is tracking your movements. The company will buy the tickets. After you are safely on your way, I will cancel your trip and get a refund."

"That should give us enough time to lay out our plans for next year," added Parker.

CHAPTER 16

Canadian Pacific Railroad Across Canada

THE FREIGHT WAGON rolled onto the wharf before first light. The handful of trunks and bags were hoisted into the forward hold of the *Maximilian*. An hour later a small boat arrived at the dock next to the ocean going ship. Two women and a man dressed appropriately for the logging camp they had been visiting scampered up the long ramp and across the dock to reach the ships boarding ladder.

"Anyone following us would need a private boat to keep up," said Parker.

Regular passengers began to arrive for the trip north and the lines connecting the ship to the wharf were cast aside and the ship began to back slowly. When the ship cleared the dock, a small harbor tug slid up next to the bow and began to push the bow around toward the open water. Danielle, Annalee and Parker, now changed into appropriate traveling attire, sat sipping tea in the captain's private cabin, well away from any portholes.

The trip to Vancouver took most of the day, the *Max* arriving only an hour before the scheduled evening departure of the Canadian Pacific eastbound train. The VIP passengers for the only private car in the train were transferred quickly to the shore and then to their waiting Pullman car.

"Your names please," asked a tall graying black man in a tailored uniform. "If you are traveling incognito, the first names only will do just fine."

Danielle stepped forward and introduced herself and then her traveling companions. "Please do not use the last names until we are well on our way," she directed, "We want our trip to be a surprise to all but the Crier family."

Two men handed their luggage up through the freight door as the purser ushered them into a parlor that might have graced the finest home in British Columbia. The whistle from the engine announced their departure and the car began to move. "We did not go through customs," offered Parker.

"No need," replied the purser, "I assured them that our private car passengers were visitors on their way to Montreal to work on a business venture that would be good for Canada. My name is Toby. Anything you need, well, it will be my pleasure to find it for you."

"Toby," offered Annalee, "my husband and I have never traveled by private car. We have the owner's cabin available on the ships that sail under the family name, but this is a first for us."

"I will endeavor to make it a memorable experience Mrs. Gritt. Here let me show you around the car and introduce you to the staff."

A small girl with a coffee and cream complexion took a drink order from the travelers as the train began to gain speed. "Normally we serve supper at eight," she offered, "but we can delay it if you would like to freshen up or sample our excellent liquor cabinet for a bit longer."

"How long until we reach Montreal?" asked Parker.

Toby arrived with a tray of oysters and cheese next to a loaf of rye bread. "The train will creep through the mountains and make a dozen stops over the next two days. Once we get out on the plains the engineer will push it up over fifty miles an hour. Montreal in a full five days."

"We should be in Montreal before the Northern Pacific train gets to Grand Forks. That will put Maples at least two days behind us even if he doesn't follow Crier's instructions to go to Denver," observed Parker.

"Two of us will be going on from Montreal," said Danielle. "Parker and Annalee will be going straight through to Boston. Can you arrange passage for them."

"It will be my pleasure," answered Toby. "I will ask Mr. Crier if we can attach the car to an eastbound train, that way you will not have to pack and unpack again."

The travel itself could not have been more comfortable; sumptuous meals and drink service, from a staff that only appeared when summoned.

They arrived in the huge Montreal Station at three in the afternoon. A carriage awaited their car and a representative of the Grand Trunk Railroad. Their Pullman was to be detached within the hour and moved over to a Grand Trunk train operated by their subsidiary, the Central Vermont Railroad. Anna and her husband would be in Boston in just over a day.

"May I offer you three a final glass of champagne?" asked Toby.

"That would be delightful,"

Parker reached into a large leather brief case at his feet and pulled a small wooden box from the bottom. He handed the case to Danielle. "This is what you might call, a just in case gift."

Danielle opened the box to find a small pistol and a box of twenty cartridges.

"It's a Webley Police Revolver in .45 caliber, loaded with five rounds. It's the same revolver that most of the police in Great Britain and here in Canada carry. You can shoot five rounds in about five seconds, but at close range, you probably would not have to pull the trigger twice. I keep it in the house in St. Michael for Anna, but we both think it would be a good idea for you to slip it into your purse until this thing with the Criers and Maples is sorted out."

"It will not be needed, but thank you," replied Danielle. "I'll return it when I get to Boston."

The carriage pulled up to the entrance of the Windsor Hotel on Dominion Square where a doorman helped Danielle down and three bellboys rushed to unload her luggage. She reached into her purse for a tip for the driver and the hotel staff.

"That will not be necessary," smiled the driver. "Mr. Crier has taken care of everything." The driver handed a small envelope to the head bellman. "Antonio here will take good care of you Miss Post."

The bellman ushered Danielle past the small line at the front desk and onto a waiting elevator. The operator stopped the car at the top floor. Danielle stepped out into a hall with only eight doors. She was ushered into a suite overlooking the river and the Jubilee Bridge that connected Canada to the ice free ports of the northern United States.

"Your luggage will be here in about fifteen minutes," advised the bellman. Our floor maid is at the other end of the hall. Just pull the bell cord if you need anything. Have a pleasant stay."

On the table in the sitting room was a letter from Malcom Crier advising her that he would call for her at eight.

Danielle tossed the hat she had purchased in Seattle on the

huge feather bed and dropped her wool traveling coat over a chair. She unbuttoned her tight collar. In the corner she found a small bar and a bucket of ice. She poured herself a sherry and seated herself on a window seat overlooking the river. A moment later the luggage arrived along with a maid who began unfolding Danielle's clothing and transferring it from the bags to a huge bureau, or the walk in closet.

Danielle watched until the maid unfolded her new lavender dress, the one with the white lace around the neck and the cuffs. "Could you please have that pressed for me, I will need it by seven-thirty. Also, could you have a hairdresser come up at seven?"

As the maid left, Danielle reseated herself at the window just in time to see a train cross the bridge, with a pullman car attached just in front of the caboose. For the first time in a long time, she felt truly alone. She took the Webley from its box and unloaded the weapon. She then stood and dry-fired the weapon a dozen times to get the feel of it before reloading it with five bullets. *That did not make me feel any better,* she thought, *but a hot bath will.*

Malcom Crier dressed in a brown tweed suit escorted Danielle into a private club. Although not a member, the club offered exchange privileges with the one in Washington he frequented. They were whisked to a secluded table in a private drawing room. In less than a minute the waiter was back with their drink order. Moments later, the wine steward followed the waiter toward the kitchen with their orders.

"You look lovely, Miss Post," commented Malcom. "By the way, Abraham and Aunt Gilda send their best wishes. They wondered if you were going to visit New York during this trip. They wanted to host a dinner to allow you to meet some of their colleagues who are interested in Alaska."

"I will make time, but not until I have seen my parents for a few days. Before I see them though, I want to really understand the position of your family on what is going on up north. Your Alaska Investors Group is somehow connected to some ugly problems, especially your man Maples."

"If you would not mind," asked Crier, "I would appreciate dinner with a lovely woman without any business. We will have plenty of time for that in the morning. Now, how was your trip?"

Danielle thought about the question for a minute before answering. "I just spent a week at sea to get from Juneau to Seattle in the governor's cabin. It was even nicer than the owner's cabin. But the trip from Vancouver, three-quarters of the way across the continent in your car was even better. I arrived more rested than when I left, and Toby and the rest of the staff made us feel like royalty. Thank you and your father for making the Pullman available to Parker and Annalee and me."

Malcom smiled and nodded. "How long will you be here in Montreal?"

"I was planning on only three or four days."

"Then you will be able to thank my father in person. His ship will be in Boston tomorrow and he will be returning in the Pullman immediately. As for myself, it was my pleasure."

"So, your father isn't here?" commented a disappointed Danielle.

"He made an emergency trip to England to visit my grand-father. Sir Rodney has been very ill."

The dinner of lobster from Nova Scotia with fresh vegetable and rice noodle salad was a bit of a disappointment after the meals on the train. It occurred to Danielle, that the difference was the service. At the club, the waiter hovered in the background while on the train the staff somehow appeared only when someone was about to call for them.

Malcom was a perfect host, his impeccable English gentleman manners put Danielle at ease. It turned out that he also had a perfect English dry humor that more than once left Danielle worried that her laughter might split a seam.

The evening wrapped up with a schedule for the next day that included a business meeting at the family offices in the morning, and a tour of Montreal planned for the afternoon.

Malcom escorted Danielle to the elevator. "By the way, Samuel Maples has not responded to the directive to go on to Denver. Frankly, we do not have any idea where he might be."

"I thought your father sent that cablegram."

"He wasn't available. Maples is his partner, not mine, so I sent it in his name."

Danielle paused at the elevator, "I hope your grandfather is getting better. I am sure that you and your father are quite worried."

"Miss Post, nothing could be further from the truth."

CHAPTER 17

Montreal, Canada

IT WAS A short walk to the offices of London Capital. The trees in Dominion Square were dressed in their best yellow and soft pink except for the Maple trees which carried their pride of Canada bright scarlet. The flowers in the gardens were all folded over, turning brown and the manicured lawns wore a coat of white frost that glistened in the early sun.

The directory noted that the offices were on the fourth floor. Danielle chose the stairs instead of the elevator. The huge glass double doors opened into a surprisingly small office suite. A graying woman who Danielle estimated to be in her late fifties greeted her from behind a huge oak desk to the left of the small reception area. The small sign on the desk read, *Mrs. Robinson*.

"You must be Danielle Post," said the woman. "Malcom just received a troubling cable and rushed out to visit the company attorney. He asked that you be made comfortable until he returns, which should be in about an hour. If you did not have a large breakfast, perhaps I could treat you to morning tea in the lobby café."

"I have eaten like a queen for a full week Mrs. Robinson. If I keep this up, I will be the size of the fat lady in a carnival. I skipped breakfast this morning."

"Then a spot of tea might be just the ticket and perhaps a scone. And please, my name is Madeline."

"Thank you, Madeline."

"Give me a minute to tell Igor that I will be out."

The two women were seated at a small round table with a Wilton tea pot steaming in front of them. "Malcom tells me that you are an attorney, Miss Post. More than that, an attorney practicing far from our civilized world."

"I am an attorney, said Danielle, "and Juneau, Alaska is certainly not Montreal, but it is no wilderness village either. We have hotels and restaurants and regular steamship service to Seattle and the rest of the world."

"Well, that's nice to hear. Malcom's father worries about him every time he travels to one of the out-of-the-way properties. Richard is always trying to be the father that he never really had."

Danielle, her curiosity aroused, used a trial trick taught her by one of her favorite professors in law school. "Oh?"

"I suppose it is best that you know just whom you are dealing with," continued Madeline. "The Crier family is not your ordinary family. I have worked for Richard since he moved here from London. I want you to understand that I am not one to gossip. Much of what I do for London Capital requires me to take actions that I think Richard or Malcom might do if they were not out traveling."

"Every successful business usually has a woman like you somewhere close to the men who run the firm. I learned long ago that if you really want to know what's really going on, it is worth the effort to find that person. Seldom, however, do they offer a nice tea before I ever start to look."

Madeline smiled and buttered one-half of a hot scone. "Miss Post, you are an unusual young lady. Let me tell you the most important thing you need to know about London Capital and the family. Richard hates his father. Sir Rodney treats his family like Chinese coolies, in fact he treats everyone except a handful of hand-picked associates the same way. Sir Richard placed Richard's mother and her two sons in a nice estate in the English countryside soon after Ricard was born and then ignored them. Oh, he was a good provider, they never lacked for money. Richard only saw his father once or twice a year and then for only a day or two."

Danielle paused a moment. "That had to be tough on Richard and his brother."

"After they graduated from college he ordered them into the family business. His lever was a threat to cut off support for their mother if they defied him. Many of his directives contradicted what their mother taught them. Frank, Richard's older brother, was given the worst of the directives. Each competitor who disappeared or partner who sold out after receiving an offer they could not refuse drove Frank deeper into his cups. One day he left Richard a note apologizing for not protecting him more and then he disappeared."

"My God, what did that do to Richard? I mean, did the burden shift over to him? Is he now the one who orders such actions?"

"Richard has refused to carry out many of Sir Rodney's directives. It so infuriated the old man, that he sent a personal representative to North America to be Richards field associate.

Richard believes that there may be more than one agent in the business mix."

"I would wager, Madeline, that I have met the one. Is it Samuel Maples?"

"You know Mr. Maples?" asked a shocked Madeline Robinson.

"His actions and behavior are a great part of why I am in Montreal today."

"Miss Post, Richard has worked very hard to isolate his son from the seamier side of the empire. I doubt that he knows what Maples is about."

"By this afternoon he will. I have a copy of a warrant from the Marshal in Juneau for Mr. Maples' arrest. Obviously, it is not enforceable here, but it should paint a clear picture to Malcom of the tactics the firm employs in Alaska."

"Miss Post, please do not press Malcom too hard. Richard will be here in the next couple of days. There are a several recent events that could change everything. You might find better solutions if you wait until Richard and Malcom have an opportunity to chat. Let me see if I can arrange a dinner at the Crier home for the day after tomorrow. That would give you an opportunity to raise your issues with both father and son at the same time."

"You take your position most seriously, Mrs. Robinson."

"I was referred by Malcom's aunt. I worked for her husband for several years before falling in love with one of his business associates, a Frenchman from Montreal."

"The referral must have come from his aunt Guilda," responded Danielle.

"You continue to surprise me. Do you Know Guilda?"

Danielle laughed and brushed a crumb from her lower lip. "I got to know Guilda and Abraham last summer on their trip to Alaska. I will visit them sometime over the holidays. I very much like them both."

"And what about my advice on how and when to address Malcom with your concerns?"

"As I said earlier, I often search for someone in a company who can help me understand what is really happening. It would do little good if I then ignored what they told me. I will give Malcom a hint of what is to come, but until his father is back, I will withhold the bloody details. For today I will focus our conversation on the big picture in Alaska."

Madeline paused, turning toward the window. "Do not misinterpret my conversation about Malcom, Miss Post. He is a smart and tough young man with winning credentials. It is just that his father could never ask him to compromise the beliefs that he and his mother taught him. Richard believes that no one should have to go through what he and Frank experienced."

"I do understand, Madeline. I like Malcom Crier."

"That is a fine thing," replied Madeline, wearing a Mona Lisa smile.

The business meeting was short and to the point. Danielle related that there were even more troubles than she had discussed with Malcom during his Alaskan trip. She also related her most recent conversation with Governor Karp about opportunities, and the needed changes in how the territory was governed. They agreed to continue the conversation after lunch. Madeline interrupted them on their way out the door.

"Malcom, your father was very interested in having a candid conversation with Miss Post. Since he will be home tomorrow evening, I would suggest a family dinner tomorrow night. The three of you can have a private conversation and Richard can size up this young woman."

Malcom turned to Danielle and smiled. "Would that be all right with you?"

"I came to Montreal to meet your father. It was your idea. Dinner sounds delightful."

Madeline caught Danielle's eye and winked. "You two go have a nice lunch and then I would recommend that you find something fun to do for the afternoon. I will call the house and get the ball rolling."

"Why do I have a feeling that I have just been the mark in a conspiracy?" laughed Crier.

The afternoon was spent on a whirlwind tour of the city of a quarter-million people. After weeks of sitting in the lap of luxury, Danielle chose to get outside. After a short visit to the hotel for a change into a more casual suit and more comfortable shoes the couple set out for the Mount Royal Park, a polished outdoor setting on the edge of the city. Miles of trails beckoned as did the scenic railroad and dozens of small food vendors, including one that served the best ice cream that Danielle had ever tasted.

"I have reservations at the Garrick Club for this evening," offered Malcom, "that is, if a very funny play is of any interest."

"That sounds like fun. I have not been to the theater since I left Boston."

"Then I will pick you up for an early dinner at five. That leaves us plenty of time to get to the club by seven."

Danielle smiled and squeezed Malcom's hand, "I am not going to be hungry by five or even seven."

"Then I arrive at six-thirty, we go straight to the Garrick. If we are hungry after the play, we can find a pub and a pint," offered Malcom.

"Wonderful, and I may be ready by the time you arrive if your driver can get me back to the hotel in the next half-hour."

The trip home took the carriage through Montreal's Magic Mile, a growing neighborhood of huge mansions and elegant buildings. "This reminds me of Boston and the old shipping and whaling family monuments to themselves," observed Danielle.

"Please do not say that around my father," requested Crier. "It really irritates him that my grandfather keeps the North American operations on a thin budget, and he has never been able to move my mother out here where many of his business associates live. Grandfather planned for his son to return to England upon his demise and take over the family estate."

"What's not to appreciate about inheriting an English country estate?" asked Danielle.

"My father will never again live in England, and certainly not in the home where he spent so many miserable years and where his mother committed suicide."

"My Lord!" exclaimed Danielle, "I had no idea."

"Miss Post, my grandfather married my grandmother as a marriage of convenience. He really was never much interested in women, and my grandmother lived that lie until two years ago when he brought a young negro boy home with him from Cape Town. That's where the firm's African mining office is located. The scandal killed my grandmother."

"My grandfather buried his wife and moved into the country home with his young friend. I would appreciate you not judging us Miss Post. My father and mother have worked very diligently to create an honest and reputable life here in Canada. We will not be tarnished by the sins of my grandfather."

"I will not and would not judge you or your family, Malcom. What I will do is pick out an outfit that is far less risqué than what I had planned for tonight, just to protect your reputation."

Malcom turned away; his face red, unable to suppress a nervous laugh.

That evening came and went in a flash. Malcom was the perfect host, but quiet. Danielle laughed until her sides ached. Later, over a platter of fish and chips and a beer, she put her hand on Malcom's. "Are you always so reserved. It is hard on a woman's ego when the man she is with is on the moon."

"I am sorry," replied Malcom. "It is not you, Miss Post. You turned every head at the club, and I was your escort. It is just that everything just changed, I believe for the better, but perhaps not."

Danielle waited for Malcom to add on to his cryptic message, but instead he waved at the waiter and made a large checkmark in the air with his finger. "Danielle, Miss Post, I will be tied up all day tomorrow with accountants and attorneys preparing for my father's return. It might be a good day for you to do that shopping that you discussed. I can have the coach available for you whenever you would like to start. If you would like, I could probably talk Madeline out of working tomorrow so that she could act as your guide."

Madeline and the coach arrived at the appointed time, and the two women started their day with Madeline's favorite scones and tea at a small restaurant run by a French couple who treated Madeline like a member of the family. The dialogue was all in French which for Danielle was very difficult as her French was beyond rusty. She did manage to pick up a question inquiring as to whether Madeline and Anrue would be at some French func-tion on Sunday."

"So, your husband's name is Anrue?"

"Oh, Miss Post, I am not a married woman, not in the sense that you would normally discuss it."

Danielle had always detested the taste of her own foot, and try as she might, she could not come up with a response.

Madeline laughed. "It is all right my dear, let me explain.

Anrue's wife is really quite mad, a patient in the mental hospital. She moved into a different world more than twenty years ago. Anrue, being a good Catholic, does not believe in divorce, so we worked out an arrangement. My address is in the rooming house directly next to his home. I do get my mail there, but other than that we are inseparable."

Danielle smiled and began to slip her heavy cloak over her shoulders. "Madeline, it is time for you to help me find the perfect dress for this evening's festivities."

The Crier home was what you would expect for a well to do businessman's residence on Saint Hubert Street. A butler met her at the door sweeping her new winter coat from her shoulders directly into a large walk-in closet off from the sitting room. She placed the large purse she carried on a shelf above where her coat hung. A maid in a blue uniform led Danielle to a chair next to a huge fireplace with a roaring fire. A moment later, Malcom slipped in from a side door, with an elegant elderly woman with piercing brown eyes on his arm.

"Miss Post, this is my mother, Dorothea. Mother, may I introduce Miss Danielle Post of Boston and Juneau in the Alaska territory."

"Welcome to our home, Miss Post," offered Dorothea. "My son has told me a great deal about you, and as at least to your beauty, he has not exaggerated."

Danielle blushed, offering her hand. "Please, my name is Danielle, but my friends call me Danny. I would like it if you would use that name."

"And my friends call me Dee," countered Dorothea. "We will have a libation first and then a dinner. I hope that you like venison, our chef has been fussing over it since early this morning."

"It is one of my favorites," replied Danielle, then turned to Malcom. "Did you harvest the deer yourself?"

"Oh no," he laughed. "I am not much of a marksman. Unlike in the states where it is growing very hard to find wild game in the butcher shops, here in Canada it is still a staple. I have the word of the chef that this animal was harvested in the prairies where it fattened on grain all summer. Most of our meat comes from the west in refrigerated rail cars."

A tall man in a dinner jacket bounded down the stairs in the corner of the room. "You must be Danielle Post. I am Richard Crier." He signaled at the maid who began to slowly spin a bottle of champagne in a sterling ice bucket on an oak stand. "A glass of champagne at the fire before dinner."

Danielle didn't really know whether it was a question or a command, which really didn't matter. Richard's smile and mannerisms finally convinced her that he had meant it as a question.

"I brought a case of Rothchild home from England," continued Richard. "It is hard to find here even though much of this community is French. The government duties on French wines reflect two hundred years of conflict between England and France," he laughed.

Malcom waited until all of them had selected a glass from the tray offered by the maid. He then held his glass up and waited until his mother, father and Danielle had touched his glass. "To an excellent meal and then a candid conversation."

The meal wrapped up a little before nine and the group adjourned to the huge office in the back of the house where a smaller fireplace blazed away and a tray of Scotches, Bourbons and liquors rested on a small table surrounded by four overstuffed leather chairs.

On the back wall were two more chairs. Next to the fireplace, between the two windows, was a rolltop desk with a cashier's chair. The outside wall was all windows including a glass door opening onto a manicured yard. Malcom helped Danielle to the seat next to the fireplace.

"Malcom advises that you enjoy a brandy and a cigar after a meal," commented. "I appreciate a woman who sets her own limits and rejoices in sharing them with the world."

Richard handed Danielle a small snifter and then took a large oak box from his desk and flipped the lid open. Inside she found six compartments, all with different cigars.

"I recommend the shorter, thin cigars unless you appreciate a more robust flavor," he offered.

"You three will have to excuse me," interjected Dorothea. "I have never learned to appreciate the smell of burning tobacco, in fact it makes me sneeze. I will enjoy my port in the kitchen where I can help the staff wrap up from dinner."

"Please thank them for me," said Danielle, "the meal was amazing."

A moment later, the two men and Danielle were seated around the table and cigar smoke drifted toward the draft of the fireplace. "Miss Post," started Richard, "my son indicates that you have several things to share with me."

"I do sir, and if I could get your maid to bring me the purse in your front closet, I brought several things to show you," she replied.

Danielle reached into the large leather purse and retrieved an accordion file. Then the maid set the purse on a chair at the back of the room.

Each section was labeled, 'Yukon, Southeast, Opportunities, Legal.' Carefully she took a set of sheets held by a clip from the Opportunities section and passed it to Richard. "Before we chat, a bit of background is in order."

Next, she took the sheets from the file section marked Yukon and passed them to Malcom. "While you were in Alaska we discussed several problems in the fisheries industry. Here are several letters from the marshal in the Yukon River village of Falcon and several other testimonials and reports. You may find they trend with what you already learned in Southeast."

For ten minutes Danielle enjoyed her cigar while the men read through the documents. When Richard placed his papers on the table in front of him, she replaced them with the clip of sheets from the Southeast Alaska pocket. Malcom thumbed through the report that his father had just completed.

Next, she handed him the section from Legal, which Malcom studied in great detail, finally retrieving a pad and pencil from his father's desk to make some notes. For half-an-hour the men studied the notes while the smoke from their cigars slowly vanished as the men ignored them.

"These carbons are a bit hard to read Miss Post," commented Richard, "However, the overall message is quite clear. Our firm is not responsible for the troubles that you bring to our attention. In the past, the company has made some transgressions, primarily in South America, but our investments in Alaska are all above board."

Malcom looked over at his father. "The reports from the marshals almost all refer to activities of your man Maples' father. While in Juneau, he operated out of a tavern by the name of the Golden Goose. Samuel Maples seemed to own part of that business and the owner; this Rattler Wilson took orders from Samuel. This Cobra Wilson is most certainly his brother. He must have been involved with Samuel as well."

"Malcom, we will not enter into conjecture here."

Danielle's patience in waiting for months to address the problems boiled over. "Gentlemen, people who I am very close to have tangled with the vicious web your company is involved in. Some have even been attacked. You can read the reports from

Falcon and from Juneau. This man Maples is in this up to his neck. You cannot ignore the sworn statement from Mr. Wilson about those who killed his brother or the warrant from Marshal Walker or the letters to the Department of Alaska Territories from Marshal Hickox."

"Calm yourself young lady," said Richard Crier. "We will get to the bottom of this. I just want it to be clear that neither Malcom or I are not personally involved, nor have we sanctioned any of this, if in fact there is really any illegal activity going on." He refilled his and the others brandy snifters and then relit his cigar.

Malcom stood and walked over to the glass door that opened onto the yard. He watched as the first snow of the winter begin to fall. "You and I both know Father, that there is a …"

The butler was at the door. "A late caller sir," he said.

"Tell the caller to come back tomorrow," replied Richard. "We are in the midst of an important conversation and do not wish to be disturbed."

"A bit too late for that, Richard." Samuel Maples stepped around the butler and entered Richard's office.

The butler grabbed Maples by the arm. "Sir, I asked you to wait in the entry. You will have to come with me."

Maples grabbed the man's hand and twisted the fingers back and around until the butler dropped to his knees. "Touch me again and I will cut off this hand and take it home as a trophy."

"It is all right Edgar, please head on home for the night," directed Richard.

Maples walked over to the fire and helped himself to a tumbler of scotch. "It is not nice to see you again Miss Post."

"That's enough Samuel. Miss Post is a guest in this house. I would prefer to meet with you privately in the morning," ordered Richard.

"Tonight, would be better," replied Maples. "I visited Toby when I got in this evening. He told me about Malcom sending the pullman for Miss Post here. I had planned on traveling with her and her friend Parker Gritt on the Northern Pacific."

Malcom snuffed out his cigar in the huge crystal ashtray on the table. "Miss Post contacted me and was worried that that is exactly what you had in mind. She is afraid of you Samuel."

"Miss Post has shared a number of files with us this evening, Samuel," said Richard. "They paint a very ugly picture of some activities in Alaska. Did you know that the marshal in Juneau has sworn out an arrest warrant for you? A warrant for murder."

Maples walked over to the fireplace, standing between Malcom and Danielle.

"Really. Who did I kill?"

"Some man by the name of Cobra Wilson up on the Yukon. There is an eyewitness and a testimonial from his brother in Juneau. The witness is one of your own men according to this Rattler Wilson. He admitted being there when you shot this Cobra fellow," replied Malcom.

"Are these reports true, Samuel?" asked Richard?

"Most likely, old chap."

"You work for me, Samuel," directed Richard. "You were to keep our dealing above board in Alaska. There was plenty of opportunity without any of your bullying. Besides, we do not want to tangle with law enforcement in the States."

"That's what you wanted. Your father was right, you are still a weak child. Well, I work for Sir Rodney, not you or your fancy pants son. I have communicated every activity to his office in London. Before I even went up to the Yukon, we exchanged telegrams from up on the Stikine. His directions were to maximize the return for the company. How I did that was left up to me."

"Samuel, that was months ago."

"You're right, Richard. I haven't been able to reach the old man since I got back to civilization, but I don't need to. I have worked for your father for twenty years. It always worked out. I keep twenty percent of the profits from projects that I work on, and he makes more because the pie is cut in fewer pieces."

"Not anymore Samuel. My father is deceased," replied Richard. "Tomorrow morning, we will meet at the office, and we will arrive at an equitable divorce. That is unless you want the firm to assist Miss Post here in bringing to justice those who have created so much havoc in Alaska."

Maples tossed the half-filled glass of scotch into the fire, which erupted shooting flames almost to Danielle's chair. He took two steps and backhanded her out of the chair onto the floor. "You have been a royal pain in my arse, miss Post."

Malcom pulled Danielle from the floor and carried her to one of the chairs at the back of the room. He then straightened himself and took a step toward Maples.

Get out now Samuel," ordered Richard. "You may stop at the office tomorrow morning at ten. I will have ten thousand pounds sterling for you. After what Miss post has told us, you are lucky to be getting anything."

"Miss Post talks too much. That is about to end," barked Maples. From his sleeve he produced a small two shot Derringer and pointed it at Danielle.

"No!" cried Malcom as he dove in front of Danielle. The Derringer cracked. Malcom collapsed in front of Danielle's chair.

Maples walked over to where Malcom lay bleeding from a wound in his thigh. He pointed the small gun at Malcom's head and then at Danielle. "I have a deal for you Richard, one you cannot turn down. You will make out a bank draft for ten times your original offer and give me the passwords for your father's safe deposit box in London. The alternative will be to kill Miss

Post and then I will reload and finish the job on your son, the hero."

"All right Samuel, all right," answered Richard. He stood and turned toward his desk.

Danielle slipped from her chair and reached for her purse.

"What are you up to, Miss Post?" asked Maples, pointing the small pistol at her head.

"I'm placing my handkerchief over Malcom's wound and see if I can stop the bleeding."

Maples turned and started toward Richard, who was fumbling with a book of bank drafts at his desk. "I'll have it for you in a minute, Samuel. Do not hurt anyone else."

Samuel was only halfway across the room when Danielle pulled her Webley from her purse and fired, the bullet striking Maples below the shoulder, breaking his arm and flinging his Derringer into the fireplace. Maples turned, shocked, as Danielle fumbled to bring the heavy pistol up to shoot again. Grasping his dangling arm, he bolted past Richard and crashed through the glass door. In the distance, the bells of the constable's surrey could be heard racing toward the house, summoned by the butler after Richard's code words, 'home for the night' signaled him.

CHAPTER 18

Montreal, Canada

"YOU ARE REALLY quite surprising, Miss Post," commented Dee Crier. Both women sat on the same side of the hospital bed where Malcom was resting. "Is shooting a pistol something you do for entertainment in the wilds of Alaska?"

Danielle smiled and fingered the Webley in her purse. "No Ma'am. Last night was the first time I have ever fired that pistol. Parker and Annalee Gritt gave it to me as we pulled into the Montreal station. His brother has taken me shooting in Alaska, but it was just target shooting. Parker was worried about Maples. He would have stayed to help me, but his wife is with child, and he needed to get her home to Boston."

"So, you might have hit my Richard instead of this Maples fellow?" she asked.

"Little chance of that, Dee. Maples was only ten feet away and Richard was on the far side of the room. I doubt that I could have hit Richard even if I had been aiming at him; maybe if I fired all five bullets, but probably not."

"I am not sure that I'm comforted by that."

"Nor am I." Richard Crier stood just inside the door flanked by a tall man with shaggy red hair erupting from under the boller that seemed to sprout from his head. "Ladies, this is lead detective Flanigan of the Montreal Constabulary. Constable, my wife, Dorthea and Miss Danielle Post, the woman your officers mentioned in their report."

Flanigan tipped his hat to those assembled. "Miss Post, I am most pleased to make your acquaintance. Would you possibly have the pistol that you used most effectively last night?"

Danielle handed the weapon to the policeman.

"A fine close-in piece, the Webley," he said. Flanigan ejected the spent brass from the first chamber and turned it in his hand. "I am quite sure that our fugitive is in great need of medical attention. Miss Post's pistol is the same as I myself carry. That .45 snub nosed bullet must have smashed the bastard's arm."

Flanigan rolled through the cylinder. "Excellent gun safety, the hammer on an empty chamber and all." Flanigan retrieved an extra cartridge from his coat pocket and replaced the spent brass he had removed and then rotated the cylinder until the hammer again rested over the one empty chamber. He then handed the gun back to Danielle.

Danielle examined the weapon again before returning it to her bag. "The Gritt family taught me to shoot, first in Boston and then in Alaska. Until I check it myself, I will always assume that a gun is loaded, and the safety catch is off. That is correct is it not Detective?"

"It is, Miss." Turning to Dorthea, he asked "how is the patient this morning?"

"The doctors say he lost a great deal of blood. He will not be out of danger until the bullet is removed, but first he must get stronger. Getting pressure on the wound right away and keeping it on probably saved Malcom's life. Again, Miss Post sprang into action with just the right medicine."

"Dee, Malcom threw himself between Maples and me just as that man tried to kill me with that hidden gun of his. If Malcom had not been the first to act, I would not be here with you right now."

Constable Flanigan smiled and took a notepad from his lapel pocket. "I believe that our fugitive has fled beyond our jurisdiction." He flipped through several pages before finding the page he was looking for. "The company dicks in the railyard found fresh blood by the tracks of last night's freight to Portland, Maine. We all suspect that your Mr. Samuel Maples jumped a freight with only minimal medical attention and crossed the border."

"So, he has gotten away cleanly," responded Richard.

"Perhaps. I have asked the railroad to telegraph all along the line to keep a lookout for a man with a bleeding arm or the body of one along the tracks."

Danielle offered a legal opinion. "Even if you can identify him and if someone takes him into custody, you still cannot get him back into your custody. New Hampshire or Vermont will not turn him over to you, will they?"

"Miss Post, the railroad police have their own set of rules. If Mr. Maples were to get into their custody somehow, I suspect that he will accept an offer to travel in a nice warm box back to Montreal. We shall see."

"I wish I had killed him," responded Danielle.

"For many, it would have probably been easier, but not for you. First, you would have to remain in Montreal until a post death hearing. And then you would have spent months if not years troubled by taking another's life. The only ones who do not feel remorse are those who enjoy it. Eventually, even many of those killers can't live with themselves. I will need your statement in the next day," continued Flanigan.

"For now, I would like to stay here with Malcom, at least until he is out of danger," answered Danielle.

"I know where you are, just don't forget," replied the detective.

Danielle arrived at the hospital the following day precisely at eight. The nurses enforced a strict visiting code. Malcom's private room and the family's years of support for less fortunate patients bought only a little flexibility. Dorthea and Danielle had been ushered from the room at seven the night before, early enough for dinner at an Italian restaurant on the next block. Malcom had not regained consciousness that first day, but the doctor didn't seem worried. "He is strong, and his heart rate is good. We'll keep him quiet while his body shakes off the shock."

As Danielle entered the room the private nurse the family hired was hovering with a spoon in hand. "Master Malcom, you will eat your oatmeal. That bullet must come out. It is lodged against your femoral artery. The doctor will not operate until you regain your strength."

"Wilda," responded Malcom with a slurred voice, "I hate oatmeal. Bring me some ham and eggs and I will eat like a horse. But oatmeal…"

"May I help?" asked Danielle.

The nurse turned and squinted at Danielle, a funny look on her puffy face. "The doctor ordered no greasy food for Master Crier, and oatmeal with honey and milk is good for a digestive system that is recovering from loss of blood and shock."

"I am no nurse," replied Danielle, "but Mr. Crier here saved my life, and I will save his even if I have to kill him."

The nurse turned and handed the bowl to Danielle. "He is all yours. I have been up all night with this stubborn young man, and I am going home."

Danielle seated herself on the edge of the bed. "Malcom Crier, if you do not recover, I will never forgive myself. Now eat so that you can leave here through the front entry instead of the back."

The nurse pulled her heavy wool coat from the closet and picked up a purse the size of a small traveling case. "I will be back tonight, Master Crier. I will be here precisely at eight and I expect that the report from the nurse's station will be sterling. If not, you will have to suffer my forty years of dealing with stubborn patients and it will not be pretty." With a laugh, she left the room, closing the door behind her.

Malcom reached over and took Danielle's hand in his. "What happened last night?" He slurred. "All I remember is Maples pulling a small pistol with huge barrels and the rest is a blur."

"I will tell you everything after you eat your breakfast."

"I will eat, but only if you can help me find a ham and cheese sandwich later."

"If you eat it right now, I will smuggle in a sandwich this afternoon. Deal?"

Danielle's morning was spent with Malcom as his mother and father, and a dozen others arrived to spend time with the patient and to wish him well. Madeline Robinson made her appearance late in the morning. Danielle slipped out at noon and found a restaurant that would make her the sandwich she had promised. By the time she returned Malcom had eaten a bowl of chicken soup and taken his afternoon medication and was fast asleep.

"I need to send a couple of telegrams, Madeline. Malcom once told me that the firm had its own telegraph station."

"I need to get back anyway," said Madeline. "I have Richard's buggy and driver. You are welcome to ride over to the offices with me. Igor will be happy to send your messages. Richard will be returning to see his son later; you can ride back with him."

A few minutes later the two women were on their way. "If you are going to unwrap that sandwich you have hidden in your purse," commented Madeline, "I am famished, and I would appreciate half."

Danielle pulled the wrapped bundle from her purse. "How did you know?"

"Miss Post, he eats a ham and cheese sandwich for lunch almost every day. He can always con someone into some grand deal when he is hungry."

⚘

At the same time in the small New Hampshire town of Berlin, a crew coach from one of the logging camps pulled up in front of its small community hospital. A large gruff man with a crooked nose stepped from the wagon and then helped Samuel Maples to the ground. "Much obliged," he muttered to the driver.

Taking Maples' strong arm, he pulled the weight of his boss against his, and half-carried the smaller man toward the hospital entrance. Approaching the front desk, the man was surprised to find nobody there or in the hallways leading away from the counter. "Just find someone and be bloody quick about it," ordered Maples.

Maples had traveled from Seattle with the former boxer and disgraced town marshal. They had been introduced by one of Maples' business partners, Albert Marathon. Maples spied a small silver bell. "Never mind, I will take care of it myself," he said, grasping the bell with his good hand and ringing it as if to drive off attacking demons.

From the far end of the hall a door banged and a tall young woman in a white uniform started toward the men. "I am so sorry. We have had no visitors all morning, so I was taking my lunch."

Spying Maples' blood-soaked sleeve she quickened her pace. "What have we here?" she asked.

"Mr. Maples here got himself shot by robbers. He needs a doctor really bad."

"Our doctor is out making his rounds, but I can send someone to find him. You just wait right here while I find the orderly."

Drew waited until the nurse headed down the hall. "I got the story right, didn't I boss? We was on the train, headed for Montreal. We met two men who told you about a logging operation for sale and we agreed to go take a look. We rode in their buggy until they stopped and pulled a gun."

"That's it. Remember, you don't know where we were. I will tell the rest of the story, if necessary, you just listen and remember."

The nurse returned moments later. "It may take a bit to find the doctor. Let me get you to the surgery and onto a table where you can rest."

"Drew, give me your shoulder again," ordered Maples.

A half-hour later a short round man in a pair of striped overalls and a stocking cap burst through the door of the surgery. He quickly examined the wounded arm which the nurse had stripped and cleansed. "Bring this man some opium and find my cutting gown," he snapped to the nurse.

"I am Dr. Piper," he continued. "That arm is infected, and the circulation has been cut off for too long. It will have to come off."

Maples tried to sit up. "That is my writing arm and my shooting arm doctor, I cannot lose it."

"Your name sir?" asked Dr. Piper.

"Samuel Maples and I am the field representative for a group of investors who have me traveling all over the world to look at opportunities. I need to write reports and sometimes even defend myself."

"Mr. Maples, perhaps if you had better defended yourself, or your man here had helped, this would not be necessary. As it is, the arm is already dead. If you don't want the rest of your body to follow lie down and let me do my job."

The doctor poured a measure of sedative into a large spoon and tipped Maples' head forward allowing him to swallow it. "Now, while we wait for that to take hold, tell me what happened."

"We were on a train from New York to Montreal and two men approached us with a story about a timber operation for sale. We agreed to go look. They took us north for an hour or so and when we came to a deserted section of the road one pulled a gun and demanded money. I am carrying a rather large sum of cash which isn't mine, so I yelled run and took off. The ugly bloke shot me. That's it."

"Your clothes look like you were riding under the train, not in it," said a skeptical Piper. "This wound is more than a day old. I served as a regimental surgeon in the Cuba war, I have seen more than my share of bullet wounds."

Maples' eyes were beginning to gloss over. "We ran into the woods and got lost." He was having trouble framing his words.

Maples slipped into unconsciousness. The doctor finished washing his hands and slipped into a white coat. "That's some story." he said to Drew.

"We was lost Doc, lost for a day. When we found the road, we walked until that coach from one of the camps found us and brought us here. You heard Mr. Maples."

"It's time for me to get to work, sir. You will have to wait out in the lobby. This will only take an hour. I have more experience with this type of wound than any man could ever want."

Drew picked up Maples' coat and headed for the lobby. Finding himself alone, he took the heavy wallet from the lapel pocket and opened it. Inside was more than three-thousand dollars. There was also a page from a telegraph pad, addressed to someone in London. The text was in English and above each word was some form of code. The text was enough for him. "Had to shoot two of our own men. One to protect our group and the other because he betrayed me."

Drew closed the wallet and returned it to the coat. He waited quietly until the nurse summoned him to the room where Maples had been moved.

The doctor came in a few minutes later. "That went well. It will be a challenge to learn to write with his left hand, but men have been doing it for centuries. Do you have a place to stay?" asked the doctor.

"I don't even know where we are," replied Drew.

"This little berg is called Berlin, New Hampshire. For two dollars a day you can sleep in the next room. We only have two other patients besides your Mr. Maples here. There is a good café next to the river where a man can eat for about a dollar a day."

"How long until my boss wakes up?"

"Oh, another hour or two, and he should be ready to travel in a week. I will have the local constable come by this evening to take your statement. He will want to look at any evidence you may have. Maybe he can catch the men who did this." The doctor left the room shaking his head, an incredulous smile on his face.

Drew waited for the nurse to show him to the room next to Maples' and then sat down to think through what he should do. He again took the wallet from the torn jacket and took out all the papers and examined them. He pocketed the telegram he had read earlier as well as one from Malcom Crier asking Maples to go to Nevada. He then fumbled through Maples' pants and pocketed three ten-dollar gold pieces, returning three more to the pocket.

He walked past the café and out onto the bridge over the river where he leaned against the rail as he carefully tore the telegrams into tiny pieces and dropped them into the river. He then turned back toward the café.

"Is there any place that I can wash-up?" he asked the waitress, as he seated himself at the counter.

"Most of our customers work down at the mill," she responded. "We have a washroom behind the building. You will have to go back out and around the outside. Do you know what you want?"

"How about a great big bowl of that beef stew wrote up on your board there, and some bread and strawberry jam. Oh, and coffee."

"That will be fifty cents. The coffee is on the house."

When he returned to the hospital, the town constable was waiting. The interview took less than ten minutes; the constable was just happy that whatever had happened did not happen in Berlin. "If you think of anything else that might help catch the thieves just stop by the office tomorrow."

"You can count on that, officer," replied Drew.

"Got to go then," responded the officer, "momma's going to have my favorite pot roast on the table in fifteen minutes."

Hours later, Drew heard mumbling from the room next door. He opened the door to find Maples sitting up, two feather pillows behind his back. There were tears running down his face.

"I am going to kill the one responsible for this," he blurted at Drew.

"That Dr. Piper said that if the arm did not come off you would die," offered Drew.

"I am not talking about him. I mean that witch with the hidden gun at Crier's."

"Are we going back to Canada then Mr. Maples?"

"No, that would be far too dangerous. Miss Post is from Boston. We will find her in Boston."

"Mr. Maples, I done a lot of hard things, but I ain't never killed a woman."

"You just stand by me, I will take care of everything," replied Maples.

"I am here ain't I? I could have gone off, even taken your money, but I am here," answered Drew.

"Smart boy you are. Has the law been here yet?"

Drew relayed the story of the constable's visit.

"Unless they get a bunch more patients, the doctor said I can stay here for two dollars a day."

The nurse's footsteps grew quieter as she moved down the hall to check on the other two patients.

"Drew, I have some gold pieces in my pocket. Use those for the expenses until I can get out of here."

Drew smiled and nodded his head. "We're gonna need some clothes. I reckon that might cost a bit. If it's all right with you, I can pick each of us up a new suit tomorrow. They won't be fancy like you're used to, but they'll get us by. Besides, working man's clothes will help us fit in."

"You do that Drew, and thanks for standing by me. Some in the past didn't and it makes me very angry. Now get out of here and let me get some sleep. Oh, and Drew, if you get the urge for a cold beer, keep it at one. We don't need any more trouble."

After bringing breakfast to his boss, Drew rented a buggy and retraced their route to the rail siding where they had been ordered off from the caboose. The railroad man they bribed had grown increasingly worried after a railroad detective informed him of the bulletin on the fugitive. They had abandoned most of their belongings in the hotel in Montreal. Anything that might identify the men, along with Maples' papers had been stuffed into a canvas shopping bag of food that Drew had purchased and hidden in the woods before they began walking toward Berlin.

It took a couple of hours to find the exact fallen log used as a hiding place. Wading around in the marshy ground, he searched from one end of the log to the other. The bag was nowhere to be found. A well-worn game trail lead from behind the log through the trees toward a backwater from the nearby river. Drew followed the trail until it ended at one side of a slough. The trail continued the far side, but deep water made it impossible to cross. Backtracking he examined the few sections of trail where the soggy ground rose high enough to be just muddy. In a couple of places, he could see the prints of a small bear that appeared to be dragging something. "I hope you enjoy that sausage and the bread you little bastard. I'll pay the price for your dinner I'll wager," he yelled toward the river.

Two hours later, he walked through the doors of the hospital just as the duty nurse returned to her station. "You will not muddy the floors with those boots, sir," she barked. "You may remove them and carry them to the janitor's station down that hall," she continued pointing. "After you clean them up, you can set them on the radiator in your room to dry."

Drew stood frozen in the doorway. "I need to do some shopping, and I haven't any other shoes."

The nurse rummaged around in a large wooden box under the counter and came up with a badly worn pair of leather slippers. "I don't know if these will fit, but someone left them in a room months ago. If they are not the right size, I have one more pair in the lost box."

Drew stuffed his feet into the undersized slippers and headed to the janitor's closet to clean up. When finished, he slipped into Maples' room hoping that he was asleep. Maples opened one eye and motioned his man to the chair next to his bed. "Did you bring the bag back?"

"Nope boss, it got drug away by a bear or something. I followed the trail until it went into a river."

"Don't worry about it. Your acquaintance Albert in San Francisco has copies of all the papers. Do you think there's any chance of someone finding that bag and tracing it back to us?"

"There is no way, boss. Once that bear tears the bag apart to get at the food, everything will be shredded and what little is left will be out in the marsh where he was headed."

"That will have to do. Now what do you think of the town?" asked Maples.

"It seems to be a quiet place with mostly folks who work in the timber. I heard that there are many city folks who come here in the winter to play in the snow. Seems like nice folks here now, the kind of people who mind their own business."

"That doctor recommends that I stay here for at least a couple of weeks. He wants to make sure that the wound is healed enough that I don't get an infection. Besides, it hurts bloody awful, and I wouldn't want to deal with it without the pain medicine. Maybe we should find a small place to rent for a month. I could start learning to write with my left hand and maybe even start learning to handle a pistol again."

Drew smiled, relieved that the lost bag was not going to turn into a life-threatening situation. "I can look around in the morning. If city folks come up here in the winter, there must be places where they stay."

"Go rent one, Drew. Now I intend to get up and start walking tomorrow, I want out of this place as soon as I can. You run along and find us those clothes we talked about yesterday. And Drew, see if you can find us a couple of Colts and some shells without attracting too much attention. Take what you need from my wallet."

"You got it boss. You know it is hunting season here now. There is an old gravel pit on the edge of town that the locals use to sight in their rifles. No one will think anything of someone shooting targets there."

"That is good thinking. Now run along. When you get back, I will want you to help me write a couple of telegrams and then put them in code. We need to brief some of my colleagues before the Criers do."

CHAPTER 19

Sitka, Alaska

THE NATIVE TRADITION of a meal shared with the entire community, had been adopted by the community of Sitka for special occasions. The fall celebration marking the end of the fishing season and the departure of the wealthy tourists, was celebrated together by both the brown skinned and white skinned citizens. The churches used the occasion to summon their mission staff for recognition.

The Reverend Max Guildham and his wife Irma stood in the serving line at what the villagers referred to as a Love Feast, and the rest of the community called Thanksgiving. The governor and his wife were seated at the first table as each family was called to present their contribution to the feast. Next to Kate, Belle Medev fidgeted as the Guildhams called one of the last presenters to introduce her dish, a huge pumpkin pie.

"Is there something troubling you, young lady?" asked Kate.

"I just got into town last night and I didn't prepare a dish," replied Belle.

Kate slid out her chair and slipped up behind the head of the head of the Society of Mission Friends, as he called the last presenter. A moment later she returned to her chair. "Your contribution is all taken care of."

Max Guildham held up his hands to still the participants. "Before serving commences, I would like to introduce Belinda Medev, the teacher at Kukwa and one of our star pupils, to present the blessing. Belinda, if you will lead us all in thanking the Lord for his bounty."

Belle stood and folded her hands in front of her. "Dear Lord, bless the food we are about to enjoy and protect all here and those of our community who are away. Please lend your hand to those who have taken up the mission of righting the wrongs that men inflict on one another. Bless those who have just joined us this year and those who now reside at your side. Finally, please save us all from the sin of gluttony. Amen."

Belle seated herself, those around her chortling. The Reverend Guildham called for each family to send a member to help serve.

Governor Karp began carving the turkeys that had arrived on the last Rus Am ship. In minutes joyous folks with plates overflowing began to reseat themselves. Soon, the laughing and voices were masked by the scrape of knives and forks on metal plates. The governor reseated himself.

"Miss Medev, perhaps we can spend a minute together in my office before you return to your village?"

On Saturday morning, Belle walked the five minutes to the governor's office wrapped in a new Filson wool coat delivered to her that morning from the Gritt Rus Am store. She had gone there to inquire about Chad's trip east. He'd departed Sitka on the *Juarez* the week before her arrival. The store clerk passed Belle a letter from Chad appointing her the company agent for Kukwa, in a new marketing effort by the shipping firm. The appointment included a hundred-dollar prepaid account in the company store and a wrapped package. Opening the package, she found the red plaid wool coat and a note that simply read, *To keep you warm on cold winter days. Perhaps not the height of fashion in Oregon, but very practical in Alaska. See you in the spring. Chad.*

A smile still filled her face as she closed the door of the governor's office where she was greeted in the reception area by Marshal Walker.

"Didn't I see you at the Love Feast with my auntie Margaret, Marshal?"

"Is Maggie Mitkof your aunt?" asked Walker.

"Marshal, almost everyone in the villages is related somehow. But to answer your question, yes Maggie is my mother's baby sister. She married a Navy bosun and moved to Kodiak with him fifteen years ago. She worked for the Navy Department. She was visiting family in Kukwa three or four years ago and returned to find a note from her husband. His enlistment was up, and he had headed home. Told her that the folks in Atlanta would never accept a Native wife."

"What a rotten story," replied Walker. "She's a very sweet person, kind of reminds me of one of those beautiful Cherokee girls back in Texas."

"She's worked for the tribal police since returning to Sitka. Is that how you met her?"

"Actually no. She walked up to me on the dock one afternoon while I was slashing away at a salmon that I had just caught. After she laughed herself out, she finished filleting the fish for me and then offered to cook it."

"Sounds like my aunt. She is not the bashful type. You like her?"

"I am a lot like your friend Chad. A gentleman never talks about such things."

Belle smiled. "You here waiting for the governor too?"

"Yup, he should be done with his little talk with Judge Dishner in a few minutes. The judge is slowly coming around."

Before Belinda could answer, the door to the governor's office opened and the judge launched his round body across the room, stopping to gaze at Belle. Finally, he tipped his hat as he opened the door to the street. In a minute, he was on his way toward his home, a bit of a bounce in his step.

Governor Karp leaned through the door of his office and motioned for Belle and Walker to join him. He was talking before either of them could find a chair. "The judge and I just spent the first positive ten minutes together in more than a year. When Chad Gritt left here, he took a stack of reports and letters from Magistrate Tome, me, and the marshal with him. At the last minute, the Judges clerk caught Chad and added a letter from Dishner. I don't know what was in the letter, but someone sent me an anonymous note that indicated the judge was urging Washington to send an investigation team to Alaska. It also urged his bosses to make sure that they read all the other correspondence that both Parker and Chad Gritt were carrying to Washington D.C. I asked him here this morning to thank him for keeping an open mind. That's all that I could say, since I am not supposed to know about his letter."

"So, you are using Chad as a courier?" asked Belle.

"That I am Miss Medev. Between the reports from up on the Yukon and ours here, I am hoping that we can begin changing the minds of some of those who control our lives. Most of them get all their information from lobbyists and legislators in the pockets of the big companies. They will never come here themselves, but they won't want to be tainted by the kind of scandals that our reports allude to."

"Probably right Governor, I reckon they will cut and run especially after some of this starts to hit the press," offered Walker. "I suppose that it won't hurt the cause if some of those stories come from the offices of Senator Fess Bolt."

"Who is Fess Bolt?" asked Belle.

"He is married to Katarina Gritt, sister to a gentleman you know well."

"The store said that Chad, Captain Gritt, will be back before the end of February. Do you think he will really bring help?"

"It will take years to get the major change that we all would like to see," answered Karp. "In the interim we will have to be satisfied with small steps. My letter simply requests that the laws as written be enforced, and that the president's office send a team up here empowered to look into both the one-sided interpretation of the law and corruption in their appointed representatives. I have invited them to start with my office and those of us in the panhandle. Then, when the ice is out, move on to the Yukon."

The meeting took only a half-hour. The governor stopped Belle at the door. "Miss Medev, I would normally never discuss the things that we just covered with a schoolteacher from a small village. I am counting on you to keep this conversation under your hat. I am also counting on you to keep the peace in Kukwa. It seems to be suffering more than seems fair; it could become a tinderbox. We will lose the entire fight if a real war starts between the North Pacific folks and the villages."

❧

The Northern Pacific Railroad terminal in Great Falls was the hub of activity for the town. Chad tapped the conductor on the shoulder. "Do I have time to stretch my legs a bit?"

"Captain Gritt, we are here for two hours while we drop the extra engine from our climb over the Rockies. We also have a crew change so; I will be on my way home before you get back."

"Got a recommendation on someplace close where I can get a quick dinner. Not that the food in the dining car is not satisfactory, I could just use a change of pace."

"A block south and two to the east is the Silver Pagoda, Chinese food. Really good Chinese food. The owner came here cooking for the coolies who helped build the rail line and stayed. He will serve you with chopsticks, one of his jokes. Just ask for silverware."

The dinner of chop suey and rice more than satisfied Chad's craving for a menu change. He turned toward the rail yard and then started to stretch his legs along the tracks. For a third time he pulled the tiny piece of paper from his shirt pocket and read again the fortune. "All great decisions come from both the head and the heart."

The unusually warm November night with the last of the light from the setting sun at his back made the exercise of walking on the rail ties a pleasant game. He walked until he almost tripped on a large piece of hose laying on the railbed. Reaching down to throw it off to one side he froze. What he thought was a piece of rubber was instead half of a four-foot rattlesnake cut cleanly by a passing train. "What the hell are you doing out this time of year?" he asked to no one in particular. "Bet you wished you had stayed in your nice warm den."

Thinking that where there is one there may be two, Chad turned and headed back to the station. "At least if a bear kills you, he will eat you," he yelled at the coyote running off to his left.

Reboarding the train, he found a telegram envelope tacked to the note board next to his berth.

Chad, I hope this finds you early enough. I am leaving for Washington the day after tomorrow. Your brother-in-law has set up a hearing to investigate the troubles in Alaska. He wants this issue on the table before the Christmas recess. Parker will be joining us. I will be meeting Malcom Crier in New York on the way. We will be spending a couple of days with the Guildhams to brief them on the Alaska troubles. We should be in D.C. by the weekend. Malcom Crier is arranging for our accommodations. Katarina will know more. I would recommend that you alter your ticket and meet us.

P.S. The press has picked up on the troubles and is raising hell. Danny.

By the time Chad could find the conductor the train east was rolling. "I will have new routing for you by morning Mr. Gritt," he offered.

"Thank you. Just mark the itinerary 'straight into the fire.'

CHAPTER 20

Berlin, New Hampshire

IT WAS SNOWING, the kind of day where you could clear your porch in the evening with a broom not a shovel. The large two-story house that Drew had rented for himself and Maples sat on a large city lot on the edge of Berlin. The dirt road to the gravel pit started directly next to the house. The tracks from the front porch to the side gate and then up the dirt road were filling with snow but still provided the two newcomers with enough evidence to find the occupants, after five minutes of banging on the door produced no answer.

The two men summoned by Maples had ridden the train from Baltimore. Both had been working as night watchmen at the port when the telegram had arrived. Both had left their jobs with only a day's notice to accept Maples' offer of two thousand dollars for a month of work. Neither was surprised to hear the sharp crack of pistol shots coming from in front of them. Turning a bend in the road they could see two men aiming at a line of bottles lined up on a log.

"Hans, the big one shooting right-handed is pretty good, but the smaller one shooting with his left hand can't hit a wall at thirty feet."

"Careful now, Dirk. Even a blind dog can find the bone given enough time," laughed his partner.

Both were shocked to find the toughest man they knew struggling to reload by placing his revolver under his shortened arm and plucking cartridges from a shirt pocket with his left hand.

"What in the hell happened to you, sir?" asked Hans.

"My God, what does the other guy look like?" added Dirk.

Both men had fought in the Boer war in South Africa. Unlike Maples, they had started out on the side of the Dutch settlers. They had been captured by a small unit, commanded by Maples, and when faced with a fourth day of torture and the assurances that their families would be hunted down by Maples himself, had turned. For two years they had informed on the movements of the Freetown Militia, intelligence that had decimated a unit of one-hundred-twenty of their former neighbors. As the war wound down, they had pressured Maples to capture rather than kill the handful of comrades still in the field, a position that had quietly infuriated their commander. Their attitude changed when a short note from the two men to Maples had been found on the body of a fallen British sergeant. They had escaped a Boer search party sent to arrest them only after Dirk's mother had screamed for them to run from her front door. Both had watched helplessly as the parents were arrested, and their homes burned by Dutch irregulars. They had learned later that both of their fathers had been shot.

What started out as treason had evolved over the next weeks into a vendetta against their former allies. They led small British units against every hideout of their former comrades and had insisted on Black Flag, no prisoner terms for their former friends and neighbors.

After the war they had stayed with Maples as he helped a friend muscle his way into the diamond trade. Later they had taken assignments from Maples on behalf of Sir Rodney Crier, first in Africa and later in South America.

Eventually, they moved to the United States where Maples set up a trust that paid them each three-hundred dollars a month on top of what they could earn in legitimate jobs. Their only requirement was to handle the occasional engagement assigned by Maples. Both were married with children. Their families never suspected that the occasional 'bank repossession' they were called on to assist with, was really something much darker. All they knew was that the monthly pension check from the 'British Army' gave them a standard of living way beyond most of their peers. The bonus pay for successful 'repossession jobs' every year or two paid for beach houses and vacations.

"Care to show Drew here how we used to do it?" asked Maples.

Hans broke two bottles and then broke the largest pieces again. Dirk did the same. Drew, not to be outdone, broke the four largest remaining pieces, then broke two more.

"Samuel, you obviously have not taught your American friend the safety of always leaving one chamber empty," said Hans.

"Or to always save the last bullet for yourself if you are about to be captured," added Dirk. "But the man can shoot."

"Dinner at the café by the bridge gentlemen," directed Maples. "All friendly talk among old friends. Then we will pick up a bottle and return to the house to discuss the job."

Three hours, and half a bottle of scotch later, the men found themselves sitting around a pot-bellied coal stove. "I still cannot believe that a woman managed to get a round off with you in the room," observed Dirk.

"My fault entirely," replied Maples. "I took a two-shot Derringer to what I thought would be at most a knuckle breaking session. I had the two men pegged right. The woman was a wild card that I didn't know was in the deck. And I can now hit the end of an apple box with my left hand, so do not insult me with smart-ass comments."

"You keep the pay coming and we will remember our 'yes sir, no sir' routine Samuel. Although I think we all may be getting a bit old and gray for this life," replied Hans.

"I think this may be our last hurrah together," sighed Maples. "Sir Rodney has passed on. His idiot son and grandson are taking over, and they are not men of irresistible force. I have informed my agents and banker that we must collect what we can and liquidate what I have in my name. I shall see if I have moved fast enough to control the secret accounts that I had set up with Sir Rodney. In any event, the trust in place for my old South Africa colleagues will pay you until you pass and then go to your families."

"That is what we agreed on when we came to the States," said Hans.

"And for this mission, I have already wired the agreed upon fee to your local bank. As one final bonus, I have opened a safe deposit box here at the Bank of Berlin. After Miss Danielle Post is dead, and when I get confirmation, I will wire you the location of the key. You will find another two thousand for each of you in that box. Consider it a retirement bonus. Now we need to get you as much information as we can on Miss Post and her home in Boston."

"Samuel, I have not shot a woman since the war, but I owe you," said Hans. "A life for an arm."

"And enough money to retire doesn't hurt either does it Hans?" added Dirk.

"You say this is all about problems in the Alaska territory, Samuel?"

"That's right, I have been active in fishing and mining up there for three years now. If the accounts, that I set up are still intact, I should be able to collect between sixty and seventy thousand. Drew, I am counting on your help, especially now that we know that there is a price on my head. You get ten percent of what I collect to give you a fresh start."

"That is real fair of you Mr. Maples," replied Drew. "You know that you can count on me."

"Samuel," interjected Hans, "when is the last time you looked at a newspaper?"

"Before we came to Berlin."

"You might want to pick up a copy tomorrow or find a library where you can look at last week's copies. Some congressman in Washington is holding hearings on problems in Alaska. The press is full of it. They are calling witnesses who were recently in the territory."

An hour in the library the next morning told Maples all he needed to know. He found Drew, Hans, and Dirk on the front porch watching kids sledding on the hill below the house, a pot of coffee and a bottle of brandy on the step below them. "Buy you a cup," asked Drew, offering Maples a chipped ceramic mug.

"No. Come in the house. We need to move up our plan. Hans and Dirk, you're going to Washington D.C. not Boston, and we need to get you out of here as quickly as we can. Drew, go get me a train schedule. You other two, let's go over just how to get this done one more time."

Maples saw the two men off that afternoon, two hundred in expense money in their pockets. While he was at the train station, Drew tracked down their landlord and advised him that he and Maples would be out of town for a couple of weeks and then pre-paid for another month's rent.

"Mr. Maples, I don't really understand the extra rent. We aren't coming back here, are we?"

"No, we are not. But if someone gets on our trail, or if someone backtracks our Washington D.C. partners then I want them to think we are coming back. They might just sit here and wait for long enough to let our real trail go cold."

᪐

Guilda Guildham demanded that both Malcom and Danielle stay in their home, which turned out to be the entire top floor of an eight story hotel on Park Avenue. Malcom had recovered from his wound before Danielle left for Boston, but he now walked with a cane. Danielle had only five days at home before the telegram had been received from Katarina Gritt Bolt announcing the coming congressional hearing and requesting her presence. Her promise to return home quickly had drawn a question from her mother.

"Is that nice Captain Gritt going to be with you then?"

"I don't know mother. I suspect that he will, but he is very anxious to return to his beloved land of rain and snow."

"And you, my dear Danielle, are you not anxious to return yourself?"

"I will not be in any great hurry to leave again for the wilds. I will be going back, but not until March."

"That is good to hear Danielle. Your father and I miss you terribly. And your father is not well; his heart condition is slowly growing worse."

"My friend, Malcom Crier, has several physician friends. Perhaps father should visit one of them."

"There are no better doctors in all the country than here in Boston. And with the endowment set up in your brother's name for training physicians, we have every possible accommodation at the medical school. Harvard College rewards generosity. Perhaps when you return you could visit your old law school. Your adventures in the Alaska territory would be very exciting to students. That old curmudgeon advisor of yours, I believe his name was Marsh, will be in the heart ward himself when he hears where you are practicing."

As Danielle stepped from the train in New York, Malcom was along the tracks waving his cane above his head. In minutes, her luggage was carted to a coach waiting in the 'police exclusive' zone. Two officers helped load her trunk in Guilda's custom coach and a moment later the driver had the two on their way uptown.

"I arrived last night," said Malcom. "Aunt Guilda had a fabulous kosher dinner waiting. She wanted a huge dinner downtown tonight to introduce you, but I talked her into postponing it until tomorrow. I just happen to have tickets to the hottest play in town and reservations for dinner. Just a token of thanks for all your help and attention while I was in the hospital. Oh, and not one word about the ham and cheese to my aunt."

"You don't owe me a thing Malcom Crier. It is I, that owe you, probably my life," replied Danielle.

"Then consider dinner and a show with me as payment, Danielle."

"I am a bit tired from traveling, but I am game."

Danielle did not see the two Pinkerton agents who had been shadowing Malcom climb into a waiting buggy and follow only a few yards behind the elegant coach.

Guilda was unruffled by her nephews' disruption of her plans. She met Danielle at the front door with the hug of a mother greeting a long-lost child. "Breakfast with Abraham to talk business, then a bit of shopping Miss Post. We want you dressed so that those lechers we send to Congress will listen to you, instead of filling their heads with thoughts of conquest."

Guilda pulled on a tiny hidden string behind the front door, and a maid stepped into the hallway and bustled toward the front door. "Christina, you are to take care of our guest from Alaska while she is visiting us. Anything she needs. Now please show her to the room next to my nephew's and wait for Norman to bring her things. Christina, this is Miss Danielle Post of Boston and the Alaska Territory."

The canopy bed almost disappeared in the enormous bedroom and Danielle wouldn't have noticed it at all were it not for the pale pink gown draped across the mattress. She picked up a note card pinned to a hatbox at the foot of the bed.

Common sense shopping tomorrow, but tonight just fun. I believe that I guessed your measurements just right, but if not, Christine is an excellent seamstress. One should start their theater season in a Ponce Pickard. Guilda."

"My family is well-off, Malcom," The waiter was seating Malcom and her in the corner booth of a packed tavern only minutes from the theater. "Well-off is different from wealthy. Is tonight on you or the Guildhams?"

"A bit of both, I must admit. Dinner reservations are easy if your family financed the Spanish chef's dream of his own restaurant. The box in the theater belongs to my aunt and uncle, as does the coach. They usually attend every opening and every closing. In between the theater resells their box with the revenues going to the company. Tonight, I was the buyer and as to finding the best table in a crowded after theater club, that is a function of a twenty-dollar gold piece in the initial handshake. That works everywhere. Are you enjoying yourself Danielle?"

"In my wildest dreams of coming back to civilization, I would never have had a vision like tonight. The answer is yes. I am enjoying myself immensely."

Malcom Crier reached across the table and took Danielle's hand in his. He didn't say a word, just smiled and a minute later laid her hand back on the table. Waving to a waiter, he ordered a bottle of Krug Champagne and as an afterthought asked for the cigar girl. "Let us wrap this up with a flourish that will set the rumors flying. Maybe we'll even make the social columns in tomorrow's papers."

After wine with dinner and at the intermission of the play and a bottle of champagne, Danielle was asleep the minute that Christine finished hanging her dress and left the room. Two hours later she found herself sitting in the over-stuffed chair watching the late-night traffic of New York on the streets below. Her return to bed led to two or three hours of restless sleep before Christine appeared at the door with morning coffee and began to lay out the clothes that Danielle had requested the night before.

As Danielle suspected, Guilda was an equal partner in the family enterprises. In less than two hours Danielle and Malcom recapped the reports and documents from the north. Abraham took notes throughout the discussion, but in the end, it was Guilda who spoke. "Abraham, Richard Crier and of course, Malcom here are tough and hard-nosed businessmen. They ask no favors and honestly seldom offer them. But they are honest and do not hurt people or break the law for money. They would not hesitate to protect themselves or someone they hold dear, but they would not knowingly do the things you have been discussing."

"Miss Post," commented Abraham finally, "I will begin tomorrow to see what might be done behind the scenes to remedy the greatest of the abuses you bring to our attention. Mining Capital Development and the Alaska Investors Group have significant influence over some of the ventures that you are concerned about. They will compete fairly in the future. Don't expect us to throw away the advantages that our capital or the law provides. But those who are responsible for actions beyond legal advantages will be looking for employment elsewhere before next season begins."

"Thank you Mr. Guildham and you too Guilda. Will you turn over any evidence of illegal activity to the authorities as you begin the clean up?" asked Danielle.

Guilda smiled and waited for the two men to respond. Finally, she took it upon herself. "My dear, Malcom is just starting out and Abraham and Richard are far too old for jail. No, we will not incriminate ourselves if it comes to that. What we can and will do is steer any investigation to evidence that directly implicates those directly responsible. Oh, and we will help with some outside investigating."

As Danielle pulled the covers up around her chin that night, two new Pinkerton men replaced the two who had shadowed them while shopping and at dinner and a concert. Each pulled a different colored stocking cap over his ears as it began to snow.

There had not been time to bring the family pullman down from Canada, so Malcom had secured a private cabin on the express from New York to the nation's capital. Two nights of restless sleep had taken a toll on Danielle and after only a couple of hours of rehearsing her testimony her eyes took a needed break. Crier gently pulled her head to his shoulder and in minutes the young woman was asleep. Three hours later a knock at the door forced Malcom to slide away from a task that he was thoroughly enjoying, gently lowering Danielle's sleeping head to the seat.

"Mr. Crier, we have thoroughly searched the train and there

is no one aboard that fits the description of this Maples guy, nor do we find any obvious hired muscle aboard. My guess is that if this fellow is going to take a run at either you or Miss Post, he has not had time to get anyone aboard this train."

"Thank you Mr…, hell I do not even know your name," replied Malcom.

"For the term of our engagement, all of us will be Mark or Luke to you. The taller will always be Mark, today that is me."

"I am not sure that I quite understand," offered Malcom.

"Quite simple, even a Pinkerton needs sleep. We will be replaced by other agents when we arrive, and eventually we will again, replace them. Sometimes you won't even know who is watching, but rest assured that at least two of us will be close by. We have arranged for a room adjoining yours and Miss Posts, so even at night we will be there. Just remember to lock your room and not open the door to anyone you do not absolutely trust. Please pass that on to Miss Post."

"I understand, and I am grateful, but I think my father's concerns are greatly exaggerated. I think that Samuel Maples is making tracks to pick up his stash of funds and then on his way out of the country," laughed Malcom.

"Perhaps, but our orders make it clear that your father believes that this man is a man of vengeance. Still, if you and Miss Post would like to have lunch in the dining car, I am comfortable that you are safe."

The lunch of poached sole and vegetables was not paired with the recommended German white wine. Danielle made it clear that she had imbibed all that she desired until after the hearing. The second pot of coffee went almost as fast as the first. "Please excuse me for a moment. I must find the women's room," laughed Danielle.

Malcom pointed to the end of the car opposite the door

where they had entered. Danielle never noticed a balding man in a brown suit rise from a table not far away and head in the direction that Malcom had pointed. A second man at the same table got up and moved to the other side of the table where he could observe Malcom.

CHAPTER 21

Washington D.C.

CHAD GRITT'S TRAIN arrived at the Baltimore and Potomac station in the nation's capital at midnight. His sister and brother-in-law were on the landing. "We wait for another hour," offered Katarina after giving her brother a huge hug. "Parker is coming in on the train from Boston."

"Is Annalee with him?" asked Chad.

"No," answered Katarina, "she decided she and the baby needed rest."

"Smart girl, that one," added Fess Bolt.

"Are you and Parker staying with us tonight or do you want us to drop you at the hotel?"

"Your place will be more comfortable than the old Willard," answered her brother.

Katarina had always possessed a laugh that would turn heads from across the room. "You would really be uncomfortable at the Willard. How long has it been since you were here?"

"Five years. It's hard to believe it's been that long," answered Chad.

"Not for me," snapped Fess. "That is three elections ago and a hundred years of hard lessons about how this place works."

"What's that got to do with the Willard Hotel?" asked Chad.

"The owners are tearing it down to build a new and grander hotel. I am happy to drop you there if you want, but you are in for a night of concrete mattresses and steel pillows."

"Where am I staying then?"

"Your new friend Malcom Crier has reserved rooms at the Arlington for everybody. Seems you now travel in a circle where opulence has replaced our old common-sense standard," replied his sister. "He and Danny checked in this afternoon."

"I would probably sleep better at the house tonight, it's been a long trip. We can check into the hotel tomorrow morning. I am assuming that the official meetings will not start until Monday."

"The committee chair will not gavel us into session until ten on Tuesday. That leaves us tomorrow to catch up and Monday to stir the pot before the hearing," laughed Fess.

Chad looked his brother-in-law in the eye suppressing a laugh. "Just what have you got up your sleeve?"

"The lobbyists, especially those representing the fishing industry in California, have been hard at it trying to suppress this hearing since I talked the chairman into taking up the matter. I thought that a press conference at the hotel, where citizens who have lived in Alaska could present their story and a bit of the evidence that the committee is going to see, might ensure that that testimony and evidence doesn't get locked away in some file cabinet when we are through. Any such conference must of course be called by you and the others who are to testify so that no members of the committee can be accused of prejudice."

"Just how would a citizen go about setting up such a press conference?" asked Chad.

"Theo, the general manager of the hotel, never misses an opportunity to promote the property. A brief meeting between him and you and probably Parker and Miss Post should do the trick. You know how it's done, you chose his hotel to begin the movement to develop the wealth that is Alaska for all Americans, etcetera. It's just too bad that the press isn't really engaged, maybe you chose the wrong hotel."

"How much did you win the last election by?" asked Chad.

"I think his margin was just over twenty-seven points," replied Katarina.

Fess continued, "If we can get to him early tomorrow, the press conference should be announced in the morning papers on Monday."

"But tomorrow is Sunday," answered Chad.

"Theo is like the oak paneling in a hotel parlor, he is always there."

Sunday was not a day of rest, or for that matter a day of church going. Instead, Parker and Chad arrived at the hotel early. The bellman delivered a note to Danielle Post's room and returned with a folded reply five minutes later inviting Chad to join her. "Parker, since the company is paying the bills, perhaps we should share a room. See what you can do and check us in," asked Chad as he headed to the stairway.

His tap at the door was met with, "Who is it?"

"Danny, it's Chad."

The door opened and Danielle, wrapped in a robe, extended her arms. Chad gently kissed her neck and then pulled away to scan the hallway. "That is not what I expected after three months apart."

Chad looked at her. "I thought I heard a door opening or

closing. A gentleman should never allow a woman's modesty to be compromised. But I must have been hearing things."

The mood broken; Chad helped himself to a cup of coffee as Danielle disappeared behind a large painted screen to dress. "Katarina and Fess have invited us to dinner this evening. I haven't spent much time with them or the kids in five years, I would like to accept," he advised.

"That would be great. Would Malcom be welcome?"

"Of course. How was your trip so far? I mean, aside from the shootout in the Crier home?"

"I am having a wonderful time. My parents are immensely pleased, and I think, relieved to have me back. I have shopped in Seattle and Montreal. In New York, Guilda Guildham could not have been a better friend. The first night, Malcom had box seat tickets to a play and dinner reservations at the hottest restaurant in town. The second night, the Guildhams took both of us out for dinner at their private club. You know, just an intimate little meal with thirty of their friends and business associates."

As Danielle emerged from behind the screen, the bright red skirt and sweater she wore somehow failed to light up her face. "I miss this more than even I knew," she continued. "Now what is the plan worked out by that scheming best friend of mine and your brother-in-law?"

Chad spent a few minutes outlining the strategy to engage the press. "We can discuss the hearing and what we should cover when we visit the press over lunch. Will your friend Malcom be joining us?"

"Not today, he has been away from his office since he traveled to Montreal to meet me and his father. He has called in his staff for a Sunday briefing and tomorrow he will go back to work."

"Doesn't he have a home here? I would have thought that he would want to stay there rather than in a hotel."

"This Maples guy is very dangerous. Both Malcom and his father, who I like very much, believe that our lives are in danger. Malcom wants us all close together so that we can watch out for each other. He even bought me my own Webley so that I could return the one Parker and Annalee loaned me."

"I hope that he is wrong," replied Chad. "I didn't even pack a pistol.'

"The hotel has security, and once we are in the congressional hearing room we will have security."

"I doubt that we will need either," continued Chad. "For all you know, this Maples guy may be dead. At the very least, he will be headed back to the west coast to gather up his winnings before getting out of the country."

"Probably true. The Criers and the Guildhams are certainly through with him, but they aren't going to incriminate themselves."

"There you go. With money like theirs, they probably have a private detective or two on his trail already. Now let's go find Parker and this Theo man. The sooner we get this all set up, the sooner we can find a Sunday brunch. I haven't eaten since I changed trains in Baltimore yesterday."

Theo Roess was everything that he was reported to be. Within a half hour of the visit, he had handwritten notes on the way to more than a dozen reporters. He had taken it upon himself to announce the news conference for three in the afternoon the next day. He even volunteered one of the five ground floor dining rooms for the event.

⁕

After two days of canvassing the hotels, Hans and Dirk were no closer to locating either Malcom Crier or Dannielle Post, both staying in rooms reserved and paid for by Business Development Partners. "Let's grab a bite and then see if we can find out where exactly this hearing will be," suggested Hans."

"Damn, Hans, that means dealing with capital security either before or after we kill her. I did not take on this job to spend my retirement in a cage or a hole in the ground."

"Dirk, you should know that you are not going to die of old age in your bed."

"Maybe," continued Dirk, "but I always look for a fighting chance. I do not want to be trapped in a building with a dozen federal cops shooting at us."

The two men left the rooming house where they had prepaid for a month. Just down the block was a small café run by a black couple where the food was wonderful and most of the rest of the customers were also black. Dirk flipped a quarter to the paperboy on the corner, tucking a paper under his arm until he was seated. "Not much chance of anyone in here pointing us out in the social circles where Crier or Miss Post circulate."

Dirk ordered ham and eggs and grits, something that he had learned to enjoy after moving to Baltimore. Hans settled on pancakes and bacon. Dirk opened the paper. He didn't say a word, before he folded the paper to highlight a front-page note. He handed the paper to Hans.

"I cannot believe how stupid these people must be," offered Hans. "They either know nothing about security or have no idea that they are at risk. They're announcing a press conference at a hotel and even a time."

The meals came in only minutes. The two Boers left a two-dollar tip for a dollar breakfast. "I say we walk over to the Arlington and lay out a plan. Someone will know where they are setting up. The only thing that could be better would be if the conference was at night, the shadows make it easier to disappear," offered Hans.

"I love that American saying. You know, don't look a gift horse in the mouth," replied Dirk.

The two men were in and out of the Arlington in less than an hour. Their working man's attire was met with more than one stare from staff, but other than that, they were invisible. The movement of the four Pinkerton agents now assigned to the security detail, two following Malcom and two sitting outside the elegant row house that was the home of Katarina and Fess Bolt, insured that no one at the hotel found their visit out of the norm.

An hour later, Hans and Dirk found themselves in a pub only four blocks from their rooming house.

"In through the front door with the crowds, then straight to the hallway next to the dining room. We can hide inside the alcove where the waiters normally work. When we see Miss Post, we will only be about twenty feet away, an easy shot. The alcove exits back into the hallway, and we are only fifty feet from the staff entrance."

"Sounds right to me, Hans, but we should go find ourselves a rack suit and hats in the morning. Maybe even a couple of those folders that the reporters all carry," nodded Dirk. "It's much easier to get close in a crowd."

"If we stash our work jackets and hats just outside the staff entrance and split up to come back to our room, the cops will be looking for some other guys. We can probably catch a boat to the Maryland side of the river and then catch a train on the other side," continued Hans. "We go south and then catch a boat back home from down the coast. I wouldn't want to leave a trail back to Myrna and the boys."

Dirk ordered another pitcher. He had found that three or four beers helped him sleep the night before an operation.

On Monday morning, the Gritts and Danielle reviewed their testimony and the documents that would be entered into evidence at the hearing. They had taken the recommendation of Congressman Bolt and presented all those documents to a photographer. According to Bolt, more than one controversial package of evidence had disappeared after hearings. The photographer had committed to have a dozen sets of prints ready by the time of the hearing.

They had learned that five other witnesses, all provided by the opposition would be testifying. Bolt also provided a short profile of the other committee members and highlighted those who they could expect to give them hard questioning. "Kill them with kindness," was his advice.

By the time of the press conference, the three felt that they were as ready as possible. Nothing had prepared them for the crowd in the dining room. Reporters from across the country had crowded into the room. Nothing sold papers or pleased editors more than a good scandal and the press could smell one in this story. Theo Roess himself gaveled the room into quiet and then announced the topic and introduced Chad Gritt as the first presenter.

"Let me set the stage by first giving all of you a brief geography lesson on the Alaska Territory, as learned over three generations of doing business there by my family. Then I will outline for you the problems in Southeast Alaska where my firm operates a passenger and freight marine service that ties the communities together and that region to the rest of the country. Later, my brother Parker will discuss how similar corruption is hindering the development of the Yukon country, eight-hundred miles to the north, a country larger than the state of Texas. Finally, Miss

Danielle Post, a woman whose family has roots in Alaska, but who's pedigree extends to the Harvard Law School, will present specific documentation from the Presidents own representatives in the territory."

The three had shortened their outlines to about ten minutes each to keep the audience engaged. Even if there were extensive questions their goal was to keep the session to under an hour. They had also held out certain legal documents including the indictments, believing that they would have greater impact on the committee the next day if the press had not already reported on them.

By the time that Danielle was escorted to the podium by Malcom Crier, a familiar face in Washington, the crowd was shouting out questions. They hushed as the elegant young lady dressed in a dark wool pin-stripe suit stepped in front of them and began to speak.

"I cannot get a clear shot," whispered Hans. "Those other two men are in the way."

"Be patient my friend," replied Dirk. "I'm going to move along the wall and see if I can find a clear shot."

Ten minutes later, Danielle wrapped up her prepared comments by advising the reporters of the copies of the documents. "My colleagues, Parker and Chad Gritt will meet you at the table in the back of the room to take names and addresses. We will send those of you who want a copy by tomorrow."

Chad and Parker stepped from the raised platform and headed toward the aisle along the wall where Dirk stood, a double-action .38 pistol clutched in the hand at his side. For some unknown reason, Parker's attention was drawn to the man in the ill-fitting suit. "Look at that guy," he whispered to Chad, "his tailor must also sew feed sacks."

Chad lunged past his brother toward the man. "Gun," was all he said.

Parker watched as the man began to lift the weapon, then he launched himself after his brother.

Behind him he heard Malcom Crier shout out a warning as he saw Hans step out of the alcove, taking aim at Danielle. "No!" he shouted as he launched himself at the young lady knocking her off from her feet just as the .38 in Han's hand went off. A reporter from the Post seated in the front row gasped.

Dirk was faster than either Parker or Chad, clubbing Chad on the side of the head and then trying to bring the weapon to bear on his target. Parker launched himself at the attacker just as Dirk fired. The bullet hit Parker in the chest, knocking him down.

Malcom lay atop Danielle, who was struggling under his weight. Hans started toward the couple, stumbling as Chad grabbed his foot. Hans swung the pistol down and fired, the bullet skimming the top of Chad's head. Before he could pull the trigger, a third time a tall man positioned across the room shot him through the heart. "One down," yelled Mark, "no shot on the other."

Dirk watched his old friend drop in his tracks, blood exploding from the center of his back. He took a step toward the door to the hallway raising his arm to empty his pistol into the human pile that was Malcom and Danielle. Before he could pull the trigger, a shorter man in the back of the room fired, hitting him below the ribs and slamming him into the wall.

Before Luke could fire again, Parker Gritt lunged back to his feet, blocking the shot. Dirk lunged for the door and out into the hallway. In seconds, he was out of the employees exit and running through the alley. He stopped and retrieved his work coat and hat from beneath the pile of leaves where he and Hans had stashed them that morning. He quickly threw off his suit coat and hat and replaced them with working man's clothes. He pushed the discarded clothes under the leaves with his foot as he buttoned the work coat. He stashed his pistol in a specially sewn pocket and pulled the stained work cap down almost to his eyes. Gripping the wound in his back with his gun hand he began to walk calmly down the alley.

Inside the press conference, the stunned group finally began to move. At the back of the room, Luke waved to a balding man, who the day before, had the same name and pointed toward the hallway door. He then rushed through the milling reporters toward the stage where his partner was already helping Danielle to her feet.

Parker reached into his lapel pocket and retrieved the folded papers from his speech. As he unfolded them, the small bullet dropped to the floor. He lifted his brother into a sitting position. Blood spilled from his torn scalp. In seconds one of the reporters was at his side, a heavy blue bandana in his hand. He pressed it against the wound as Chad's eyes flickered. "Damn, that hurts."

On the stage, Malcom Crier lay on his stomach, his teeth clenched. Danielle pulled away from the Pinkerton detective and knelt next to Malcom. She reached into her large bag and pushed past the loaded Webley to reach her hanky. Malcom watched as she quickly folded the cloth.

"No, you don't Miss Post, not there you don't."

Seconds later an older man in a gray suit took the handkerchief from her hand and pressed it down on Malcom's wound. "Right in the arse, couldn't be a better place to get shot."

"I am Dr. Piedmont, the house physician," he told a bystander next to the stage. "Hold this in place while I check on the other patients."

Danielle looked up from Malcom and finally focused on

Parker holding his brother, his head and shoulders covered in blood. "My God, my God," she said as she followed the doctor.

The reporter holding the bandana over Chad's wound gave way readily to the doctor. He turned to Danielle. "Names O'Reilly, formerly with the 8th cavalry. I think this lad will be just fine. I've seen scalps cleaved this way more than once. Should only leave him with a headache and a new part on his hair."

"I concur, Mr. O'Reilly," offered the doctor. "I think we should send this man to the hospital overnight just for observation, but I don't think there will be any permanent damage."

"Doc," stammered Chad, "I have a congressional hearing tomorrow morning. I came all the way from the Alaska territory to testify."

"I think you will testify; if I am wrong, do you prefer a solemn ceremony or a wake?" replied the doctor.

"What about my other friend Mr. Crier?" asked Danielle. "This is the second time in two months that he has saved my life."

"He'll have a sore butt and will need to sit on a cushion for a few weeks, but that should be all," replied Dr. Piedmont.

Theo pointed to the wounded reporter. "I didn't see the third one."

Piedmont rushed to where the man, still seated in his chair, his head tilted back, blood pumping from between his fingers. He examined the man, then pulled the pencil from the reporter's hand and carefully inserted it into the wound to slow the bleeding.

Turning to Theo Roess who hovered only a few feet away Piedmont continued. "We probably will want a couple of ambulances Mr. Roess, but we got lucky. No permanent loss of customers."

Luke pointed toward the body next to the Alcove. His

partner swept the room with a practiced gaze and then nodded. Luke walked over and began to rifle through the pockets of Hans' coat, finding a key to the rooming house. He passed the key to the balding man who had just reentered the room after searching the alley where Dirk had fled. "We are going to stick with our charges," he commented. "It will be up to you and your partner to find the shooter."

The evening found Katarina and Fess pushing through a throng of reporters in the waiting area of the hospital. "I'm sorry, but no reporters are being allowed on the third floor," commanded an orderly.

"I am Congressman Bolt, and my wife here is the sister of one of your shooting patients."

"Elevator to the third floor and check in with the nurses station."

They found Parker and Danielle sitting in two straight-backed oak chairs next to the elevator. To their relief, both were smiling. "What's the scoop, as one of the reporter's downstairs would ask." said Katarina.

"Our brother is already stitched up, a mild concussion and a split scalp. I have seen worse on the Rugby field. They are in there now trying to get him to eat. Malcom is in surgery where they are removing a bullet from his bum. They expect a speedy recovery."

"I heard that there were three shootings," interjected Fess.

"A reporter sitting behind Danielle took one below the shoulder, but it missed the lung. He is out of surgery and back in his room," responded Parker.

"It sounds like you had an army on your side," continued Fess, "what the hell is that all about?"

"Richard Crier had wired the Guildhams from Montreal," offered Danielle, "worried about me and his son. They apparently knew this Maples man. They hired a security detail from the Pinkertons. Malcom knew they were there from the time that I arrived in New York, and he made the decision to expand the detail when we got to D.C. I never even knew they were around."

"I would like to thank them personally," commented the smiling Congressman.

Danielle pointed at a man in a brown suit sitting in a chair between two rooms.

"First a word with the troops and then I think that I will start with the reporter. He wouldn't happen to be from Massachusetts, would he? Hell, it doesn't make any difference, his story will make the papers."

Ten minutes later he was back. "That Luke fellow doesn't talk much. Smiled and said something to the effect that it was all part of his job. He did indicate that the Pinkertons were assisting the police in finding the other shooter."

"And the reporter?" asked his wife.

"He's with the Post, and in the next hour they will have another reporter here for his story. He is all fired up about the assassination attempt to shut down the congressional hearing about corruption in Alaska. I am sorry about people getting hurt, but you will not believe what the publicity from today is going to do to elevate the hearings."

A few minutes later the three were escorted into Chad's room. "You should have ducked big brother," laughed Katarina. You look like you did when you were fifteen and you crashed that bicycle that Father bought you into the cement hitching posts in front of the house."

Parker smiled at his sister and shook his head. "I don't know, Sis, I think that Chad's thick skull is the only reason that Danielle is still with us. That and Crier's butt. The other Pinkerton, the one who calls himself Mark told me that the pistol that he took from the dead man had thirty-one notches filed into the grip. The men who came after you were professionals."

Chad wiped a tear from his eye. "I refused the sedative and this hurts like hell. I don't want to be thick headed at the hearing in the morning."

"Thank you, Chad Gritt." Danielle kissed him softly on the forehead. "If you don't feel up to it, Parker and I can handle the hearing."

"Not a chance, Danny. I don't think the hearings had anything to do with those two shooters. I think that it was pure revenge on this Maples' part, but it isn't going to stop me from why I came here."

"Chad," interjected Fess, "maybe this is just revenge, but I wouldn't put it that way if you are asked tomorrow. If the committee thinks this scandal may include attempted murder, then even those opposed to any action in Alaska will be real quiet until this blows over."

CHAPTER 22

Washington D.C.

THE PLANNED SMALL hearing room had to be abandoned due to the throng of press pushing to get in. The chairman gaveled the assembled into session an hour late and took the unusual step of swearing in Danielle, Parker and Chad together. At the table reserved for the opposition only one witness appeared flanked by two attorneys.

Copies of the documents presented to the clerk were handed out to each of the committee members as Chad opened the hearing.

"Twice the size of Texas, more coastline than the rest of the country combined, nodding to the congressman from Minnesota he added, a land of a million lakes. The land that much of the country once called 'Seward's Icebox' is now served by steam launch throughout Southeast Alaska and the area of Cook Inlet. The Yukon is served in the summer by five steamboats. Each region is served by at minimum weekly steamship service in the summer and in the case of Southeast service every three days.

All three of the speakers here have traveled all the way from the territory because we are convinced that this committee and those in the executive branch responsible for governing the territory do not want the treasure of Alaska controlled by unscrupulous businesspeople who are supported by bureaucrats who are confused by your directions or worse, in the pocket of those business cartels. We don't think it is the intention of the federal government to allow a few to steal the wealth of the citizens."

Chad's prepared statement ran longer than the time allotted, the chairman more than agreeable to continue his fascinating testimony. Moments after he finished, the chairman stopped all questioning and instead directed Parker to commence with his prepared remarks. "We will wait until these three patriots present their concerns before we each take our individual shots. I will insist on extraordinary courtesy considering their long trip to be here knowing that some, who did not want us to hear this testimony, might use force to stop them."

Parker outlined the opportunity being literally washed from the streams and rivers of the vast Yukon basin. He carefully avoided any mention of what was going on east of the border in the Yukon territory. "Stolen claims, the law being used to throw hard working immigrants off from diggings that some had spent years finding, gangs of bullies beating honest men into submission." He concluded with the affidavits of those who participated in the forged document smudged ink test. "The men who prepared the statements that you are now reviewing, are not against capital, rather they believe that the men who have risked everything including their lives should be the ones who work with the captains of our industry to bring the capital to bare. They should share in the winnings."

Danielle presented the documents prepared by the marshals,

magistrates, and the governor. "You can see from these reports and even arrest warrants that the authorities in Alaska do not have the resources or legal foundation to address these issues. The people themselves are legally powerless since they have no vote, no local jurisdiction, not even the right to legally found cities or gain title to their own homes. It is remarkable under the circumstances that Governor Karp and those under his direction have been able to keep vigilante actions to a minimum."

The first question after the presentation came not from Fess Bolt, but from a congressman from California. "Miss Post, I am sure that you consider yourself a competent lawyer, but I think that even you would admit that your limited experience, your failure to even appear before your peers for an examination before the bar, limits the depth of your evaluation. Tell me, what possible harm is coming to the people of the territory from strong willed businessmen dragging the territory into this century?"

Danielle smiled and rearranged the pile of notes in front of her. "Congressman, every attorney can practice yielding a sword or a shield. They can represent those who need the protection of the law or those who wield the loopholes in the law for their own gain. You may correctly assume that I am of those who believe in the shield. Recently for example, you led many of your colleagues in beginning the process of righting some of the wrongs inflicted on Native Americans, and I believe that the catalyst for your actions was a real empathy for what happened to the Nez Pearce only a few years ago. In Alaska, self-sufficient native villages, villages with a strong Christian faith, some with schools funded without the help of this Congress are being starved because the captains of the fishing industry use methods that put only an additional two cents per can of salmon in their pockets. They leave little for the traditional users of the resource to put in their stomachs. They are hurting. And it costs the treasury because we now ship food to people who only a few years ago fed themselves and worked to send their best and brightest off to college."

The questions continued for more than two hours before the chairman swore in the fourth person registered to testify, a man who represented the small clique of fisheries companies that controlled almost all fishing in the Pacific. "I will be very brief," he said. "The firms that I represent provide meaningful and rewarding work for hundreds of workers from South America to the Alaska territory. We use methods that minimize the cost of the product that we bring to American citizens. We follow the age-old economic theories that preach maximizing profits. That is how this nation was built, and how it will remain strong. With that said, I commit to you that our industry will undertake a thorough review of our practices in the Alaska territory to find and correct any legal abuses and to ensure adequate food resources are available to its people."

Fess Bolt rose from his chair, and as he often did during hearings, sat on the back of the chair, his feet resting on the seat. This put almost his entire body above the table in front of him and his collogues.

"The chair recognizes congressman Bolt."

"Thank you, Mr. Chairman," began Bolt. "Now, let me get this clear. You are saying that there are most likely some transgressions in the fishing community, but the folks you represent do not think that this government should have jurisdiction or take any action to deal with those transgressions?"

"Congressman, we do not know of any specific transgressions that rise to the level of illegal activity. But we have a responsibility to find out. This is especially true since the collapse of the fur seal trade has left the treasury few funds to operate the government in Alaska. This Congress is not going to fund close supervision over the canneries along three-thousand miles of coastline. More importantly, you do not have to."

"I see, and if the practices continue to leave the local Natives hungry, or those same people just trying to feed their families die, then what would you suggest?"

"I can't imagine that sir. But this Congress appropriates sums every year to feed the Indians from Washington to Florida. The cost of helping the few thousand Indians in Alaska would not add much to that sum. Besides, those programs have freed up vast territories where the Indians chased wild resources inefficiently. Those lands are now used for farming and timbering and mining. That will happen in Alaska as well."

Bolt continued, "so we allow not only the companies in fishing, that you represent, to run roughshod over the people of Alaska, but also the mining consortiums and the timber interests. That sir will not be the story of the development for much longer, there will be a rule of law and hopefully this committee will instigate investigations and modifications to the laws to protect those people."

"Congressman, we are not the enemy. You need not spend precious resources regulating industry that is doing exactly what the country asks for. We will develop that land and create wealth and infrastructure so that someday Alaska will be full of citizens."

The hearing was interrupted by a congressional aid slipping up to the speaker's chair with a folded note. "Ladies and gentlemen, I have just been informed that a Treasury boat accompanied by two Pinkerton detectives intercepted a stolen oyster boat. They believe the man in the boat was the wounded man from the attack on our Alaskan friends here. He apparently shot himself in the head when approached."

The buzz in the room turned into an uproar as dozens of reporters bolted from their chairs to file stories. The chairman, unable to restore order immediately, gaveled the session into a ninety-minute recess for lunch.

"I will treat you to lunch in the dining room," offered Bolt. "If you three try to go anywhere outside the building right now you will be mobbed for comments."

They were at the table only a minute when the committee chairman pulled up a chair. "You know the real truth, that flunky from the fishing lobby is just about right. Even if we introduce legislation today to really strengthen the law and enforcement, it will not be passed until at least next year. Then it will take another couple of years to get any funding. There is no will in this Congress for any form of home rule for the territory or the funding that it would take to implement it."

Danielle groaned while the Gritt brothers just scowled.

"Am I wrong Fess?" asked the chairman.

"No Albert, you are not. What I was going to suggest to my friends here is that they take a few minutes and jot down three or four specific things that they would like to see done, things that will not cost too much. Just like your old friend Governor Karp suggests, we move forward one bite at a time."

The people at the table all ordered lunch and the congressmen spent the next hour firing questions about Alaska. "Be patiently impatient and please pass that sentiment on when you return," offered the chairman. "When we resume, I will ask each of you for one specific idea, or an action you think will make a difference. You have stirred the pot, and someone will get thrown to the wolves. That alone will not help much. Give us something that we can do to help but make it so reasonable that no one on the committee will object."

That evening the Bolts, and the three Alaskans were joined for dinner by two other congressmen and their wives in the Grand Dining room of the Arlington. At a table not far away,

Luke and Mark picked at their meals while surveying all the other diners and the three doorways to the room. As dinner wrapped up, Danielle rose and folded her napkin. "I leave you in the capable hands of the Gritt brothers who know far more about the Great Land than me."

The wife of a congressman from Georgia smiled up at Danielle. "Wherever you are off to must be so important that you would abandon a table with so many handsome and powerful men."

"Danielle smiled a nervous smile. "I am off to the hospital to visit a good friend."

As she left the room, another Mark and Luke materialized in the lobby, only this time Danielle knew instantly who they were.

At the table, Katarina stood. "Please excuse me, but under the circumstances, Danny could probably use a friend. Fess dear, I am assuming that I might find you in the men's smoking bar later."

Danielle was already seated in the coach when her friend flagged down the driver. "Care for some girl chat on the way?"

The two women were recognized by Dr. Piedmont who was just leaving. "I was just checking on my two patients, although each now have found physicians of their own."

"It's a bit past visiting hours, Doctor, but I had hoped to see Mr. Crier before the lights go out," whispered Danielle. "By the way, Katarina Gritt Bolt, this is the physician, Dr. Piedmont from the Arlington who took charge after the shooting yesterday. My Lord, was it only yesterday."

"Mrs. Bolt, I am assuming the wife of Congressman Bolt, am I correct?"

"Yes, and I wanted to thank you for helping my big brother who just can't seem to keep his big head out of trouble."

"And how was Chad this afternoon?"

"He will be fine, doctor. He didn't seem much the worse for wear at today's hearing."

"I read about it in the evening paper. Seems they got the second shooter as well. I found out that the Pinkertons had discussed your safety with the hotel security office and had asked them to stay out of the way."

Danielle looked at Katarina and then at the doctor. "Probably for the best. There were already four men with guns in that room; a couple more and it might have been a blood bath."

"Exactly," replied Piedmont. "Now, let me escort you past the orderlies to the third floor."

Malcom was flat on his stomach as Piedmont escorted the women into the room. Dressed in hospital pajamas, unshaven and a bit pale, he was the epitome of someone that needed a bit of tender loving care. Danielle seated herself next to the bed while Katarina waited at the door. "Malcom, how are you feeling?"

"A lot better than the last time," he answered. "Better than the two men Maples sent."

"Maybe, but perhaps they are in a far better place."

"Not unless Hell is a far better place than its reputation indicates. How did the hearings go?"

"According to Fess they went as well as can be expected. Kat, you were in the gallery."

"Good evening to you Mrs. Bolt. I am quite sorry about all of this. How is your brother?" asked Crier.

"Well enough to shake up a full congressional committee. I think that Parker and Chad made the case, but it was Danielle's handling of the questions that made the day."

"Are we about to write off our investments in the territory then?" asked Malcom.

"No, I doubt that anything earth shattering will come of this hearing. There will be an investigation or two and a bit more scrutiny, but Alaska will wait for some time for any fundamental change," answered Danielle.

Danielle leaned forward and placed her cheek on Malcom's shoulder and began to cry softly.

"What is this all about?" asked Malcom.

"I feel blessed that the Lord put you next to me both here and in Montreal. I would not have been at the hearing today; I probably would not be anywhere at all."

"Danielle, I am no knight in shining armor," offered Malcom.

"You are to me. It's more than you putting your body between me and those two terrible men, it is how you put your personal gain aside and helped us. The leadership of you and your father on the Alaska issues is spreading. Witnesses from the big mining companies didn't even appear."

Katarina looked down at her friend. "I think I'm going to check up on our favorite reporter."

"Danny, I asked you not to judge my family by what my grandfather and his hired hands were doing. Abe and Aunt Gilda seem to know more about Samuel Maples than either my father or me. They were the ones who hired our bodyguards. I suspect that they are busy cleaning up the mess as we speak."

"Malcom Crier, do not sell yourself short. I can't believe such a funny man can have such an analytical side and when the time comes, the heart of a lion."

"I could give you the same compliment. Straight from the frozen north to the lights of Broadway and from terror to congressional testimony without missing a beat. I did nothing that the other men in your life like Captain Gritt would not have done."

"Malcom, the difference is, the territory that you are comfortable in, and the weapons each of you have chosen." Danielle sat up, wiping the tears from her cheek and chin. "Doctor Piedmont said that you will be getting out of here by next week. I sent my parents a note that I will be heading home tomorrow, but I will be back in a few days. Let me take care of you at least until you are mobile again."

"I would like that Miss Post. My mother wants to send that nurse who helped me in Montreal to be at my bedside. I already told her no. I was going to hire someone locally, but I must admit I enjoy your company."

"Malcom, what about security? I mean, I look at every man on the street and wonder if he was sent by Maples."

"Danielle, I think it is over, at least for us. The man who tracked down the fugitive briefed me this afternoon. He thinks these two men were long term associates of Maples. When they recovered the body of the second man they found two traveling bags in the boat. The clothes fit men the size of the two in the hotel yesterday. They also found a note about a safe deposit box for a bank, and old railroad tickets from some place called Berlin New Hampshire to Washington D.C. There were also notes with both of our names and descriptions along with a newspaper announcing the hearings. He thinks that they were old South Africa hands based on the weapons they carried. Both had British army serial numbers."

"Perhaps, dear Malcom, but what if they are wrong?"

"The Pinkertons told me that Guilda had changed their mission. Two men are already on the way to Berlin, and their entire network has been put on alert to find Maples. If they are chasing him, he won't have time to send more trouble our way. As of tomorrow, I asked the Pinkertons to cancel their watch over me. I will ask them to continue to shadow you until you feel safe. And Danny, I am so sorry that this all happened."

Katarina slipped her head around the door frame. "You two aren't going to embarrass me now, are you?"

"Not on your life Mrs. Bolt," answered Malcom. "I have already caused this beautiful young woman too much trouble."

Danielle reached down and kissed the back of Malcom's head. "I will see you in the morning, before I leave."

"That Post reporter is a really nice man," offered Katarina as the two women reached the steps of the Hospital. I promised him an exclusive if he travels to Alaska next spring. He wants to do a series on what is really going on there. I know that Parker and Chad won't mind at all. Will you be willing to participate?"

"Katarina, I don't know for sure that I am going back," answered Danielle.

"I thought that might be your answer. Just do me the favor of telling my brother yourself. And, if you end up here, we will make a name for ourselves in this town."

At noon the next day Katarina saw her brothers and Danielle off for their trip to Boston.

❧

At the same time all the way across the country, Samuel Maples and Drew stepped down from their train in Oakland. Maples flagged a cab and directed him to a small waterfront hotel. "I will send a note to my partner in the city asking him to meet us for lunch at a place not far from the ferry terminal. Let's get checked in and then go find a cold beer and some dinner."

Drew paid the cabbie and started into the lobby where his boss was registering for two rooms.

"Shooters try to disrupt a hearing in the capital, read all about it," sang out a paper boy on the corner.

Drew dropped the two bags and rummaged through his

pocket for a dime. Finding only a quarter he dropped it in the boy's hand. "Keep the change."

He began reading the front-page article until he had the key points down. Walking into the lobby he handed the paper to Maples, pointing out the headline story. "Look at this Mr. Maples, two men killed by Pinkertons in Washington D.C. What do you make of that sir?"

Maples never changed his expression. "Let me read the story. We can discuss it at dinner."

CHAPTER 23

Boston, Massachusetts

THREE BUGGIES WERE waiting when the train from D.C. rolled into Boston. Annalee and her parents were there to pick up her husband while Danielle's mother waited in a hired cab for her daughter. Maria Gritt was the only one waiting on the landing. After her three decades in Boston, she now spoke her Spanish tinted English with a Boston accent. "I will hug my youngest son before he disappears across town."

She wrapped Parker in her arms. "Your bride waits just across the street," she volunteered. "I expect you two for dinner after Mass on Sunday."

Turning to Chad, she extended her hand.

"That's it, mother? Parker gets a huge hug, and I get a handshake?"

"You chose to go directly to Washington without stopping first to see your madre."

"Mother, I was on my way home when Danielle here sent me a telegram informing me of the hearings. I had no choice."

"Of course you did, you could have left Sitka in time for Thanksgiving. Instead, you feast on railroad food by yourself. A mother cannot help but worry."

"It seems to me that I have heard this refrain before," replied Chad, "when I was eight or ten or twelve and you greeted father returning from somewhere or another. Where is Dad?"

"No, 'hello mother how are you?' No kiss, just a question about your father?" joked Maria Gritt.

Chad wrapped his arms around his mother and gave her a huge kiss on the cheek. "I just thought he would be here."

"He is making the rounds. Since the story of the shooting at the press conference hit the papers more than one of the bankers that he had lined up to help with the financing have gotten cold feet. No one wants repayment for their Alaska investment in plomo."

Chad looked confused. "Plomo?"

"You have forgotten your Spanish. Don't you remember the age-old Spanish question. *Plomo u oro?* Lead or gold?"

Turning to Danielle, Maria continued. "I am so pleased that no harm came to you my dear."

"I seem to have had guardian angels Mrs. Gritt. I think you know one of them."

Maria stepped back two steps. "Chadwick, please take off your hat and give your mother a look."

Chad did as requested, bending his head toward his mother. "Miss Post, it has been my experience that it takes much more than a bump on the head to stop a Gritt."

Chad turned to Danielle, his face a bit red. "Dinner and whatever I can get tickets for on Friday?"

"That would be lovely," replied Danielle, "now I must run. The telegram from my mother was twinged with a bit of panic. It's time that I show her that I am all in one piece."

"We will walk you and Parker to your rides." Maria slipped her arm under Chad's and led the group through the station and out to the street on the other side.

As Parker disappeared into the coach with his wife and Danielle was embraced by her mother, Maria turned to Chad. "It would be nice if just one generation of this family didn't have to land in the middle of a fight."

Chad laughed, "no shipwrecks, no revolutionary armies, no Tlingit warriors, what Parker and I face is child's play Madre."

"Perhaps. You must fill me in completely on the way home. Honestly son, I worry that your fight may be far more dangerous. In the past, your grandfather and father at least knew who their enemies were. Now, tonight is Yankee pot roast, but on Sunday mole poblano. Dinner for twelve."

Maria called out to the driver in Spanish and the coach began to roll. "Maybe a bit of my Spanish will come back being around you and the staff," commented Chad.

The Gritt home sat on a sprawling lot with sweeping views of the ocean, only blocks away from the home built by Chad's grandfather of the same name. That home had been divided into two residences after the death of Grandmother Katarina. One side was the winter home of Parker and Annalee, and the other was available for Chad and his sister when they were in Boston. The coach house had also been converted into a spacious cozy home.

The coach stopped at what the family all referred to as the 'old house' and dropped off Chad and his luggage. Chad left the two bags at the curb and shouldered the heavy trunk and headed up the stairs to the front door. An aging Black woman swung the door open. "I surely did miss you Master Chad," said Claire Smith. "Welcome back."

"Let me drop this trunk, Aunt Claire and I will greet you like I feel."

Chad skipped down the stairs and wrapped his arms around the woman and lifted her off the ground. "It's good to see you too. How are the kids?"

"They good. But they be without a mama if you don't take it easy on these old bones."

Minutes later, Chad found himself seated in the kitchen of the coach house with a cup of tea and a huge slice of honey cornbread. "Tell me about Ott and Sally."

"Ott Jr. is now a master on one of your family's new screw ships, mostly on the run to the Caribbean and back. You just missed him. It would be nice if you are going to stay long enough for you to meet his family. He got married just after you left. Like you and his father, he was in no hurry. He and Angalie got themselves a strapping son."

"Sally is still married to that Cajun preacher man down in Louisiana. I hope she be about done with havin' children, I can't keep up with more than the six in that house already," laughed Claire.

"And you, Aunt Claire? How are you? I mean, what projects are you up to now?"

"Master Chad, I am slowing down. I still keep an eye on the old house, and I still teach Sunday school. The only thing new is I finally finished my college degree, after twenty years of trying, and I am on the school board of the colored high school."

Claire's husband Ott died on the same voyage where Chad's father met his mother. Claire, just as Ott before her, became a member of the Gritt family. Her two infant children grew up with the Gritt kids living in the converted coach house. From the moment Claire learned of her husband's death she took control of the family. She started cleaning the offices of the company while she learned to read and write. Within three years she was a clerk, and in ten she oversaw vessel scheduling. Her passion for education rubbed off on her children, who in turn, became role models for the younger Gritt children.

"What time does your mother expect you for pot roast?"

"How did you know it was pot roast?" asked Chad.

"First day back, it is always pot roast. It is a family tradition. Then I bet your mama be fixin' some of her country's comfort food for Sunday supper."

Chad rose and kissed the woman on the cheek. Aunt Claire, I remember so many moments like this when I sat in a kitchen with you and ate your honey cornbread. Hundreds of days when you were helping my grandmother while my parents were away at sea. I pray that my own children will have that experience."

"How you doin' on that Master Chad?"

"I don't know, I thought I did, but today I am not sure."

"Sounds to me like you a man who thinks he needs a wife when he really wants a partner."

Chad smiled. "I am off to take a bath and get myself organized. I'll only be home until a bit after Christmas. Are we on for a New England boiled dinner?"

"I already bought a new dress for that."

Chad walked the short distance to his parents' home, stopping to buy wine on the way. The streets were filled with carts and carriages and people rushing home after work. In the distance the sound of a train whistle overwhelmed the hum of the city and the groan of steam engines on the bay. The bells chiming six o'clock caught up to him as he reached the front door. "Welcome home," offered his father as Chad swung the door shut behind him.

"What's with the cane, Dad?"

"Nothing to worry about. The doc says that I have about

worn out my knees. No more ice skating or rugby for me. I only use the cane when I have been out walking. On a day like this with temperatures in the forties and no rain, I walked downtown."

Chad threw his coat over the top of the clothes tree behind the door and kicked off his shoes. "I brought wine for dinner."

"Thanks, I forgot to pick up any on my way home," replied senior. "Your mother hasn't lost a step in reminding me when I screw up. She's in the kitchen with Lupe the new cook. Join me in my office for a bourbon, after you meet your responsibilities. I'm looking forward to you telling me why we need a million-dollar line of credit."

Fifteen minutes later, Junior and Senior were seated in over-stuffed leather chairs next to a smoldering fire quietly sipped their drinks.

"Southeast Alaska is going to continue a steady growth," started Chad. "But up on the Yukon, next year is going to be crazy and two years after that the folks will look at that year as the calm before the storm."

"Parker and I talked about what was going on across the border. He deposited more than three-hundred thousand dollars into the company accounts in Seattle. He will need another six-hundred thousand just to purchase the inventory he already has orders for. Your sister is still the company president, but since Fess began to move up in Congress, I have been arranging most of the financing. We can handle the six-hundred thousand and another six hundred if needed without any lines of credit."

"We are going to have a lot more competition in the general marine business in the next couple of years. I want to warehouse in Juneau and supply the smaller communities with our weekly runs. That will take more than half of our reserves. I also want to look at an inventory each spring in St. Michael to meet what

Parker believes will be an exploding demand up the Yukon," continued Chad.

"We can handle it, son."

"But we will not be able to deliver it. We need another paddle-wheeler and enough lumber delivered to St. Michael to build tow barges. The heavy machinery that will come with development is going to take more capacity than we have. When we get upriver, we will sell the barges for lumber at a very good profit."

"That much activity is going to draw in a lot more competition," observed his father.

He continued, "up on the Yukon, there are going to be five boats that we know about next year, including our two," he continued. "Commercial is running two and there is one new boat owned by some British and Canadian investors."

"There would have been two more," offered his father. "One Commercial boat and one owned by the Canadians sank on the run to northern Alaska."

"I worry every time we send a ship to St. Michael. That part of the North Pacific is brutal on a regular ship, let alone a flat bottom river boat. We made a good decision to put the new boat together in St. Michael."

"You still haven't discussed your strategy for overcapacity, in a boom there will be more capacity than the market will bear when the rush turns into production," observed senior.

"We make hay for three years, cement our relationships with those who are building lasting companies, just as we have always done. We will pay off the floating stock in two years or less. At the end of the third year, we put part of our fleet on the market. We should be able to triple our original investment selling to groups who think they have missed out on the boom."

"It worked for your grandfather during the California boom. It should work again. I will arrange for drinks with our bankers.

They will want to know just what triggered that attack at the Arlington Hotel. You don't seem worried about a repeat."

Chad's discussion of the attack and its roots was interrupted by Lupe's tap at the door. "Maria sent me to tell you that if that beef roast gets cold you will have to eat it with tortillas," she laughed.

"This cook speaks better English than the last two," commented Junior.

"I insisted on it," replied his father, "I get tired of never hearing my mother tongue around the house."

"I thought Grandmother Katarina spoke Russian first," joked Chad. "But I understand."

❧

The meeting with the four bankers started at four in the afternoon at the Warren Tavern in Charlestown. With the lunch crowd gone and the evening patrons yet to arrive, the men found all the privacy they needed. Each banker represented a different institution, but as was the tradition in Massachusetts for three hundred years, all were close friends who shared the risks and rewards of Boston's well-seasoned business community. The Gritt family with only a hundred years of history were relative newcomers with a good track record.

"Welcome home young man," toasted Mathew Colodas, raising a pint of dark ale. Like your father and grandfather, you appear to be bulletproof."

"Thank you, Mr. Colodas," replied Junior, removing his sea cap, exposing the stitches in his scalp. "I have not forgotten my manners; I am just a bit self-conscious about the wound. Obviously, I am not bulletproof, just hardheaded."

"It's almost the twentieth century young man. Feel free to wear the cap inside if it makes you feel better. Now tell us why we should let this old man next to you talk us into putting up a million dollars. And, just for the record, hardheaded runs in your family."

Chad outlined what was going on in Alaska and the Yukon territory. He was careful to filter out things told to him in confidence, and to delete specific locations and names, citing confidentiality commitments. A deal was struck when the timeline for repayment was shortened to four years and a bonus. All were on board except for the youngest bankers at the table.

Milton Wiseman was in his early fifties, a small man with a round face, graying curly hair and wire rimmed glasses. "Captain Gritt, I am still not comfortable that helping your family does not put all of us at risk. Even if the risk is not directly to us, if something were to happen to you, who is looking out for our money?"

"Mr. Wiseman, the trouble in Washington City was one of revenge after a falling out between some investors. The man responsible was wounded by Miss Danielle Post as he threatened two men she was visiting with. As an act of revenge, he sent two of his associates to kill Miss Post. My brother and I were just in the wrong place at the wrong time. This same renegade has been creating havoc in the territory but since the falling out with his partners he is on the run. And, since the incident in the Arlington Hotel, the Pinkertons are part of the group chasing him. I am not worried, and I am certain you are not in danger."

"Wiseman, a little gun play might be a nice contrast to your life of collecting old books and rare orchids," laughed Colodas. "If you are not convinced, I will take your share."

"No," laughed Milton, "I'm in, but if someone comes looking for trouble over this, I will give him your home address."

⚜

The Bijou Theater had changed hands since Chad or Danielle last found themselves in the front row seats. The new owner had converted the theater to boisterous plays and challenged the old axiom that it 'won't play in Boston' by introducing outrageous and even bawdy vaudeville. Chad picked up Danielle from her parents' home at seven, in order to make the seven-thirty curtain.

The show lasted more than two hours and ended with a chorus of actors poking fun at the president and Congress. At the end of the performance, the owner, Benjamin Franklin Keith, remained on stage after the mandatory curtain call. "Ladies and those of you who think you are gentlemen but really come to see what the girls of our troupe wear beneath those petticoats, we have two distinguished guests in the house."

Chad's head began to swivel to see who Keith was talking about. He grasped Danielle's hand as he spotted a man who might have been the governor in disguise seated in the back of the room.

"In our front row are Miss Danielle Post and Mr. Chad Gritt. A big hand of applause for two traveling Boston citizens who just last week faced death to draw attention to the kind of corruption that keeps those buffoons we send to Washington City in expensive suits and with call girls. Stand up, you two, and let us salute you."

Moments later, the couple who had not moved a muscle were dragged to their feet by the patrons on either side of them.

An embarrassed Chad and Danielle turned to face the crowd who cheered wildly.

"Perhaps you could arrange to stop by the office before you return to the Alaska Territory. I would love to have you meet with a couple of our staff writers. Your story would make a great plot for a play. Anyway, thanks for reminding us that citizens can make a difference," continued Keith.

After leaving the theater the couple sought out some privacy by losing themselves in the roar that was the Green Dragon Tavern. "Maybe this is the same table that Paul Revere and the Sons of Liberty used to plot the American Revolution," said Danielle. "I keep looking around to see if we're being watched."

"Don't let it bother you, Danny," said Chad. "We intentionally set up the press to give our story some momentum so we can't complain that it did."

A bottle of very expensive champagne in a silver ice bucket arrived at the table only minutes after their seating, long before they expected to attract a waiter in the crowded room. "I didn't order this," said Chad looking up at the waiter.

"Compliments of the house. It's been about a century since the Green Dragon hosted conspirators putting their lives on the line to right the wrongs of tyranny. Just like a century ago, you may imbibe and plot in private, no one here will utter your names," laughed the waiter.

For two hours the couple sipped champagne and snacked on chowder and bread. The second bottle of champagne arrived with a note.

When you return from the frozen north the next time, please let us know you are coming, and we will arrange a more private table.

"That brings up a subject that we need to discuss," started Chad. "I intend to catch the train the Monday after Christmas for California. That's only about three weeks from today. We talked about you going with me so that we could take on the town. Are you still up for it, Danny?"

"I am not sure yet. Next Monday I'm going back down to Washington to follow up on Malcom Crier's recovery. I expect that I won't be back until just before Christmas. We can talk about it then."

Chad rubbed the top of his head gently. "I am wounded too."

"Please don't make this more difficult," pleaded Danielle. "You know that I owe Malcom my life twice over. The least I can do is to make sure that he is back on his feet."

Chad sipped his wine, staring across the room. "Danny, tell me the truth. Are you coming back to Juneau next spring?"

Danielle paused. "I still don't know. I can give you a dozen reasons not to, and only one that pulls me north. I promise to sort it out. That's all I can commit to right now," replied Danielle, tears in the corners of her eyes.

Chad took a deep breath. "You don't know just how much I understand. Now let's get out of here. I propose we meet with Mr. Keith at the theater before I head back. It might be fun to help him with this play idea." Chad kissed her cheek. "You taste like Sitka Sound," he said, rising.

As they made their way to the door, a tall man with red hair saluted them from behind the bar.

Making up the Sunday dinner party were Annalee Parker and her parents, along with Katarina and Fess, just home for the congressional recess. Claire Ott, Chad, and the Parish Priest also came. At the last minute, Danielle had decided to spend the day with her parents.

Maria Gritt and Lupe spent days preparing the meal that was the official state meal of Maria's home state in Mexico. Usually, mole poblano was prepared only on major holidays, but in a family who made their living at sea, any day that all three children were at home was a holiday for Maria.

Claire smiled at Chad and patted the empty chair between them. "You smile Master Chad; the Lord knows what is good for His children."

For Chad, the next week was a blur. The bank loans were

finalized, and Chad took advantage of his father's experience to define the expansion needed and a manpower plan to make it all possible. He was pleasantly surprised to receive a telegram from Danielle advising that she would be back in Boston in a couple of days and asking him to set up a meeting with Ben Keith at the theater.

Danielle also sent a telegram to the dean of her old law school, offering a short student assembly on the law in a remote territory. "Miss Post here is one of our most inspirational graduates. As you can all see, she's faced more than one obstacle and prejudice in her field of study."

The meeting with Ben Keith turned into a very enjoyable waste of time as the theater owner and his writers had already concocted a short play from the headlines. The content would be hilarious, but probably not helpful to the cause of political overhaul in Alaska. "You may assume that we are taking some artistic license with the story," laughed Keith. "If we don't sell tickets, the story will not have any legs. Could I use your names on the flyers and advertising banners? You know, saying that you found the story amusing and worthwhile?"

Chad and Danielle accepted complimentary front row seat tickets for another new play opening the day after Christmas. This one harpooned the push by American Planters to overthrow the Hawaiian monarchy, in the name of saving the Hawaiian people. They enjoyed diner at a tiny waterfront restaurant where they specialized in lobster. Both Chad and Danielle carefully avoided any serious conversation, which made it a wonderful experience.

Chad's date the following day was with an older woman who had picked another historical site for their evening. Claire Ott's favorite restaurant was the Union Oyster House. No one made a better New England boiled dinner of fresh seafood and vegetables. The huge pot arrived at the table with a giant slotted ladle and large bowls.

"Can you imagine, Master Chad," started Claire, "corn on the cob in December? I am loving this."

Chad had not been very talkative, even on the carriage ride. "Probably imported from Cuba on one of our ships," was all he said.

"You thinkin' about a nice young lady?" asked Claire.

"Actually, I was thinking about two different young ladies. As different as can be."

"You eat now, young man. All that is botherin' that head of yours will sort itself out real soon. Pass the bread now."

"And how would you know that Aunt Claire?" asked Chad.

"Chad, it's not much different than when Ott Junior was where you are now. First, it's all the young ladies, then it's just two. There comes a time when a traveling man finally realizes that it would be nice to have a real place with your own folk to come home to. Ott Senior figured that out, and I was the one chosen, and by God, I was happy, and we were happy. It was way too short, but every day I think of him. He will never get old like me; he will always be that handsome well-educated man who sailed away with your father in 1866. It will sort itself out because you will figure out what makes you happy. On the other side, you better believe that the young ladies are also trying to figure out what will make them happy."

Telegrams flew between Gritt Rus Am offices and others who might play into the strategies being fleshed out in Boston. The decision was made to transfer the *SS Havana* from the Caribbean run to the Alaska run the following spring. Her heavy bulk design made her the logical choice for a route where more money could be made hauling equipment and supplies than passengers.

The next day, Claire sent a dozen telegrams to maritime

lobbyists that she knew from Washington looking for a replacement ship for the Boston-Caribbean sugar and rum run. The industry had gone on a building spree the previous decade and many companies run by investment bankers found they had more capacity than they could afford.

The second set of telegrams sent—the ones looking for a third riverboat—was met with more than a hundred offers to sell. That industry was suffering even more. First was a drought, which left many routes without enough water to float a boat, or worse, left boats vulnerable to logs and rocks that holed the hulls. Second was a huge building boom that left the industry with a third more boats than could profitably operate. And worst of all was new competition from the railroads.

Parker and Katarina had spent hours developing a specification for what might be an ideal boat for the Yukon. None of the boats offered to fit the bill perfectly, and worse, none of them could be easily disassembled for transport on a steam ship across the North Pacific.

Chad Senior sat in his office on Christmas eve, with his three children. "One more hour of business talk before I drag all of you off to Mass," ordered Maria as she passed by the door. "It is a most sacred holiday, and this family will not spend it talking about business."

"Send a telegram to your Uncle Carl in New Orleans," suggested Senior. "No one knows more about the river and the boats than Carl. Tell him what you need and offer to send him and Susan to Seattle, to see to the loading. Susan will drive my brother crazy to find just what we want, just to spend a month with her son and the family. Just don't tell Travis or he may move north."

At the Gritt household, Christmas blended Mexican and German traditions. The family attended both evening and morning mass, while the scent of fresh Mexican pastries filled the air. The German-style tree glowed with yellow and orange and red ornaments. Outside, a full-sized manger scene from Mexico drew hundreds of Bostonians, with the women serving spiced wine and cider to the crowd.

After the presents were opened, and breakfast finished, the women retired to the kitchen to clean up while the men loaded baskets of gifts into two carriages. A half hour later, accompanied by the parish priest the presents were delivered to the children at the Catholic orphanage, along with a bank draft large enough to operate the facility for a month.

After Annalee and Parker departed to spend the evening with her parents, the rest of the family finally took a moment to relax. Chad took a cup of tea out onto the porch to watch the families filing by the front gate. When he hadn't returned in a half-hour, his mother, wrapped in a wool shawl, followed him.

"You seem a bit lost this evening," she said.

"No Mother, not lost, I'm thinking of how different Christmas was last year, you know, in Sitka. We had fresh snow and most of the town gathered in the community hall. Even the Russian Orthodox people joined us for carols and dinner, even though they don't celebrate Christmas until January. Danny was there, and we talked about missing our families. It is much more rugged and crude, but tonight, I miss that as well."

"Chad, your father and I only spent two holiday seasons in Alaska. Your father would have spent the rest of his life there, but I simply could not. It's alright, I mean to have both."

After the play the following night, Chad and Danielle adjourned back to the Green Dragon, which, unlike their last visit, was less than half full. This time, no one seemed to notice them, which was a blessing. They ordered a pitcher of ale and a meal of fish and chips and sat quietly, staring at one another. Finally, Danielle broke the silence.

"I am going back to Washington with Fess and Katarina when they return from Europe. I want to continue to push for some action in Alaska."

Chad smiled.

"I still haven't decided whether I will be traveling back with Parker and Annalee in March," she continued. "I may be growing weary of all of this civilization by then, but maybe not."

"I will miss you if you decide to stay here, but this has become a wonderful place to visit for me, not my home," answered Chad.

"I know. I will wire you as soon as I know what I am going to do. You know that I love you?"

Chad leaned across the table and kissed her but said nothing.

❧

"I hear that you and Fess are off to Europe, sis," laughed Chad the next morning. "Must be great to travel on Uncle Sam on those congressional junkets."

"Actually, we are going at the invitation of Grandma Katarina's little brother. He invited Fess to discuss the troubles brewing in Russia, especially in St. Petersburg. He is now the commercial attaché at the embassy in Washington. He was called home just before the holidays for consultations. He thinks the Gerhardt estate is in jeopardy, and I know he's worried about his children. There's a backlash against the monarchy that seems to be growing."

"You know, sis, you and Mother keep harping at me about starting a family. If Grandma Katarina's father could marry a young wife and start a new family after she married our grandfather, it probably isn't too late for me quite yet."

"Chad, you might want to actually catch one of the women

in your life while you can still run fast enough to catch her," said his sister, laughing uncontrollably. Two days later, Chad found himself on the train to New Orleans for meetings.

CHAPTER 24

Oakland, California

THE OAKLAND WATERFRONT was a bit seedier than that on the other side of San Francisco Bay. The town took pride in its working-man roots, relishing its difference from the suit and tie crowd only five miles away.

"Drew, find yourself a seat at the bar where you can keep an eye on our table," directed Maples. "The partners in the Alaska Investors Group are all very private men, but also men who would not hesitate to settle a disagreement with a pistol. Its best if you do not know much about them. We wouldn't want one of them deciding you were a loose string."

Maples carried a gin and tonic from the bar to a table. The J.M. Heinold's Saloon had been new the first time he had visited. The owner had slowly improved the furnishings, salvaged mostly from broken ships. What had started as a seaman's saloon had now taken on some polish, but not much. Maples had operated out of the saloon for the last two years.

The small saloon was only half full on that Thursday evening.

The owner Johnny Heinold sauntered over from the elevated stool where he kept an eye on the floor. "I thought that was you Mr. Maples, welcome back. You expect company for dinner?"

Maples stood and extended his hand. "Johnny it's nice to be back. But do me a favor. The name is Mapolonias, you know, Greek. I haven't had the courage to correct you. I didn't want to insult you after the tremendous service that you and your help provide."

"I am damn sorry about the mix-up Mr. Mapolonias. What happened to your arm?"

"Johnny, I may need that storage room again. I would be happy to give you a couple of months' rent in advance. It worked well as an office last visit. As to the arm, it got crushed in an accident."

"Sorry, I would be damned happy to make whatever arrangements you may need."

"You know Johnny, my close friends just call me Mule. I would like to count you among them."

"Mule huh? That somehow fits. Well Mule, I am a bit short-handed tonight. If it is all right with you, I have a young kid who comes here to study. I am trying him out helping with the tables. Normally he just busses for me. He's not the type of person that anyone asking questions would ever pay any attention to."

Maples looked over at the bar where a rough looking kid in a white apron stood watching his boss. He waved the kid over.

"Jack, this is Mr. Mapolonias, one of our regulars when he is in town. You take real good care of him, and he is always worth a good tip. Now remember, you only work on Tuesday and Thursday nights, and I get to see your grades at the end of the term. If you don't keep them up, I will have to let you go."

Johnny winked at Maples as he turned away.

"You got a last name, Jack?"

"London Mr. Mapolonias, the name's Jack London. You must travel a lot, sir, Mr. Heinold says you're a regular, but I've never seen you in here before."

"I do kid, I used to travel a lot in South America, but for the last three years I have spent my summers in the Alaska Territory."

"Wow, what's that really like? I mean, is it all Esquimax and igloos and snow like they say?"

"Not all of it, but it can be cold. The men up there are tough, and they work hard. The land is so vast that you couldn't walk around it in a lifetime," answered Maples.

"Do you like it, sir?"

"I do, maybe someday you can go take a look yourself."

"I would like that, I think. I've never been out of Oakland. What exactly do you do up there Mr. Mapolonias?"

"You shouldn't ask so many questions, kid. There are a lot of men on the waterfront who have stories that they consider private."

"I'm sorry, sir. Can I get you anything?"

"Just bring me another gin and tonic and keep an eye out for a man about my size and age with an eye patch. When you see him, send him over."

"Will do, sir. Maybe if you're going to be here a while, you can tell me some more about Alaska."

Maples didn't answer, he simply picked up the small traveling case he had placed next to his chair and began fumbling for a folder.

Five minutes later, Jack was back with Maples' gin and Alfred Marathon who was dressed in canvas pants and a green work shirt.

"Alfred," started Maples, "you look like anything except for a successful banker."

"Samuel, after that mix-up in Washington City, I thought it prudent to disappear in the crowd when I am around you."

"You know about that, do you?" asked Maples.

"The papers listed their names a couple of days ago. Both Hans and Dirk gone. I thought those two were invincible."

"For the record," Maples flexed his shortened right arm, "they were just trying to clean up a mess that I got myself into."

Marathon smiled, "Too bad about the arm, that's a pisser. Couldn't think of two men who I would have rather had cleaning up that kind of mess for me. Looks like the mess is still out there. You getting careless in your old age, Major?"

Like Maples, Alfred Marathon had been a soldier in the British army. Unlike Maples, Alfred had not been English. He was born in New Jersey where his wealthy parents had shuttled him from one private school to another as he spread a trail of trouble. After graduating next to last in his class at Princeton, his parents sent him to Europe, some say to avoid questions about how a student who never went to class managed to get his degree.

In England he fell in with a group of well-off friends and the stipend that his father sent every three months allowed him to live a fun but unrewarding life. One day three of those friends walked into the pub where they met every night and announced that they were joining the army to go kill counterfeit Nederlanders in South Africa. Those friends had pulled some strings to secure a temporary commission as a lieutenant for their American friend and the four set out on their latest lark. Five months later, the three friends were all dead and Alfred was becoming a bitter and brutal warrior.

He had served for three years, the last two under Maples. After the war, he worked with Maples in the diamond industry. It had been Marathon who had first met Sir Rodney Crier and introduced him to Maples. After his parents were lost at sea, and he had inherited one-third of their estate, he partnered with Crier to establish the Marathon Bank in San Francisco as a vehicle for financing projects in the Americas. Marathon, Maples, and Crier formed the Alaska Investors Group partially with funding from Abraham Guildham. The last partner added was Miguel Coronzo, the embittered son of a Mexican family who had lost almost everything in the most recent Mexican revolution. Miguel had been recruited by Maples years before to ensure his directives were carried out in South America, no matter what they were.

Marathon waved to the kid at the bar.

"May I bring you a drink?" asked Jack.

"Make it a tall scotch neat, and a beer chaser," replied Marathon, "and some menus."

Marathon scowled at Maples. "That one of yours at the bar, the big one who looks like a prize fighter?"

Maples nodded his head. "You referred him to me through your assistant. Don't you remember or are you getting old?"

"And that kid, what his story?" continued Marathon. "Johnny scraping the bottom of the barrel? I am not too sure that I trust a kid to keep his mouth shut."

"Leave the kid alone. He's just fine. Asks a lot of questions, but only about the country of Alaska."

"Let's get down to business then, Samuel, what do we do about the death of Sir Rodney? And just as important, how much trouble are you in up north?"

Maples saw no reason to hold back anything from his best ally, at least the best remaining after Sir Rodney's death. He outlined the problems including the need to leave two of their own in holes in Alaska. He was even candid about the warrant issued by the magistrate in Juneau and his meeting with the Criers including turning his back on Danielle Post.

After he wrapped up, the two men waved the young Jack London over and ordered dinner and more drinks.

"Samuel, there is another problem brewing," snarled Marathon as he drained the last of his beer chaser. "When we agreed to take in Abraham Guildham as a partner in the Alaska Investors Group, it was because Sir Rodney saw it as a vehicle to leverage his son Richard into becoming one of our partners. We never discussed our methods with him. He is old school, insisted on meeting even Miguel. Last summer you toured Alaska with him and his wife."

"No debate there Alfred," replied Maples.

"Did you know that Guilda hired the Pinkertons to protect her sister's husband and her nephew?"

"I never even thought about who had hired them. I assumed that it was that Danielle Post or her friends the Gritts."

"It wasn't them," continued Marathon, "Abraham himself wired me and told me that after the dustup in Montreal, Guilda had demanded that Abraham sever his connections with you and protect the family. I was contacted by the local Pinkertons while you were still on the train. There is a five-thousand dollar reward out for your capture."

"Damn, that is going to be a lot more difficult to deal with than one troublesome woman in Boston."

"It is, and it is going to make wrapping this all up in a neat bundle much more difficult," added Marathon.

"What do you mean wrapping this all up?" asked Maples.

"That's why you are here isn't it? That's why you're using a different name with everyone you meet. You know that it's time for you to cash out and retire somewhere that they won't follow you, before you end up like Hans and Dirk."

"You are correct, of course Alfred. What has Guildham asked you to do?"

"Samuel, you did go a bit over the edge when you tried to shoot the young lady in the Crier home in Montreal, and after shooting Guilda's nephew you then threatened to finish the job."

"Alfred, you weren't there. Richard Crier had been listening to that bitch from Alaska. He tried to buy me out for ten thousand pounds. That's less than five percent of what my share is worth."

"Samuel, we have had each other's back for years, and I have yours now, but we need to do what you came here to do. We have to collect what we can and get you out. I don't think Abraham is looking for blood, but his wife is. I think he will be satisfied if your name never comes up again."

"Why don't you just buy me out Alfred?"

Young Jack arrived with new drinks and the news that their meals would be out shortly.

"What will you take for your share?" asked Marathon.

"You and Sir Rodney own sixty percent. My piece is surely worth at least a million dollars, but I will take a half million. I have another hundred thousand in personal loans out there. You know, like the loans to the Wilson brothers in Alaska. I can live very well in Argentina on five or six hundred thousand."

"Samuel, I don't have a half million."

"Don't give me that, Alfred, you are worth three or four times that plus your share of the partnership."

Marathon smiled. "Samuel, money doesn't work that way. What I have is either invested or is out on loans through the bank."

"Borrow it then."

The smile on Marathon's face became a laugh. "Samuel, do you know how long my bank will last if word gets out that I am personally out trying to borrow a half million dollars. The run on the bank would wipe it out before the end of the month. Beyond that, I can guarantee that your balance in my own bank is many times what my own is. You are not destitute. You have time."

Maples watched as two hard faced men took seats on either end of the bar from Drew.

"Alfred, I see that you brought a couple of yours as well, so let's not let this get out of hand."

"Agreed, my old friend. I am working on a plan to have one of my bank clients look at buying out your share. It is going to take some time. He has the money, but he works really slow. He may even want to tour Alaska this spring before he writes a big check."

"And in the interim, what do you expect me to do, sit in a hotel room?" snapped Maples.

Young Jack arrived with one platter. "Be back in a minute with the other one."

The two men each took a break to start their dinners. Maples noticed that Drew was also starting to carve away at a big steak, but he also noticed him carefully sweeping his gaze between the two men at the ends of the bar. *Good for him,* thought Maples.

"No, my old friend, I think that with forty people in the San Francisco office of the Pinkertons, sitting around anywhere in the area would be bad for somebody's health, theirs or yours. Take a week or two, I can send them on a couple of wild goose chases without ruining my credibility. I'll have Miguel track you down here. Arrange to go down to South America for a couple of months and close out your accounts down there. Take a look at the operation in Columbia and see if taking full control of that might be a fair trade off for your other equity."

"Alfred, my specialty is acquisitions not operations. I'll take a look, but I think I would rather have the cash, still the short trip to South America to let things cool down is a good idea."

Maples waved at the waiter and ordered one more round. When young Jack arrived with the drinks, Maples stopped him. "Jack, often things are not way they seem or people not what they appear, still that can sometimes work to your advantage."

Jack looked at him with a confused expression.

"My friend Al here works in a big building across the bay, and we are working on a couple of business ventures in Alaska. If word were to leak out that we are working on these projects, someone might try to cut in front of us. We will need to have someone deliver packages back and forth over the next few days, somebody who would like to hear more about Alaska and who can keep their mouth shut. It will pay five dollars a day plus ferry expenses, and it can be done before or after school. Are you interested?"

"Sure Mr. Malponias, I am your man."

When Jack had moved away, Marathon leaned across the table. "Samuel, I have moved your yacht up to Monterey Bay and am having her repainted white. I have also renamed her."

"What the hell is that all about?" asked Maples.

"The Guildhams know her well, and the Pinkertons may be looking for her. They also may be watching the border crossings. The *Retirement* might be a good way to get across the border. In the interim, let me know what you need to plan your trip."

Marathon rose and instinctively extended his right hand, which Maples awkwardly grasped with his left. "Samuel, I have found my out, I intend to remain here as a respected banker. You look like a gentleman hacienda owner if I have ever seen one. I ask you, friend to friend, don't sink us both."

As Marathon headed for the door, the two minders dropped a few coins on the table and followed. Drew picked up his unfinished steak and his drink and carried over to where his boss sat trying to write some notes with his left hand. Maples was chewing so hard on his lower lip that Drew could see drops of blood.

"I take it that the conversation didn't go very well, Mr. Maples."

"Drew, while we are here, I am going by the name of Mapolonias. That just got more important. My friend tells me that the Pinkertons are looking for me."

"I don't like the sound of that. Those folks are relentless, and they work smart. I know."

"Tell me what you know."

"Mr. Maples, they were the folks that figured out that I had taken a bribe to let a railroad bandit operate out of my town. I walked away from the office, and they agreed to lock up their file somewhere."

"Does this change our arrangement then?" asked Maples.

"Nope, so far, I ain't done anything to point them at me and you haven't asked me to. In fact, I probably owe them a little payback, but I am not looking for it."

"Alright then, here is the plan. We will meet with another of my old partners in the next couple of days. Johnny is renting me the storage shack out back to use as an office. We will be sending information back and forth to the man who just left. He is helping me put together the information to go collect about $50,000 that I am owed in South America. That will get us out of this area for a couple of months until the active search blows over."

"Mr. Maples, I thought we was headed for the Alaska Territory. I was looking forward to seeing that country."

"We will be going north, but not until late spring. We will wait for breakup."

"Breakup what," asked Drew?

"When the ice goes out. We will go to Southeast Alaska first, then make a short trip up the Stikine River to the Cassiar gold fields. I have a partner there who owes me. Then I will need to visit two partners in the southern Alaska territory who should be good for ten thousand each. By late May, we will be at the mouth of the Yukon where I have a steam launch stored. I want to beat the first steamboat up that river to collect from two more old associates."

"Mr. Maples…I mean, Mr. Mapolonias, that's a lot of travel, and those Pinkerton folks are really good about watching ship and railway stations."

"Drew, have you ever traveled by private yacht?"

A huge smile appeared on the big man's face. He shook his head, no.

"You will like it. We'll head south within a couple of weeks and then later use the same transport north."

"What do you want me to do for now, Mr. Mapolonias? You want me to be the go-between for you and the man who just left?"

"No, Drew, I'm going to use that kid at the bar as a courier. Tomorrow, while I am here, I need you to go find out where Bay Couriers buys their hats and jackets and buy one of each that will fit that kid. Oh, and find one of those bags that the couriers wear on their back."

"I can do that tomorrow. What's next?"

"Drew, I may need a bit more muscle in the spring, but I'm not sure. Just check around and see who might be available."

The next day young Jack tapped on the open door to the storage room behind the saloon. Maples had placed an old door over the top of two beer kegs as a desk. He sat leaning in an old ship's chair that he had borrowed from the saloon, a new black Stetson pulled down over his eyes and new cowboy boots propped up on the desk.

"You look real different, Mr. Mapolonias."

"My friend last night said that I would make a good rancher, so I thought I might try out the look."

"I never heard of a cowboy with an English accent before," said Jack.

"Good observation kid, I'll have to work on that. Let's start with a new moniker."

"I don't know what that is."

"A new name. From now on just call me Mule. That sounds like a smashing rancher name. Now, are you ready to go to work?"

"Sure am."

Maples handed Jack a large leather bag. "See how that fits on your back, you may have to adjust the buckles."

Jack fumbled with the straps for a few minutes before he got them right.

"Now inside the bag is a hat and a coat, the same as the Bay Couriers use. Try them on.

A moment later Jack stood in a slightly oversized coat and a round cap with a chin strap holding it in place.

"I don't get it, Mule; I don't work for those couriers."

"Remember last night I said that some other businessmen were watching that other fellow and me? Well, they won't think a thing when you walk into a bank in that outfit. Just don't wear it here on the Oakland side. Find a place to put it on while you are on the ferry or in the terminal on the San Francisco side, then change back when you return. That should throw off anyone who is watching."

"What if someone does come up to me, Mule?"

"You run like hell, boy. But I doubt that will happen. That's why we are being so careful."

"I understand, sir. This would make a great story like in one of those dime novels."

"That it would. Now inside the bag is a large paper envelope that has been sealed with wax and a special stamp. The man on the other side, Mr. Alfred, will have an identical stamp for any envelope he gives you. It assures that either of us can tell if the envelope has been opened. You take this to the Marathon Bank and give it to the security guard who sits next to the elevator, then you wait for him to come back. He will give you a sealed envelope. Put it in the pack and bring it straight back to me. If you make the three o'clock ferry, you should be back on the four o'clock sailing from the other side."

Jack took the hat and coat and carefully folded it and placed it back in the bag. "Uh, Mule, you wouldn't happen to have the address of that bank?"

Maples reached into his case and pulled out an envelope. He tore the return address off and handed it to Jack. "Move it, kid. If Johnny doesn't see you doing your homework by five, he'll skin us both."

Jack arrived back at the storage shed at four-forty, out of breath. A tall man with black hair sat across the makeshift desk from Maples. "Just leave the whole bag with me, Jack." He flipped a ten-dollar gold piece to the courier. "This pays for today and your expenses for the next trip. Just check in tomorrow at about the same time."

After the kid disappeared into the back door of Heinold's Saloon, Maples continued the conversation he was having with Miguel Coronzo.

"Miguel, we will be collecting some old debts that our contacts in Columbia, Bolivia and Peru still owe me. You should probably go along to assure them that the South America Investors Group is not going out of business, and they will be expected to do what they are told. Still a couple of them may object to paying off large loans with no notice, so we will need three or four tough hands to make their choice clear."

"Major," replied Coronzo, "you and I can probably handle it."

"No Miguel, I want no trouble, and it has been my experience that sending a crystal clear message avoids trouble. You have anyone in mind?"

"We will recruit locally. For the right price, I can get anyone. For five hundred in gold, I can get a whole company of army, including their commander," he laughed.

"That won't be necessary. I was thinking more like a couple of men for fifty apiece."

"No problemo mi Captain. Alfred said we were taking your boat. Maybe we can do some fishing on the way down and maybe a stop or two. I know three or four places where we can stop with no questions, places where beautiful company comes with the room."

"I guess we are in no big hurry. We don't need to be back until March. It will just be the crew, and three of us. I am traveling with a defrocked sheriff, a good man, you will like him."

"I noticed that Pickering isn't around," offered Miguel. "What happened to him?"

"Pickering got himself into a place where he was expendable. I assure you that it was quick and painless."

Coronzo dropped the line of questioning, knowing exactly how such decisions were made.

"When do we leave?"

Maples closed the folder in front of him and stood up. "Have your kit on the dock at seven in the morning ten days from now. I will buy you a tequila at Johnny's, but I recommend somewhere else for dinner."

The two men walked past young Jack sitting at a table by the door. His nose never left the text in front of him. Maples waved at Drew sipping a beer at the bar.

"Miguel, this is Drew, you two should get to know each other since you are going to be traveling together for at least a couple of months."

Jack made four trips across the bay over the next seven days. Arriving after the last trip he found Maples again sitting with the black Stetson tipped over his eyes and his boots up.

"Here's the bag, Mule," he called out.

"Thanks kid, you have done great work. I'll be gone for a couple of months, and when I get back, I may need your services again."

Maples pulled the jacket and the box hat from the pack and hid them on a board that he had tacked up in the rafters in the ceiling. "We will leave those here until I get back. You can keep the bag to use at school." Maples took a twenty-dollar gold piece from his leather vest and flipped it across the room. "You never met me, or Mr. Alfred and you have never been in the Marathon Bank. Got it?"

"Yes sir, Mule. You can count on me and when you get back, I'll be the one studying at the table next to the door. Thanks, and have a fine trip, sir."

CHAPTER 25

Louisiana And California

CHAD SPENT THE next two months visiting family in the south. His uncle Carl had married the widow of a Confederate officer after the Civil War and was now master of the Reece Plantation estimated at ten square miles. During the war, Carl had been a Union naval officer patrolling the Mississippi River. He'd maintained friendships with rivermen from New Orleans to Indiana. The purpose of the trip was to find a third steamboat suitable for the Yukon River, but much of the trip was spent just catching up with family and doing some quail hunting.

The riverboat business had never recovered from the over-expansion during the war. Every major city had boats for sale, but moving a boat from the Mississippi to Alaska, around the tip of South America seemed a suicide mission. Chad's uncle, Travis Gritts's father, proved to be the perfect contact. Within weeks, Gritt Russ Am Company was the owner of a brand-new boat, ordered by one of Carl Gritt's old friends, a boat the new owners could not afford to finish. The thing that made the boat perfect for the Yukon route was that it had never been assembled.

Within weeks Chad was on his way back to California. The boat would be shipped by rail to Seattle as soon as the shipyard could finish crating it. Carl remained in Indiana to supervise the shipment, after which he and his wife would accompany it across the country.

❧

When Chad finally arrived at the station in San Francisco his cousin Travis and Camile were there to meet him.

"How are my folks?" asked Travis. "Did my mother and my sister talk your ear off?"

Chad tugged first on his left ear, then his right. "Nope, they are still where they were before I arrived at Reece Plantation. Besides I spent most of my time with your dad. We ran up to Indiana to buy a new boat for the Yukon. We had a great time. I wish my father's health was a good as yours."

"The farm keeps him outside and active," replied Travis.

"That, and quail hunting, I could learn to love that."

"You met Tobias then. That is the most self-made man that I have ever known. After the war, after the slaves were freed, I remember him sitting in the back of the courthouse just to listen to how educated men talk. When my father convinced my mother to sell him and his wife the land they built their house on, he was still working ten-hour days on the farm. Yet he managed to build that house in less than six months. He owns a sporting goods shop in the city, right next to the boat terminal, and that's how he gets most of his hunting clients."

Camile tugged on her husband's arm. "Travis, you talk about that uppity old Negro like he was a family friend. I'm hungry."

"My dear, let's get cousin Chad to his hotel and then lunch."

"It just dawned on me that I didn't make any reservations for a room," said Chad."

"Nothing but the best for the family," snapped Camile. "We are at the Palace. We took liberties and made you a reservation there after they squeezed us in. I also made a reservation for Miss Post."

"Danielle is in Washington City. She won't be joining us. I like the Palace, it's just a bit more than we normally spend," replied Chad.

Travis, standing behind his wife gently shook his head.

"You're right of course Camile. The Palace is perfect for our business meetings."

Travis smiled and nodded his head. "We are off to the Palace then. Here let me grab the trunk."

The Palace was aptly named. The front desk was gracious in cancelling the extra room reservation and found Chad a room on the fifth floor overlooking the entrance on Market street. The bellman led Chad to a huge elevator the size of a hotel room in less expensive hotels, and in less than fifteen minutes Chad was back in the lobby where Travis waited.

"My wife still has a bit of the Deep South in her. Her father came over from Italy before the war between the states and married her mother who had moved to New Orleans from Cuba. The restaurant they started made a small fortune before the war and a great fortune during the war catering to Union officers. Camile takes great pride in being part of plantation society. There isn't a month that goes by without her reminding me that the reason she married me was the Reece."

Chad just listened.

"Camile will be down in a few minutes. I asked the concierge for a late lunch spot where Camile can be seen with the elite. I hope you don't mind, but it will keep peace in the family."

"Lead on," replied Chad. Claire's comments about a wife or a partner echoed in his head. "Where are we going then?"

"The place is called the Cliff House. Mayor Sutro just finished it, and it is *the* place to go. My hero medal will get a bit of polish from my wife."

The place was everything that it was represented to be, especially the clientele, which represented the elite of California and travelers from across the West. What it was not was a private place to discuss the Gritt Russ Am business needs for 1897. In fact, the social calendar laid out by Camile made it almost impossible for Travis and Chad to work on anything for business. On the fourth day after Chad's arrival, Travis surprised his wife with rail tickets to her parents' home.

Camile's departure the following morning came with an angry scene at the train station that did not end until Travis agreed to join her later in the month. When he finally connected with Chad for a late breakfast, Travis was calm enough to carry on a realistic conversation.

"I left the Reece Plantation because, like my father and you, I need to make my own life. I fully intend to reinvest in our firm and someday, when the hub of the business moves west, I want to be the Gritt who runs the show. I am never going back to the swamps, and while my wife heard that before we married, I think it's finally sinking in. I guess we both have some decisions to make, and her spending another two weeks with her mother may make it easier. Anyway, I am sorry about wasting your time this past week."

"There are some challenges with operating what is basically a family business. I have my own challenges, but for right now they will take a back seat to what needs to be done this year," replied Chad. "We have about a month's worth of work here, but if we split it up, we can finish in a couple of weeks. First, we need to divide the shopping list."

For the next ten days, Travis concentrated on vendors while Chad met with mining engineers and mine owners trying to anticipate the needs of the Yukon miners over the next three years. The greatest help came from an equipment broker who had been active the previous year, buying up surplus in Idaho and Nevada and reselling it to a group with mines in Latin America. The two men agreed to meet on the Friday before Travis was to leave, to lay out a plan for The Marx Company to supply Gritt Russ Am.

"I want to bring along my banker if it will be alright with you," asked Chapman Marx. "He has some experience with Alaska and the Yukon."

"How about dinner? You buy, since we appear to be the customers," laughed Chad. "The manager of our Seattle office is here, and he will be leaving over the weekend. Count on the drink bill being a bit larger than the dinner tab."

"My kind of business meeting," responded Marx.

Travis and Chad arrived at the University Club a few minutes early and were surprised to be ushered immediately to an almost empty dining room where Marx and another man waited. Chad introduced Travis, and Chappie introduced his friend.

"Gentlemen, this is Alfred Marathon, the president of Marathon Bank. Al, this is Chad Gritt and his cousin Travis Gritt.

Marathon extended his hand.

"Chappie here says you've got experience in Alaska and even in the Canadian gold fields," said Chad. "Could you tell us a bit about that?"

Marathon smiled and reached into his lapel pocket for a long thin cigar. "You know the firm that I helped bankroll gentlemen. And I know a bit about you two as well."

The surprised look on the two men faces was exactly what Marathon had expected, though not altogether welcome. "I am a very junior partner in the Alaska Investors Group."

Travis was confused, but Chad grasped the meaning immediately. "Mr. Marathon, you have a partner who is not on my friends list. In fact, the only lists he appears on belong to law enforcement."

Now it was Chappie Marx's turn to be confused. He turned to Marathon. "Who is he talking about Al?"

"Our investment group includes an old acquaintance who was our northern operations manager. He managed to get himself in trouble with the Marshal Service in Alaska."

"More than that, I think. Your Samuel Maples is also being hunted by the Pinkertons for that dust up before the Alaska hearings in Washington City," said Chad.

"Mr. Gritt, Mr. Maples is no longer part of our group."

"Then are you helping rain in that crook, Mr. Marathon?" asked Travis, finally catching on.

"Our old partner is not wanted for anything in California, so no, I am not playing sheriff. What I can tell you is that Maples has left the country."

The subjects that evening would have made front pages across the country. The Problems with Sontag's North Pacific canneries, presented by Chad, yielded a response identical to that given Danielle by Abe Guildham.

"We will, of course, will look into the problems, Mr. Gritt, but we reserve the right to operate in the most efficient manner allowed by law," offered Marathon.

The problems in the gold fields along the Yukon brought a similar answer. "I am told that there will be some form of investigation next spring, and that will determine if Maples' methods have crossed a legal line. In any event, the Alaska Investors Group will protect our interests in Alaska in the courts and in Congress."

After an excellent dinner, where the tension between Marathon and Chad could be cut with a knife, Travis finally intervened. Turning to Marx, who had also eaten in silence, he changed the subject.

"Mr. Marx, it will be you and I who juggle the actual business dealings between our firms. Our sailing schedule for next year will allow me to communicate with our offices in the ice-free parts of the state on a weekly basis. Up on the Yukon, it will be every two weeks between May and October. Any inventory that you have, can be put into flyers distributed across the territory."

Chappie Marx smiled for the first time that night. "And any orders that come down to your Seattle office can be wired to mine. I will respond immediately, even if it is just to let you know I'm searching for what you need."

Marathon sensed that the time was right for an olive branch. "Mr. Gritt," he addressed Chad, "We are not expanding in Southeast Alaska next year, and our two ships should support all our activity. In the north, however, our plan to operate a riverboat on the Yukon ended with the loss of a boat we sent last summer. Without that boat there is no reason to add a ship for use between San Francisco and St. Michael. We will be looking for a shipping company to support our operations."

"Mr. Marathon," stammered Chad, "I can see how a group can end up with a bad apple from time to time. If your group really is going to operate above the law, we would welcome the business. Travis would be your man. But if you are going to need any volume moved, now would be the time to schedule it. Our season is expected to be very busy."

"When will you start service on the Yukon?" asked Marathon.

"The ice on the upper river usually goes out by the fifth of May, but the lower river ice jams normally don't clear for a couple more weeks. You could probably run a small boat up the river by the twentieth, but we will be operating a week or so after that."

The dinner ended with warm conversation between Chappie and Travis, and silence between the other two participants. A curt handshake sent them on their way.

"Travis," said Chad, "I do not trust that man Marathon."

"Chad, his money will spend like any other man's. I won't take on anything that doesn't pass the smell test."

"Let's walk a ways. I can use the exercise," suggested Chad. "Then a brandy and a cigar at the hotel."

"Maybe two brandies," laughed his cousin.

When the two men finally wandered into the grand carriage entrance and checked at the front desk for messages, neither was surprised to find a note from Chappie Marx offering to buy breakfast the next morning.

"I didn't have any idea that Alfred's group had troubles like we discussed," Marx admitted over a plate of scrambled eggs. "I've got a line of credit with him, but that's all."

"I wasn't accusing Marathon of any specific, Chappie," replied Chad. "But that group he's part of is a pack of wolves taking advantage of weak laws and little enforcement in the territory. It's probably best if his bank isn't part of any transactions between you and us."

"I may need his line of credit to purchase what you need," offered a worried Marx.

"Then, you may need a second banker, one that will look at our orders as collateral. We maintain accounts with Wells Fargo just around the block from the hotel."

"Marathon has made it hard to use anyone but him. I can't move more than ten thousand from my own accounts without paying off my credit line," argued Marx.

"Chappie, we can't run your business, but we may become a big customer. I can tell you that the Alaska Investors Group clubs anyone who opposes them into submission," snapped Chad. "We're going to keep a real close eye on anything we do with them."

Travis drained his coffee mug and waved at the waitress for a refill. "For now, I wouldn't challenge Marathon. Leave your South American business with Marathon Bank. If your business with us grows, you should be able to deal with your debt to Marathon within a year or two."

"I'll scramble to come up with enough to open an account with Wells Fargo," said Marx.

Chad smiled and covered his cup as the waitress started to refill it. "I am not due back in Seattle until March. Let's take a run over to Nevada and look at that load of hydraulic pipe we discussed. We can run it through a new account at the bank and start to build a history between our two firms. If you open the account with a thousand dollars, we should be able to bump that up to five before I leave."

"That would really help," smiled Marx.

A day later, Travis was off to join his wife, and Chad and Chappie were in Nevada.

CHAPTER 26

Oakland, California

Nothing had changed at the waterfront saloon. Drew tugged open the heavy door then followed Maples to his favorite table in the corner.

"Happy to see you again Mule," snapped young Jack London as Samuel Maples took a seat at his regular table. Minutes later, Drew took a chair across from him where he could watch the door. Remembering what the two men drank, Jack closed the textbook in front of him and called a drink order at the bartender.

"This is the first day away from Miguel Coronzo since we got on the boat. I don't miss his company, boss," stated Drew.

"Miguel has his place, but I won't miss him much either," replied Maples, as their drinks arrived.

"That man confuses tough with just plain mean, boss. I never saw a man cut off a woman's ear in front of her husband before. It stinks. That fellow had already agreed to get you the money within a week."

"Drew, my Spanish is lousy, and you don't speak the language. He must have thought Paco wasn't serious."

"That bag Miguel carries should be enough. Who wouldn't take you seriously when you dump a sack of cut-off ears and fingers, even a nose on someone's desk?"

The two men ordered dinner.

"Jack where is Johnny this evening?" asked Maples.

"He tries to take Sunday off, Mule. He works from seven every morning and usually closes the place after midnight. I don't know how he does it, sir."

"Me either, kid," replied Maples. "Anyway, we'll need the storage shed for a week or so, but not until tomorrow.

"You going to need me to run pouches to the bank again, Mr. Mapolonias?"

"Probably, but not tomorrow. Anybody suspicious been in asking questions about us while we were gone?"

"Nope. Just the same crowd as usual," replied Jack.

"That's good to hear kid, that means nobody has picked up on our business deal in Alaska. Just keep your ears open. Hell, they may even hire private detectives to track down this deal, you never know what they may claim, so stay mum Jack."

"For sure Mule. You can count on me."

That same evening Alfred Marathon was having dinner with Miguel Coronzo.

"How was the trip?" asked Marathon. "I am assuming that our partner collected what was due him or you wouldn't be back. I figured you to be gone three months, and your back in ten weeks."

"Samuel hired me to persuade people, and I am really good at it, Mr. Marathon," responded Miguel. "I am glad that I went, Samuel has changed. He doesn't have the same old fire. He's forgotten the difference between asking a subordinate and telling him."

"*Mister* Marathon? You've never called me 'mister' anything, Miguel."

"I guess that has changed too. You are now a big banker and after this trip it's clear that you now run the partnership. Samuel is going north for a few months, and after that I doubt that we will ever see him again."

"Samuel has business in Alaska, the same kind that he had down south. His presence is starting to create problems. I want him to finish what he must do and get out of the country. If anyone tosses him in jail, it could create trouble for all of us."

"Mr. Marathon, he is getting a bit soft, I guarantee that. He is also getting sloppy," said Miguel.

Jack's first trip across the bay occurred two days later, this time accompanied by Drew. In Jack's courier pack was an invitation for Marathon to join Maples at the Heinold's Saloon the following afternoon. In the bag that Drew carried was just over sixty pounds of gold coins, about thirty-thousand dollars' worth of gold. While Jack waited for the return pouch, Drew rented a safe deposit box and placed six canvas bags of coins inside.

Jack was surprised when the man from the saloon, now dressed in a suit, returned with the courier pouch. "Young man," he said to Jack, "would you mind waiting in the lobby while I have a short conversation with your partner here?" Marathon flipped the courier a silver dollar.

Ten minutes later Drew found Jack coming from a shop two doors down, a paper bag of chocolate candy clutched in his hand.

"That man is an interesting man," was all Drew said.

The following afternoon the man from the bank, along with two toughs walked quietly into the saloon. Johnny seated the man at a back table and slipped out the back door to find Maples in the storage shed.

"Alfred, it's nice to be back, even for a short stay."

"Samuel, I saw your man at the bank yesterday. I am assuming that it was the lion's share of your winnings from the south that he put into a deposit box. Smart. You do not want to travel with that much gold."

Maples ordered drinks for the two, then watched as Drew took a stool at the bar.

"That's right. I assume that you and Miguel debriefed. My creditors paid me in full. I think they would have anyway, but Miguel used his skills to insist on it. I think it fair that the partnership pays for his services since I am selling my share for such a grand discount."

"I paid Coronzo the hundred dollars a day that we agreed on. I wanted to talk to you before I reimbursed him for the thousand dollars in expenses that he requested," said Marathon.

"Miguel found five men who traveled with us for just over a month. I paid their expenses and a weekly fee for entertainment. I suspect that Miguel paid them the standard rate for soldiers. A thousand sounds about right for the lot."

"What do you need from me then Samuel? I mean to set up your trip north. It isn't a good idea for you to stay in the bay area any longer than necessary."

Maples licked his finger and began to run it around the lip of the glass in front of him.

"Tell me what's on your mind Alfred."

"I have been visited by the Pinkertons four or five times since you left. I suspect they are staking out the bank and the house, at least occasionally. I also met your old friend Chad Gritt."

The whine from the top of Maples' glass increased as Samuel increased the speed of his finger.

"Samuel, stop that racket, you know it gets under my skin. Sounds like the whine of bagpipes."

Maples picked up the glass and drained it. "And just how did that happen to come about?"

"It turns out that his company is contracting with one of my clients to find mining equipment to ship north. If you ever find yourself in the same room with Chad Gritt, I hope you have mastered shooting with your left hand."

"Don't worry about it, Alfred. Gritt seldom carries a revolver. I suspect I'll be the only one who is armed. What did you tell him?"

Marathon began to work on his beer chaser before answering. "I told him the truth. I said you had left the group and that you were out of the country. I also offered him some shipping business for next summer."

"Smart, ruddy damned smart of you. Keep your friends close and your enemies closer," responded Maples.

"Samuel, Mr. Gritt is not my enemy. He knows that I consider him a competitor, and I know that he sees me tied to you. But he is your enemy not mine. The warrant in Alaska makes your task there dangerous and the screw-up with Hans and Dirk tainted the whole group. You are an old comrade Samuel, and I want you to collect your debts quickly so that I can take my new investor to Alaska. That is the key to buying out your share. But when it gets right down to it, you need to get out of here."

Maples pulled a fat Cuban cigar from his jacket. "I would offer you one, but I know you carry your own."

Maples lit the cigar and rolled it in his fingers. "For twenty years I have done the real dirty work for the group while the rest of you used your winnings to live a fine life. Now it's my turn to fade away, not into society like you and Sir Rodney, but really away where I can try to live my remaining years like the man my mother always wanted."

"Samuel, I thank you for all you have done. I want you to be able to fade away into whatever life you want. But Miguel says you are losing your edge. How much is really on the line up north? Is it five thousand, ten thousand? Is it worth a fight, or worse?"

"Alfred, It is north of twenty thousand dollars. I lost the bag with all my notes when I was wounded. I need for you to send over the copies of those notes that you are holding. I am going to collect it and if by chance I can even the score for my lost arm, that will be a bonus."

"Alright, send your boy for the notes tomorrow. I figure that about twenty percent of what you collect is mine anyway. But get this figured out before Gritt or one of those Pinkertons does. Once you collect what's due, swing by and draw your funds from the bank. I will cash out your account and put the funds in that deposit box your man rented. Go south Samuel, far south. I will wire you your share from the group when I get a deal done."

"Alfred, I should be out of here in a week or so. I will need to recruit some men to help me collect, just like Miguel did."

Marathon waved at the bartender and ordered two more drinks. "Take Miguel with you. Let him supply a couple of men. Hell, you, Miguel and that man of yours at the bar should be enough but let Miguel hire a bit of insurance if you want."

"And who is paying for Miguel?" asked Maples.

"The Alaska Investors Group is good for the first five thousand, any more is on you," answered Alfred. "And Samuel, go easy on Sontag at the cannery. He owes the group way more than he owes you. We need him for this year's salmon pack, and he is already bitching. That Rattler Wilson you set up as his contact won't even talk to him."

"I'll slip into that part of Alaska as quietly as I can and then go north," responded Maples. "I'll see about a replacement for Wilson and for his brother up in Falcon. You got anyone in mind?"

"Not offhand," replied Marathon, "but if I find the right men I will wire you up in Puget Sound country. I assume you are not going to base your trip out of Seattle, with the Gritts and the Pinkertons watching for you there."

"Right again, I will slip into the city for a day or two to close a couple of bank accounts, but I was thinking of Bellingham as a base. I'll wire you when I get there."

"That Gritt fellow offered a bit more intelligence than he knows. He thinks the ice will be out at St. Michael by the twentieth of May, but their first trip won't be for another week. You have an extra week or two to get organized before you head north. Now, what about Miguel?" asked Marathon.

"My man there at the counter doesn't like Miguel very much, Alfred. I think I will look around a bit before I make that commitment," answered Maples.

"Samuel, Miguel has covered your back for years. I would feel better if he was along. He is a known quantity."

"How about I let you know in three days. In the interim get me those files. And, Alfred, do you still have that stack of photographs from Alaska Territory that I sent down a year ago?"

Marathon nodded.

"Send them over with the kid. I want to give them to him for all his help. Don't worry, I will sort them, to make sure there is nothing in them that traces to you or me."

As Marathon rose to leave, the two men at the ends of the bar both converged on Drew who put his hand on the colt in his pocket. Each of the strangers extended their hands in a kind of professional courtesy and whispered something in his ear.

As the men left, Drew picked up a nearly full drink and sauntered over to Maples' table.

"What was that about Drew?" asked the boss.

"Just saying goodbye, Mr. Maples. They said that they probably wouldn't be back."

"You hungry, Drew?" asked Maples.

"I could eat a horse, boss. Could we go back to that Irish pub we went to last time? I could go for a couple of Irish whiskeys and a huge bowl of stew. Anything but meat off a grill or something with chiles."

"I need to talk to you about chillis, Drew. We can talk while we walk. Have you got a couple of men we can really count on for the trip up north, men who won't be tempted by the reward or who will take off at the first whiff of gold?"

"No one comes to mind, but I can check around tomorrow, over in the city," answered Drew.

Seven days later the eighty-foot steam yacht *Retirement* pulled out of Monterey Bay headed north. On board were the captain, an old British coastal patrol officer from the China fleet who had been with Maples for twenty years, and the same three Chinese crewmen who had served their captain since the boat had been purchased. Also on board were Drew and Maples but not Miguel Coronzo. He would be taking the train north when the *Retirement* found a home in Puget Sound waters.

Maples had reluctantly accepted Coronzo when Drew could not find any men he trusted. Coronzo had insisted on bringing two of his countrymen.

✑

The same day that the *Retirement* sailed, Chad Gritt boarded the steamer *Maximilian* for his return to Sitka. After unpacking his kit, he made his way to the bridge, and extended his hand to the ship's skipper, Pat James.

"Just like I was part of the furniture, Pat," offered Chad. "I have nothing to do until we get home, but I'll be damned if I am going to miss out on a few days on the bridge of a ship."

"You have been gone too long, Chad. Let's see if we can get the salt level in your blood back to where it belongs," laughed James.

That evening at dinner, Chad pulled a folded telegram from his pocket and reread it. So, Danielle wasn't coming back to Alaska, at least not to stay. He looked again at the name of the young man who would be traveling from Boston to take over her law practice the third week of June. He didn't recognize the name. Her telegram was short and to the point. She was probably going to stay in the East and pursue the life of her dreams. She could no longer be satisfied watching him chase his dreams. It ended with, *love, Danny.*

After dinner he found himself the only one on the deck, as the ship plowed through a spring snowstorm. The wet snow coated the upwind side of his body in minutes. Brushing himself off, he moved to the opposite side of the ship where he was sheltered from the wind. In the distance he could see the illuminated sweep of a lighthouse through the snow. Danielle's telegram opened two emotions at once. As the ship's purser emerged from the door beside him, Chad wiped the dampness caused by the bitter wind from his eyes.

The ship's arrival in Sitka did little to sweep away Chad's melancholy. It was snowing, huge flakes of wet snow, driven by a twenty-knot wind. The dock crew tackled the freight transfer with the same professionalism that he had drilled into them, and the few arriving and departing passengers spent only a minute or two exposed to the weather. Finally, one of the men pushing a cart of luggage from the ship stopped and extended his hand.

"Welcome back, boss."

"Where is everybody?" asked Chad.

"Hell boss, no one knew you were coming, how would they?"

One of the things that made Sitka different from much of the territory was the mild winters, where the temperature seldom dipped below freezing and never stayed there for long. Still the temperature inside the old Gritt family home was the same as the snowy air outside. Chad struck a match and ignited the fire he had preset before leaving in November. The Russian style fireplace surrounded by inches of cement and tile would take hours to warm the house.

With that fire started, he moved into the kitchen and built a fire in the wood cook stove. The small split sticks would heat the cast iron stove much faster. Finally, he retreated to the bathroom in the back of the old house and built a third fire in the round iron stove that served to heat the water in a large tank on top. Pulling a short ladder from a closet, he climbed to where a hand pump with a short hose attached, sat on a pipe from the floor. He worked up a sweat filling the tank on the stove and then he filled the large tank attached to the wall above the toilet. He knew that with three fires burning, the inside of the house would be cool but bearable by late evening.

He carried his two bags and trunk to his room and began to unpack from four months of travel. He hung his suits in a small cedar-lined closet in the room and picked up the round of sailor bread that sat in the bottom of the closet to draw away the moisture from the damp air. He replaced the hard tack with a new piece from a metal container that he had carried from the kitchen.

Moving to the living room, he opened a large crate and began stacking the two dozen books from his travels on the shelves that ringed the room. Two hours later after a hot bath and a change of clothes he pulled his heavy plaid hunting coat over his shirt and headed for Kuzenofs for a hot dinner.

By the time his meal was served, word of his arrival had leaked out and the restaurant filled with old friends anxious to hear about his trip, especially about the problems in the nation's capital. Within a couple of hours, he had run out of stories and news. He had just paid his bill when Governor Karp bolted through the door.

"I just heard you were back," said Karp, "I just wanted to invite you to breakfast tomorrow at the house. You can fill me in on your trip and I'll update you on what little news I have."

"That sounds like the best offer I have received since I got back Lyman. Now if you'll excuse me, I am going home to pull the quilt off my bed and roll up in front of the fireplace. I'd sleep in my bed, but it will take until tomorrow to warm up the bedroom."

The following morning, Chad was up well before the dim light from the overcast day slowly crept into the room. He made a pot of coffee, shaved, dressed, and was in the company offices long before anyone else arrived. By the time he left for his nine o'clock breakfast with the governor he was satisfied that everything was running well. He noticed that the *Miles Pierce* was away, and a quick check of the scheduling board told him where the other ships were.

Katherine Karp greeted Chad at the door with a huge hug. "It's been quiet around here since you left, young man. You still like cinnamon rolls?"

"I thought I smelled a bit of heaven when you opened the door," answered Chad.

"The quiet has been a blessing," offered the governor walking into the kitchen where Kate had just poured three cups of coffee. "Let's hope it continues."

Over cinnamon rolls and coffee and canned fruit cocktail, the two men covered Chad's trip, dwelling on the events in Washington. The governor had more current news than the man who only a week before had been where the telegraph, railroads and newspapers seemed to make the world fly by at an ever-increasing pace.

"There will be a federal marshal, a treasury detective, and a federal prosecutor on your company's first trip to St. Michael. They will be on the *Denali's* first trip up the Yukon as far as Falcon. They are going to follow up on the reports from Marshal Hickox. Seems that you got somebody's attention about the problem with mining claims and our judge up north."

"That's good to hear, it appears that Danielle Post is shaking some branches because that decision hadn't been made before I left Washington.

"How is Miss Post?" asked Kate.

"I think she will be fine, but it doesn't look like she is coming back," answered Chad. "You can take the girl out of the city, but you can't take the city out of the girl."

"Young Captain Gritt," started Kate, "you can take the young man out of Alaska, but for men like you it is a marriage. Some women cannot tolerate another wife. I suspect that Lyman and I will go back south someday, but if we had come here when we were young…"

Lyman laughed, then wiped a bit of coffee that dribbled from his chin. "I for one, am sorry to lose that girl. She made this a more beautiful place."

Kate flipped a spoonful of cinnamon role at her husband.

"What is the status of things here?" asked Chad. "What

about the villages and the canneries? Anything new between Kukwa and the North Pacific folks?"

"The North Pacific Transportation unloaded a new pile driver at their cannery last month. They're busy mounting it on a barge. I understand that they're going to start driving new pile in Kukwa this month and then move on to the other damaged traps. The foreman that they sent told Marshal Walker that their new design should allow them to open a gate to allow unneeded fish to escape."

"We shall see," replied Chad. "Danny feels confident that the Criers will push for that, and it appears that it is mostly their money, and the Guildham's, behind North Pacific. I met their banker in San Francisco, a guy by the name of Marathon, and I don't trust him any more than I do, Maples."

"What is the status of the infamous Mr. Maples," asked Kate?

"According to Marathon, he left the country."

"But you don't believe him, I take it," replied the governor.

"Marathon is not the kind that will lie to your face, he is too polished and cautious for that. It's more what he doesn't say, or what he leaves out, that concerns me," Chad replied.

"Then he'll be governor of California someday, I suppose," laughed Karp. "Sontag left before you did last fall. He was due back last week. The way he plays his hand, it won't take long to see if there's any real change."

"The *Miles Pierce* is due in today, and I will probably take her right back out tomorrow. I have about twenty tons of freight to move. I'll be gone a week. Marathon actually sent some equipment for Sontag's cannery on the *Maximilian,* so I need to make a stop there. This must be some kind of test, for us and for them."

"You can spread the word that the worst of the troublemakers is reported to have fled the country. Tell the villages that this won't end the trouble, but perhaps it will ease a bit." offered Karp.

Three days later the *Miles Pierce* made its way toward Kukwa inlet, after two earlier stops and a stop at the North Pacific Cannery. Chad learned that Patrick Sontag had been called to San Francisco before his return. The new pile-driving barge was already pounding in the foundation for a new warehouse.

The foreman, a jovial man named Oscar, reconfirmed the design for the new fish traps, showing Chad a set of drawings that featured a wire tunnel from the center holding pen to the river side of the trap. It included a door that could be opened from the top of the pen to allow escapement.

"I'm a bit worried, Mr. Gritt, about the reception that I am going to get at Kukwa Inlet," spat Oscar, around the chew of tobacco tucked in his cheek. "The guards and keeper here never stop talking about the bad blood. I'm a lover, not a fighter, and I have eight kids to prove it."

"There is real bad blood, said Chad. "Find a way to make amends with the village."

"Got any good ideas?"

"A couple. First, invite the chief and a few other villagers to meet with you and look at the plans. Second, last year someone blew up the center piles on the dock the government built for the village. Helping rebuild that dock might be a good peace offering."

Kukwa felt different this time. As the boat edged up to dock only men were there to greet them. Chief Medev caught the bowline, while the young shaman, Peter Jones, secured the stern. The villagers had spiked long planks across the gap where the center pilings had been destroyed. Both men were surprised when Chad Gritt emerged from the pilothouse.

"Where is Macky?" asked Medev.

"He's been working all winter while I traveled. He deserves some time off. He and his wife are taking their four children out of school and heading to California for some sunshine."

"How long you stay here?" asked the chief.

"John, I'll only be here for the night. I've got a dozen crates of freight for you, including supplies donated to the school from friends in Boston."

"Glad that man in Washington town cannot shoot straight," said Medev, "maybe you not come home at all."

Chad made his way down the ladder from the bridge and climbed onto the dock. He extended his hand to the chief and then to Jones. "We'll wait for more tide before we unload. In a couple of hours, the boat will be level with your dock, and it will be easier."

Chad looked around the silent village. "Where is everyone?"

"Some people come into town an hour ago. They say that the cannery is going to build a new fish trap. They also say that they saw your boat at the North Pacific Cannery. Everyone is at the meeting house to decide what to do."

"Why are you and John on the dock then?" asked Chad.

"We think maybe we wait until the people argue too much, then we go and calm things down. Tlingit like *chechako*, first angry and then we use our head," answered Jones, speaking for the first time.

"That is why John is chief, and you were chosen to follow old Joe," said Chad.

"If you would like to come aboard, I have a set of plans from the foreman of the crew that is rebuilding the fish trap that I would like to show you. It may make a difference in what you say to the people."

Oscar had loaned Chad the plans as part of a strategy to arrange a meeting with the leaders of Kukwa. He rolled them out on the table in the lounge and talked the two leaders through the changes.

"This part shows how the cannery plans to leave a passage from the holding pen to the edge of the trap to allow the salmon to escape once the tender is full. This square represents a door that the trap operators will open to allow the fish to come upriver."

"That is good," said Medev with a smile.

"That is good if the men at the trap open the door," snapped Jones.

"I can't guarantee it, but there is more," said Chad. "Congress is concerned about the villages, but there will be no law change this year. Instead, North Pacific wants to avoid problems, with you and with Congress. I met with some of the owners, and they promise that they will allow enough fish to get to your river to feed the village and to protect the spawning stock."

"Captain Gritt, you now deliver freight to the cannery. You are no longer one of us," Jones said coldly. "The talk of men far away is only talk."

"Peter," came a sharp voice from the door. "Peter, you should apologize to our friend. What would you have him do, to prove that he cares about us?"

Chad turned to find Belle at the door, her face crimson.

"It's all right Miss Medev, Peter and all of you should be skeptical. Damn, I am skeptical, but the men whose money is behind the North Pacific Company all indicate that they will order change. The man who is mostly behind the problems is no longer with that company, maybe even no longer in the country. Did I say *damn*? I am so sorry, Belle."

Belle laughed. "That word is probably the first word in English that the boys in Kukwa learn," Captain Gritt. "I spend time everyday helping them unlearn it."

Chad turned to Chief Medev. "John, the owners of the cannery shipped some freight with our firm just to send a message that they're not our enemies. They could have waited two weeks and sent the same freight on one of their own ships. The foreman of the crew that will drive new piling for the new fish trap wants to meet with the village. I think these plans are his way of saying he is not your enemy."

Peter brushed past Belle and headed for the ladder. Chad watched him go, worried.

Chief Medev touched Chad's shoulder. "It is all right, I think. It is hard to be shaman when our people are torn between the old ways and the new laws. A hundred years ago if the shaman said we'd been wronged and we needed to even the score, the people would have readied for a raid. In those days a raid ended when a battle had been fought or a hostage or two had been captured. Today the enemies make all the laws, and they are powerful enough to destroy the whole village."

"It is time to go visit the people and tell them what I have learned," Medev continued.

"Captain Gritt," started Belle, "can you stay for dinner? The blue grouse are hooting in the big trees. I shot two. Grouse is much better than chicken."

An hour later, the meeting broke up with some still determined to stop the construction of a new trap and others happy that there might be another solution. Men headed to the dock to help unload freight. Four of them carried two large boxes to the school.

"Belle, one of these boxes if from the Society of Mission Friends, all the way from Seattle. The other is from Danielle Post who sent it to you from Boston. I didn't know she'd sent it until I reached Seattle, and I have no idea what it contains."

"Is Miss Post back in Juneau, then?" asked Belle.

"I got a telegram from her just before I left. She isn't coming back right away."

Belle turned toward the kitchen, hiding a smile. "I must go see what else will go with the grouse. The birds are hanging on the back porch Captain. Would you mind plucking them for me?"

Well after midnight, Chad rolled up in a blanket on small bunk behind the wheelhouse and was instantly asleep.

Belle, unable to sleep, used a hammer to claw open the top of the crate from Danielle Post. Inside were dozens of books and five paper parcels tied with string. On top of the first parcel rested a letter. She took it with her to bed, opening it on the way.

At dawn, Belle was awakened by the sound of the *Miles Pierce* making its way slowly out of Kukwa Inlet. She smiled and went back to sleep. She would ring the school belle a little late this morning.

CHAPTER 27

Puget Sound, Washington

The *Retirement* crept into Port Townsend, Washington late in the afternoon. The boat had inched its way up the coast from California, stopping twice to wait out weather. Turning east into the Straight of Juan de Fuca, the craft headed straight toward its planned destination of Bellingham until Maples ordered a sharp right turn toward Port Townsend.

"Drew, I think it is prudent that we change our routing and our timing just in case those Pinkertons or somebody else has a welcoming committee planned," laughed Maples. "Would you accompany Captain Kilcher to the harbormaster's office and register us for a full months stay? Then check on the schedule for passenger ferry service to Seattle."

The following day, Maples sent a telegram to Alfred Marathon requesting that he arrange for Miguel Coronzo to arrive in Seattle two weeks from that day and directing Miguel and his campaneros to a cheap hotel at the waterfront.

Captain Kilcher, Drew and Maples spent the following day

drawing up a list of supplies needed and a schedule for the trip to Alaska. The next day, while Kilcher began filling the larder, Drew and Maples caught a boat to Seattle. Arriving late, they checked into a nice hotel downtown and, after dropping their bags, made their way to an ugly sailor's saloon across from pier three. Taking a seat in the back of the dark bar, Maples ordered drinks for both of them.

"Boss," asked Drew, "what are we doing here?"

"I am waiting to see which of the five men I hired to help a survey crew in Alaska walks in the door first. I need someone to keep an eye out for Coronzo. I don't dare use these men again in Alaska, the Juneau marshal knows their faces, but one of them will want to earn a quick fifty by sending us a wire when Coronzo gets here."

Three hours later, the deal was done and Maples and Drew retreated to their hotel where they ate a late dinner. The next day they visited a bank in Seattle where Maples withdrew all but fifty dollars from an account.

"Why did you leave the fifty in the bank?" asked Drew as they were leaving.

"Just like the rental house back east, if anyone is tracking us, I want them to think we are coming back. Three years from now that money will be donated to a school or church."

Two days later, the two men visited another bank in Tacoma, and again left a small balance in the account. Five days after leaving Port Townsend, the men arrived back at the dock, only to find the *Retirement*, missing. A sharp series of steam whistles from across the bay caught their attention. The boat was tied up to a coaling dock, taking on every bit of coal her bins could handle.

For the next ten days, the men stashed tons of supplies into every spare corner of the boat, spending their spare time reading and loafing around the old shipping and logging town. The men worked on toughening up their bodies with long walks in the beauty of the Olympic Peninsula's rain forest.

On the fourteenth day, two things happened. First, the man that Maples hired to watch for Coronzo sent a telegram that Miguel and his two companions had arrived. The second thing forced a change in plans.

Arriving at the boat after visiting the telegraph office, the men found a note from the harbormaster. Ten minutes later, Drew found the man sitting in a deck chair outside his office soaking up the spring sun.

"Don't know if it is important to you or not, said the harbormaster, "but a couple of folks passing themselves off as Pinkerton detectives were in my office this morning looking for a boat from California that sounded a lot like the *Retirement*. They had a different name on the telegram they were working from and were looking for a boat of a different color. I told them I had not seen the boat. They left a card asking me to let them know if I did see it. They were in a big hurry to get up to Port Angeles, so they didn't walk the docks. I expect them back through after they visit the harbors out on the peninsula."

"Thanks for the tip, but it doesn't mean much to me," answered Drew. "We fueled a few days ago, so I suspect the boss to be heading back south soon, but thanks for the tip."

An hour later, Maples himself delivered a second bottle of premium scotch to the harbormaster.

"Thanks, sir," offered the harbormaster. "I can't afford twenty-dollar liquor on what they pay me."

"We brought a case, and I am the only one who drinks scotch," said Maples.

The following morning, the boat crept out of the harbor at dawn. Instead of turning left toward the open Pacific it continued straight north. Four hours later, she tied up at the dock in the inner harbor of Victoria, on Vancouver Island, just on the Canadian side of the Straights. After a couple of inquiries, Captain Kilcher hired a tiny harbor tug to tow the boat to a small shipyard. He arranged to have the boat pulled into a large warehouse.

Drew and Maples checked into the Dalton Hotel where they made a third reservation for Kilcher. A few hours later their captain found them at the prearranged Garrick's Head Pub.

"I dropped my sea bag at the hotel and came right over," opened Kilcher. "Our timing is lousy with the fishermen all pestering the shipyard to get them ready for their season. It is amazing what a couple of fifty-dollar gold pieces can do to rearrange a schedule."

"What does the schedule look like?" asked Maples.

"They will clean and repaint the bottom starting tomorrow. The conversion of the owner's cabin into a dormitory for Coronzo and his companions can be done at the same time. The reinforcement of the main cabin roof and the new crib for a steam launch will have to wait until we buy one. They will build the cradle and the launching boom to fit the new boat. New paint will have to wait until that is done."

Drew sat quietly while the captain and Maples discussed the work to be done. Finally, he couldn't control his curiosity and interrupted. "I thought we were heading north right away. Why are we working on the boat?"

Maples scowled at his subordinate. "On the way over from Port Townsend, we decided to add a small power boat to the old girl, so we can move around without drawing the attention that an eighty-foot boat draws. While we were at it, we decided to change how the boat looks."

Turning to Kilcher, Maples continued, "since she will soon belong to you, what did you decide to name her?"

Kilcher laughed and drained his mug of ale. "The rest of our trip will be aboard the *New Life,* and our new hailing port will be right here. It helps to be a Brit."

That afternoon, Maples cabled Alfred Marathon and advised him that they were rearranging their schedule and asked Marathon to tell Coronzo to sit tight and wait for further instructions.

Kilcher saw to it that his three Chinese crewmen were comfortable in a tiny inn on the edge of China Town and that each had spending money. When he returned to the Dalton Hotel, he brought a recommendation for dinner.

That evening the three men dined on Peking duck, roasted pork and Chinese vegetables at a restaurant that reminded Kilcher of his time in China. At the end of the meal, and two bottles of rice wine, the check arrived with fortune cookies. Maples carefully cracked his open and laughed. It was written in Mandarin. He handed it to Kilcher.

"It reads, *'the time has come to settle your affairs'* whatever that means."

Maples took the tiny slip of paper and slipped it into his shirt pocket. "How about we go back to the Garrick for a night cap?"

The following day, the men were back at the waterfront scouring the docks and boatyards for a power boat that could haul six men safely but was small and light enough to lift onto the deck house of the larger yacht. By four in the afternoon, the men realized that they were going to need help finding what they needed and headed for the boat yard where the crew were already hard at work scraping the growth from the hull of their transportation north.

"I figured you'd be back," commented McMahnon, the owner of the boatyard. "There be no shortage of power hulls around the harbor, but few light enough to lift fifteen feet."

Kilcher began filling his pipe, waiting for the Scotsman owner in overalls to continue.

"I can steer you to one Molly of a boat that will do your work. The price will be a pretty penny, but worth the money."

"Alright, show her to me," snapped Kilcher.

"She will cost two hundred plus a fifty dollar finder's fee for pointing you in the right direction."

Kilcher looked over at Maples who nodded his head. He reached into his pocket and produced a fifty dollar gold coin. "The fifty is only going to leave my hand if we like what we see."

"Right you are then, follow me."

The owner walked to the far end of the warehouse where he began to tug on a heavy canvas tarp. Minutes later, a beautiful small launch of twenty-four feet emerged from a cloud of dust. A small, riveted boiler with a firebox at one end, sat in the middle of the narrow hull, connected to a gear box and a shaft that pushed through the oversized keel. On the other end of the shaft was a large bronze three bladed propeller. The smokestack lay sideways across the steam tank hinged so that it could be folded up for travel or down for storage.

"She was built to run loggers from a camp to the timber on the outside of the island. She'll carry six or eight at a solid ten knots. I took her in to repair a hole in her hull. She found a deadhead at flank speed. By the time I finished the repair, the owners had gone broke. Most likely, gents, they ran the whole shebang like they built this boat. Too light for the job, hoping to save a copper or two. But she will do just fine as a carry aboard. She weighs about fifty stone. You can lift her with a single boom and swing her over the stern. The boom and plumbing for a steam winch will cost you another two-fifty."

Two weeks later the *New Life* slid down the ways, now painted a soft blue. The crew practiced launching the steam launch with the boat tied to the dock. The launch had also been painted the same blue and now sported the name *Little Life* on her stern. A folding frame that would support a large tarp over the seats lay lashed to the seats as Kilcher and Drew ran the fast little boat around the harbor before declaring her a delight to operate.

"Her boiler will not handle coal, too hot," directed the mechanic who had carefully adjusted and lubed the running gear. That night the boatyard filled a large wooden box in the stern of the small boat with chunks of scrap wood.

At three in the afternoon of the following day, Coronzo and his companions caught a cab from the pier where their ferry from Seattle docked. They were met at the entrance to the Dalton Hotel by Maples. The men unloaded their luggage but before they made it to the Hotel entrance, Drew pulled around the corner in a rented wagon.

"Load up," directed Maples.

"I thought we were going to be at the Dalton for a week," snapped Coronzo.

"Change of plans my friend," replied Maples. "There are no rooms available until later. We might as well familiarize your men with the old *Retirement*. They need an orientation run."

As the wagon arrived at the boatyard, the Chinese crewmen met the men and unloaded their luggage. "Take what you can," directed Maples and the crew will carry the rest. We don't dare leave it here or it will be gone when we get back. Drew, kindly return the wagon."

Two hours later the boat was pushing north at its best cruising speed. Coronzo made his way to the bridge where Kilcher and Maples stood at the wheel. "When are we heading back?" asked Miguel. "My men are getting hungry."

"We should be back about August I think," answered Maples. "I suppose we will have to feed your men earlier than that. Chin picked up some nice beef steaks. I figure dinner about nine."

Tommy, who had been with Kilcher since his time in China had the helm as the boat chugged between the bright lights of Vancouver on the right and Nanaimo on the left. The captain had joined the passengers in the main salon where a huge tray of smoked salmon and several loaves of French bread sat next to three bottles of liquor.

"Just think of it as jerky made from salmon," laughed Drew, watching the faces of the three Mexicans as they sampled the salmon. "I had never eaten it until a few days ago."

Miguel introduced Juan and Tiko, explaining that they knew little English, but adding that he would be there to interpret. Both men had the same hard look that Miguel carried. Both carried knives on their belts. Drew's trained eye also picked out knives in the tops of the men's boots. Miguel laughed as he talked about their pay for the three months they would be gone.

"A new Colt, a model 94 Winchester and three hundred dollars each plus another two hundred when the job was done," he advised. Alfred fronted me a thousand each. I consider the extra a bonus," he told Maples.

"If that is fine with them, it's fine with me," advised Samuel.

"Now why are we on our way already my friend," asked Miguel. "I told Alfred that I would keep him posted on our progress."

"Miguel, since we arrived in the area, the Pinkertons have been dogging us. I don't know how, but I can't see any reason to stay anywhere for more than a few days. Besides, it will be safer when we are beyond the reaches of the damned telegraph."

Miguel pulled the plug of a tequila bottle from the rack on the edge of the table and passed it to Juan. "You think Alfred is tipping off the detectives. No way that is happening, believe me, Samuel."

"I didn't say that, but there is no reason to make it easy for them to catch up. I spent over a thousand dollars to disguise the boat because the Pinkertons had a description of it. Those guys are good."

Miguel translated into Spanish for the two new members of the group. Then he turned to Kilcher.

"Captain, what then is our schedule?"

"Samuel has it all in his head, Señor Coronzo. My job is to move us north and wait until Samuel tells me to change direction."

"Samuel, I don't like traveling blind. That is not how we have ever worked before," snapped Miguel.

"Get used to it Miguel. Until we reach Alaskan waters where I am confident that one of our new shipmates can't reach a tele-graph, I will be the only one who knows the plan. Even the captain and Drew are in the same predicament."

Miguel smiled through his bushy mustache. His dark eyes surrounded by leather-like skin darted around the table. "You were always a step ahead of those around you Samuel. I guess that is how you remain alive after all these years. Now how is Chin cooking that beef? I hope it's Mexican style with chilies and beans."

Drew erupted in laughter. "Chin couldn't find a single chili in Victoria."

The *New Life* crept north along the inside passage, working through narrow passages and anchoring for the night in remote coves, riding out two spring storms in sheltered bays. Kilcher avoided any of the villages and fishing communities along the coast of British Columbia. Maples had directed that they stop nowhere that might allow a message to reach a telegraph. The trip through sheltered waters was all that kept Juan and Tiko on board. Neither had even been on the ocean before and for the first two days they traveled with their heads draped over the railing and the next two in their bunks cradling a bucket.

By the fifth day they had begun to get their sea legs. That afternoon the boat slipped out of the protected waters of British Columbia and started across the open waters of Chatham Sound where there was no protection from the booming swell of the North Pacific. By the time the boat reached Revillagigedo Channel, they were again feeding the fishes.

Like all who travel the sea, motion sickness started later and ended earlier with each episode. By the time the boat anchored in a small cove near Annette Island, the two men had recovered enough to join the others for dinner.

Maples had spent enough time in Latin America to speak the language sparingly while the two new crew members had spent the last few years in Los Angeles. Maples learned enough over dinner to determine that the men had crossed the border from Mexico only minutes ahead of a platoon of federales sent after them after a botched bank robbery in Mexico.

Both men were veterans of the continuous conflicts in their country starting with the civil war between the Juaristas and the monarchists thirty years before. Both men had their roots on poor peasant farms in central Mexico where each received a smattering of education in Catholic schools, before being recruited as child soldiers. In ten years of following one strong man or another they had lost any sense of values that their Catholic education had provided. Either would have slit Chin's throat for the lack of chiles in the galley if Miguel hadn't pointed out that there was no other cook aboard. One thing both men shared was an ability to take orders from a superior.

"We are ahead of schedule," remarked Maples as dinner wrapped up. "Our first stop will be in Wrangell, but only for a day. Tomorrow, we will sleep in a bit and then do some maintenance. Miguel, I want Juan and Tiko sanding the decks before we move on."

Miguel passed on Maples' instructions to the two men, drawing a groan.

After Miguel and his hands had retired for the night, Kilcher found Maples smoking on the open bridge wing. "The decks are immaculate," he started, "they need no work, Samuel."

"No Captain, but the two new soldiers need to learn who really is in command here. When the chips are down, I want them reporting to me not Miguel."

After a leisurely breakfast, Maples and Miguel led the two men to the bow. Maples handed each a block of pumice and then taking one himself, knelt and began rubbing the block over the teak decking. Standing, he ordered the two men to finish the job he had started.

Miguel laughed and shook his head and walked away while Maples stood first next to Juan and then Tiko watching their work. He would return every half-hour until the job was completed. As the men sanded the last board, he handed them two brooms to sweep away the dust. When they finished, he nodded. "Bueno," he snapped, and handed each man five silver dollars.

From the anchorage at Annette Island, it took two days to reach Wrangell. While Kilcher arranged for more coal, and Drew and Chin headed into town to find any fresh food, Maples wandered to the office of the Stikine Transportation Company to check on the schedule for the riverboat. The ice had gone out of the Upper Stikine only a week before and the boat was on its second trip of the season. The boat would depart on the same schedule as the previous year. He booked and prepaid passage for five for the fourth trip, in ten days. Finishing, he found Miguel and his men drinking an Olympia beer in the small saloon on main street.

"Miguel, we need to outfit you three for an overland trip, and then a trip down a large river." He took a list and a pencil from his pocket and handed it to Miguel. "Check off what each man has with him, and the rest we will find in the local mercantile."

"You must be looking for gold," offered the clerk, as he piled boots, raincoats, long underwear, wool coats and sweaters on the counter. "We ain't had many prospectors outfit with us since the Cassiar started to play out. You going to need food as well?

"No, I think we are well set there," replied Maples. "You have any snowshoes?"

"Nope, if you are going north, you can probably find some in Haines. If you are going up to Telegraph Creek, the trading post has them."

"What about cartridges?" asked Miguel. "The boys and me only brought one box each."

"I have a case of thirty-thirty shells in the back and maybe some odds and ends of other rifle cartridges," answered the clerk. "I carry some ammunition for Colt pistols. What do you need?"

By early afternoon, the *New Life* was riding a high tide through the Wrangell Narrows on the way to Juneau. Kilcher would have never run the narrows alone, but a supply boat from a logging camp had agreed to lead them through the rocky winding passage. That routing had shaved more than a day off from the planned three-day trip to Juneau.

The boat ran to the southern end of Gastineau Channel. In the distance, the town of Juneau lay on the right side of the channel and the Treadwell mining community of Douglas lay on the left. Instead of moving up the channel, Kilcher turned the boat west and then north around Douglas Island. Just before dark the boat dropped anchor in Auke Bay just north of Juneau.

Gastineau Channel ran past Juneau connecting with Auke Bay. However, the channel north of the town was very shallow with only a few feet of water over miles of sand flats even at high tide. An hour before high tide the next morning the *Little Life* reached the city dock in Juneau and tied up next to the government boat on the float. Two men climbed the ladder to the dock. Drew took the small map from his pocket and unfolded it, sharing it with Miguel.

"I'll go visit the marshal in his office," offered Drew, "while you find the Golden Goose and that man Rattler Wilson. The two men parted a few blocks into town.

Drew found the marshal sitting feet up in the office adjacent to the magistrate's office. He pulled off his stocking cap and rustled his hair, then rushed into the marshal's office.

"Marshal," he said, "I was heading into town to find that lady attorney. I'm with a new cannery group looking at building over in Freshwater Bay. Me and another were on the way here when one of those sailboats they use for fishing flagged us down crossing Icy Straight. When we pulled up close to them, five men with rifles pointed guns at us and told us to clear out. They weren't going to let anyone else build fish traps anywhere near their village. I think they were Tlingit people. You better go have a talk with them right away. If they go pointing rifles at our crew down in Freshwater Bay our men are going to shoot."

Marshal Walker dropped his boots to the wooden floor and walked over to a map tacked up to the inside of the front door. "Show me where this happened and which way you think the men with rifles went."

Drew reached into his pocket for a small cigar case and offered one to the marshal before taking one himself. The marshal struck a match and held it while Drew lit his cigar and then ran the flame right to his fingers lighting his own.

Drew poked his finger right where Icy Straight intersected with Lynn Canal. "Here is where they waved us down. We poured the wood to the firebox on our boat after they backed off and scurried north. The last we saw that other boat was heading down Icy Straight." Drew slid his finger a bit west and south. "It looked like they were headed toward the village of Hoonah."

"If I can find Skipper, we can take a run over to Hoonah and check on things. I will be gone a couple of days. I probably should go down to talk to your folks in Freshwater Bay before I head home. It takes two armies to make a war."

"Marshal," continued Drew, "I'm heading back tomorrow and can deliver your message. That would probably be better anyway, since those men weren't there when we were threatened. My boss Mr. Mapolonias will be in Juneau in the next week, I will make sure he comes by."

Walker pulled his wool jacket from a peg behind his desk. "Guess I better get on with it while it is still fresh in the minds of the men who threatened you. I got to admit, with some of the traps literally starving the villagers, my sympathy lies with them, but I won't let them take the law into their own hands. No one should die over fish."

As the marshal started through the door, Drew grabbed his arm. "Can you direct me to the office of that lady attorney before you go?"

"Her name is Danielle Post, but you won't find her in her office. I hear she is still in the East. When she left, she planned to be back on the June twenty-third run of the Gritt boat from Sitka."

"Thanks marshal, I will pass on the message to Mr. Mapolonias and make sure he stops in Juneau when he can."

Across town, Miguel sat on a stool in the Golden Goose nursing a beer. The bartender had been more than cooperative in offering answers to the dozens of questions that the newcomer seemed to have about the town and its people. He had confirmed that the town had two attorneys, but one, a woman, was out of town. The bartender was waiting for the owner of the Golden Goose to come in for the day. He had moved from an apartment upstairs to a house near the channel only a month before.

As Rattler Wilson pushed through the door, the bartender pointed him out. Miguel picked up his beer and followed Wilson to his office.

"Can I help you?" asked Wilson staring up from his desk.

Miguel pulled an envelope from his pocket and handed it to Wilson. "Your old boss, Samuel Maples has been pushed out of the Alaska Investors Group. I am helping clean up the old mess. The letter in front of you is the transfer of your loan. I am the new owner of the note, and I came to collect the debt. I don't intend to come back."

"Mister, I don't think you mentioned your name…"

"Miguel Coronzo, Mr. Wilson. I used to work with Maples, but now I work for the other partners."

"Well Mr. Coronzo, I don't have four thousand dollars just now."

"Mr. Wilson, I didn't expect you to keep that kind of money in your saloon. I am sure you will have to stop by your bank or something. In Mexico, where I am from no one would dare keep that kind of currency with them. There are too many very tough men who would want to take it away even if they had no claim. I have other things to do in Juneau, so why don't I stop by tomorrow afternoon to collect what is mine?"

"Mr. Coronzo, I don't know if I can raise four thousand in a day."

"I am sure you can, sir. It will just take a bit of effort," offered Miguel. "I will see you tomorrow then."

A half hour later, Drew and Miguel steered the *Little Life* back toward the shallow passage to Auke Bay. Their two-hour stop in town had taken most of the day, and the tide was falling. The men watched silt billow from behind the boat, as the propeller drug through the sand of the shallow passage. Both were relieved when the water cleared indicating they had finally reached deeper water. There had been a weathered old man lighting the firebox of the government boat as they had departed, bringing a huge smile to Drew's face.

"That hombre Wilson is not going to be very cooperative," observed Miguel.

"That's too bad for him," replied Maples. "I recruited him and his brother more than three years ago and I liked both. I hope he doesn't think he can renege on our agreement like his brother. I left him for the bears up on the Yukon. Rattler may take a bit of persuading, but he will pay up. He keeps at least four thousand in a safe behind a picture in his office."

"I think the marshal took the bait," commented Drew. "When we left, there was smoke coming from that government boat. The marshal should be out of the way for a couple of days. That was a great plan boss; none of us want to tangle with the law."

"It's possible that Rattler will round up a couple of locals. The three of them won't be any match for the four of you. I would recommend you get there a little early," directed Maples.

Drew found a seat at the bar next to the door to Rattler Wilson's office and ordered a beer. He struck up a conversation with the bartender whose shaking hand dribbled beer all the way from the tap. The four men had crossed the sandbar on the way to Juneau an hour before high tide in a driving rainstorm. They had erected the folding frame and stretched the tarp provided by the Victoria boatyard to provide some shelter, but it did little to protect them. Drew's seat in the back at the tiller had protected him from the south wind leaving him only damp compared to the others.

"Damn nasty out there today," laughed Drew. "I am with a cannery crew looking at a new site out on Chichagof Island. I am glad I came in yesterday and not this morning."

"I need to restock the beer cooler," commented a nervous bartender. "I'll be in the back a few minutes."

As the man disappeared through the door to the storage room, Drew shouted, "mind if I grab a bar rag to dry off a bit?"

"Help yourself," yelled the barman.

Drew rounded the end of the bar and glanced at each shelf until he found what he was looking for. He quickly slipped the sawed-off double-barreled shotgun from below the till and removed the buckshot shells and slipped them into his coat. He then grabbed a bar towel and returned to his stool just as the bartender returned with two cases of beer.

"This seems like a quiet little place for a mining town," offered Drew.

The bartender began pushing beer bottles into a sheet metal bin full of ice. "It usually is. Everybody pretty much minds their own business. Me and the boss there," he continued pointing at a closed door to the left of the bar, "can handle any trouble that starts in the Golden Goose."

"You two been together long?" asked Drew finishing his beer and motioning for another.

"Not real long. The boss hired me after he started seeing my sister last winter. He was kind of going through a tough time and Cheryl Ann got him into her prayer group."

"Sounds like quite a gal. He sounds like a lucky man, your boss."

As Drew started his second beer, Miguel pushed through the door taking off his rain hat and shaking it. "Is Mr. Wilson in, kid?" he asked.

"He's in his office, but he don't want to be disturbed," replied the bartender.

"He will see me, kid, he has no choice." said Miguel.

Miguel made his way toward the bar as Juan and Tiko pushed into the saloon.

"The kid says that his boss doesn't want to be disturbed mister," snapped Drew. "He knows the man since his sister is dating him."

Miguel snapped something in Spanish to Tiko who rushed past his boss and began to bang on Wilson's door. At the same time, Miguel took a stool directly in front of the young bartender. Juan moved to the other side of Wilson's door just as it flew open, and Rattler emerged with a pistol at his side. The young bartender nervously pulled the shotgun from the shelf in front of him and cocked both hammers.

"I figured you might bring some help," snarled Wilson, "now it's time for you and your two men to hightail it out of here before Paul there spreads you all over a wall with that twelve-gauge."

Drew chugged the balance of his beer. "I thought you said that this was a peaceful town," he directed to the bartender.

Turning to Wilson, he continued, "I don't think the kid there is going to shoot anyone without these." He produced the two shells from his pocket.

Before Wilson could react, Miguel lunged across the bar and grabbed Paul by the hair. He dragged him face first across the bar and pinned his head. In an instant, he flicked a knife from a sheath behind his head and sliced half of Paul's left ear off and then flipped it to the end of the bar in front of Wilson. Frozen for a moment, Rattler looked up from the ear to find both Juan and Tiko pointing pistols at him.

"Samuel told me you might be a little difficult to collect from, Mr. Wilson. If you don't drop that pistol by your side and produce my money, I will cut off the rest of his ear and then go to work on his other one. Your choice. If we have to pry that whole safe out of the wall of your office and carry it out over your bodies, we will, but I only came to collect what is mine."

"I'll get you your money, just don't cut the kid," snapped Wilson. He laid his pistol on the bar and turned back into his office.

"Mr. Wilson, bring an extra four hundred. You makin' this tough, calls for a collection fee for the boys here."

"You know you won't get away with this," snarled Wilson, "The minute you're out of here, the marshal will be on your trail."

"Not right away," replied Drew, "I arranged for him to be out of town for a couple of days. And just for the record, I am real sorry about Miguel here cutting on the kid. You can blame yourself, but I am sorry just the same."

Rattler counted out four thousand four hundred dollars from a canvas bag and placed it on the bar. "There is no way out of this town," he growled.

"Then we will still be here when the marshal gets back," answered Drew. "All you have to do is find us."

Ten minutes later, the four men were back at the boat and Rattler and Paul found themselves locked in Wilson's office.

Juan had stoked the firebox before leaving the boat. Before seating himself, he threw four more small pieces of wood into the box. "Reverse," ordered Drew as he swung the tiller to back away from the dock. "When we get under way, it is probably a good idea to bail some of the rainwater out of this tub before we reach the shallow water."

Three hours later the small boat was securely lashed to its cradle aboard the larger yacht, and the vessel was underway, headed for Chatham Straight and the west side of Admiralty Island. "We take the backdoor route to the North Pacific Cannery," snapped Maples. "Mr. Sontag should be back, and he owes me ten-thousand dollars."

"Samuel, Mr. Marathon didn't want to rough up Sontag. He says he needs him," growled Miguel.

"Miguel, it isn't Alfred's money, at least not what is owed. I suspect that Alfred will ask Sontag to be my replacement, and that's just fine with me," answered Maples. "Sontag will have just over thirty thousand dollars in the cannery safe to pay expenses this summer. He will have to give Alfred an IOU for what he gives us, but he won't fight, he will just complain by letter to Alfred and ask for another ten thousand in operating funds."

When the *New Life* reached the cannery Sontag wasn't there. He had gotten in from his trip south and a couple of days later had headed to Juneau. No one knew when he was returning, which was just fine with Maples who had a key to the safe.

Two days later, the *New Life* rubbed up against the pier back in Wrangell.

"What are we doing back here?" asked Drew. "I thought we were headed for St. Michael. The Yukon should open up within a month and I thought you wanted to be the first one up the river."

Maples laughed. "I still need to collect two thousand from my agent in the Yukon. Besides, the ice goes out of the Yukon from east to west. We are taking a steamboat to Telegraph Creek in the morning and then going overland to the Yukon while the lakes are still frozen. If my timing is right, we will reach the villages around the Choindike before the river opens. We'll buy a couple of boats or canoes and follow the ice into Falcon. The judge there is holding four-thousand dollars that Rattler Wilson's late brother owes me."

Maples counted out four hundred dollars from the Juneau money and handed it to the men who helped collect it. "I only want what is mine. The collection in Telegraph Creek and Falcon should go easy. Tonight, go paint the town, just be back by midnight. We have our gear to get ready before tomorrow morning. Unless you want to stand in the rain all the way up the Stikine, we need to be at the dock early."

Maples waited until Miguel and his men disappeared into town before he tugged on his raincoat and followed them.

The small inn in the center of town had evolved from a bunkhouse with meals during the Cassiar gold boom into a small eight room hotel with a five-table diner. The man at the front desk was both shocked and pleased to see Maples. Zeke Twilliger had known Maples from a time when both traveled by train from Santa Fe to San Francisco. Zeke had been a purser for the Railroad and Maples had just finished up a trip to the southwest looking at mining properties. When the train reached the San Francisco station, four policemen and a representative of the railroad were waiting on the siding. Zeke had taken one look at the group and abandoned his position at the door of the first-class cabin and bolted off from the train on the other side. He had dodged through the railyard and disappeared while the men on the landing waited for his appearance. Maples had taken in the whole scene, and when questioned by one of the policemen, he said that he didn't think the man was on the train.

Maples had found Zeke the same way he had connected with

Drew. Alfred Marathon had circulated word in the underbelly of the city that he was looking for someone with specific talents and he was willing to pay a hundred dollars for the right introduction. Two days later, Zeke had tapped on the door of Maples' office was surprised to find one of his passengers waiting, a pistol on the desk. Maples found that the railroad suspected that Zeke was skimming funds from the saloon car.

"I didn't take much, I was just trying to get enough together to buy a small restaurant of my own," whined Zeke.

Maples made him an offer he couldn't refuse. He would put up another five hundred dollars to the three hundred that Zeke had stuffed in his pants. Maples would get him out of the city and together they would set up a restaurant in Wrangell. Zeke became one more link in the communications network that supported the Alaska Investors Group. In Wrangell they had stumbled on the old bunkhouse and purchased it for three-hundred dollars. For another three-hundred dollars, Zeke had slowly remodeled it into a presentable inn.

"I didn't expect you back until summer, boss," said Zeke.

"I am up here on my farewell trip, Zeke. I am retiring and closing out all my loans."

"Mr. Maples, I don't have five hundred this time of year. I barely hold on every winter," replied Zeke. "I can scrounge up a couple of hundred, maybe. If I can send you payments over the next year I can pay you back."

"I will take the two hundred, don't worry about the rest, the place is yours." Maples took a promissory note from his lapel pocket and picked up the pen at the register and marked it paid in full. "I do need a favor though; I am going up the Stikine tomorrow and I expect that some men will be by here in the next couple of weeks looking for me. I need for you to tell them that you saw me depart on the same yacht I usually travel on and that I went south."

"You bet I will cover for you. That still won't make it equal to all you've done for me," replied Zeke. "Anything else you need?"

"I just need that old sea bag that I left here last fall. I am going to need some traveling clothes."

Zeke brought an old stuffed canvas sack out of the storage behind the counter and dropped it on the floor at Maples' feet. As he stood, Maples blasted him in the face with his fist.

Zeke staggered back to his feet. "What was that for? I said I would help, and I meant it."

"Now your story will be believable. I have had to rough up a couple of borrowers to get paid. You can now tell them that I wouldn't take no for an answer. You dug the five hundred out of your underwear drawer and I left. It gives you a reason to tell them where I went," said Maples.

Zeke rubbed a dab of blood from the split in his left cheek and nodded.

"Thanks Zeke, and good luck," offered Maples. "From now on you try to stay an honest man." Maples extended his hand and Zeke shook it.

The next morning, a wagon full of gear stopped at the dock where the small paddle wheeler was getting up steam. Four men followed the wagon and began carrying the gear aboard. As the small sternwheeler turned to the north, heading for the mouth of the Stikine River, Kilcher pulled the *New Life* away from the dock and followed the little boat until it turned toward the river. Kilcher swung the helm over and pushed the yacht out toward one of the outlets from the archipelago that was Southeast Alaska heading north. He had a month to make it to St Micheal where he would wait.

CHAPTER 28

Juneau, Alaska

CHAD BOUNDED UP the stairs of his Juneau office and found everything at his desk exactly like he'd left it. He tugged the checkered handkerchief from his pants pocket and began to knock down the layer of dust.

"Kind of a mess," came a drawl from the door.

"That it is, Marshal," replied Chad. "It seems crazy that winter is the dusty time in Juneau. Must be because the summers are too wet for dust. How you been?"

"Good," responded Tex Walker. "But the crazy time seems to be starting early this year."

"It never ended for me this winter," laughed Chad. "The problems with the North Pacific folks and especially that Maples fellow just followed like my shadow."

"We heard all about that little ruckus you got yourself into in Washington. How's the head?" asked Walker.

"I'm just fine. I just moved my part to cover up the little furrow that the bullet made. It could have been a lot worse. If it weren't for the Pinkertons that Abe and Guilda Guildham hired to protect their nephew Malcom, it could have cost Danielle and my brother their lives. I wasn't even a target, I just forgot to duck."

"Well, I'm glad you ducked enough. You hungry?"

Chad looked at the pile of four-month-old work on the desk and smiled. "Come to think of it, I am hungry. You buying?"

"Nope. Let's stop by the Golden Goose, Rattler has a story you need to hear, and his pay is a lot more than mine. Then we'll go visit the Chinaman."

A half hour later the three men were seated at a window table in the Crossing Café. The owner Johnny Chung arrived with a pitcher of fresh lemonade. "Knew you were back here," he said to Chad. "You always bring big sack of lemons. Is Miss Post here too?"

"Not now, Johnny, maybe she'll come back and maybe she will stay in the east."

"I will be sad if Miss Post stay there. We got everything on the menu board, but those damned Irishmen not eat up all the corned beef I brought in for their holiday. Probably will last until June. I got corned beef with cabbage and potatoes on special for fifty cents. Best I got today."

Soon the Johnny was back with three heaping platters of corned beef. Chad was startled when Rattler Wilson held up his hand and began saying grace.

It took only ten minutes for Wilson to outline the incident at the Golden Goose. Then the marshal added his strange encounter with the fishing company representative who had sent him on a wild goose chase to Hoonah.

"Once I found nobody in Hoonah who knew anything about threatening fishing company folks in Icy Straight, I took a little jaunt down to Freshwater Bay. Hell, there was nobody anywhere around that bay. Certainly, no camp of men surveying for a cannery," snarled Tex.

Wilson finished chewing a mouthful of corned beef. "I went to find the marshal right after the four men came collecting Maples' debts left the saloon. That is, after I got Paul over to the doc to get his ear sewed up. You know the doc sewed that piece of ear back on. I hope it takes. I don't think Paul is too worried, but it may get Cheryl Ann to quit chewing on me for a while. Anyway, the marshal wasn't in town as he just said."

Chad wanted to hear more about Rattler Wilson and Cheryl Ann Hannahan but didn't ask. Instead, he turned to the marshal. "You obviously think the two events are tied together?"

"No question about it," replied the marshal as he signaled the owner for more lemonade. "Both of us figure the big fellow who sent me chasing my tail and the man who slipped into the Golden Goose early and somehow unloaded Paul's shotgun was the same man."

Rattler picked it up, "and there is no question that he was with this Miguel and the two Mexicans who came to collect the debt. The thing is, I know Samuel Maples, and he wouldn't have hesitated for a minute to slice up a young kid to get something he wanted. Before he got serious about Alaska and the Yukon he was in Latin America. Those three must be part of the same kind of network he put together here, only from south of the border instead of north."

"You think they're still working for him?" asked Chad.

"I do, and so does the marshal," answered Wilson. "Pat Sontag was in the saloon a few days ago. He just got back from San Francisco where he was made acting manager of the Alaska Investors Group until they hire a replacement. Evidently, there was a falling out between Maples and the rest of the owners. Now Maples is what Sontag called 'cleaning up.' That tracks with him coming here for four thousand dollars. Sontag owed Maples ten thousand."

Chad had been listening for most of lunch. He pushed his plate away. "So, you think that Maples was here calling the shots, Rattler?"

"Both the marshal and I think he was here. He must know about the warrant, so he didn't want to tangle with the marshal. He sent those four toughs into town, but you can bet he was close by calling the shots."

"I should have figured it out at the dock before I left for Hoonah," added the marshal. "There was a steam skiff at the city dock all spruced up and painted a nice little blue. There were no other boats I don't know at the dock. It isn't the type of boat you would find in a cannery camp or even a logging operation. It was just the right size to load on top of a big yacht like that Maples fellow brought up here last summer."

Chad asked for the bill from the Johnny who started to buss the table. "You no like my cooking anymore?"

"Nothing wrong with the meal, Johnny," answered Chad, "just a bit too much coffee this morning." Chad pointed at Rattler Wilson when the bill arrived.

"Tell me Mr. Wilson, where else would this Maples man be headed before he leaves the territory?"

"He has contacts in Wrangell, a man that the marshal met last summer while he was looking for that missing miner. He has a man up the Stikine at Telegraph Creek. You know about Sontag. He will also probably go after the four thousand your brother left with the judge in Falcon. He isn't the kind of man to walk away from anything."

The marshal turned to Wilson, "and you think all of these men owe him?"

"I know they do. That's how Maples recruits. He finds men

with real financial or legal trouble and offers to stake them if they do his bidding when called on," answered Wilson.

Walker smiled, "are you in trouble with the law, Mr. Wilson?"

"Not in this territory or even in the United States," answered Rattler. "Me and my brother could have been in trouble in Montreal in a different life. We both coordinated things for Maples here in the territory, but we didn't steal nothing, and we didn't kill nobody. I admit we were damned tough to deal with from time to time, but that ain't illegal."

"The marshal here would have liked to arrest Maples for that killing up north," snapped Chad, "but when it gets right down to it, this Coronzo fellow may really have been collecting a debt that he bought."

"Captain Gritt, that man is not a financier. "He is a paid hard man, just like my brother and me were. Maples is here in the north somewhere, and he has at least four bad men working for him," answered Wilson.

"Then he will collect what he can in this area over the next few weeks and wait for the ice to go out of the Yukon to collect that debt. He will try to get there before the marshal in Falcon gets a copy of that warrant," smiled Chad. "The governor tells me that the first boat to St. Michael will have a couple of deputies on it headed for Falcon anyway. When they come through Sitka, I will encourage them to deputize a few more men before they head up the river. They should catch up to him."

"I am not too sure," replied the marshal. "We know that he is comfortable going cross country to the Upper Yukon. Maybe he'll finish here and then go up to Telegraph Creek and try to follow the ice downriver. He may be leaving the St. Michael area about the same time your brother arrives with detectives."

"Seems like a lot of work to collect a debt, especially if he just wants to close up shop and get out of the country," offered Chad.

"That's the other part of what happened here the couple of days that Maples' men were in Juneau. They really canvassed the town looking for Danielle Post. More than a few folks told them what we heard."

"And just what was that?" asked Chad.

"That Miss Post was due into Sitka on one of your ships the third week of June and that she would probably be coming over here with you on the *Miles Pierce* as soon as she could," answered Walker.

"Did Miss Post actually manage to put a slug into Maples?" asked Wilson.

"She did that, in front of a couple of his former partners," replied Chad. "Why?"

"I know Samuel, Captain Gritt," started Rattler, "he was after her, not that Malcom guy in Washington City. He will never let it sit, that a woman got the best of him. She is in real danger."

"Gentlemen," replied Chad, "I do not really think that Miss Post is coming back to Juneau."

"But Captain Gritt," snapped Wilson, "Maples doesn't know that."

❧

The trail from Telegraph Creek ran north for about a hundred miles over rolling terrain and then split with one route turning more westerly toward Atlin Lake and the other continuing mostly north to Teslin Lake. Maples' man in Telegraph Creek, Burger, found two local Indians with dog sleds to haul the gear over the trail while he and Maples and the four other men in the party had taken turns braking trail on snowshoes. The group had broken camp that morning and headed for Teslin Lake. Once the sun finally crept over the horizon the outside temperature crept up to the zero mark. By noon, it was a balmy twenty-five above as the two guides halted for tea.

Before Maples climbed the stairs to Burger's office, he had ordered Drew and Juan to hike a mile out of town and then cut a length of telegraph wire from the poles leading into town. The men cut it into ten-foot pieces and then scattered it on the way back to the river landing. Maples knew that it would take days to replace the wire and by then he would be well on his way north. He would insist that Burger go all the way to Falcon with him, which assured that he would not send any messages that could lead to a welcoming party at the mouth of the Yukon.

As the two guides built a fire and put the billy on to boil, Samuel exercised his strategy to ensure the chain of command came through him and not Miguel. On the trail, it was easy. It was clear to Juan and Tiko that Miguel was just as cold and miserable as they were, and that Maples was the man with the knowledge to keep them alive. Today's lesson was how to lash three freshly cut poles between two spruce trees and then weave spruce branches together to break the bitter wind screaming across the tundra.

The trip to the Choindike river would be another five-hundred miles, about fifteen days of traveling and then another five days to reach Falcon. If everything worked out, they would stay on the ice all the way. If the river broke up early, they would need to find boats or canoes at one of the villages along the Yukon. Maples would have to rely on Drew and the Indians if they needed the boats as early as the mouth of the Choindike. The last time he was on the Choindike, the miners' committee had told him to 'never come back.'

The tea and a handful of smoked salmon and a piece or two

of biscuit renewed everyone's spirits except Miguel who glowered at Maples and especially the Indian mushers as he again lashed his snowshoes to the oversized leather boots stuffed with three pair of socks. "Samuel, we ride while the Indios ride on their sleds. We should be taking turns riding. That would be fair."

Maples had heard the same refrain for the past two days. In fact, it had begun the first night that they reached Telegraph Creek when Miguel first looked out over the snow-covered terrain as he sat shivering in the poorly heated storehouse that was the only building large enough to accommodate the group. It didn't help that Maples himself had imposed on his local agent and had spent the night in a real bunk in his well heated cabin and not on a hard wooden floor. What Samuel hadn't told the others was that the stump of his missing arm ached miserably in the cold. He could barely control the urge to massage the frozen fingers his brain wanted to take care of, on a hand that wasn't even there.

As the men packed, Maples tried for a final time. "Miguel, you and I walk because the Indians know the dogs and the sled. Neither of us knows how to control them. If we lose a sled full of supplies, we could all be lost. Just be thankful that you are not carrying a seventy-pound pack while we walk."

"I didn't agree to walk hundreds of miles through the wilderness. I signed on to ride in your nice warm boat and help you collect your money. I do it for you and for Alfred. My father would roll over in his grave to see a Coronzo walking instead of riding."

"Miguel, you are free to turn back any time you want. The rest of us are going to finish this trip. I intend to pick up the four thousand in Falcon and then we walk no more," snapped Maples.

"If the Indios can drive the sled, I can drive the sled."

Maples needed to diffuse the growing confrontation. "In two days, we will camp a half day above the small roadhouse on the end of the lake. The following morning you may take one of the teams. If you cannot handle the team, the furthest it will run is to the roadhouse. After that we shall see."

The morning of the third day found the men camped on an eastern facing slope. The temperature quickly soared to above freezing. Huge clumps of melting snow dropped out of the trees around camp, often landing on the men as they packed up. Before anyone was on the trail, all felt the dampness of the snow that had sifted in around their collars.

True to his word, Maples paid one of their mushers a five-dollar bonus to strap on snowshoes after making his team ready. Miguel walked with him patiently for ten minutes while the musher tried to explain the dogs, the harness and their control. Finally, Miguel could take no more. He leaped on the back runners of the sled. Maples caught him by the arm.

"If you get in trouble, tie the rope from the back of the sled to a tree and wait for us," he said.

"Mush!" yelled Miguel, smiling from ear to ear.

The well rested dogs lunged at their harness, but the sled went nowhere. The sled owner pointed and began laughing until he was doubled over.

"Miguel," barked Maples "you will have to pick up the snow anchor buried next to your feet."

Miguel waited for the dogs to settle down, a drawn look on his face. Then he pulled the wooden block with spikes driven through it from the snow and dropped it into the sled in front of him.

"Mush!" he yelled.

The rested dogs bolted into a run down the trail. Miguel had lunged forward just before falling off the sled and hooked his arms around the upper crossbar. As the sled rounded the first bend, the men in camp found themselves laughing until their sides hurt. The last they saw of Miguel was him draped out behind the sled, his knees dragging in the snow as eight dogs roared over a small hill.

Hours later, the hikers found the sled on its side, the dogs in a tangle of brush and Miguel sitting at the base of a tree where he had tied the anchor rope. Miguel's pants were torn at the knees, and his face was a mass of scratches. His pants from mid-thigh down were soaked as were his boots from where the dogs had dragged him through the soft snow of the trail and the overflow on the small streams that they had crossed.

It took hours to sort out the team and get the sled load repacked. Maples took Miguel's bag from the second sled and tossed it to the man. "Change your wet pants and put some dry socks on with your new rubber boots."

Miguel threw the pack back into the sled and grabbed his snowshoes and began strapping them on.

"You don't want to leave those wet boots and socks on," offered Maples. "When the sun starts to set, with these clear skies it is going to turn cold fast. Our stop here means we won't get to the lake until late."

Miguel ignored him and finished lacing on his snowshoes. He then headed down the trail.

The group finally reached the tiny roadhouse. The owner helped the men water the dogs and then helped the mushers stake the dogs in the trees around the cabin far enough apart that they wouldn't fight over the dried salmon chunks that made up their dinner. When he returned to the cabin, he found four of the travelers sitting against the wall soaking up the heat. Miguel sat in front of the small metal stove tears running down his face while Tiko tried to pull the frozen boots over the frozen socks, stopping every few minutes to hold each foot closer to the fire.

Drew and Burger dug out a slab of bacon and a pan of frozen beans that the men had cooked the night before and began preparing dinner.

"If I had knowed you all was comin,' I would have thawed a bear roast out of the cash," offered the owner. As it is, I got flapjacks and some berry preserves for breakfast, but I am plumb out of coffee."

"We have coffee," offered Maples. "We can spare a pound when we leave, and some sugar too."

Maples stood next to Miguel as the last sock was peeled from his feet. "You got some frostbite on those toes, but I don't think you will be losing any of them. Probably going to be damned sore to walk on, and you are going to lose a bunch of skin. We will bandage them up before you put on socks in the morning."

"I got some headache powder," offered the owner, "nothing stronger though." The old sourdough pulled off his right boot and then his sock and pointed to his foot. "Could be worse young man, you might have to amputate a couple of toes, like me."

After dinner, Maples opened a hinged wooden box and set two bottles of brandy on the floor. In a minute the sourdough found a collection of glasses, cups and empty bottles and lined them up next to the brandy. Maples handed one bottle to Miguel who sat groaning against the front door.

"Drink about a third of this and maybe you can sleep."

He then uncorked the second bottle and divided half of it among the rest of the crew, taking none for himself. He watched until Miguel chugged about a third of the bottle and then he pulled it from Miguel's hand.

"You have another couple of weeks on the trail, you may

need this later," he said recorking the bottle. "It will be worse over the next three or four days."

Turning to the roadhouse owner he asked, "you have any axle grease to lube up those toes?"

"Nope, but I got some bear grease in a tub in the cash. I will chop off a block. We can warm up a bit for tonight and tomorrow, but don't thaw the whole block or it will rancid up on you."

By late morning the men intersected the trail of a hunting party who had killed several moose along the lake and packed the meat into heavy freight sleds for the trip down the Teslin to whichever village they called home. The guides estimated that they were three days ahead and unless a major snowfall set in, their packed trail would make the trip to the Yukon easier.

The first two hours of the trek brought an avalanche of cursing and snarling from Miguel. Before leaving, they had smeared bear grease over the toes that were already turning black and then wrapped clean cloth around them. With three pair of heavy socks over the rubber boots, Miguel's feet were warm, but the lashings of the snowshoes over the soft rubber rubbed his damaged feet. It wasn't that the pain had lessened as they walked, it was more that he was blocking it out. Maples watched the fire in Miguel's eyes as he trudged silently.

That man would kill me in a heartbeat if he didn't need help getting back to civilization, thought Maples. *A year ago, I would be thinking just like him.* Maples reached across to rub the stinging fingers on his right hand almost shocked to again find it missing.

Their route was the same as Maples had taken the year before, straight down Teslin Lake and then down the frozen river to where it dumped into the Yukon. The trip was easier by canoe. "No more hills or valleys gentlemen," he offered. "Just a dash across the ice all the way to Falcon."

Over the next five days much of the skin on Miguel's frozen toes sluffed off and under the daily applications of bear grease new skin began to form. By the tenth day he had learned to walk with the pain as only an angry man could. The normally boisterous Coronzo was reduced to a handful of words daily. As they traveled the air slowly warmed leaving large areas of water over the ice, some of them deep enough that their guides detoured onto the banks to avoid them.

From the mouth of the Teslin River, the party turned downriver on the Yukon, occasionally encountering other travelers, but staying to themselves. It was almost a shock to come around a sweeping bend in the river and find a large Indian village on the right and behind that the growing town, that Dawson was becoming.

"We stopping for the night?" asked Miguel.

Maples stopped the sleds and conferred with the guides for a few minutes. "No, we push on."

"I am stopping right here," snarled Miguel. "I want a drink and a warm bunk for a few nights and some real food."

"Suit yourself, Miguel," continued Maples. "You won't find a drink here, or even a meal. By this point everything worth eating and drinking has been consumed. The folks here are just holding on for the first steamboat of the season. But feel free to stay, you can probably find someone who will sell you some boot leather soup for five dollars and who will rent you a beachgrass mattress in their cabin for another five per night. You can catch a ride south when the riverboats start downriver. Just don't expect us to wait for you down in St. Michael."

"What the hell do you know, Samuel," snarled Miguel. "How do you know these folks are hurting? They may have warehouses full of food."

"When we left Falcon last fall, there were miners coming in

from all over the territory to get out of the country so that their partners, who were staying to watch over their claims, would have enough to eat. Besides, didn't you notice that the tracks of that hunting party never turned off. They led straight to here. The miners are hiring the Indians to bring meat into the camp just so they have something to eat. Still, Miguel, stay if you will."

Maples gave the go ahead for the mushers to start downriver and one at a time the men on snowshoes turned away from the cabins on the shore and followed. Finally, Miguel turned and followed. Maples was only half surprised.

The Yukon below the Choindike flows two-hundred yards wide between huge sweeping hills covered in spruce and birch. The well-worn trail that had led the men to Dawson continued downriver. Each day the groaning of the ice beneath them grew louder. The Indian mushers didn't seem worried even when large leads opened in the ice. Each night they made camp on the shore as late as they could, and the group was off at first light each morning. With light from four in the morning until eleven at night that meant little rest. The weather warmed every day, and by late morning the men were traveling in shirtsleeves. Their rubber boots proved to be a godsend as the snow over the ice first turned to mush and then to standing water. It was almost dark when the small group pulled off from the ice just above the small Indian village upriver from Falcon.

"You men make camp here for the night. Burger, you come with me. We will make arrangements for all of you in Falcon. Plan on being there for breakfast," directed Maples. "There's a saloon at the far end of town, I will meet you there."

It took almost two hours for the seasoned men to walk the last eight miles into Falcon. The river ice groaned continuously as they walked. They arrived at Wilsons saloon just as the bartender was closing. Maples smiled at the man he had last seen the previous fall.

"Is Pug Wolcott around?" asked Maples.

"Pug drowned his self, right after you left last fall Mr. Maples. Some of the locals were hounding him after the marshal and Parker Gritt brought Cobra's body back to town. Some of Cobra's friends wanted to talk to Pug especially after Gritt walked in with a bill of sale for the saloon."

"I held the note on the saloon, and I transferred it to Pug when it became clear that Wilson wasn't paying me back," replied Maples.

"I know that Mr. Maples, but Gritt had a bill of sale and Pug got himself dead. I do Know that Mr. Gritt left four thousand in gold for paying off your debt with Marshal Hickox."

"I'll look up the marshal in the morning. I am just passing through with some friends like Mr. Burger here. Are you still open for a drink?"

"Come on in, we can use some cash money customers," replied the barkeeper. "The marshal is out of town at a new strike downriver. He personally goes out to survey every new claim before he accepts any paperwork."

Over two whiskies, Burger and Maples continued a conversation that they had started on the walk to town.

"So, I am still going to be employed by the Alaska Investors Group," smiled Burger. "Good luck on your retirement Mr. Maples."

"Thanks. You'll have a new regional manager, but they didn't tell me who it will be before I left," answered Samuel.

"I will bet that the two mushers you hired to get us here can sell their sleds and teams for a real premium if they want to," continued Maples. "You three could ride the first boat upriver when it comes through and then go overland back to Telegraph Creek."

"That's what we planned on," replied Burger. "We can buy a canoe at the mouth of the Choindike and paddle up the Teslin. I haven't made a trip like that since I came west with the Hudson's Bay Company twenty years ago. It might be fun. Once I get back home, do I still contact the same folks that I used to telegraph for you?"

"It will be the same people who have been keeping in touch with you over the last couple of months," responded Burger.

"Samuel, I haven't gotten a telegraph message since December. That one was from Richard Crier. I haven't heard a peep from Sir Rodney in months."

"Do you have that code book I gave you when you started?" asked Maples.

Burger rummaged through his small pack and handed a tiny leather bound book to Maples.

Maples walked over to the potbellied stove in the center of the floor and tossed the book into the fire. He took his seat and picked up his drink. "That code was just between the few of us who Sir Rodney hired. He passed on last fall, so it won't be needed anymore."

Maples waved at the bartender. "Is Mr. Smyth in town, and the judge?"

"I think so Mr. Maples. Do you want me to go find them for you?"

"No, that won't be necessary. I'll surprise them in the morning. In fact, it will probably be best for all of us if you don't tell anyone that I am here for now. Mr. Burger and I will need a place to stay, maybe the storeroom here in the saloon?"

"Why don't you use old Cobra's cabin? No one is using it

since his demise." The thinly vailed threat from Maples had not missed its mark.

"Thanks for the idea. Now what have you got around here to feed two hungry travelers?"

The rest of the party was sitting on the steps of the saloon when Burger and Maples arrived that morning. "We're heading to the restaurant to get some breakfast, and then I want Drew and Juan to go find Judge Wildham. Miguel, you and Tiko find Jack Smyth. I'll point out their cabins on the walk to the restaurant. Meet Mr. Burger here at the saloon. He will show you where to take them.

Natasha's hadn't changed, nor had the owner's angry look as she recognized Maples. All of Maples' men ordered ham and eggs. After weeks of camp food, he did the same. The grinding noise from the river brought Maples out of his chair as he finished a third cup of coffee. He turned from the window. "We got here just in the nick of time. That ice is bulging and starting to move."

Natasha's husband sauntered into the dining room. "That ice will start moving seriously tonight and by tomorrow night it will be running chunks of ice. A man could probably head downriver in two or three days if he was willing to take it slow, to stay behind the ice. You going downriver Mr. Maples?"

"I generally travel where I want and when I want, Grigore. But to answer your question, my friends and I will be going downriver after I take care of some business here. Mr. Burger over there in the corner and his two Indian friends who agreed to guide us here from the Stikine country will be needing a place to stay until they can catch a boat upriver."

"Mr. Maples, I am not looking for trouble, but if you can get your business done before the marshal gets back and starts asking questions, it might work out for the better. I think you could be on the water before he gets back."

Two hours later, Judge Wildham and Jack Smyth found themselves standing in front of the table in Cobra Wilsons old cabin. Behind them Drew and Miguel blocked the door while outside Tiko and Juan rested on the rough bench soaking up spring sunshine.

"I asked you two here to announce my retirement," started Maples. "This trip is just to clean up some old dealings. Jack, I lent you two thousand dollars to get set up here, and I am going to need it back."

"Samuel, I don't have two thousand of my own right now. I sent most of my money out to the bank in Seattle last fall," said Smyth.

Without any word from Maples, Miguel buried his knife in the table in front of Smyth.

"Honestly Samuel, all I have is about six thousand from last fall's clean up at the mines. It all belongs to the Alaska Investors Group."

"I'll take the heat for you, from the group," replied Maples. "You draft up a promissory note to them for a couple of thousand dollars and draw that amount in gold." Maples picked up a folded sheet from a stack in front of him and slid it across the table. "I will cancel your note as soon as you make the payment. You keep working for the group and everybody is happy."

Smyth started to respond but stopped as Miguel reached over his shoulder and pulled his knife from the table.

"This would be a good time to cancel this debt, Jack. It's a good deal. You don't want to pay the penalty that not paying up might bring, besides you will be free to renegotiate your deal with whoever they pick to replace me."

Smyth pushed his chair back and started to rise.

"Two more things," started Maples. "We'll need your help to get the boat into the water as soon as the ice moves and the group will probably be happy if you run the boat down the river so that it can be brought back here. Also, Drew there at the door and I will be bunking with you until the ice is out."

"Samuel, you don't need to treat me like this. I thought we were friends," replied Smyth.

"I like you too, but I'm in a hurry, so I don't have time for negotiations," snapped Maples.

As Smyth opened the door, Maples ordered Drew to accompany him.

Maples looked at Wildham. "Now Jack, you and I go back more than ten years. You need to know that Sir Rodney is gone and that my relationship with his son and grandson is not what it was. I know that I met you through them, but they don't know about our agreement, and they don't know much about how we built the business here. I just want you to know that I am not going to tell them, and neither are you."

Wildham laughed and turned to Miguel. "Will you give Samuel and I a minute alone please?"

Miguel waited for Maples to nod his head and then stepped out into the sunshine.

Wildham turned back to Maples. "You know I have the four thousand that Parker Gritt left to pay off your note on the saloon. You can pick it up anytime. Smyth there has paid me a thousand dollars for every claim that I helped with just as you told him. I keep your twenty-five percent in a folder in my safe. I will put it with the four thousand. Send your man Drew. I don't like your Mexicans."

"Thanks, just remember that none of this ever happened," smiled Maples. "One more thing, it's going to get crazy upriver next year. You might consider relocating where the picking could be better. There are some problems brewing with the U.S. government. You might do well to change jurisdictions."

"I appreciate it my old friend, but if the group is still going to be doing business here, I think I will stretch it another year and then go south. I am damned tired of the cold, Samuel."

Wildham opened the door and headed for his office whistling. Miguel stepped back into the cabin and closed the door.

"Mr. Maples, you should never have treated me like you did. If you weren't leaving already, I would cut your heart out for dragging me across the ice. "You always told me about the whole plan before but now you don't trust me."

"Miguel, it's not you that I don't trust, it is the Criers and Alfred. I know that it would be better for them if I disappeared. They don't want to risk their lily white reputations, and you still work for them. Its Burger and that damned telegraph. I am just doing what I taught you years ago, I'm watching my back."

Miguel slid the knife he was holding into the sheath behind his head. The look on his face didn't make Maples feel any better.

"When we get back to San Francisco I will add a thousand to the three thousand that you are being paid by the group. But between now and then, I need you to be the good soldier you have always been."

Miguel smiled. "I have always taken orders haven't I, Samuel. Just don't order me around in front of Juan and Tiko."

"Let's go open the saloon Miguel. By the way, how are the toes?"

"I have learned to ignore the pain."

Grigore's prediction was perfect. On the late afternoon of the third day the heavy ice flows disappeared downstream and only small chunks of bank ice were in the river. Drew and Smyth had spent the previous day servicing the boat and all the men had stacked their gear in the small cabin. With the help of Grigore's horses, the men slid the boat from the blocks where it had survived the winter and across the mud until it floated. Within an hour they had the firebox hot, and enough steam to back away from the bank and turn downriver.

Before the boat could build speed, a group of men rushed to the shore. Bill Hickox began to wave for the men to return. When they ignored him, he pulled his pistol and fired into the water in front of the boat. Seconds later three men with Winchesters sprayed the bank at the marshal's feet with shots sending him running.

"Damn it, Samuel, the marshal knows that I am with you," snarled Smyth. "Now I will have to come up with a good story before I can return to town."

"I paid for this boat, Jack," snapped Maples. "I was going to leave it for you and the rest of the group, but instead I think I will sell it downriver." Maples pointed at Smyth and flipped his hand. Moments later, Miguel and Juan stood laughing as Smyth floundered in the bitterly cold water.

"I can't swim screamed Smyth."

"Learn or die, Jack," yelled Maples as the boat picked up speed.

The men caught up to the ice pack just before dark and decided to make a camp where a clear stream entering the Yukon created an eddy. In an hour the men had a fire roaring and were dining on a string of fat grayling that Drew had caught on a feathered hook and line he had found in the toolbox. Maples sat with his back braced against a huge cottonwood as the rest of the men lounged around the fire, passing a bottle of bourbon that Maples had taken from the saloon.

"Mr. Maples," started Drew, "we've been together for months now and I know that you are a hard man, but usually a man who is fair with those around you. Well," he continued," I don't understand why you would throw that Smyth man out of the boat."

Maples smiled through clenched teeth. "Drew, you do not rank high enough to question my decisions."

"How about me Samuel," asked Miguel. "I tossed him over, but I agree with Drew. I don't know why except it was your orders."

Maples pulled the cigar from his clenched teeth. "Mr. Smyth was of no more use to me, but he was right. He can still be of use to my former partners, the same men who pay you Miguel. If he made it back to shore, he won't have to explain anything to the marshal. And we will not have to listen to him bitch all the way down the river."

The men stopped twice a day and salvaged wood for the steam engine. Two Swedish saws were put to work cutting the small logs and branches stacked on the bow to fit into the firebox. Each day their leisurely pace allowed them to run a bit longer before they caught up to the massed ice. Each time they passed a village or trading post people stood on the bank surprised to see a powered boat going downriver. As they reached the Yukon delta, they found the southern and central channels clogged with ice jams, but luckily the northern channel, the one that turned toward St. Michael was clear.

Rounding the point at Stebbins they found the *New Life*

anchored just offshore of St. Michael. Maples was at the tiller as they ran the boat up to the boarding ladder hanging over the side. It took only minutes to load their gear onto the yacht.

"Drew, you and Miguel run the launch over to town and sell it for whatever you can get for it. You can split the money between yourselves."

Turning to Kilcher, Maples asked, "How long until we can get underway?'

"We can have steam in two hours Samuel."

Turning back to the men in the launch Maples added, "We are underway in two hours. You will have to get the new owners to run you back out or wait for the first southbound ship."

The *New Life* was pushing hard, just offshore of Point Romanzof the next day when they spied a heavily loaded ship northbound along the offshore ice pack.

Maples settled into his overstuffed chair on bridge, a new cigar between his smiling lips.

CHAPTER 29

Sitka, Alaska

IT WAS GOOD to have lunch with Parker, Annalee and their infant son. The brothers had finalized their plans in Tacoma while supervising the unloading of the railcars carrying their new steamboat. They were in Sitka for only four hours before reboarding the heavily loaded *Maximilian* for the trip to the mouth of the Yukon.

The ship carried a handful of passengers and a letter from Danielle. Chad knew all along that she might not be coming back, but it was still a surprise when he opened the letter and confirmed that she wouldn't be on the *Juarez* later in the month. He was surprised by the announcement of her move to Washington. He was even more surprised by her engagement to Malcom Crier. The 'all my love' that closed the letter did little to soften the feeling of loss.

The dock crew watched their boss slinging boxes and pushing a hand-truck like a man possessed. By the time the *Max* disappeared to the northwest, there was nothing left to put away.

Chad flipped a ten-dollar gold piece to his foreman and asked him to treat his crew to a cold beer. Then he retreated to his office where he soon ran out of paperwork. He pulled on an old raincoat and started down the beach trail angry and sad. Aunt Claire had been right, Danielle had figured out what was right for her.

Governor Lyman Karp made his way to the old Gritt family home with two folios tucked inside his raincoat. The rain that had started that afternoon had been only a prelude to a May storm that rolled in from the west. Across the bay all the islands had disappeared in the mist. The gale drove the rain through every seam of his heavy rubber coat and attempted to lift the oversized rain hat from the governor's head. The huge spruce trees among the houses shuddered with each gust. Any one of the two-hundred-foot trees could crush a house if its roots tore from the water soaked ground.

Lyman didn't even knock. He bolted through the door, slamming it against the wind three times before it latched. He tugged the soaked coat and hat from his body and hung them on pegs behind the door, then kicked off his rubber boots. Finding his host absent, Lyman pressed his body close to the heavy ceramic stove in the parlor and watched the steam start to rise from his soaked canvas pants.

Five minutes later, Chad barged through the back door and dropped the crossbar to make sure that it didn't blow open. "Remember that planked salmon dinner that I promised you, Lyman? Well, it is going to be fried fish. I managed to get the fire going under the shelter a couple of hours ago, but then the wind picked up. I tried for the last half hour to keep it going, but all I have is hissing steam from rain on partially burned logs."

Lyman smiled. "I like my fish fried my friend. If it still comes with canned pork and beans and frybread." He picked up the bottle of brandy that sat on a warming shelf built into the chimney. "I am assuming that you have a couple of snifters stashed somewhere."

Chad reached into a China cabinet next to the back door. "Right, you are old chap, warm brandy on a wet night."

He handed the governor the snifters and headed for his bedroom. "Let me find you something to wear so that you can hang those pants up to dry."

The small talk that started the evening turned quickly to the real reason for the meeting. Lyman took a typewritten page from one of the portfolios and handed it across the kitchen table to Chad.

Chad read the top line and looked up at Lyman with a confused expression.

"Marshal Walker went down to Wrangell to follow up on the Maples incident that you and Rattler Wilson talked about. The transport company confirmed that Maples and four other men went up the Stikine and they haven't come back. Maples' agent in Wrangell got himself all beaten up objecting to Maples trying to collect an old debt without any notice. He confirms that Maples came in on his old yacht. When the marshal pressed Maples' man, he changed his story, Maples was headed for the Yukon."

Chad sipped his brandy, chasing off a shiver from the wet collar of his shirt. "I'm not surprised, but that means the two government policemen and those two Pinkerton men headed for St. Michael may be too late to intercept Maples."

Lyman propped his stocking feet up on a kitchen chair next to the fire to dry his damp socks. "The government men are still going up the Yukon. They have an arrest warrant for Judge Wildham. That assumes that the proof that Marshal Hickox says he has is real. I don't know about the Pinkerton men, maybe they'll just be turning around or maybe they will go up the river too."

"All that makes sense, Lyman, but what is this Pardon for Rattler Wilson I am holding?"

"Wilson is a different man than before his brother was killed. The marshal indicated in his letter that Wilson now calls himself R.A. not rattler, and that he is engaged to Cheryl Ann Hannahan."

"I guess, if I use all my imagination, that I can see Wilson with the prettiest member of the Christian Women's Service Society. But I still don't understand the pardon," said Chad.

"Wilson went down to Wrangell with the marshal. On the way, he confided that he knew about the shooting of old Joe in Kukwa and about the death of those two fishermen that Johanson lost last year. He swore that he told the guards he hired that no one was to get hurt, but he knew just the same. He told Walker that Samuel Maples had stopped at the cannery himself. According to Wilson, Maples told the men that they were to use any means that they wanted to make sure that Sontag made his quota. Maples even authorized Wilson to pay each of the guards an extra five hundred at the end of the season to keep them quiet."

"That's quite an admission," said Chad. "Why give the man a pardon if he is part of three murders?"

"Chad, I was a newspaper editor, not an attorney before I went to the Congress from Vermont. As an editor, I would look at this story and consider Wilson a great source for a far bigger story. I suspect that as an attorney I would also consider giving him leniency if he would help me go after the man responsible for all this. That's what the Pardon is all about."

"Did you discuss this with Judge Dishner?" asked Chad.

"No, no I didn't. With the evidence mounting that the judge

up north isn't fully on our side, I didn't want to include Judge Dishner until I know for sure that he isn't working with Maples."

"So how do we find out?"

"We get Wilson to fill in any blanks that need to be filled in. The Pardon should make him feel comfortable doing that. Then we have to catch this Maples fellow and see if he will sing his heart out to try to save his life."

Chad got up and headed to the kitchen where the wood stove was finally hot enough to cook on. "You know Lyman, he doesn't strike me as a man who will be easy to catch and even if we do get him into custody, not the kind to offer evidence."

"We win if we catch him, even if he hangs without uttering a word," replied Lyman. "We have just the bait he is looking for."

"And what is that?"

"You know that Danielle Post shot the man don't you?" asked the governor."

"I do, and I know that Maples sent a couple of professionals to kill her and Malcom Crier in Washington. I was there," said Chad, rubbing the scar on his head.

"Did you know that Maples lost his right arm from that wound?"

Chad turned from the frying pan of bacon drippings. "That means he lost his writing and shooting arm."

"It also means his career is over." Lyman rummaged through the second folder on his lap. "According to this Zeke Twillinger in Wrangell, Maples is up here collecting money from a half-dozen men he loaned money to, then he is retiring. I can't imagine that he will leave without trying to square his debt with Miss Post."

Chad stirred the can of beans heating on the stove. Then he slipped a pan with leftover frybread from his morning's breakfast into the oven. Finally, he lifted two huge fillets of king salmon from a pan of flour and dropped them into the hot bacon grease.

He grabbed the huge metal saltshaker from the shelf next to the stove and then the pepper and seasoned the fish.

"Lyman, Danielle is not coming back. When the *Juarez* comes in, there will be a young man aboard who is taking over her practice, but no Danielle Post."

"Is she staying in Washington?"

"She is, how did you know?"

"Kate and I have known Malcom Crier for a decade. He is a very persuasive man my friend. He isn't going to give up his life of comfort and culture to go prove that he has what it takes, in the last frontier. To the Brits, moving from an estate in the English countryside to anywhere in North America is like you or me moving to Alaska. He has proven everything he needs to prove. Now all he needs is the perfect partner."

"I wish I could dislike the man, but instead I respect him. Did you know that he was wounded twice, once in October and again in the dustup in Washington? Both times he was defending Danny. Hell, the first time I wasn't even there," replied Chad.

"Chad, it sounds like Danny has chosen well for what she wants in life. Malcom will be there when she needs him, even if it is just to refill her champagne glass at an opera intermission."

"But Crier barely knows Danny."

"Chad, Malcom's Aunt Guilda was taken by Danny from the first time she met her. She chose well for her nephew. They live a different life than you or me."

Chad smiled and refilled his brandy glass and then Lyman's. "And if she was here now, she would again be a target for Samuel Maples. But she is not here, she is safe. And we have no bait."

"Are you taking the *Miles* on your normal loop tomorrow?" asked Lyman.

"I am, first to Kukwa then the canneries and then Juneau.

I won't be going up the canal this trip. I should be back in five days."

"Are we ready to eat yet?" That smells great, and I haven't eaten since early."

"Grab a plate from the cupboard next to the sink. The silver is in the drawer below and get in line."

Moments later, the two men were standing at the counter in the kitchen shoveling dinner into their mouths. When Lyman came up for his first full breath, he smiled at Chad.

"Chad, you don't work for the territory, but I think you want this man as much as those who do. I think you and the marshal and maybe Mr. Wilson will come up with a plan. Talk to them while you are in Juneau. Remember, Maples doesn't know that Miss Post isn't coming back."

❧

Late the next day the *Miles Pierce* slid up to the newly repaired dock in Kukwa. Ivan and Chad began loading crates into a cargo net that had been lowered from the dock. Low tide left only a foot of water below the hull of the small ship. "Did you bring my rifle back from the gunsmith?"

Chad looked up to find Belinda Medev looking over the edge of the dock.

"Nice to see you too Belle. No, he wasn't through with the repair on the trap."

"Then I guess I will have to pick it up myself," laughed Belle.

Chad looked up as the net came down for the second load of freight. In it were a trunk and two smaller cases.

"You going somewhere, Miss Medev?" asked Chad.

"I am, Captain, I am going all the way to Sitka with you. School is out and I have an end of term meeting with the Society of Mission Friends to plan for next year. Now move away from the ladder you two, I'm wearing a dress."

Chief Medev stopped sorting the small bag of mail that had arrived and took his daughter's hand. "When you get back, we will start planning for your small house in Shaman's Cove." The chief went back to the mail as Belle started down the ladder.

Belle stepped from the ladder and gave Chad a big hug.

"Daughter, you got a letter."

Belle looked up as her father dropped a large envelope. She started to open it, just as it started to rain, so she retreated to the cabin.

"You take good care of Belle, Captain Gritt," said Medev. "When you bring her back, you stay awhile. We go to catch King Salmon, white man way."

"You have a deal, Chief John. Macky should be back by then, so I won't be tied to the wheel."

Chad piloted the boat out of the inlet, past the new fish trap. Then he handed the ship's wheel over to Ivan and headed below to find Belle.

"How are things with the men at the trap since the fish came in?" he asked. "Are they letting enough fish get to the river?"

Belle folded the letter she had been reading and carefully knotted the silk scarf that hung around her neck. "The run is weak this year, but there is more Chinook in the river than a year ago, so I guess the answer is yes."

"I hope that continues. We have some freight for the North Pacific Cannery and quite a load for Johanson, so we won't be in Juneau until late tomorrow," added Chad. "Then we will spend a full day and night there. The governor has some things he wants me to discuss with the marshal."

"That will be just fine with me. A friend has asked me to do her a favor while I'm there, so I will be busy all day. But I will be free in the evening," said Belle.

"Perhaps then you will have dinner with me at the hotel?" asked Chad.

"I would love to Captain Gritt, if they will break their no Indian rule again."

"I can assure you that you will be welcome for dinner as my guest, Belle. I am sure that I can get you a room too if you need one."

"That won't be necessary. Danielle Post has offered me her spare bedroom whenever I am in town," answered Belle.

"Belle, Danny will not be there. She isn't coming back to Juneau," replied Chad.

"I know. She wrote me and sent me her key." Belle produced a door key from her jacket pocket. "She sent me a letter several weeks ago telling me that she probably would not be returning. Her letter today confirmed that, and she asked me if I would pack her clothes and the other personal things and send them to her in Washington City."

Chad looked a bit shaken, and started to ask Belle more about Danielle's letter, but he was stopped when Belle pressed a finger against his lips. "Someday, maybe we will talk more about this, but not now. I am happy to help her."

When the *Miles Pierce* left Juneau three days later, five large travel trunks were stashed in the almost empty hold. As was normal in the spring, there were few passengers to connect to the southbound ships. Beyond the marshal and Rattler Wilson and Belle, the only two passengers were a mine mechanic with his wife, who had only arrived only a few weeks earlier. She was leaving with or without him.

As the small ship crawled into the Sitka dock, Marshal Hickox bounded onto the bridge. "Chad, I think we guessed right. I think that boat that we thought was a fisheries research vessel anchored in Katlian Bay right below old Sitka belongs to Maples."

"I remember that boat from last year," answered Chad, "it was one of the prettiest natural cedar yachts that I have ever seen. It sure as hell wasn't blue."

"That's what paint is for young man," continued the marshal. "But I can tell you flat out that that little blue steam launch at the city dock is the same one that I saw in Juneau."

"If that's the case, we need to hide you and Rattler until we figure out what they are up to."

"We could just go board that big blue boat since we know that Maples is probably aboard," observed Hickox.

"Marshal, four men with Winchesters could hold that boat forever. We would need a cannon to sink her. And we don't know who else might be aboard. Maybe some folks with nothing to do with what Maples has been doing."

"We don't have a cannon anyway. So, I guess we wait until they tip their hand," closed the marshal. "You have any idea where we can disappear to?"

"You both can bunk at my place. If they don't have anyone in town you can get out a bit, but until we know, you will cook for yourselves."

The *Miles Pierce* reached the dock just as the sun slipped below the overcast in the western sky. A copper glow illuminated the town, especially the onion dome on the Orthodox Church. Chad arranged for a buggy to take the miner and his wife to the hotel. The reverend Gillam was there to pick up Belle. Chad made his way to the office while Ivan and the dock crew unloaded the freight and put the boat to bed. Hickox and Wilson sat in folding chairs on the bridge waiting.

Chad climbed the stairs to his office above the dock. A big

man with shaggy hair rose from his chair. "You, Captain Gritt," he asked extending his hand. "My name's Drew and I am here representing the North Pacific Company and its manager."

"Pleased to meet you," answered Chad. "How can I help you?"

Two hours later he watched three men descend the ramp at the public dock and disappear under the canvas top of the small blue launch. The steam whistle sounded on the launch, and it pulled away from the dock.

Chad walked out of his office and waved at the bridge of the *Miles Pierce*. Minutes later, he had his traveling gear and that of Wilson and Hickox in the back of one of the company's freight wagons and the three of them set off for the Gritt home.

"They had a man waiting in the offices. He indicated that the *Juarez* would come in with some freight for Sontag and more importantly he told me that he just bought a load of lumber for the trap and brine operation that North Pacific is building. He asked me to haul the lumber to the saltery for them and the freight for Sontag since some of it is supposed to be used at the new facility in Humpy Cove. I told him we could deliver his freight on the passenger run to Juneau the day after the *Juarez* docks."

"So, they have a fish salting plant planned," laughed Hickox.

"For that amazing insight you buy the first round at Kuzenoffs.

On their way to the Inn, Hickox paused. "Just because they left for now doesn't mean that they won't have someone watching when the *Juarez* comes in, to make sure that Miss Post is aboard."

"I have an idea or two on that," replied Chad. "The *Juarez* isn't due for three more days, so I have that long to make one of those ideas work. Now walk Marshal, you are buying the first drink."

❦

A young woman dressed in rough men's clothing stood in the light rain as the passenger ramp was lowered on the *Juarez*. Chad was the first person up the ramp. Next, four men made their way down the ramp and disappeared into the lobby. Then the young woman hoisted her canvas bag and carried it up the ramp.

Twenty minutes later, Chad escorted a woman dressed in a long lavender dress and a fur coat to the ramp. The woman stopped for a moment as Chad gently kissed her cheek. She pulled the broad brimmed hat down tightly around her face to protect her makeup from the damp and descended the ramp on Chad's arm. He helped her into the governor's coach which waited across the dock and then Chad bounded back up the ramp. The coach pulled away from the dock at a trot and wound through the streets to the governor's home where the young woman again pulled the hat down around her face as she rushed to the front door where Kate Karp waited.

When Chad finally wrapped up with the captain of the *Juarez* and wandered back to the offices, the same man who had been there three days before waited. With him was a second Latin looking man who walked with a pronounced limp.

"Captain Gritt, I just wanted to reconfirm that the freight and my lumber will be on your sailing tomorrow," said Drew.

"I contacted the mill this morning. Your lumber will be delivered as soon as we clear the *Juarez* to continue its trip north. We will load the lumber and your freight tonight and we will be off at dawn." Chad pulled a chart from the chart rack and spread it on the counter. "Let me reconfirm exactly where you want it delivered."

Drew pointed to the place that he and Chad had already marked. "Miguel here will be waiting for you at the fish trap. I may be working with Mr. Sontag at the cannery. You can deliver the freight not needed at the trap there."

Chad nodded and rolled the chart up and returned it to the rack. "Thank you for the business."

"Miguel will see you late tomorrow then," said Drew as he turned for the door. His friend, walking like he had a hundred small cuts on the bottom of his feet followed.

A lanky young man in a suit rose from where he sat, taking in everything and made his way to the counter. "Are you Captain Gritt, Chad Gritt?"

"I am, and unless I am mistaken you are Mathew Pushkin," responded Chad. "Danielle asked me to keep an eye on you until you settle in. You will have to wait a week to go to Juneau. We'll only have one passenger on the trip tomorrow."

"That's fine with me Captain. Danielle suggested that I spend a few days here getting to know the governor and Judge Dishner before I start practicing. As it is, it will take years to fill her shoes."

"Mr. Pushkin, unless you wear Italian shoes with button up fronts and pointed toes, you will never fill Danny's shoes. Don't try, just fill your own, that's how this territory works. You need a place to stay?"

"No thank you, sir. I will take a room at the hotel and then I think I will spend the afternoon just walking around. There hasn't been a Pushkin in Sitka since my father left the day after the transfer of ownership. He was an officer in the Russian navy."

"Welcome young man, you know that my grandmother was Russian," offered Chad.

"I do, sir. Danielle told me all about you. She said that no one could help a chechako be more at home here than you."

The next morning, Wilson and Hickox arrived at the dock before light and made their way down a ladder into the hold. There they pried the lid off a box and retrieved five rifles each with a box of ammunition. They concealed two on the bridge and the other three in lockers at the bow, midships and at the stern.

The ship's crew arrived an hour later. Then the only passenger arrived in the governor's coach. The young well-dressed woman had a shawl wrapped around her face as she boarded the *Miles Pierce*. Moments later, one of the dock hands retrieved a travel case from the coach and what looked like a long tube wrapped in canvas and followed the woman into the main salon.

The boat was ready to get under way the minute the last of the freight had been secured on the aft deck.

"Thank you, Belle, for being our decoy," offered a smiling Hickox. "I doubt that anyone was watching this morning. We think they will go after Miss Post at the fish saltery, but maybe not. They may be waiting in Juneau. If that's the plan, they may be watching this morning. They know that they can get to Juneau more than a day faster than the *Miles Pierce* can."

"I just hope that this all works," replied Belle. "This Maples guy is responsible for the death of my grandfather."

Belle made her way up the ladder to the bridge after the ship was well out in the bay. Chad was at the chart table. Under her arm was the canvas roll which she leaned against the bulkhead behind the door. Chad looked over to Macky at the wheel.

"I figure about three in the afternoon. It will be almost dead high tide when we get there."

Macky grunted. "It will be a damned hot afternoon with clear skies and not a breath of wind."

Both men's estimates were right on. North Pacific's salmon salting plant was in Humpy Cove on the mainland north of the main cannery. Three large streams flowed from towering mountains into the cove, but unlike most of the streams in the area, only two species of salmon used them for spawning. Both species made better salted than canned fish. The boat slipped past the completed dock and then backed slowly until Ivan could toss a rope to a man who waited near the stern. Moments later, Chad signaled the stoker for slow ahead as he pushed the bow against the rough deck where another man took a rope from Macky and tied it off. Both men on the dock wandered back to where a stack of crates were piled.

Chad nodded to Belle who stood quietly on the bridge. "Stay down and out of the way. We don't want any shooting, but if it starts, I am not going to let you get hurt. I am going below."

Miguel had started out on the dock by the time that Chad reached the rail mid-ships. "We have your lumber," yelled Chad.

Seconds later, the two men who had secured the lines bolted from behind the crates with rifles in their hands and behind them came two more men, a one-armed man holding a pistol and the other man with two rifles, one of which he tossed to Miguel.

"Captain Gritt, we meet at last," said the man clutching the revolver in his left hand. "I don't want any of that lumber we shipped. After we take what we really came for you may do with it whatever pleases you."

Chad looked down where a Winchester rifle lay on the deck and then back at the men on the dock. "I know what you came for Samuel Maples, and Miss Post is not aboard."

Maples raised the pistol and aimed it at Chad only thirty feet away. "My men saw Miss Post leave your ship from Seattle. We know she is with you. Being a hero will only mean that I kill you and take your ship. I will find that bitch."

Before Chad could respond, Belle Medev, still in her elegant lavender dress and her huge hat stepped out onto the wing of the bridge. She reached up and pulled the hat from her head and tossed it out toward the deck. "Unless Miss Post is now part native, I think you are going to be very disappointed."

"Throw down that pistol Mr. Maples," came a call from the back of the pilot house. "You are under arrest." Hickox moved out of the shadows.

Maples pulled the trigger of his pistol. He had practiced a lot, but he was still a naturally right-handed man, shooting left handed. The bullet smacked the rail in front of Chad just as he reached for the rifle at his feet, blasting tiny splinters into the side of his face. The bullet deflected high, creasing Chad's skull. He lunged upright and tumbled over the rail barely holding onto his rifle. In less than three seconds all five men on the dock were shooting, mostly toward the marshal who had dropped to his stomach trying to return fire.

From both ends of the boat, men emerged with Winchesters as did a second man from behind the wheelhouse. Macky fired wildly from the bow while Ivan did the same from the stern. While they never hit anybody, it gave Wilson and Hickox the moment they needed to pick a target. Hickox tumbled Juan off his feet while Wilson took aim at the big man in the center who was pointing his rifle at him. A moment of recognition crossed both men's faces as they pulled the trigger. The big man dropped with a bullet through the chest just as Wilson was thrown to the deck. Hickox finally found Maples, who was scrambling back toward the crates firing his pistol at the center of the boat. Hickox squeezed the trigger and watched Maples grasp his stomach and drop to his knees then crawl behind the crates.

Miguel and Tiko backed away from the boat scattering their shots. Miguel slipped behind the crates, but Tiko, now the only target visible was too slow. He was slammed to his back. Chad levered another cartridge into his Winchester. Then he ran the sleeve of his shirt over his face trying to clear the blood that ran into his eyes.

Miguel looked behind him. The same hidden ramp from the beach that had allowed the men to approach the boat without being seen now offered an escape route. Miguel watched as Maples clutched the top of a crate and pulled himself upright.

"Miguel let's get out of here," snapped Maples.

Miguel flashed a brutal smile at Maples who knew instantly what it meant. Then he shot Maples squarely in the chest pitching him from behind the crates.

"Maples is yours," he yelled, but I am going to take your Captain Gritt as payment for the loss of my men." Miguel pushed the crate forward to clear a shot at Chad, who was barely back on his feet, clinging to the boat railing. The three shots slamming into the crates couldn't penetrate the layers of wood. Just as Miguel started to pull the trigger the crate in front of him exploded. He was dead before his body fell.

Belle flipped open the trapdoor of her old 45-70 rifle and flipped the spent brass from the huge slow-moving bullet into the water. The whole affair had lasted less than a minute.

Belle dropped the rifle and raced down the ladder for the deck where she collided with Macky coming from the bow. Together they leaped over the rail to reach Chad.

"You don't look so bad, Captain," said Macky as Belle held Chad's bloody face in her hands. "Looks like he missed both your eyes. The rest will heal."

Belle carefully wiped away the areas where Chad's face was bleeding, stopping to pull three more splinters from his wounds. She pressed the lace hanky in her pocket against where the bullet had reopened the scar on his head. She then shook her head and kissed him on the forehead. "Chad Gritt, when will you learn to duck?"

Macky and Belle looked up to find Hickox helping Wilson, his right thigh covered in blood, limp past them.

"Help me down," asked Wilson, as he sat next to the big man who had shot him and who he had shot. "Reed, what are you doing here? I thought you were just a guard at Sontag's cannery until you could go home this fall."

Reed wiped the blood from his lips. "Mr. Maples recruited me and sent me north before I ever met you. He offered me five-hundred dollars to help him here and a ride back south. Rattler, you knowed how much I missed my wife and the little ones."

Wilson pulled up Reed's shirt and examined the wound. "You aren't going home Reed."

"I tried to pull off Rattler," whispered Reed. "I just got caught up in it."

"Me too," replied Wilson. "You got that money on you?"

Reed could barely lift his arm to pat his coat pocket. Wilson retrieved the bank notes.

"You have any more at Sontag's," asked Wilson?

"Another thousand and some coin," stammered Reed his breath now ragged.

"I will get the money to your wife. Reed stopped breathing. Wilson closed his eyes and then his own. "God, this man has sinned like most of your children, maybe worse. But in the end, he was really trying to be a servant of the Lord. He was a church going man when he was in Juneau. Like me, he just never had much practice on how to be your servant. He deserves a hearing up there."

The marshal walked on checking the other men down on the deck. None would need a doctor.

"Who was that man?" asked the marshal.

"His name was Reed. He was the first man Maples sent up. He was a convicted murderer. Maples bribed some guards to spring him from jail before they hung him. He was Maples' trigger man in southeast. He was once a Catholic priest who got himself caught up in the Mexican wars. In the end he was trying to find God again like me."

The marshal helped Wilson to his feet. "Was he the one who shot old Joe, and killed those two men from Johansons?"

"I don't know for sure," responded Wilson. "He told me a few weeks ago that the man he killed in California had raped his wife. He also said that he could live with that, but not the others. He didn't offer more, and I didn't ask."

"Let's get Wilson here, over to Sontag's. He has an infirmary. He will limp for a while where that round ripped muscle, but all he needs is some opium and a needle and thread."

Turning to Macky, he asked, "What have you got to weigh these men down. We bury them at sea on the way, all except Maples. We take him with us."

"A length of tie down chain around the waist should do the trick, but Marshal, I don't know why we don't take them back to Juneau and give them a Christian funeral."

"These men were all connected to the Alaska Investors Group, one of the most prestigious investment companies in the territory. They were led by a mad man, and it got them killed. Still, we don't need to give the press a reason to taint the whole group. The governor would have tried them if they had surrendered, but he didn't want to. Its better if this just goes away."

"What about Maples?" asked Belle. "Why are we taking him back?"

"First, he is a wanted man, and we need to clear the warrant. But mostly, I want to show Sontag that Maples is done. I want him to send the investors a letter that makes it clear what can happen if they let things get out of hand."

The *Miles Pierce* jockeyed up to the dock at the North Pacific Cannery and tied up behind the blue yacht. Sontag and the big man, Drew, met the boat.

"You didn't tell me that Samuel Maples was with your group," snapped the marshal as he stepped onto the dock. He tried to ambush us at the saltery. You have some explaining to do."

The marshal put his finger in the middle of Drews chest. "It might be that you will rot in some prison in Seattle mister."

"Hold on, Marshal," said Sontag. "My friend here was worried about what was going on with Samuel, just like I was. He refused to go with him. There was no way to warn you."

"That's right, Marshal," interjected Drew, "When we stopped to collect what Mr. Sontag here owed Mr. Maples a couple of months ago, we learned about the saltery, that it was overbudget. Hell, I never thought a thing about buying lumber and shipping it. Maples was still part of the Investment Group as far as I knew. When I saw Maples and Miguel and the other two carrying rifles for the boat ride to the saltery I refused to go. That's why Maples hired the other man."

"He is telling you the truth, Marshal," added Sontag. "I will swear to it."

"They all died for Maples' revenge. We buried the other four at sea, but Maples is rolled up in a tarp on the back of the boat. It will be better if none of this ever happened. You understand me gentlemen?" barked the marshal. I will take Maples back to prove he is dead so that I can cancel the warrant."

"Marshal," started Drew, "wouldn't it be better if even his death didn't have to be advertised?"

"What do you mean?" asked Chad, who had just joined the marshal, barely able to stand, the world spinning."

"Well, Mr. Sontag here and Me and Captain Kilcher from the boat could all give you sworn statements that we knew Maples, and he is dead, then you wouldn't have to take Maples to Juneau. We will take Maples' body back to California to show the rest of the investors that he was no longer the rogue who was getting them in trouble."

"That sounds like a good idea to me," offered Chad. "The governor doesn't want any more mess than he already has from this. Now I need to go lie down."

Two hours later the *New Life* pulled away from the dock. In the forward freight hold was a wooden barrel holding Maples' body, packed in salt. Drew and Captain Kilcher stood quietly on the bridge watching the cannery slip away in the mist.

"What is our best time to Seattle?" asked Drew.

"We can make the run in five days if the weather holds," answered Kilcher. "Now tell me, did you tip off the marshal and get my old friend Samuel killed?

"I never spoke a word to the marshal since I sent him on that wild goose chase in Juneau," answered Drew. "That isn't a crime in the territory. But honestly, I wasn't going to be part of murdering a lady."

Kilcher smiled, "I wasn't very happy about the idea myself. If Maples had let me go with you to Sitka, I probably would have talked to the marshal. I didn't have the courage to try to face down Samuel or Miguel. I am sorry to lose an old friend, but I am pleased not to have to travel with Miguel or his hired thugs."

"You know captain, you now own a fine craft, but you are out of a job. I could see you liked it in Victoria, maybe a place to start over. Including the five thousand we got from Sontag, there is almost twenty thousand in that wall safe in Maples' cabin. After the cost to get us back south, there will still be about seventeen thousand left. I suggest we split six to you and eleven to me," said Drew.

"I thought Maples collected ten thousand from Sontag," snapped an irritated Kilcher.

"I gave Sontag back half. When I saw the *Miles Pierce* coming, I knew what had happened. We needed his help. I told him the other five thousand was really from the Group," answered Drew.

"That still doesn't explain why you get eleven and I get six."

"When we get to Seattle, I will jump on a train for the East. You go find the Pinkertons and hand them that barrel down below. Maples is worth five thousand. The body and the statements from the marshal and Sontag should be all they need. See, eleven apiece. Just don't tell Marathon anything. I will take the blame if any is assigned, but not until I get several thousand miles between Marathon and me."

Kilcher extended a hand. "You got a deal. Besides, I don't like the idea of handing Samuel's body to the business partners who got him killed."

"What do you mean?"

"While you were talking to the marshal, that young woman, Belinda, wandered down to where I was sitting on the dock. She explained just how the whole thing happened. Samuel got himself wounded by the marshal, but Miguel killed him right in front of everybody. He then tried to kill Chad, so she shot him."

"That's right my friend, replied Drew. "Miguel killed by a young woman. With what happened to Maples and now Miguel, it makes you real shy of feminine company."

"At least any with ties to that Captain Gritt."

CHAPTER 30

Southeast Alaska

THE *MILES PIERCE* surged up against the dock in Sitka. Chad was diagnosed with a concussion from taking two blows to the head in six months. The therapy was bed rest and light work until the symptoms disappeared. Luckily, there was a nurse available who already had experience nursing the patient from previous wounds.

It gave the newly minted celebrities time to socialize. Belle Medev was escorted to the annual social of the Society of Mission Friends by Chad Gritt, who now sported a cow lick where his hair used to part. All of Sitka turned out for the event.

A few days later, Chad escorted Belle again, but this time to the Juneau Chamber of Commerce dance, where for the second time his date raised every eyebrow in the place. For the second year in a row, the woman on his arm was the most beautiful woman in the hall. Because of her place at the governor's table, those present recognized only her Russian heritage.

While Chad and Belle were dancing away the evening, the

Maximilian made a port call in Juneau on its return from the Yukon. On board were federal officers and the two Pinkerton detectives who had traveled up the Yukon with them. The marshal and the governor received a whispered message as they waited for the orchestra to finish their break.

The men were ushered into a small conference room, where the governor and the marshal waited. The detectives were satisfied that their search for Maples was over after reading the affidavits from Drew, Sontag and the marshal. While the governor and the marshal sipped coffee, the two federal officers returned to the ship and fifteen minutes later reappeared with Judge Wildham in handcuffs.

Karp glared at the judge who sat across the table. "Why would you risk your legal career for a few thousand dollars?" he asked. "This posting was a good prelude to a far better appointment back in the states."

The judge glared back, "I am guilty of nothing, Lyman. No jury in the country will convict a sitting judge for exercising his own judgement in such a difficult situation. And that's all I am accused of."

"Get him out of here," ordered Karp.

The two federal officers pulled Wildham to his feet and led him toward the door. One of them turned before leaving. "He was just as defiant in Falcon, despite files of proof against him. I don't know who he thinks is going to come to his rescue, but this case will destroy the career of anyone who does."

Karp returned to the dinner, a scowl on his face. "What is wrong dear? asked Kate.

"I just spent a few minutes with an old acquaintance who I once thought was a friend. Now he is in real trouble and not only am I not going to help him, but I am also the one who will swing the biggest club as he runs the gauntlet."

"Well, dear, let me cheer you up. Look at Captain Gritt and Miss Medev on the dance floor. How long do you think he is going to pine over Danielle Post?"

"Pine over who?" asked Karp.

⤮

Three thousand miles to the south, a large scruffy man walked into the J.M. Heinold's Saloon and took a seat at a back table after stopping to chat with the young boy studying near the door. Young Jack London carried a double shot and a mug of cold beer to the man.

"Where is Mr. Mapolonias?" asked Jack.

"He plans to be here tomorrow, and he asked me to arrange for you to get a message to the bank that he would like to meet with his partner at four tomorrow. He suggests you use your disguise, so you don't attract any attention."

"I will be happy to help. Those photographs that Mr. Mapolonias gave me really made me excited to go visit the Alaska Territory. Do you suppose that he can take time to tell me about his trip?"

"Probably not," replied Drew. "He's so busy he's almost a ghost, if you know what I mean. Anyway, I'll have an envelope for his banking partner at the desk of my hotel when he gets here to see Mapolonias. Please wait until he arrives and run over to get it. It will tell him everything he needs to know."

"You can count on me sir. You want another beer?"

"Sure do." Drew took a twenty-dollar gold piece from his pocket and flipped it to young Jack. "After this last trip, Mr. Mapolonias is getting kind of forgetful, so here is payment in advance."

"Gee thanks, Mister. Hey, I don't know your last name, Drew."

"If Drew was good enough for Mapolonias, it will have to be good enough for you, kid. Now, go fetch that beer."

At three-thirty the next day, Drew walked into the Marathon Bank dressed in a tailored suit and handed the teller his safe deposit key. The teller checked his signature and led him into the vault where Drew emptied the safe deposit box. From the case he carried, he took two stockings filled with sand, placed them in the box and then closed it and returned it to the clerk.

An hour later, he was on the train to Santa Fe. As he sat sipping on a glass of champagne in the club car, he toyed with the safe deposit box key in his pocket. The trip back to New Hampshire where another safe deposit box waited would take five days. Drew smiled.

The waiter slipped up beside him. "Your table is ready Mr. Cargill. I haven't seen you in a while. Did you ever find that man your banker client hired you to track down?"

Back at the saloon, Alfred Marathon waited nervously for Maples' arrival. The young courier who had disappeared soon after his arrival returned with an envelope.

"That Drew fellow said to give this to you, sir."

Marathon opened the envelope and then smiled. He waved at Jack who brought him another bourbon and a beer. He then called to the two men who had accompanied him to the saloon. "You two can head on home now, everything here is just fine."

He then chugged the double shot and picked up his beer. He read the note for a third time. It read, *Everyone you were worried about is dead. I never pulled a trigger, so you don't owe me a thing. I am paid in full. D.C.'*

**READ THE NEXT BOOK IN THE
GRITT FAMILY SERIES,**

FROM RUSSIA WITH BLOOD

AUTHOR'S NOTES AND ACKNOWLEDGEMENTS

My adopted home state has a fascinating history. Most scientists believe that the Americas were first populated by those crossing the land bridge that once existed between what is now the Russian Far East and Alaska. The beginning of human history in North America begins in Alaska. The entire Gritt Family Saga series includes pieces of history from the 1820s to the present.

After the Russian "occupation" of Alaska in the 1700s, the people of Alaska were subjugated by foreign nations. The purchase of Alaska from Russia at the end of America's Civil War began a transition back to more local control, but not before decades of American federal government neglect and, even worse, carpetbagger-like corporate exploitation. This book tells the story of how the local native population and newly arrived American citizens fought back against a handful of corporate titans determined to milk the wealth of the territory for their own benefit.

My thanks to the Sitka History Museum and the Anchorage Museum for their help in documenting the period. The corporate records of companies such as the Alaska Commercial Company, which transitioned from Russian to American ownership, offer a view of commerce that wasn't much less exploitive than the fur trade in the Pacific Northwest in the 1800s. In the late 1990s, Elizabeth A. Tower wrote a great book, *Icebound Empire*, which was a major catalyst for my personal quest to understand the exploitation of Alaska and how Alaskans fought back. It helped me guide the companies I was running at the time so that we made life better for our communities while also making a profit.

As to the creation of *Robber Barons*, I, as always, first want to thank Carmen for her tireless help in turning a rough manuscript into a book. The dozen advanced copy readers who helped polish the story not only helped refine the narrative but also the historical accuracy of the book. But any recognition for the content must emphasize the people of Alaska, especially the native people whose resilience and values shape a unique culture.

All of my books, so far, have been shaped by Damonza, a unique company in New Zealand that turns the vision of each book into a distinctive cover and transitions my scattered prose into a format that makes the books easy to read. Well before the first commercial copy of the book is released, my publicist, BTS Designs, begins their work to help make the public aware of the book in a market where a million new titles are published each year. Thank you, James.

Which gets me back to Carmen. Thank you for doing so much of the commercial work it takes to succeed as a writer, work that since I retired from the corporate world, I don't like to do. You make both my career and life better than I deserve.

www.rodgercarlyle.com
Goodreads author Rodger Carlyle
Amazon author Rodger Carlyle